A Blood So Sweet

Summer Riley

Copyright © 2024 Summer Riley

All rights reserved.

ISBN: **9798876959980**

DEDICATION

To my Husband for always loving and believing in me, especially when I don't love or believe in myself. I'm lucky you remain my #1 Super Fan.

And to all my fellow lovers of the dark and of all the things that reside there.

And to those who didn't believe I would ever write a book. This is my second with more to come. Spite is the most amazing motivator. Thank you.

CONTENTS

i.	Acknowledgments	
1	Chapter One	Pg 1
2	Chapter Two	Pg 8
3	Chapter Three	Pg 17
4	Chapter Four	Pg 25
5	Chapter Five	Pg 33
6	Chapter Six	Pg 44
7	Chapter Seven	Pg 54
8	Chapter Eight	Pg 65
9	Chapter Nine	Pg 78
10	Chapter Ten	Pg 87
11	Chapter Eleven	Pg 97
12	Chapter Twelve	Pg 107
13	Chapter Thirteen	Pg 118
14	Chapter Fourteen	Pg 130
15	Chapter Fifteen	Pg 138
16	Chapter Sixteen	Pg 147
17	Chapter Seventeen	Pg 156
18	Chapter Eighteen	Pg 163
19	Chapter Nineteen	Pg 173

20	Chapter Twenty	Pg 184
21	Chapter Twenty-One	Pg 188
22	Chapter Twenty-Two	Pg 200
23	Chapter Twenty-Three	Pg 212
24	Chapter Twenty-Four	Pg 224
25	Chapter Twenty-Five	Pg 236
26	Chapter Twenty-Six	Pg 249
27	Chapter Twenty-Seven	Pg 259
28	Chapter Twenty-Eight	Pg 272
29	Chapter Twenty-Nine	Pg 280
30	Chapter Thirty	Pg 289
31	Chapter Thirty-One	Pg 298
32	Chapter Thirty-Two	Pg 307
33	Chapter Thirty-Three	Pg 317
34	Chapter Thirty-Four	Pg 327
35	Chapter Thirty-Five	Pg 334
36	Chapter Thirty-Six	Pg 342
37	Chapter Thirty-Seven	Pg 349
38	Chapter Thirty-Eight	Pg 356
39	Chapter Thirty-Nine	Pg 366
	Epilogue	Pg 379

ACKNOWLEDGMENTS

I would like to acknowledge all my family and dear friends who read this story and offered invaluable feedback. It's because of you that this story was completed and released.

I would also like to acknowledge all the Kindle Vella readers who read *A Blood So Sweet* while it had its run on Vella. Thank you for making it a Top Fav each month.

Beautiful cover art created by PandaCapuccino on Instagram and tumblr by same name.

TRIGGER WARNINGS

Blood (duh, it's a Vampire story). Age gap (yeah, he's a Vampire). "Sugar Daddy" Trope (he's a sexy, rich Vampire). Swearing (I like to curse and so do my characters). Sex. Open door sex. Explicit sex scenes. Mentions of abuse (physical, mental, verbal, sexual). Kidnapping. Character death. Physical Fights. Gore(ish). Fantasy characters. And love.

CHAPTER ONE

"Desperate times call for desperate measures," Brynn said with a sigh.

Tapping on the Benefactor icon on her phone, her hazel eyes opened wide as she saw the brightly colored notification on her home screen. Five matches. She had only had the app for a week and already had *five matches*. It had taken her best friend, Jenni, two whole months for a single match.

Maybe her luck was finally changing.

Sitting back in the worn armchair, she took a quick glance around the busy coffee shop. Although no one was paying attention to her, she brought her phone closer towards her freckled face in the hopes that no one would see her screen. She still felt wrong for creating a profile on the controversial dating app.

Pushing past her hesitation, she clicked on her first match. His name was Paul, and he looked old enough to be her grandfather. He claimed to be a shipping tycoon, whatever the hell that meant. From his pictures, he was an avid fisherman who spent most of his time on a yacht in the Caribbean. His verified net worth came in at five million. Five million that Brynn could see he had to share with at least three ex-wives, a handful of children, and a dozen grandchildren.

It was an automatic *no* for her.

Moving onto the next candidate, she almost laughed at how cliche he seemed. If she didn't know the strict vetting that came with being a Benefactor, she would've sworn he was a love scammer. On the screen he looked too perfect. A land developer from Dubai, Cicero was the most handsome silver fox she had ever seen. He was also a car snob through and through. Almost all his pictures were of him either draped upon, or behind the wheel of some very expensive sports cars. With his Gucci sunglasses and tailored made Dunhill suits, it was clear that he took his image very seriously. Even with a good cleanup, she knew she was too rough around the edges for him.

Swiping away Cicero's message, Brynn continued to her third match. Tapping on his profile, she sucked in a sharp breath as her eyes settled on his main picture. To her shock, his debonair good looks blew Cicero completely out of the water. With dark hair that framed a chiseled face, serpentine green eyes, and a toned body that strained against his Tom Ford three piece, he was the embodiment of her fantasy man. Clicking on his full profile, she took her time reading his stats.

Name: Nikolai (Nik) Draven
Age: 37
Height: 6 feet, 3 inches
Weight: 203 lbs.
Hair: Brown
Eyes: Green
Ethnicity: Eastern European
Marital Status: Widower
Children/Grandchildren: None
Occupation: Entrepreneur, Philanthropist
Net worth: 4.4 billion U.S. Dollars

Rereading his net worth for a second, and then a third time, Brynn choked on her own spit. Holy shit. How in the world could a thirty-seven-year-old entrepreneur be worth that much money. And what the hell was he doing on a sugar daddy app?

These were red flags, right?

Letting her curiosity get the best of her, she closed out of the app and went straight to Google. Typing in his unusual name, she was surprised to find only one result. Clicking on the business webpage, she scanned through the dry article. Apparently, Nikolai Draven had purchased the multi-million-dollar application design firm Alpha Web. The same design firm that just so happened to have created Benefactor.

"Oh my God," Brynn whispered. "Tasting from your own supply? Kinky."

Never one to shy away from glaring warning signs, she swiped back over to the Benefactor app. Once again clicking on Nik's profile, she continued to read more about the mysterious billionaire.

Wants: I'm looking for companionship with a young woman, 22-28 years old. Someone with a good head on her shoulders, that's strong and independent, but also doesn't mind being spoiled and shown the finer things in life. Must be a night owl, and in overall good health. I'm not ashamed to admit that petite brunettes are my weakness. Sex isn't a requirement, but I'm not opposed to adding it into our arrangement. If I've matched myself with you, please know that I'm very interested, and would love to meet you for a drink to see if we are compatible.

Pulling her lower lip between her teeth, Brynn gave his profile another go. If he was looking for a feisty brunette in desperate need of financial spoiling, well, she was his girl. It would be stupid of her not to reach out. Her eviction notice was going to magically disappear on its own.

Deciding to take the plunge, she hovered her finger over the 'message' button. Just as she was gathering the courage however, she was pulled away by a familiar voice.

"Hey Brynn!" Jenni said cheerfully, taking a seat on the couch flanking Brynn's chair. "God that exam was a nightmare…I'm so glad it's over! Have you turned in your paper, yet?"

Looking at the bubbly blonde, Brynn shook her head. Honestly, she hadn't even started the damn thing. She had been forced to take on a third job at the Breakfast Spot next to campus. She didn't have time for anything anymore. Not even sleep. It was by a complete miracle she was passing the two classes she was taking this semester.

"Not yet," she admitted.

Raising a brow, Jenni gave her friend a critical face. "Brynn…it's due in four hours!"

Letting out an exasperated sigh, she couldn't help but roll her eyes. As if she didn't know? She could write the stupid thing in forty minutes, tops. It wouldn't be good, and her professor would probably have some words to say to her, but it would be done. Everything she did was with a bare bone minimum these days. That's all she could do at this point in her miserable life.

"I know…I know," Brynn replied, waving her hand dismissively. "I'll write it in a little bit."

Staring at her friend, Jenni softened her features. She always felt helpless when it came to Bynn. She wished the stubborn girl would just let her help with some of her bills. She hated to watch her slowly drown in debt.

Catching Jenni's blue eyes, Brynn shrugged her shoulders. She knew exactly what she was thinking, and she really didn't want to have another argument about it. Besides, it wasn't Brynn's money to give away.

"So, how's Donald?" Bynn asked, wanting to change the subject.

Painting on a bright smile, Brynn physically gushed at the mention of her Benefactor. She knew she shouldn't brag, but she couldn't help it. The past six months had been the best six months of her life.

"Oh my God, so good! He just signed a seven-figure deal with the city to expand the Marketplace…and he's trying to move forward with that hotel deal in Vegas! I'm really hoping he wins that bid…he promised to buy us a condo at The Palazzo if he gets it," she replied, wiggling in her seat. "But, oh! I don't think I told you this…Don told me that if I get an A in Analytics, he's taking me to get this…Ibiza! Ahh! Can you believe that? Me…partying on a yacht in Ibiza? Do you think I'll see Calvin Harris? Ahh! What if I see freaking Beyoncé?!"

Holding in a disbelieving laugh, Brynn tried her best to be happy for her sweet friend. Jenni of all people deserved this; she shouldn't be so jealous of her windfall. She had seen pictures of Don, the girl really was working her ass off to secure her future.

"That's amazing, Jenni! Well, if you see Beyoncé, tell her I said hi!" Brynn said with a wink.

Arching a brow, Jenni slapped the arm of the fraying couch. "I should ask Don if you could come too!"

Shaking her head, Brynn brushed off the thought. With her luck, Don would probably try to rope her into some seedy threesome. Even being in Ibiza with Beyoncé wasn't worth that disgusting prospect.

"No, no! That's your gift, you've earned that one…and besides, maybe I'll be going on an all-expense paid vacation soon, too. Who knows?" She said suggestively, tucking a chestnut lock behind her ear.

Gasping in surprise, Jenni clapped her hands together. "Ah! Brynn! Did you match, already?!"

Nodding her head, Brynn pulled up Nikolai's picture on her phone. Holding the cracked screen towards Jenni, she lifted the corner of her lips into a cocky smile. Her friend's reaction to her match's picture was priceless. A look of pure shock and envy rolled into one.

"No way! No freaking way! This is your match, Brynn? Are you kidding me?!" Jenni asked, grabbing the phone for a closer look. "Ooh…he's Daddy material, for sure!"

"I know, right? We were just matched today! But girl…read his bio," Brynn encouraged.

Swiping her finger across the screen, Jenni quickly scanned over Nik's stats. Pushing out a disbelieving huff, her mouth dropped open in complete astonishment. Turning the phone back towards Brynn, she pointed at his net worth.

"Four point four BILLION dollars?!" she squealed, not caring if the coffee shop patrons overheard. "BILLION?! Oh my God, Brynn! Holy! Shit!"

Shushing her friend, Brynn grabbed her phone back. Giving a small laugh to those that turned to look at them, she waited for them to go back to their coffees before answering Jenni.

"I know! Isn't that crazy! Not only is he insanely hot, but he's insanely rich!" she said, dropping her voice low. "Do you think I should message him? I mean…yeah, I should. Right?"

Blinking at her friend, Jenni gave her an incredulous look. Did she really just ask her that?

"Girl…I swear to God, if you don't message him right this fu—"

"Ok! Ok!" Brynn interrupted, pressing the message button on the app. "I'm doing it! I'm doing it!"

Watching with wide eyes, Jenni beamed for her friend. She couldn't remember the last time Brynn had been so excited about something. Her life was going to change and change for the better. She just knew it.

Hesitating for a long moment, Brynn tried to think of what she should write. She didn't want to sound too desperate, or too easy. He was a playboy billionaire who probably wanted a cool girl. She could be that, right?

"Uh, what should I say?" she asked aloud.

"How about hi," Jenni suggested with a tiny shrug.

Nodding in agreement, Brynn typed a simple greeting into the message bubble. Nothing too forward, nothing too strong.

Hi, Nik. How about that drink?

"Ok, I did it…now I guess I just wait, huh?" she asked, trying not to stare at her screen.

"Yep, it's just a waiting game, now…but I'm sure he will message you back soon," Jenni reassured, pushing the strap of her purse back onto her shoulder and standing from the couch. "And when he does, you need to text me ASAP, ok?"

Watching Jenni prepare to head to her next class, Brynn gave her a knowing grin. She was her only friend and honestly, the only semblance of family she had. Who else would she tell?

"Yeah, of course," she replied.

Blowing a kiss, Jenni turned on her heels. Walking towards the door, she glanced over her shoulder. "See ya, now write that paper!"

Waving her off, Brynn let out a long sigh. Right. The damn paper. How could she forget?

Bending down next to her chair, she pulled her laptop from her torn backpack. Turning it on, she struggled to find a comfortable position in her seat. Heading straight into Google Docs, she began to type mindlessly away about her opinion of Anne Boleyn. She had only finished two paragraphs when she heard a sudden *ding!* coming from her phone.

Picking it up from her lap, she pressed on the message notification on the Benefactor app. Reading her match's reply, she instantly felt giddy. She wondered if this was the beginning of her new life. She sure as hell hoped so.

Brynn. Hello. I was hoping to hear from you. Yes. Let me buy you that drink. I'll make the reservations and get back to you. I can't wait to meet you.

Xx, Nik

CHAPTER TWO

Pressing her back against the elevator wall, Brynn took in a large breath as it made its descent into the belly of downtown Phoenix. She has always wanted to try this place. It was a modern speakeasy with an old-fashioned twist, completely hidden one hundred feet underground. Unfortunately, reservations were extremely hard to come by, and forty-five-dollar cocktails were a little too rich for her blood.

Apparently two problems her possible Benefactor didn't have.

Watching the analog numbers as they ticked downwards, she toyed with the heart shaped clutch in her hand. God, she hoped she looked ok. Jenni had insisted that she borrow her lucky black bodycon dress. She couldn't remember the last time she wore something so tight, or so short. She had to remember not to bend over, otherwise someone would get a full view of her barely there panties.

Unless she wanted them to, of course.

Feeling the elevator slow, she straightened her posture. Trying her best to ignore the butterflies filling her belly, she reminded herself how important this night was. She hoped they had chemistry; it would make things so much easier.

Coming to a complete stop, she stepped away from the elevator wall. Lifting her crimson painted lips into a confident smile, she watched with wide eyes as the metal doors opened. *Well here goes nothing,* she thought to herself.

Walking out of the lift, she glanced around the dimly lit space to gain her bearings. From the first look, it lived up to its hype. Surrounded by rock walls lined with walnut bookcases, she instantly felt comfortable. Music from the nineteen-thirties danced through the cool air, masking the conversation of attractive patrons sitting along the vintage bar. It was lively and unpretentious. The perfect spot for what essentially was a blind date.

Noticing a sharply dressed young man walking towards her, Brynn felt her anxiety spike. He looked nothing like Nik's picture. Surely, he wasn't her date. She hoped she wasn't being catfished.

"Good evening, Miss. Do you have a reservation with us tonight?" the maître d asked, his tone hinting of boredom.

Letting out a sigh of relief, Brynn lifted her slim shoulders in a tiny shrug. She really needed to calm down, of course he wasn't her date.

"I uh…I'm meeting someone, he said he had reservations for us at nine-thirty? I don't see him, though…it should be under a uh, Nik Draven?" she said, shifting her weight from one high heel to the other.

Instantly righting himself, the maître d nodded his head. Knowing he had to go above and beyond in the customer service department, he forced a cheerful smile.

"Oh, yes! Mr. Draven has been expecting you…please, right this way," he said, motioning her to follow.

Stepping behind the maître d, Brynn measured her steps as they wound their way around the busy bar room. Looking around at all the different faces, she wondered where he was taking her.

Glancing over his shoulder, the maître d urged the brunette closer. "Mr. Draven has reserved a private room for you two…everyone loves this part," he said, leading her towards a hulking bookcase.

Giving the bald man an odd look, Brynn couldn't hide her confusion. Opening her mouth to ask him what he meant, she was effectively silenced when he reached out to touch a leather-bound version of *Great Expectations*. Tipping the brown spine backwards, the bookcase started to grumble. Within a handful of seconds, it slid to the right, revealing a small room hidden away from the rest of the bar.

"Oh," Brynn whispered.

Bowing his head, the maître d used his open hand to show her inside. "Enjoy your evening, Miss."

Smiling a reply, Brynn thanked him as she entered the private space. Just barely crossing the threshold, the bookcase quickly closed behind her. Leaving her all alone with the stranger sitting on the loveseat facing the opposite direction.

Swallowing hard, her eyes adjusted to the low light of the room. Letting her gaze settle upon the man's broad back, she took in a breath. Catching a whiff of what had to be his cologne, she was immediately put at ease. It was warm, with a hint of bourbon and spice. It was masculine and confident, something only a man who was secure in himself would wear.

"Nik?" she asked almost timidly, taking another step forward.

Turning his head towards the sweet voice, Nik stood from his seat. Moving to secure the button of his dark gray suit jacket, he let his green eyes take their fill of the beauty before him. To his surprise, she was even more stunning in person. He would have to give his recruiter a raise, he may have finally succeeded in finding him his perfect match.

Making his way towards the young woman, he had to stop himself from reaching out to brush her chestnut hair from her shoulders. He could tell she was nervous by the way she refused to meet his eyes. Normally, that would be an automatic *no* for him, but for some reason he found her innate submissiveness to be endearing. He instantly liked her. *No,* he realized. It wasn't just that. *He wanted her.*

It had been far too long since he had felt that way about anyone.

"Brynn, my...look how beautiful you are," he purred, his tone deep and sultry.

Laughing nervously, Brynn felt her face flush pink. Forcing herself to get a good look at her possible Benefactor, she lifted her hazel eyes from the checkerboard floor to his chiseled face. *Good God,* she thought to herself. Love at first sight wasn't something she believed in, but lust at first sight? Oh, that applied here.

"Thank you, so are you!" she replied, instantly wincing as she realized what she had said.

Lifting his full lips into an amused grin, Nik let out a tiny chuckle. It was clear that he had the same effect on her that she had on him. The night was already off to a great start.

"Well thank you," he said, giving her a wink.

Widening her eyes from his flirty display, she squealed internally. Locking her knees to keep her wobbly legs from buckling, she attempted to calm her racing heart. Geeze, what was she, sixteen? She really had to get a grip.

Studying her freckled face for a long moment, he allowed himself to relish her awkwardness. He was used to making people nervous, but she was making this fun. He wondered if other parts of her turned the same shade of pink as her cheeks.

Holding out his hand, he motioned towards the loveseat. "Please?"

Following his lead, Brynn walked towards the navy sofa. Carefully stepping from heel to toe, she gave herself kudos for not tripping on Jenni's ridiculous Manolo Blahniks. Why were high heels always so damn uncomfortable? She hoped he didn't have a shoe kink.

Taking a seat on the edge of the velvet loveseat, she dropped her heart shaped clutch to the floor by her feet. Watching Nik intently as he sat beside her on the couch, she shivered slightly as he brushed against her. It was a good thing she was on the smaller side as he took up most of the plush cushion. Not that she was complaining.

Resisting the urge to look at her thighs as she adjusted the tiny skirt of her black dress, Nik cleared his throat. Quirking his head to the small coffee table before them, he reached into the lapel of his suit to pull out a ballpoint pen. On the table rested a black leather binder embossed with his initials in a golden scroll.

"Well, this is the necessary evil of the night…before we go any further, beautiful Brynn, I will need you to sign some documents for me," he said, handing her the pen.

Taking the silver pen, Brynn arched a sculpted brow. Suddenly, everything became very real. They weren't just innocently having drinks; they were beginning what was essentially a business transaction.

"Documents?" she asked, leaning in to take the binder as he lifted it from the table.

Nodding his head, he purposefully met her eyes. "Just a legal formality…it's your basic non-disclosure agreement. I just need you to agree that anything we discuss or do tonight, or in the future should we choose to go further, stays between us."

Unable to turn her gaze, she stared into his dark emerald eyes for what should have been an uncomfortable amount of time. Listening to his deep voice repeating the explanation for a second time, she found herself wanting to agree to anything he asked of her.

Anything.

"Oh, ok…yeah, of course," she replied, blindly flipping the binder open. "I completely understand."

Giving her a warm grin, he blinked his eyes to break their contact. Watching her quietly as she skimmed through the pages, he warned himself not to become too greedy. This girl wasn't like the others. He wanted her to act on her own wants and impulses. It would end up being more satisfying for both in the end if she had free will.

Looking over the formal language, Brynn scrunched her face in thought. She had never seen an N.D.A. before but didn't see anything wrong with its terms. Basically, she had to keep her mouth shut. If she didn't, he could slap her with a lawsuit for a million dollars. Honestly, it would be like trying to squeeze blood out of a turnip if he tried. She didn't even have a hundred dollars to her name.

Deciding to ignore another red flag, she skipped through the last few pages. Turning to the last page, she hastily scribbled her name and date. Officially beginning what had the potential to be the best thing to ever happen to her. Or possibly the worst. Slapping the binder closed, she handed the signed documents and pen back to Nik.

Taking the items in his large hands, Nik drifted his gaze over her face. Staring at her deep red lips, he felt his excitement bubble. He was looking forward to learning everything about her, inside and out.

"Good girl," he praised, standing from the loveseat.

With a tiny smile, she silently beamed from his approval. For some reason, she really enjoyed hearing it. Probably because throughout her entire life, no one has ever really given her an ounce of it.

Tucking the pen back into his lapel, Nik softened his face. She looked so sweet at that moment; it was clear that she needed someone to care for her. "I'll go order us some drinks…Midori sour, right?" he asked, lifting a dark brow.

Nodding her head, she gave him a curious look. How did he know her favorite drink? Was he also psychic? A hot, billionaire psychic?

"Yeah…uh, how did you know?" she asked.

Starting to head towards the secret door, he casually shrugged his broad shoulders. "It was part of the questionnaire you filled out when you signed up for the app. I hate to admit that I've read it a few times…I'll be right back, beautiful."

Furrowing her brow, she watched him open the bookcase and slip from the room. She couldn't remember being asked what her favorite drink was on the questionnaire. But admittedly, she had been pretty sleep deprived when she filled it out.

Brushing the thought away, she took a deep breath to settle the rest of her nerves. Looking around the small room, she suddenly jerked when she remembered a promise she had made to Jenni.

"Ugh, crap," she said, grabbing her clutch from the floor.

Quickly opening the leather heart, she reached inside for her phone. Looking at the cracked screen, she spit an expletive when she noticed six messages and two missed calls from her dearest friend. She was probably freaking out, thinking the absolute worst had happened. Ugh, she was an awful friend.

Pulling up her messages, she quickly read through Jenni's texts. They became more and more frantic as they went along. Knowing her friend was probably ready to call the police, she typed a reply.

Hey Jenni-I'm SO sorry!! I didn't mean for you to worry!! I made it ok...omg he's HOT!! Like...I want his head between my thighs hot. But he's legit. I can't say more. I'll text when I get home! Luv u!

Sending the text, she pushed out a sigh. She felt like the worst friend ever for scaring Jenni. Absently scrolling through her X feed to get her mind off her faux pas, she almost didn't hear her date come back into the room.

With only one drink in his hand, Nik closed the hidden door. Stepping towards her, he was slightly annoyed to see she was on her phone. He wondered if she had already broken her N.D.A.

"Is everything ok?" he asked, standing next to the loveseat.

Jumping slightly, Brynn looked up at his handsome face. There was a slight frown that made her wonder if she had done something wrong. Crap. Did he think she was posting about him? Closing out of the app, she immediately locked her phone. Nodding her head, she shoved it back into her clutch.

"Yeah! Sorry...I just remembered that I promised my friend I would text her when I got here. It's just something we do when we meet a guy for the first time. There are a lot of homicidal monsters out there, ya know?" she replied.

Letting out a sigh, he handed her the Midori sour. Once again taking his seat, he gave her a knowing look. He hated how women had to worry about possibly being raped and murdered at any given moment. It was a flaw of human nature that hadn't evolved one iota over the years. However, now that she had him, she wouldn't ever have to fret. He would keep all the other monsters away.

"Well, I hope she stops worrying…I promise you, you're in very safe hands," he said, his tone deep and sincere.

Taking the green drink, she smiled sweetly. She hoped he wasn't lying. Noticing he didn't have a drink of his own, she narrowed her hazel eyes.

"You're not having anything?" she asked.

Shaking his head, he turned his body towards her to give her his undivided attention.

"No, I have a meeting first thing in the morning," he said. It was a blatant lie, but one that wouldn't harm her any.

"Ah, I understand…it must be important," she replied, bringing her drink to her lips and taking a small sip.

Lifting a shoulder in a half shrug, he hummed away her comment. Not caring to dive into his own life just yet, he reached out to skim her knee with his fingertips. Although he already knew much about her semi-tragic history, he was looking forward to hearing her first account. He wondered if she trusted him enough to tell him the truth.

"So, beautiful Brynn, tell me about yourself," he said.

With a shiver running down her spine from the simple touch of her knee, she took another sip of her tart drink. She always hated talking about herself. It usually ended in someone's pity. Something she absolutely loathed.

"What would you like to know?" she asked, her voice lifting.

Leaning into her personal space, Nik brought his face in close to hers. Locking his intense gaze, he reached up to cup the side of her face with his hand.

"Everything," he said, grazing the pad of his thumb over her reddened cheek. "Tell me everything."

CHAPTER THREE

Instinctively leaning into Nik's gentle touch, Brynn closed her eyes and enjoyed the tiny bit of intimacy. For some reason, she wanted to tell him her whole life's story. Every blemish, every bruise. She knew he would keep them safe. She didn't know why; it was just a feeling she had.

"Ok…well," she began, opening her eyes. "I'm originally from the Pacific Northwest…Tacoma, Washington. Home of Ted Bundy…what a claim to fame, huh? Um…my parents were really young when they had me. I think my mom was sixteen? My dad was eighteen? They were just really young and didn't know much. I remember being really poor and hungry and dirty…ugh, yeah, I was always dirty. Probably because they started doing drugs. Heroin, specifically. Anyways…there was just a lot of abuse and…well, just a lot of bad things happened while I was with them. When I was five, they lost custody of me…the state finally stepped in. Only took my dad pushing me out of our second story window while on a bender but yeah…they finally stepped in. I was put into the foster care system. Sometimes I don't know whether that was a step above being with my parents but…yeah. I was in the system until I aged out when I turned eighteen."

Keeping his deep green eyes focused on her face, Nik absorbed every word. He had already pulled all the CPS, DCF, and DCYF documents pertaining to her. He knew all the gory details about the physical, mental, and sexual abuse she endured as a child. Although she was just skimming the surface, he still felt honored that she was telling him as much as she was. It was something he didn't take lightly.

Sucking in a breath, she gave him an embarrassed look. His handsome face was so intense, he almost looked worried. Had she said too much?

"I'm sorry, I probably said too m—"

"No. No you haven't," he interrupted, letting his hand slip from her cheek. Taking her free hand in his, he gave it a gentle squeeze. "Please...go on. What happened after you aged out?"

Licking her painted lips, she nodded her head before continuing with her history.

"Ok...so, yeah. I aged out at eighteen, but I was pretty lucky. My boyfriend at the time he...well, his parents...let me stay with them until I graduated high school. That was a pretty big thing for me. No one thought I would do it, ya know? And not only that, but I also got a scholarship to ASU for their Social Work program. I thought with what I have been through maybe I could make a difference in the system or something. Anyways, that's why I'm here. The scholarship was only for a year, though. It's been rough since that ran out...I had to drop down to part time, hence me going on year five of trying to get my bachelor's degree. That's a little embarrassing...but life is expensive, ya know? I'm just trying to survive out here."

Nodding in agreement, Nik listened as she continued to ramble about the rising cost of living and having to work three jobs just to scrape by. He had once been extremely poor and knew all too well the horrors that came along with it. At that moment he wanted nothing more than to save her from it all.

"You've been dealt a bad hand, Brynn. It's not fair," he said softly.

Giving him a shaky grin, she lifted her Midori sour to her mouth and took a large drink. Ahh, there was that pity she so hated to see. Swallowing the strong liquid, she winced as it burned down her throat.

"Life isn't fair," she replied dryly.

Noticing the change in her composure, he sighed to himself. Putting up a wall was probably one of her defense mechanisms, something that could be detrimental in a relationship if she chose to continue. He would have to remember that she wasn't looking for someone who offered their condolences on her shitty life. He didn't want her to feel worse about it. He wanted to make it better.

"No. No, it's not," he agreed.

Nodding her head slightly, Brynn remained silent for a handful of seconds. Internally, she was chastising herself for being somewhat rude. She liked Nik, and he genuinely seemed interested in her. He might have more money than God, but he wasn't the enemy.

"I'm sorry," she said.

Shaking his head, he squeezed her hand one more time. It was another form of defense. She had probably apologized for a million things she shouldn't have throughout the years. He would love to work on that with her.

"You have nothing to apologize for," he replied sincerely. "Absolutely nothing."

Chewing on the inside of her cheek, she gripped Nik's large hand. It was sweet of him to say that, and she didn't know quite how to handle it. Wanting to deflect attention away from herself, she turned the questions to him. Barring what he had written on his profile, she really knew nothing about him.

"Hmm…so what about you? Tell me about yourself," she said, leaning towards the coffee table to set the remnants of her drink down.

Humming a reply, Nik leaned back against the loveseat. Trying to look as unbothered as possible, he decided to give her a small autobiography.

"Well, I'm originally from Romania," he began.

Lifting her brows in surprise, Brynn interrupted him. "Romania? Ooh…like Dracula?"

With a small smirk, he quirked his head. *Oh, if she only knew.*

"Vlad, actually. Vlad the Impaler. He's who Stoker used as inspiration for Dracula…but, yes. We do have the reputation of having Vampires," he said.

Following Nik's body language, Brynn rested her back against the couch. Continuing to hold his hand, she gave him a flirty look. "Know any?" She asked.

Raising a dark brow, he met her hazel eyes. "Dozens."

Laughing lightly, she wiggled in her seat. Oh, this was much better than talking about her sad little life.

"Oh yeah? And are they all as hot and rich as Hollywood makes them out to be?" she joked.

Suppressing a snicker, Nik nodded. His circle was full of them and the pretty little thing before him would fit right. But he was getting ahead of himself. He had a habit of putting the cart before the horse when something piqued his interest.

"They are…maybe I'll fly you to my home country and introduce you to them, someday," he replied, his voice deep and dark. "But don't worry, I won't let any of them bite you. That privilege is mine."

Widening her eyes, Brynn giggled playfully. Oh, how fun that would be. She would gladly fly to Eastern Europe to meet some fake vampires and indulge in a bit of fantasy roleplay. If that was one of his kinks, she could see herself playing along.

"Mmm…ok…just as long as you'd protect me," she said, lifting her chin slightly.

Maintaining eye contact, a serious look passed over his sharp face. If she allowed him, he would protect her from all the monsters she knew nothing about.

"I'd protect you with my life, Brynn," he replied truthfully. "You'd never have to worry about that."

Taking in a breath, she felt a sharp shiver run down her spine. He sounded so sure and confident, as if he really would protect her with everything he had. She had spent too many nights praying for just that. Maybe he was her heaven-sent miracle?

"I'd like that," she whispered.

Staring at his face for a few seconds, she shook herself from her thoughts. Wanting to get back into a playful mood, she continued with her questions.

"Ok…so, uh…you're originally from Romania…but I don't hear an accent so…how long have you been in the States for?"

"A long time…the majority of my life, really," he said honestly. As far as he was concerned, his undead life counted.

Tossing her long hair over her shoulder with her free hand, she bent her torso closer to her almost Benefactor. She was really starting to like him; he was incredibly easy to talk to. So much more than all the college idiots she had dated before.

"Oh? And why did you come? Family? Work?" she asked, wanting to know more.

Brushing his thumb across her knuckles, he moved his simmering gaze from her eyes to her red lips, and down to her now exposed neck. It was long and elegant, and it made his mouth water. He wondered how her sun kissed skin would feel under his teeth.

"Work…America is the land of opportunity and all of that," he said, unabashedly staring at her pulse point. "Obviously it worked out for me."

Licking her lips, she felt the heat of a flush pepper her skin once again. She knew what that look meant. Playing into the flirtation, she lifted her free hand to touch the bit of her throat he was staring at.

"It really did, didn't it?" she said, running her fingers along her sensitive skin. "And just how did it work out so well, hmm? Did you sell your soul to the Devil or something?"

Allowing himself to fall for her little display, he followed her fingertips as they danced over her freckles. Holding in a laugh, he nodded once. Several actually, but that was a conversation for another night.

"Yeah. Something like that," he said, holding back his rising lust.

"Well, maybe you can introduce me to the Devil after I meet all of your Vampire friends…I'd love to sell him my soul, too," Brynn said, dropping her voice.

Arching a brow, he dragged his green eyes back to her face. Little did she know that he could make that happen. "I think that can be arranged…but only if you're a good girl," he said cheekily.

Grinning like a Cheshire cat, Brynn leaned in closer to Nik. With the alcohol hitting her system, she felt herself growing bolder.

"Oh, I can be good," she promised.

Releasing her soft hand, he moved his touch to her bare knee. Inching his fingertips up her thigh, he hummed low. He had no doubt that what she was saying was the truth. The question was just how good? He wanted to find out.

"Mmm…I really like you, Brynn. I want to move forward. Is that something you would be interested in?" he asked huskily, swirling the tip of his index finger along her inner thigh.

Sucking in a breath, Brynn mentally stopped herself from jumping off the couch. Would she be interested in having a relationship with a handsome billionaire who would take care of her financially in exchange for companionship and possibly sex? *Uh, duh.*

"Yes, very much so," she said without a hint of hesitation.

Easing his fingers away from her skin, Nik gave her a wolffish smile. He was looking forward to whatever fate had in store for them. He had a feeling that whatever it was, it would drastically change them both.

"Wonderful...I'll have my driver pick you up at your place around ten tomorrow night. We'll go over the terms and conditions of our relationship, then," he said.

Perking up suddenly, Brynn furrowed her brows. Ugh. Ten? Tomorrow night? Of course her real life would try to ruin this for her.

"Oh...I can't meet up tomorrow night, I have a shift at the Kinky Kilt," she said, disappointment passing over her fine features.

Shaking his head, Nik reached up to brush her cheekbone with the back of his hand. What kind of Benefactor did she think he was? As if he would let her keep a job at some seedy bar on the Southside.

"No, you don't," he said without skipping a beat. "Not anymore. I'll handle that for you. From now on, I'll handle everything for you...the only person you will ever have to answer to is me. Do you understand?"

Mouthing the words *holy shit,* Brynn stared at him with a look of surprise. This was what she wanted, right? Someone to sweep her off her feet and take care of all her worries?

Yes. A million times yes. It didn't even matter what his terms were. In that moment, she would say yes to anything if it meant he would be her knight in shining armor.

"Yes, I understand," she said, her voice barely above a whisper.

Dropping his hand from her cheek to her neck, he trailed his fingers along the line where her artery lay. Feeling her pulse quicken, he lifted his lips into a wicked smile.

"I'm going to take such good care of you, Brynn...you'll see," he husked.

CHAPTER FOUR

Relaxing against her seat in the back of the Mercedes-Maybach S 680, Brynn turned her eyes upwards towards the large moon roof. Watching the stars twinkle in the clear night sky, she felt her head spin. Was this actually happening? Was she really going through with this? She wanted to pinch herself to make sure she wasn't dreaming.

"Are you comfortable, Miss Smith?" her driver asked, pulling her from her wandering thoughts.

Glancing at the older man's reflection in the rear-view mirror, she nodded her head. She was more than comfortable. She had never ridden in anything so luxurious before in her life. Hell, she didn't even own a car.

"Yeah, very much so, thank you," she replied.

Slowing down to five below the speed limit, the driver continued heading north on the 101 through Scottsdale. Per his instructions, he stayed four car lengths away from the car ahead of him and avoided the various potholes as they came into view. By nature, he was a careful driver, but the demands for this particular ride were a little overboard. Who was this girl? The future Queen of England?

"Good, well if there's anything I can do for ya, please let me know," he said.

"Thank you," she replied politely.

Looking out of her window, she watched the city's lights as they leisurely drove along the state route. She really had no clue where they were, or where they were going. She rarely made her way over to Scottsdale, unless a friend was buying drinks in Old Town.

"Actually…can you tell me where you're driving me to?" Brynn asked, fully realizing how odd the question was.

Turning his head, the driver paused for a split second. It was rare that a passenger didn't know where they were going. There wasn't anything in his paperwork that said he couldn't say, so he felt comfortable that he wasn't ruining some big surprise.

"The Soho, Miss Smith. We're almost there," he said.

Scrunching her face in thought, Brynn tried to recall if she knew what The Soho was. The name sounded familiar, but she couldn't quite place it. Letting her curiosity get the better of her, she reached into her black pleather purse for her phone.

Quickly typing into the search bar, she clicked on its official website in the results section. Scanning the page, her eyes widened in surprise. It was an exclusive condo building with incredible views of the McDowell Mountains. Modern and upscale, The Soho's claim to fame was its newly built penthouses. All of which had four bedrooms, three baths, and skirted around six-thousand square feet.

"Oh my God," she whispered. "Well…he is a fucking billionaire, Brynn. Where else would he live?"

Clicking through the pictures, she stopped once she came across one of the penthouses' master suites. It was massive, with a California king sized bed on one side, and a full living room set on the other. Floor to ceiling windows flanked an entire wall, showcasing a balcony large enough to hold a party of twenty. It was the most opulent bedroom she had ever seen.

She hoped it was Nik's penthouse; more specifically, she hoped it was his bed.

Letting her thoughts drift to her handsome Benefactor, she wondered how long it would take before he tried to make a move. Their night had ended with a simple, chaste kiss on her cheek before he helped her into her Uber. She had wanted much more, but he was a gentleman through and through. Maybe he would give her a quick peck on the lips tonight.

A girl could dream, right?

Laughing lightly to herself, she closed out of the web browser and locked her phone. Putting it back into her bag, she glanced out of the window as the driver exited off the 101. Making their way down the side streets, she noticed just how clean the landscaping of the various homes and businesses was. They were in a safe area, much safer than where she was about to be evicted from. She probably would never have to use the flashlight taser she always carried with her.

Slowing down the Mercedes-Maybach, the driver pulled into the center lane. Turning into the entrance for The Soho, he cleared his throat as he drove towards the main entrance of the large condo building.

"We're here, Miss Smith," he said.

Straightening herself in her seat, Brynn felt a sudden rush of butterflies fill her belly. Looking out of her window, she couldn't help but smile when she noticed Nik waiting for her on the sidewalk. Standing confidently under the lit awning of the building, he looked like an Instagram model. With his hands in the pockets of his dark slacks, and his white dress shirt partially unbuttoned, he was the epitome of what Jenni would call *Daddy*.

God, she wanted more than just a tiny kiss on the lips.

Watching the car pull up, Nik grinned as he locked his eyes onto Brynn's sweet face. After the frustrating day he had flying in and out of LA to deal with an unruly Beneficiary, he was ready to focus all his attention on her.

Waiting until the car had come to a complete stop, he reached for the handle of the passenger door. Opening it, he bent down to get a good look at her. She seemed so innocent and pure in her floral sundress, jean jacket, and worn Converse shoes. It was a stark departure from the sex kitten she portrayed herself to be the night before. Not that he was complaining, he loved it when a woman could be both a saint and a sinner.

"Hi beautiful Brynn…I've missed you," he purred before addressing the driver through the opened door. "Thank you for bringing her home to me safely. Your tip is waiting for you back at the terminal."

Turning his head, the driver lifted his hand to give a tiny salute. "Thank you, Sir…have a good night, Miss Smith."

"You too," Brynn replied.

Moving her hand towards her seatbelt, she paused as Nik leaned his large body in through the door. Opening her mouth to ask what he was doing, she was silenced by him unbuckling her seatbelt. It was an odd thing to do, but also kind of adorable. He really was a different breed of man.

"Thank you," she said, trying to quell the sharp excitement rising in her veins.

Removing the seat belt strap from her slim body, Nik gave her a sly smile. Pulling himself from the Mercedes-Maybach, he held out his hand. She had spent some time in the sun, he could smell it on her skin. He suddenly wished he could be out during the day unguarded with her, she probably looked like a Goddess in the sunlight.

"Of course," he said. "Now come, let's get you inside."

Grabbing her purse in one hand, Brynn took his with the other. Easing out of the luxury vehicle, she stepped onto the sidewalk.

Keeping her warm hand in his, Nik closed the door behind her. Giving it a small squeeze, he led her towards the entrance. "Did you have a good day?" he asked, removing a keycard from his pocket.

Catching his green eyes as he swiped the lock and opened the door, she offered him a bright smile. It was the first day in forever that she didn't have any responsibilities. She had spent much of it sleeping and sunbathing with Jenni at Don's mansion. It was a perfect day; she hoped the night would be just as special.

"It was amazing, thank you…how about you? How was your meeting?" she asked, stepping through the threshold of the condo building.

Walking to the private elevator for Penthouse One, Nik pushed out a short sigh. His day wasn't as wonderful, he hated being the disciplinarian sometimes. It was a necessary evil, though.

"Long…very long…but I must thank you. Knowing I'd get to see you got me through it" he said, using the keycard once again to call the lift.

Shifting her weight from one foot to another, Brynn turned her freckled face upwards. Giving him a flirty grin, she felt her confidence soar. She was pleased as punch to know that she hadn't been the only one pining away.

"Oh, so you were thinking of me, hmm?" she asked.

Locking onto her hazel eyes, he lifted the corner of his lips into a sinful smirk. If she only knew what kind of wicked thoughts were running through his mind all day.

"You were definitely a distraction," he said, waiting for a second while the elevator door opened. "Normally I'm pretty good at compartmentalizing but…I just couldn't seem to do that. Not that I'm complaining."

Encouraging her into the lift, he followed quickly behind. Pressing the button to the penthouse, he continued to study the fine features of her face. It was taking all his strength not to press her into the corner and turn all his dark fantasies into reality.

Swallowing hard, Brynn planted her feet as the elevator rose upwards. He had that hungry look in his eyes, the one that made her ache in the most delicious way. Would it be too bold of her if she showed him she wasn't wearing anything under her little dress?

"I'm sorry for distracting you," she said.

Releasing her hand, he lifted his to brush an errant strand of hair from her flushing face. Tucking the lock behind her ear, he let his fingertips trail down her neck.

"I'm not," he said, his voice deep and warm.

Feeling a shiver race down her spine, Brynn squealed internally. She hadn't had this type of chemistry with anyone, it was starting to drive her insane that neither of them was acting upon it. He had warned her that nothing would happen until they had gone over his terms, but still.

Dropping his hand, he purposefully leaned away just as the lift came to a stop. He could almost hear her begging him to take her and he needed to create some distance. Luckily, the elevator door opened just in time.

Motioning towards the penthouse with a quirk of his sharp chin, he softened his smile. "Please, come in," he said.

Pushing her disappointment to the side, she nodded her head. Taking a step into the beautifully furnished penthouse, her mouth dropped open. Glancing around the expansive living space, she let out a disbelieving laugh. She knew it would be amazing from the pictures on the website, but in person it was on a whole another level.

"Oh my God," she breathed.

Brushing past Brynn, Nik urged her forward with a flick of his hand. Walking to the center of the living room, he turned to watch her reaction.

"Come, take a look around," he encouraged.

Following his command, she slowly walked through the stately living room. Dropping her pleather bag on the warm wood coffee table, she turned her head from side to side to take everything in.

Although all the decor and furnishings were impeccable, they completely surprised her. They looked like they were straight out of her beloved Pottery Barn catalog. While she adored PB, she had a hard time seeing Nik using their design services. He could afford much more than upper middle-class furniture. But what did she know, really? Her seven-year-old tv was sitting on a piece of plywood held up by cinder blocks.

Moving from the living room to the dining room, her eyes widened as they settled upon a table big enough for twelve. Dressed for a full dinner service, she marveled at the antiqued bone china and crystal wine glasses. Everything was stately, yet opulent and she wondered just how many dinner parties he hosted on a regular basis.

Stepping over to the gourmet kitchen, she reached out to touch the white marble countertops as she spun around the modern space. All the stainless-steel appliances were top of the line, she recognized them from the cooking competitions she watched when she had a quick minute to herself. She had always wanted to cook a full holiday meal in a kitchen just like this. Maybe he would let her this Thanksgiving?

Observing her quietly, Nik followed her as she all but danced her way down the wide hallway. Blowing past three guest bedrooms and two bathrooms, she made a straight beeline to the master suite. He prayed she would like this room most of all.

Boldly passing through the threshold of the suite, Brynn gasped audibly. The layout was exactly the same as the website, but that was where the similarities ended. Instead of being somewhat cold and modern, it was warm and lush. Once again, everything looked like it was straight out of the catalog she had drooled over for months and months. She didn't know which she wanted to lie on first; the white, plush rug in front of the electric fireplace, or the Alaska king-sized bed lined with all the fluffy pillows she could ever ask for.

Sensing her excitement, Nik gave himself a mental pat on his back. Walking past her, he casually took her hand. Gently pulling her towards the large balcony, he glanced over his shoulder at her shocked face.

"Let's get some fresh air and talk, hmm?" he said, sliding the glass door open.

"Sure," she replied.

Letting him lead her onto the balcony, Brynn glanced around the starlit sky. Even though the darkness was hiding the mountains, she knew the view was spectacular. She couldn't wait to see the cotton candy sunrise kiss them.

Letting go of her hand, Nik turned to face her. Lifting a dark brow, he studied her as she absorbed her new surroundings. She wore an awestruck look that boosted his ego.

"Well, beautiful Brynn? Do you like it?" he asked, knowing full well the answer.

Nodding her head, it took her a few seconds before she could form a reply. She had only seen homes like this on tv or in movies. Never in her wildest dreams did she ever think she would be able to spend any amount of time in something so glamourous.

"I love it…it's stunning…I…I just can't get over it!" she said, smiling brightly.

Lifting his large hand, he moved to cradle the side of her face. Gently encouraging her to meet his heated gaze, he reminded himself to commit the moment to memory. He had many more surprises in store for her, but the first one always carried the most magic.

"Good, because it's yours."

CHAPTER FIVE

Blinking her hazel eyes, Brynn gave Nik an incredulous look. What did he just say? That this spectacular condo was hers? No, that couldn't be right. Her ears were playing tricks on her. Surely, she hadn't heard him correctly.

"What?" she asked, her voice lifting in disbelief. "I'm sorry…I…I don't think I heard you right."

Running the pad of his thumb along her freckled cheek, Nik nodded his head. The shock on her face was worth every annoying hoop he had to go through to give her this gift. Although they were entering into a relationship where this was the expectation, her disbelief was true and genuine. She truly was a breath of fresh air.

"This penthouse is yours for as long as you want to be with me," he said, his dark green eyes focusing on her stunned face. "Do you like it?"

With her mouth agape, Brynn found herself at a complete loss for words. A myriad of emotions was hitting her all at once. She didn't know whether to laugh, or to cry. Was this really happening? They had only met each other twenty-four hours prior, and he had already given her a penthouse?

Holy shit.

"I…I, uh…I love it!" she stammered. "But…I mean…we've only just met…are you sure?"

"Brynn, I never do anything unless I want to…but besides that, I know you're a week away from being homeless. There's no way I would let that happen," he said.

Dropping her eye line, she felt a wave of embarrassment crash into her. She was hoping he wouldn't find out about that. Getting the eviction letter was one of the most humiliating moments of her life. And she had had quite a few in her twenty-three years on this planet.

"Oh," she said softly.

Moving his hand from the side of her face, he gently took her rounded chin between his index finger and thumb. Lifting it, he forced her to meet his eyes. Clicking his tongue against the roof of his mouth, he shook his head. The shameful look on her face had no place here.

"No...don't you feel bad about that. It's not your fault that you rent from a scum lord that doubled your rent just because he could. I know how hard you've worked...you deserve this reward. And there is more to come. Now...why don't we go back inside and go over some ground rules, hmm?" he asked, using the low tone of his voice to lull her.

Taking in a breath, Brynn nodded in agreement. Within an instant, all her abashment melted away, freeing her to enjoy what her new life was about to bring. He was right, she did deserve this. She deserved all of it.

"I'd like that," she said, giving him a bright smile that crinkled the corners of her eyes.

Pleased by how quickly she responded, Nik felt secure in his selection. There was something unique about her that he already adored. He just might keep her all to himself.

"Good girl," he replied, releasing her chin.

Letting his hand fall, he once again took hers. Grasping it tightly, he led her back through the sliding glass into the master bedroom. Making sure she had crossed the threshold, he secured the door behind her.

"Shall we take a seat on the sofa?" he asked, motioning to the cream-colored couch in front of the glowing fireplace.

A little disappointed that he didn't want to talk business on the huge bed, Brynn shrugged her shoulders. Telling herself that the sofa looked just as comfortable, she agreed to his suggestion.

"Sure," she said.

Stepping towards the high-backed couch, he allowed her to take a seat. Making sure she was sitting comfortably, he sat down beside her. Letting his hand drift onto her bare knee, he smiled as he heard a gasp escape her berry-stained lips. Knowing her reaction wasn't due to any of his influence, he couldn't help but grin. Intruding into her mind for a split second, he caught a few flashes of her wicked thoughts. The little minx was imagining herself straddling him and riding him into oblivion. Her eagerness excited him.

He was looking forward to turning her fantasy into reality.

Dropping her eyes to her knee, Brynn swallowed hard. Watching his fingertips as they swirled a lazy pattern, she pressed her lips together to keep herself from saying something inappropriate. He was just touching her leg, why was that such a turn on?

Clearing his throat to grab her attention, Nik began the boring process of getting down to business. The quicker she agreed to his terms, the quicker he could give her what she truly wanted.

"Are you ready to go over the conditions I have for our relationship, Brynn?" he asked.

Moving her eyes from Nik's hand to his chiseled face, she tried to stamp down her erotic thoughts. Nodding her head, she reminded herself that this conversation needed to happen.

"I'm ready," she replied.

Patting her knee, he purposefully removed his hand. Leaning back against the linen sofa, he kept his simmering gaze on hers.

"Good…I don't have many rules, but the ones I do have are non-negotiable. So, let's begin…*One*. For the entire length of our relationship, you will be completely monogamous and loyal to me. You are *mine* in every sense of the word. Do you accept?" he asked.

Suppressing a squeal, Brynn watched as a serious look passed behind his green eyes. Possessiveness was usually a red flag, but she understood where he was coming from. He was investing a lot in her. And she did have to admit, the thought of her belonging to him made her toes curl.

"Yes, I accept," she said.

"Wonderful," Nik said, offering a small smile. *"Two*. Under no circumstances are you allowed to bring men here while I'm away. I don't care who they are, I don't care how innocent your reasoning is. They are not allowed here, period. And never try to lie to me about it, I will know."

Nodding in agreement, she quickly agreed to his second rule. It wasn't an unreasonable request. Plus, she didn't have any male friends, so it wouldn't be a problem.

"Good…ok, now onto rule *three*. You will maintain a three-point five GPA in all your classes. Also, next semester, you will enroll full time. You no longer have to work, so this shouldn't be a problem…and I want you to finish your degree as quickly as possible. Not that you need a degree, but I know it's an important goal for you and I want you to see it through," he said, his voice warm and encouraging.

"I can do that," she said.

"You're making this easy…I just have three more to go. Ok. *Four*. When I'm in town, you will drop everything to be with me. Barring school and schoolwork, of course…but any time not in class you will be with me. You'll accompany me to any events I may be attending, any errands I may have to run…basically, your world stops when I'm here," he said, intently watching her micro expressions.

Suddenly confused, Brynn furrowed her brow. When he was in town? For some reason, she has the impression that they would be living together full time.

"Wait...you're not going to be here every day? I thought you lived here," she said with a small frown.

Shaking his head, Nik leaned forward slightly. He loved hearing the little bit of disappointment in her voice. It bode well for him that she wanted him near.

"No, my beautiful Brynn...*you* are the only reason I'm here in Arizona. I came here specifically for you...but I don't have one home, per say. I have many. I travel for work extensively all over the world. Los Angeles, Chicago, Miami, New York, Toronto, London, Rome, Prague, Paris, Tokyo, Shanghai," he said, motioning with his hand. "And on and on and on...my business takes me everywhere. We may not see each other as often as we like but I promise that when we do, all my attention will be on you."

"Oh. Ok," she said with a sigh. "Well...ok, I accept rule four."

"Fantastic...we're moving right along. *Five*. You must maintain your health. My assistant, Yetta, will be stopping by tomorrow with various supplements and vitamins. Take them. Religiously. I would also like you to workout at the gym we have here at least three times a week...I don't think that's too unreasonable. Also, it's imperative that you up your intake of leafy green vegetables and at least once a week, I would love for you to have a really good steak dinner. Grass fed and organic, of course," he said.

Quirking her head, Brynn wanted to pinch herself. Was this really a rule? Due to her financial circumstances, she never really had the option to focus on her health. Hell, in the last few months it was rare for her to even have enough food for one meal a day. A steak dinner at least once a week? Oh, done. Her mouth was watering just thinking about it.

"I'll do that gladly...even the working out part. I hate working out, but

I will for you," she replied.

"Well, Brynn…really, you should be doing that for yourself first and foremost…but I appreciate that. I want you to live a long and healthy life," he said with a caring nod. "Ok. So. That brings us to *six*. My most important rule."

Leaning in towards him, Brynn licked her lips in anticipation. So far, his rules weren't too over the top, she was sure that his final rule wouldn't be, either.

Catching her gaze, Nik gave her a very serious look. If she wouldn't agree to this, their relationship wouldn't move forward. He hoped she would do the right thing, he liked her too much.

"As you know, philanthropy is extremely important…specifically, blood donation. That is something very near and dear to me. One of the organizations I run supplies blood to hospitals around the world. It saves countless lives every year, and I'm very proud of that fact," he said, selling every ounce of his half-truths. "My last rule is that you must donate blood at least twice a month. I have a private nurse that will come to the penthouse to make it extremely easy. But yeah…this is non-negotiable for me. Every woman that has come into my life has had to do this…and I cannot make an exception for you, no matter how much I might want to."

Scrunching the fine features of her face, she paused for a moment as she absorbed his words. His request came completely out of left field, she didn't see that coming. It was odd to say the least, but not a deal breaker. She had donated blood on a few occasions and never thought that the process was unpleasant. She could live with that one bizarre caveat.

"It's a good thing I'm not afraid of needles," she joked.

Curling the corner of his mouth into a smirk, Nik leaned his torso into Brynn's personal space. He knew she wouldn't turn him down.

"Mmm…so you accept my terms, then?" he asked, inching closer.

Drifting her eyes across the planes of his pale face, she took in a shaky breath. Of course she did, she'd be insane not to.

"Yes, I agree to all your rules, Nik. I will be yours until we mutually agree to part ways," she replied.

Narrowing his green eyes, he hummed low as he memorized the moment. Lifting both of his hands, he cradled her flushing face. "You're not going to regret this," he promised.

Melting into his touch, Brynn's heart began to race. Feeling dizzy from the heat of his gaze, she gave him a flirty smile. "Should we seal the deal with a kiss?" she asked sweetly.

Instantly accepting her invitation, Nik closed the space between them. Brushing his full lips against hers, he teased her with a barely there kiss. One that he knew would draw out the desire she was suppressing.

Feeling him pull away from the tiny peck, Brynn furrowed her brow in protest. Lifting her hands to grab his forearms, she greedily drew him back to deepen the kiss. Hungrily moving her lips over his, she encouraged him with her tongue.

Growling into the heated kiss, he dropped his hands from her face. Breaking her hold on his forearms, he pulled her torso flush against his. Listening to her quickening heartbeat, he felt his own lust rise. He knew she was a hellion under that good girl façade. She just needed a little nudge to bring her out.

Spurred on by his roaming hands, she boldly climbed onto his lap. Giving him a playful shove, she pressed him to the back of the plush couch. Straddling his muscular thighs, she moaned as he yanked on her jean jacket. Her mind was spinning, her body moving on autopilot. In that moment, he was the only thing she needed.

Pulling the dark denim from her shoulders, Nik nipped at her lips with his sharp teeth before soothing them with a swipe of his tongue. Ripping the fabric from her arms, he threw it on the floor without a second thought. Skirting into her thoughts, he hissed when he learned she wasn't wearing panties.

Fuck, he thought. She was going to test him.

With his large hands moving to her waist, Brynn whimpered as a familiar ache settled between parted thighs. Wanting more of the delicious torment, she rolled her hips in a slow rhythm opposite of her impatient mouth. Begging for more with every deliberate pass.

Pulling at the skirt of her sundress, Nik wedged his hands under the thin fabric. Roving his rough touch to her bare ass, he dug his fingertips into her flesh, using them to help her grind down against his hardening cock. Hearing her blood rush through her veins only excited him more. He needed to taste her in every way imaginable.

Wanting to take their tryst further, she drifted her fingers to his crisp dress shirt. With shaky fingers she began to work the pearlized buttons, unbuttoning them one by one until reaching his waistband. Mewling against his lips, she arched sharply as he gave her ass a sharp squeeze. Distracted by his touch, she almost didn't hear the tight shrill of his cell phone going off in his pocket.

Suddenly ripped from the heady moment, Nik hissed into the kiss. Freezing for a split second, he debated whether he should answer. He knew who was calling, and what it was about. It pissed him off to no end.

Noticing the instant change in her Benefactor, Brynn halted her wanton movements. Reluctantly pulling away, she opened her eyes. Noticing the ringing of his phone wasn't stopping, she quirked her head. Of course this would happen. *Of course.*

"Do you...do you need to get that?" she asked, breathing hard.

Narrowing his green eyes, Nik spit out a sharp curse. Knowing that the phone wouldn't stop ringing until he answered, he grudgingly released her ass to grab the phone from his pocket.

"I'm so sorry, Brynn," he said, his voice edged in anger.

Giving him a tiny grin in reply, she lifted herself on her knees to allow him room to get into his pocket. Catching her breath, she tried not to let her annoyance get the better of her. This would probably happen every now and then. He was a businessman, after all. Capitalism never slept.

Pressing his thumb on the screen of his phone, Nik brought the cell to his ear. Keeping his eyes locked on Brynn, he barked low into the phone. He hated seeing the disappointment on her face. The little brat in LA had gone too far this time.

Licking the remnants of their kiss from her lips, Brynn tried to quell the intense need still bubbling in her blood. Listening to him talk, she perked a bit when she realized he wasn't speaking English. Unsure of the language, she was able to make out bits and pieces of Latin but didn't recognize the rest. However, knowing where he was from, she surmised it to be Romanian. She wondered just who the hell he was talking to, and what about.

Pressing his lips into a fine line, Nik couldn't help but seethe. Not bothering to end the call politely, he slammed the pad of his thumb on the screen. Letting out an angry growl, he came to the decision that his arrangement with a particular Beneficiary had come to an end. There wouldn't be any pushback from the Elders, so it would be a clean break. He just loathed that it would take him away from the pretty little thing bouncing ever so slightly on his throbbing cock.

"I have to go," he said, stuffing the phone back into his pocket.

"What? Now? Seriously?" Brynn asked, her voice lifting in surprise.

Nodding his head, Nik leaned in to give her a quick kiss on her parted lips. Tasting her bitter frustration, he made a silent vow that he would make it up to her. This wouldn't happen again.

"I have to go back to Los Angeles…I will only be gone two nights at the most," he began, helping her from his lap.

Settling back onto the sofa, she smoothed her floral skirt over her thighs. Watching Nik as he stood to full height, she couldn't hide her unhappiness.

"So…do I just wait here until you come back?" she asked.

Lifting his arm, he brushed a stray chestnut strand from her eyes. Pausing for a long moment, he let out a sigh. He hated leaving her like this, when there was still so much to discuss. Maybe if he was methodical in the way he handled things, he could shave off half a day.

"You don't have to, but I would feel better if you did. My assistant will be over tomorrow…she will give you your new phone, supplements, credit card, and set you up with your car service and grocery delivery. If you have any questions, she will be more than happy to fill you in. The penthouse is stocked with anything you may need until the movers can deliver your things from your apartment," he said, buttoning up his dress shirt.

Standing from the couch, Brynn looked up at her handsome Benefactor. Two days really wasn't a long time, and she could think of a million worse places to wait. Brushing off her annoyance, she painted on a smile.

"Thank you for taking care of everything," she said.

Moving to grasp her hand, he brought it up to his lips. Pressing a soft kiss to her knuckles, he gave her a wink. She was so gracious, probably the most gracious one of all. It made him want to give her everything she desired for the rest of her life.

"And there's more to come, my beautiful Brynn. So much more…I'm looking forward to finishing what we started," he said huskily.

Swallowing hard, her legs turned to jelly under his hungry gaze. God, she would be thinking about doing just that until he came back to her. She hoped one of the bathrooms had a removable shower head attachment, it would help to take the edge off.

"Mmm…me too," she replied, taking half a step closer. "Can I walk you to the door?"

"I would love that," he said.

Squeezing his large hand, Brynn slowly led him towards the door of the master suite. Crossing the threshold, she glanced up at his face as they headed down the hallway to the front door.

"Your hair looks amazing that way," she said cheekily.

Humming a reply, he lifted his free hand to run through his unruly dark locks. Trying to smooth them into place, he arched a brow. "Does it? Well, feel free to muss it up again anytime you wish," he said.

Laughing lightly as they reached the front door, Brynn made a mental note of that allowance. Normally she didn't care for longer hair on a man but on Nik, it looked amazing. She couldn't wait to twist her fingers in it while he worshiped her.

"Deal," she replied, unlocking the door.

Pulling the hunk of metal open, she honed her eyes on his pale face. "Well…I guess this is goodnight?"

Nodding once, he leaned down to kiss her reddened cheek. Reminding himself that the quicker he left, the quicker he could return, he took a step out into the hallway connecting the penthouse to the elevator.

"Goodnight my lovely Brynn. I'll be back as soon as I can," he said, reluctantly taking his leave.

CHAPTER SIX

Grabbing a bottle of kombucha from the Sub-Zero refrigerator, Brynn let out a loud yawn. Closing the door with her elbow, she looked at the mess she had made in the kitchen. Remnants of the large breakfast she cooked lay strewn about the marble countertops. Eggs, chicken sausage, fried potatoes, waffles, an omelet; she had happily indulged in them all. It was the first full meal she had had in months.

Needless to say, she was sufficiently stuffed.

Popping open the bottle, she took a large gulp of the vinegary concoction. Making a face as she swallowed, she quickly replaced the lid and set it down among the breakfast mess. Why did everything that was supposed to be good for you have to taste so damn awful?

"Blech," she said, grabbing the opened water bottle next to the pile of broken eggshells.

Bringing the plastic bottle to her lips, she chugged down the cool water. Finally getting the taste of the kombucha out of her mouth, she weighed her morning's options. She could either spend a good half hour cleaning or sunbathe on the balcony.

"Hmmm…tough call," she said with a laugh.

Deciding the kitchen could wait a little longer, she headed for the sliding glass door. Slowly pulling it open, she closed her eyes as she stepped onto the balcony. Letting the sun hit her face, she took a deep breath of the fresh air. She absolutely loved mid-April, when the seasons in Arizona transitioned. After spending most of her life under a blanket of clouds and rain, she could think of nowhere better to be. She was a sun lover through and through.

Opening her eyes, she soaked in the gorgeous view before her. The

McDowell Mountains filled the space where the earth met the sky, their sharp peaks taking on an aubergine hue that took her breath away. She felt like a Queen overlooking her kingdom, she still couldn't believe that this was her new normal.

Squinting from the bright light, she looked around at the various pieces of patio furniture. This balcony was a tad bit bigger than the one attached to the master suite. Its vibe was more masculine, with sleek chaises and sofas made of teak with gray cushions. No doubt Nik wanted to stamp a bit of himself somewhere. Not that she minded.

Taking a seat on one of the reclining chaises, Brynn took another drink of water before placing it down on the wooden table beside her. Lying on her back, she pushed out a sigh as she melted into the thick cushions. For a split second she chastised herself for not putting on the itty-bitty bikini hanging in the closet. Her lululemon sports bra and biker shorts would be leaving her with some interesting tan lines.

She wondered if Nik would like them.

Closing her eyes once more, she relished the moment. She was warm, fed, and well rested. The only thing that could make it even better was if her Benefactor was lying next to her.

"Mmm...Nik...Nikolai...Nikolai Draven...Mister Draven...mmm," she whispered, rolling his name with her tongue. "I'm yours, Sir, do what you want with me. I've been such a naughty little girl."

Giving into her silly fantasy, Brynn puckered her lips to imitate an over-the-top kiss. Laughing lightly to herself, she wiggled on the chaise, pretending to be ravaged by her phantom lover. Lost in the silly daydream, she was suddenly caught unaware by an elderly woman hunched over her prone form.

"Brynn Smith? You Brynn Smith?" the woman asked, her voice carrying a thick Romanian accent.

Instantly snapping open her eyes, Brynn shrieked in surprise. Looking at the stranger, she screamed once again.

Scrunching her wrinkled face, the woman motioned with her hands for the young woman to calm down. She already didn't like how loud this one was. Or how odd. Pretending to kiss the air, who does that?

"Shh. Stop screaming. You scare the neighbors," she tisked. "Now, come. Inside. Too hot out here."

Trying to calm her racing heart, Brynn snapped her mouth shut. Placing an open hand against her chest, she pulled herself up. Blinking at the woman as she hobbled inside, her mind went on high alert. Who was she and why was she there?

Standing from the chaise, she cautiously followed the woman into the penthouse. Keeping her distance, she watched as she limped towards the dining room table.

"I'm sorry…who…how…how did you get in?" Brynn asked.

Letting out a sigh, the elderly woman walked around the large rectangular table. Finally facing Brynn, she reached towards two canvas bags she had placed down a couple minutes prior.

"I knock, no answer. I ring doorbell, no answer. So I use keycard," she replied, pulling out items from the bags. "I Yetta. Mister Draven assistant. He told you I come over today."

Lifting her brows in surprise, Brynn stared at the woman. *This* was Nik's assistant? She had to be at least seventy years old and was clearly not in the best health. She wondered why she hadn't retired. Nik must be an amazing boss.

"Yetta! Yes! Yes, he did…he just didn't tell me when you would be coming over. Forgive me, I'm sorry I didn't hear you ring the doorbell," she said, walking closer to the dining room table.

Lifting her brown eyes, Yetta huffed under her breath. She knew she had to be polite. Mr. Draven had mentioned on more than one occasion how much he liked her. It was a rarity for him. This girl must be different to pique his interest so much.

"Of course you don't hear me. You too busy in fantasy land," she said.

Instantly feeling embarrassed, Brynn dropped her eyes to the wooden floor. *Crap.* She probably wouldn't ever live this down; she prayed the woman wouldn't tell Nik.

"Yeah…I'm sorry about that," she said.

Shrugging her gnarled shoulders, Yetta mumbled something low. Waving away the apology with her hands, she finished taking the last bottle of vitamins from the reusable bag.

"Ok. Supplement and vitamin. Here you have woman multivitamin. B-12 vitamin. Vitamin C. Probiotic. Iron vitamin. Take after breakfast. Everyday. Here is green food powder. Mix with water. Drink. Disgusting but you must drink. Oh. Liquid IV. Yes. Also mix with water," she said, pointing at each bottle as she rambled them off.

"Oh, ok. Sure," Brynn replied. "I'll take them all."

Picking up a white rectangular box from the table, Yetta held it out to Brynn. Shaking it impatiently she gave the young woman an annoyed look.

"Here. New phone. Open it," she said.

"Okay," Brynn replied, taking the phone. "But why do I need a new phone? Mine still works."

Pointing at the box, Yetta met Brynn's confused gaze. Reminding herself to be patient with the girl, she softened her harsh features.

"For Mr. Draven to keep contact with you. Untraceable. Secure. The way he like," she said.

Nodding her head, Brynn mouthed a silent 'oh.' She supposed it made sense, but it did make her wonder why their communication had to be secure and untraceable. Were his business dealings legit?

Opening the box, she took a long look at the sleek new phone. With sharp edges and a razor thin body drenched in warm gold, it was the oddest phone she had ever seen. Taking it from the packaging, she was shocked at just how featherlight it felt in her hand. It seemed too delicate; she was sure she would break it.

"What kind of phone is this?" she asked, bringing it closer to her face. "I'm going to drop it and shatter it, I just know."

"Mmm…măr. Er…Apple Omega. Prototype. Very tough. Will not break, no worry," Yetta answered.

Holding onto her reservations, Brynn hummed critically. Swiping her finger over the screen, her eyes widened as the Apple icon flashed over the tempered glass. How the hell was he able to get a prototype?

"Password is four, three, two, three," Yetta barked.

Typing in the password, Brynn scanned over the home screen. She was taken aback by the fact that there were only five apps. Phone, messages, camera, photos, and a random period tracker called Crimson.

"Um…do you know why there's a period tracker?" Brynn asked, arching a brow.

Nodding her head, Yetta tried to sell it as casually as possible. "Mister Draven need to know when you have monthly bleed so he can prepare," she said.

"Prepare? Prepare for what?" Brynn asked, scrunching her face.

Clearing her throat, Yetta painted a blank look. After doing this dozens and dozens of times, she had never been asked that.

"He is…I think…afraid of women blood," she said. "Very common in our country. Superstition."

Mulling over her answer, Brynn was both surprised and disappointed. Nik didn't seem like the type of man that would be scared or turned off by a menstruating woman. But perhaps Yetta was right and this was just how they were in Romania. She really had no idea.

"Huh," Brynn replied. "Ok, well, I'll use it."

"Yes, good," Yetta said before leaning across the table and handing the young woman a credit card. "This for you. Black American Express. No limit. Use for anything you need."

Blinking at the credit card, Brynn dropped the phone and its box onto the table. Taking the credit card, she examined it with a shaky hand. Oh, God. She was holding an AMEX Centurion Black Card. She had only heard about this in movies, and here she was, holding one with her name on it.

Holy fucking shit.

"Thank you," she said.

Pushing out a little snort, Yetta pointed at the phone. "No thank me. Thank Mister Draven."

"Oh, yes...yes of course," Brynn replied.

Folding her arms over her chest, Yetta watched Brynn for a long moment. She could tell she didn't have a mean bone in her body. It was rare for a mistreated animal to retain its sweetness. She knew that firsthand.

"Mister Draven like you. He thinks you special," she said, eyeing the young woman up and down.

Taking in a breath, Brynn beamed inside. It was comforting to hear that coming from a third party. She thought he was pretty special, too.

"Do not break Mister Draven's heart," Yetta warned. "It took long time to heal."

Meeting her brown eyes, Brynn nodded once. She remembered that Nik's marital status on his Benefactor profile had said widower. She was sure Yetta was referring to that. It was something she did want to talk to him about, in due time of course.

"I'll try not to…and for what it's worth, I like him too," she confessed.

"Good," Yetta said simply. "Now car service. Number saved on phone. Use it. Also, grocery delivery saved on phone. All organic. All good. Call in order and use AMEX card. They deliver."

"Oh! Could you tell me what kind of food Nik likes? I want to make sure that he has stuff to eat whenever he's here," Brynn asked, smiling brightly.

Shaking her head, Yetta brushed off her question. Again, no other girl had ever asked her that. Maybe she wasn't as money hungry as the others.

"Mister Draven on special diet. No worry. He take care of himself," she said.

"Well, I…I would like for him to have something here. What kind of diet is he on? Keto? Mediterranean? Dairy free? Sugar free? Gluten free? Vegetarian? Pescatarian? Vegan? I mean…I've dabbled in a bit of every diet since I was a teen, I will gladly accommodate!" Brynn said cheerfully.

With a stern look on her face, Yetta huffed once more.

"No. No. You never been on Mister Draven diet. He take care of himself," she repeated, her voice low and stern. "Buy food for *you.*"

Furrowing her brow, Brynn surveyed the older woman. She really didn't know why she seemed so annoyed. It was just a simple question. She would just have to ask Nik herself.

"Okay," she replied, dropping the topic.

Sighing heavily, Yetta took the empty canvas bags from the table. Grasping the handles in her arthritic hand, she motioned towards the door.

"Good. Yes. Well, I go now," she said, beginning to limp towards the front door.

"Ok, I'll walk you out," Brynn said.

Following Yetta, she pressed her lips into a fine line. She wasn't sure if she had made a good impression on the woman. Some people just had a curtness about them, and it made them impossible to read. For some reason, she really wanted to win her over.

Opening the heavy front door, Yetta crossed the threshold without a second thought. Slowly stepping towards the elevator, she paused for a moment as Brynn said a polite goodbye. Glancing over her shoulder, she forced herself to give the young woman a lopsided grin.

"I see you later," she said.

Giving Yetta one last look, Brynn closed the door to the penthouse. Taking in a deep breath, she let her mind wander to the weird bits of conversation she had just had. It seemed like Nik had some odd idiosyncrasies, but honestly, who didn't?

Shrugging them off, she headed back towards the dining room. She made it to the table just in time to catch her new phone ringing. Picking up the thin device, she smiled when she saw the name *Nikolai* pass across her screen. Clicking on the answer bubble, she brought the cell to her ear.

"Nik! Hi! How's LA?" she asked, her voice lifting in excitement.

"Hello my beautiful Brynn...it's so nice to hear your voice. Los Angeles has been...taxing to say the least. But I'm finally negotiating a severance package. If it's accepted relatively soon, I'll be home to you tomorrow night."

"Oh, yeah? That's great! I can't wait to see you," she said, walking circles around the large table.

"The feeling is mutual… I hate that I left you the way I did. Were you able to get some sleep?"

"I think I was able to get a few hours…honestly, you left me pretty wound up. But one of the shower attachments in the master shower helped," she said suggestively.

"Ohhh…God, Brynn. I have to be the bad guy in a few minutes and now I'm going to be thinking about you getting yourself off in the shower without me. You little tease."

"Well, good. Serves you right," she said cheekily.

"Mmm…well, don't you dare touch yourself again until I come home."

Shivering slightly, Brynn halted her steps. Oh. This was getting fun. "Or what, Mister Draven?"

Waiting for an answer, Brynn heard a deep growl on the other end of the phone. Swallowing hard, she felt her heartbeat tick upwards.

"Or I'm going to tie you to the bed and bring you to the edge again and again…first with my fingers…then with my mouth…and then with my cock. But I will stop every single time you're just about to cum until you're just a whimpering, crying, begging mess. Do you understand, my beautiful girl?"

With her mouth falling open, Brynn had to mentally stop herself from screaming. *Holy shit.* That was probably the hottest thing any man had ever said to her. She liked it. She *really* liked it.

"I understand," she breathed.

"Good girl. Now…before I forget. My nurse, Peggy, will be by this evening around six o'clock for your blood donation. Please make sure you drink enough water so you're hydrated."

Blinking away her erotic thoughts, Bynn snapped back into the present. Blood donation. That's right. Rule number six. He really meant it when he said it was his most important rule.

"Ok, I will. I promise," she replied.

"Thank you. Well, I'd better calm my cock down and finish this. I'll text you later, ok?"

Humming into the phone, Brynn enjoyed the mental image his one little comment kicked into her head. It almost made her want to take him up on his little threat.

"I'm looking forward to it…good luck, Nik," she said.

"Thank you, my beautiful Brynn. I'll talk to you soon."

CHAPTER SEVEN

Pulling her high ponytail taut, Brynn quickly walked towards the front door of the penthouse. She was proud of herself for hearing the alarm for the door of the condo complex this time. Twice, in fact. She hoped she would get to the keypad before it rang for a third time. She hated to keep people waiting, but six-thousand square feet was a lot to transverse.

"Ahh! I'm coming! I'm coming! Don't leave!" she yelled to herself.

Finally reaching the video keypad gracing the wall, she touched the condo entrance button. Within a second, the image of a petite woman flashed onto the screen. Wearing bright fuchsia scrubs and carrying a medical bag, she looked kind and competent. Exactly what you would want in a medical professional.

Hitting the call button, Brynn flashed a smile. Although the woman couldn't see her, it was an automatic habit. Years in customer service had hammered into her brain that people could tell whether you had one on your face.

"Hi! Peggy? I'm sorry to keep you waiting, let me buzz you through! Just head to the elevator for Penthouse One and I'll send it down," she said.

Watching the woman nod her head and give the camera a thumbs up, she quickly pressed the condo door button. Making sure the raven-haired tech made it through, she touched the elevator's call button. It was amazing how secure the penthouse was, but it did make the deliveries and visits somewhat complicated.

Wealthy first world problems, Brynn, she chastised herself. At least she didn't have to sleep with her broken dresser barricading the door, anymore. She would gladly take this tiny inconvenience over the constant threat of being assaulted or worse.

Rolling her eyes at her own absurdity for complaining, Brynn unlocked the front door with a flick of her wrist. Pulling open the heavy slab of metal, she waited patiently for the elevator. It was six o'clock on the dot, she loved it when people were on time.

Hearing an electronic chime, she watched as the door to the elevator slid open. Fixing her posture, she waved to the nurse.

"Hi! Peggy?" she asked.

"Yep, that's me!" Peggy replied, stepping out of the elevator and walking down the short hallway. "And you must be Brynn?"

Nodding her head, Brynn yanked the door open wide. Giving her enough room to push past, she encouraged her with a nod.

"Yeah, hi! Please, come on in," she said politely.

Securing the large medical bag on her shoulder, Peggy walked into the penthouse. Smiling a thanks to Brynn, she halted her steps once reaching the end of the open foyer.

"I'm not sure how afraid of needles you are so I just want to calm any anxiety right away…I pride myself at getting a vein in one stick," she said confidently.

Closing the door, Brynn stepped towards Peggy. Giving a tiny shrug, she met her dark brown eyes.

"Oh, I'm totally ok with needles, but that's great to know…the last time I gave blood, it took three tries before they were able to get it. That kind of sucked but I'm way more hydrated this time, so that will probably help," she said, realizing she was starting to ramble. "Uh, yeah…so, anyways…where should we do this?"

Giving the young woman a knowing look, Peggy glanced around the open space. Pointing at a large cream armchair in the living room, she lifted a black brow.

"Does that happen to recline at all?" she asked.

Moving her gaze to the chair, Brynn nodded once. "Oh yeah! It even massages and has heat!"

"I would expect nothing less, Mister Draven likes to spoil those he cares about…ok, so we'll do the donation there. But I will ask you not to use the massage feature until after we're done. I would hate to get any stains on that light fabric," she said with a small laugh, starting to walk to the oversized chair.

"Yeah, we definitely don't want that to happen!" Bynn replied, following her.

Setting down her medical bag on the coffee table, Peggy began the process of removing her equipment. Waiting until Brynn had taken her seat, she moved her small Hemaflow Scale and collection bag to the black end table next to the recliner.

"Ok, feel free to get comfortable, just don't go back all the way," she said.

Using the control panel on the side of the armrest, Brynn pushed the armchair back. Finding a relaxing position, she settled against the plush fabric as Peggy gathered the rest of the necessities and put on a pair of latex gloves.

"Alright, I'll need you to extend your left arm and make a tight fist for me," she said.

Doing as instructed, Brynn watched the nurse as she wrapped a strip of blue elastic around her upper arm. Making sure to keep her fist tight, she waited as Peggy used the tip of her index finger to find a vein.

"Oh yeah…already found a good one! Anyone told you that you have really nice veins? No wonder Mister Draven likes you so much."

"What?" Brynn said.

"Oh, Nothing!" Peggy said cheerfully. "It's just that with your veins, you're what we call a *power donor*. It'll be super easy to pull blood from you. Anyways...I wish every donor made my job easy."

Eyeing the nurse for a moment, Brynn attempted to make sense of the odd comment. Maybe being a power donor meant she could donate blood more often? Probably not, twice a month seemed like an awful lot. Deciding to brush it off as she had with everything else, she gave her a grin.

"Well, good! I never want to make anyone's job harder than need be," she said.

"You know...the Earth would be a much better place to live if everyone followed that same line of thought. You're a kind soul," Peggy said, getting to work.

Swiping the alcohol wipe over Brynn's sun kissed skin, she brought the butterfly needle towards the crook of her arm. "Ok, just a tiny pinch," she warned.

Holding still, Brynn winced slightly as the needle pierced her skin and then another once it found her vein. She had to hand it to Peggy, that was the easiest poke of her life. She definitely knew what she was doing.

Taping the needle to Brynn's arm, Peggy turned on the Hemaflow. Making sure the machine was gently rocking the medical bag as it collected Brynn's blood, she hummed softly.

"Ok, that will do it...just try to relax," she said, removing her purple medical gloves. "It should take maybe ten minutes. I just need to make a couple of quick phone calls...I'm going to head out onto the balcony and come back in a few. Does that sound ok?"

Nodding, Brynn offered a grin. She was relieved she wouldn't have to make small talk.

"Yeah, sure!" she replied.

"Great, be back soon," the nurse said, walking to the sliding glass door.

Waiting until she heard the door close behind the nurse, Brynn let out a long sigh. Watching the collection bag as it filled with her crimson blood, she made a disgusted face. Blood didn't make her squeamish, but the feeling of it leaving her body with every strong heartbeat did.

"Ugh, so gross," she whispered.

Closing her eyes, she rested her head back against the comfortable chair. Sitting quietly for a few moments, she suddenly stirred when she felt a buzz coming from the small pocket of her shorts. Reaching for her thigh, she fished out her new phone. Reading Nik's name on the screen, she quickly pulled up his text.

How's it going, beautiful?

Instantly feeling giddy, Brynn typed a reply with her free hand.

Good! I'm currently being bled dry, lol. Here, let me send you a pic!

Tapping on the camera button, she switched the camera around to face herself. Holding the phone at arm's length, she took a flirty picture of her puckering for a phantom kiss with her bleeding arm on full display. Hitting send, she laughed out loud. Hopefully he would think it was just as funny.

It only took a handful of seconds before he replied.

God. This is so fucking hot.

Reading the message, she scrunched her face in thought. The picture was hot? Not understanding how, she shot a text back.

It is?

Very. With this one donation, you're saving three lives, Brynn. That's insanely hot.

Immediately having a lightbulb moment, she huffed under her breath. Duh, Brynn. Of course he would think that, he said his blood donation program was extremely important to him. He really did have a kind and generous heart.

Lifting her cell back over her head, she took a few more pictures of herself in various poses, making sure to showcase her arm in each one. Sending them all in a single batch, she smirked to herself. Praying that he loved them just as much, she mentally counted the seconds. She was able to reach twenty before receiving a reply.

You little tease. You're going to be the death of me. Just wait until I get back.

Oh, yeah? I dare you to do your worst, Nikolai.

Ohh. I intend to. Don't you worry.

I can't wait…when will you be back?

Soon.

Not soon enough.

I agree…I have to go. Be good, my beautiful Brynn.

Mmm, yes Sir. But only if you promise to think of me.

I always am, Xx

Feeling a shiver race down her spine, she read and reread their brief exchange. How could just a few short sentences cause her brain to go into overdrive? She couldn't wait until he was done with whatever he was doing in LA.

Hearing the sliding glass door open, Brynn stashed her cell back in her pocket. Turning her head towards Peggy as she came into view, she offered the nurse a kind grin.

"Am I done?" she asked.

"You sure are!" Peggy replied, grabbing a new pair of latex gloves from her bag. "Now that wasn't too bad, was it?"

Shaking her head, she sat patiently as the nurse grabbed a cotton swab and strip of medical tape.

"No, not bad at all…thanks for making it as painless as possible," she said, wincing slightly as she removed the needle from her arm.

Placing the cotton ball against the puncture wound, Peggy quickly secured it with white tape. Folding Brynn's arm, she encouraged her to hold it in place. Pulling the needle from the collection bag, she stuffed it in the small medical waste bin tucked in her bag.

"You're very welcome," she said, turning off her Hemaflow Scale and putting it away. "Just try to rest for a few hours. Do you have any orange juice you could drink and something sweet to eat?"

"Oh, yeah, I just had a grocery delivery, so I'll definitely have a snack," she replied.

"Good!" Peggy said, holding the blood-filled collection bag tightly in her hand. "Ok, well, I guess that's it! I'll see you in a couple of weeks,"

Attempting to stand from the recliner, Brynn was stopped by Peggy raising her free hand.

"Oh, no…you stay right there. I'll see myself out," she said, grabbing her medical bag and swinging it over her shoulder.

"Alright…well, thanks for doing this! It was nice to meet you," Brynn said.

With a warm smile on her face, Peggy headed towards the front door. Glancing over her shoulder, she called out to the newest beneficiary.

"It was great meeting you Brynn, I'll see you soon!" she said, taking her leave from the posh penthouse.

Closing the door fully behind her, Peggy took a couple of steps before digging her phone from the front pocket of her medical bag. Unlocking it, she pulled up the number to her boss. Waiting for him to pick up on his end, she cleared her throat.

"Hi Mister Draven. I'm all done with Brynn. I'll get this right over to the airfield. The courier should have it in the air within the hour," she said.

"Thank you, Peggy. Make sure that this sample is treated with the utmost care. I'm looking forward to receiving it," Nik replied before curtly hanging up.

. . .

Sprawling his large body on the light gray couch of his suite, Nik stared blankly up at the ceiling. His frustration was still bubbling beneath the surface, causing him to clench his jaw and grit his teeth. Mia had started off so well. At one point, she had been one of his favorites. A gorgeous little thing with long blonde hair, and big blue eyes. She had aspirations of being an award-winning costume designer, and he had done what he could to make that dream a reality.

But the beasts of Los Angeles had gotten ahold of her, turning her into nothing more than a junkie whore. Tainting her once heady blood with a variety of poisons that made it toxic to his kind. Sadly, she was no longer useful, and the Elders wanted her gone.

Ulysses had threatened to mind flay her, wanting to inflict as much pain as he could. He hated it when his investments didn't pan out. He had swayed the tyrant to allow him to handle her. After all, there was a bright new addition to the program. Ulysses would soon have a fresh supply; the thin promise was just enough to keep his wrath at bay.

When he arrived back in LA, Mia was on the tail end of her forced withdrawal. It had made her so sick, so incredibly weak. Her immeasurable pain was so great that for a split second, he debated on whether he should permanently end her suffering. His one major flaw kept him from following through.

And so, he had waited until she was just coherent enough to accept his otherworldly influence. It took more time and effort than he had anticipated, but she had finally welcomed her new narrative. She no longer held any memory of him, or their time spent together. And after her year-long stay at the rehabilitation center in Malibu, she would have enough money and resources to keep her clean for the next five years.

It was the least he could do.

Closing his green eyes, Nik stewed in silence. Locking Mia away in his memories, his thoughts drifted towards Brynn. Visualizing her angelic face, his anger slowly melted away, replaced by much needed serenity. He couldn't wait to hold her in his arms.

Letting his mind go wild with torrid thoughts of the brunette, he hissed an expletive when he heard a sharp rap on the door of his suite.

"Yes?" he barked, not bothering to get up.

"Uh, yeah...courier package for a...Mister Draven?" yelled the delivery man through the wooden door.

Instantly perking, Nik stood to full height in a single motion. Quickly clearing the elegant space, he felt his mouth water. *Finally*. He had been thinking of this moment since he matched himself with her on the app.

Ripping open the door, he reached into the pocket of his slacks. Taking out a hundred-dollar bill, he gave the courier a critical look.

"Has the warming bag been turned on the entire time it's been in your care?" he asked, dropping his eyes to the locked insulated bag held in the delivery man's sweaty hands.

Nodding his head, the young man swallowed hard. The man standing before him was probably the most intimidating person he had ever seen.

"Uh, yeah…yes, Sir," he said.

"Excellent," Nik replied, taking the bag from the courier and replacing it with the generous tip. "You will have no memory of this, you will have no memory of me. Now go down to the hotel bar and enjoy a drink before going home for the night."

Blinking his heavy-lidded eyes, the delivery man suddenly straightened his stance. Mumbling something unintelligible under his breath, he turned on his heels and headed for the elevator.

Not bothering to see if the courier had left the floor, Nik slammed the door of his suite shut. Stepping towards the dining room, he placed the red bag on the lacquered table. Typing in a code on the keypad, he unlocked it with a sly smile on his face. Opening it, he gently picked up the crimson collection bag.

Skimming his fingertips over it reverently, he studied it in the fluorescent light of the room. It was rich and robust, warm and dense. Containing the magical essence needed to sustain his kind within each microscopic cell.

Closing his eyes, he silently thanked Brynn for her most precious gift. This would stave off his hunger just long enough to enjoy her other human attributes.

Grabbing a goblet from the table, he carefully opened the collection bag. Pouring the warm contents into the crystal, he breathed in the heavenly aroma. It smelled like her, saccharine sweet and drenched in sunlight; causing his sharp canines to extend in anticipation.

Bringing it to his full lips, he tipped the heavy glass back. Taking a greedy mouthful of the scarlet liquid, he only let it sit on his tongue for a second before swallowing. Almost immediately, an exhilarating effect took over his readied body.

Groaning low in pleasure, his head rolled back as a wave of ecstasy overtook him. Consumed whole by her borrowed life force, he almost didn't recognize the shards of radiant light absorbing into his undead tissue. It was only when he felt the familiar bolt of molten heat slice into his core did he realize the chaos he had unknowingly unleashed.

Breathing hard, his now ebony eyes opened wide. Stunned into a thick silence, he shook his head in defiance of the terrifying truth. It had been centuries since he had come across another.

Brynn Smith was a Sun Walker.

Knowing firsthand the grim implications, his intentions with her switched on a dime. She was no longer chattel in his harvesting scheme. She was a sacred deity that needed saving from his own kind.

Setting the goblet down upon the table, he fished his silver phone from his pocket. Dialing his ever-faithful assistant, he brought the phone to his ear with a shaky hand.

"Yetta. I need you to call Leonardo and have him wipe Brynn Smith from the Benefactor Program. I need every single trace of her gone. Do you understand? Every. Single. Trace. As far as the Clan is concerned, she does not exist…yes? *Good.* And have my jet prepared, I'm heading back to Scottsdale immediately."

Ending the call abruptly, his cold black eyes fell to the crystal chalice. Watching Brynn's blood as it congealed against the glass, he made a solemn vow. He wouldn't allow what happened to his beloved Leona happen to her.

The Monsters would not claim this one.

CHAPTER EIGHT

Sitting still on the edge of the bed, Nik watched the multicolored sunrise as it played out on Brynn's peaceful face. Protected by her blood, he basked in the sun's warmth as it penetrated through the large windows. It had been centuries since he had been able to be this unguarded with the sun. He really ought to enjoy it, to fully step outside into its brilliant rays. But at that moment, he simply couldn't turn away. The glorious sun paled in comparison to the woman sleeping before him.

He would be lying if he said he wasn't terrified. If the Elders caught wind that he had found another Sun Walker, he wouldn't be able to protect her. They would do just as they did with Leona. Locking her away in their craggily fortress, they would bleed her just until the point of death. Again and again as her mind withered away into madness.

Once her body finally caved, whether from age or sickness, Serena would turn her. Unable to disobey her Sire, Brynn would have to follow the war hungry bitch's command. Not fully Vampire nor Sun Walker, she would skirt the world in between. The new treaties they signed with the Governments of the world said nothing about the Hybrid she would become. The Elders didn't care for Mortals the way he did, and they were growing bored in their old age. They would use her to unleash hell for their pure entertainment.

He couldn't let that happen.

Pressing his lips into a fine line, he tried to come up with a semblance of a plan. Although it wasn't much, he had at least a couple of weeks to play with. Just as long as they were compensated in the ways they were accustomed, none of his other Beneficiaries would miss his presence. Things would continue as they had, and his Clan would be sustained. He worried about the promise he made to Ulysses, but that was easily excused if he sold it correctly. The new girl broke his rules, it was as easy as that. He was forced to let her go. There would be another to take her place.

Only there wouldn't be, and Ulysses' patience was already paper thin.

Furrowing his brows in thought, he went over different scenarios in his mind, none of which were completely failproof. Hiding seemed like their best option. There were still places on Earth untouched by either Mortals or Vampires. They could create a life together. It wouldn't be lavish, it might not even be comfortable, but at least she could have one. And when she passed away naturally, as Mortals did, he would reenter the Clan's fold. It wasn't unheard of for him to disappear for decades at a time. Admittedly, it was a weak plan, but it had the potential to work.

Satisfied that he had a direction on which to build upon, Nik gave himself permission to enjoy the day with her. The effects from her blood wouldn't last long, he might as well savor every moment in the light as he could.

Watching quietly as she began to stir, he lifted the corners of his lips into a warm grin. She couldn't know anything was amiss. Eventually he would have to tell her, but that was a problem for a different time.

Moaning lightly as her fiery dream slipped away, Brynn slowly opened her eyes. Staring out of the window at her mountainous view, she let out a sleepy yawn. Staying still as she soaked in the morning, she was suddenly alarmed as she caught something out of the corner of her eye. Turning her groggy attention towards the edge of the bed, she immediately jumped to a sitting position.

"Oh, God!" she yelled, instinctively covering her bare chest with the thick comforter. "Nik?! What…what are you doing here?!"

Holding up his hands, Nik shushed low. Giving her an apologetic look, he moved his body closer to the spooked beauty. He felt awful for scaring her, he should have eased her into his presence.

"I'm sorry, Sunshine…I shouldn't have scared you like that. I got back a couple of hours ago but you looked so sweet I didn't want to wake you up," he said, reaching up to brush her hair from her face.

"So you…you were just watching me sleep?" she asked curiously, meeting his simmering gaze.

"Well now that you've said it out loud, it sounds really odd…but yes. Yes I was," he said, trailing his touch down the side of her face.

Eyeing him curiously, Brynn suppressed a shiver as his fingers dropped lower to trace her collarbone. Admittedly, his confession was a little creepy, but she liked the thought of him watching over her. It made her feel safe in a way that she hadn't for most of her life.

"Maybe it's a little weird…but honestly, you can watch me sleep anytime you want," she said with a flirty grin. "I'm glad you're back…I missed you. Can you stay for a while?"

Nodding his head, he scooted his large body closer. "Actually…I've cleared my schedule for the foreseeable future so I can focus all my time on you. You have me all to yourself."

With a wicked grin, Brynn leaned in towards Nik. Humming lightly, she let the edge of the comforter fall down her bare tits. Stopping just before it exposed her rosebud nipples, she tipped her head back to look at his sharp face. Even though they hadn't known each other long, he made her feel valued and wanted in a way no one ever had. It was a massive turn on.

"Mmm…I do love the sound of that…but the question is, do I get every single part of you?" she asked, her voice taking on a sultry tone.

Bending down, Nik inched towards her parted lips. Stopping just before he touched them with his own, he narrowed his dark green eyes. He loved how unabashed she was. It made him ache in the most delicious way. He couldn't wait to taste her.

"Only if I get to have every part of you, too," he husked.

"Mmm…well…that's only fair," she replied before boldly pressing her lips to his.

Returning her soft kiss, Nik lifted his hands to the sides of her beautiful face. Holding her still, he gave into his searing desire. Moving his lips over hers hungrily, he pressed and pulled, using his tongue and teeth much in the same manner as before. Hoping she would cave into the want he could feel building within her.

Moaning wantonly, Brynn melted into his touch. Swiping her tongue into the kiss, she teased him with a gentle retreat before dominating with her teeth. Biting his lower lip, she grinned against his lips as he growled a warning.

Breaking the passionate kiss, he licked his injured lower lip. Tasting the remnants of her blood still coursing through his veins, he shuddered in pleasure. She was a wicked little thing; he couldn't wait to hear her beg.

"Minx," he hissed, making her fall back into the plush mattress. "Be careful…I might bite back."

Letting out a small laugh, she watched with bright eyes as he ripped the comforter from her half naked body. Waiting for him to move over her, she reached up to undo the buttons of his white dress shirt.

"Mmm…please?" she asked, purposefully nicking his chest with her nails. "I think I want you to."

Hovering just muscular body over her, he groaned as her manicured nails grazed over his alabaster skin. Giving her a look in warning, he felt his bloodlust threaten his resolve. She had no idea what she was asking, or how much it excited him. Pulling back on the reigns of his carnal nature, he quieted her with another needy kiss.

Finished with the last button, Brynn ripped the starched fabric free of the waistband of his slacks. Helping him remove it from his chiseled torso, she moved her attention to the button and fly of his tailored pants.

"Mmm...off...take these off," she demanded against his full lips.

Not needing to be told twice, Nik pulled away from the desperate kiss. Shedding his gray slacks and boxer briefs, he flung them to the floor. Bracing his naked form over her, he buried his face against the crook of her neck. Suckling against her pulse point, he groaned as he felt her hands dip between their bodies to touch his hardened cock.

Humming sweetly, she closed her eyes as he licked the skin of her neck. Using her nimble fingers, she traced the shape of his cock before wrapping her hand around its thick girth. She didn't have to see it to know it was perfect. Just long and thick enough to fill her cunt the way she had always wished a cock would. She was wet just thinking about it.

"Fuck, Nik...if I would've known you had this in your pants, I would've fucked you at the bar," she said.

Mumbling unintelligibly against her flesh, he arched sharply in her roaming grasp. Trembling as he tried to keep his lust in check, he groaned while she began to slowly pump his length. *Gods.* If he knew she could handle his cock, he would've fucked her then, too.

Twisting her wrist once reaching the tip, Brynn teased Nik's aching cock. Using a gentle touch, she sped up her movement. Bringing her hand up and down, she teased the head with every other pass. Again, and again until she heard him spit a vicious curse.

"Stop!" he barked against her throat. "I need to taste you."

Swallowing hard, Brynn opened her starry eyes. Halting her erotic touch, she reluctantly let go of his cock. Meeting his eyes for a split second as he crawled down her splayed body, she felt her skin pebble. He had a feral look that would be terrifying if she wasn't burning up with need.

"Holy shit," she whispered, feeling his fingers tug the white cotton panties from her narrow hips.

Focusing his attention on the lower half of her body, he watched mesmerized as her perfect pussy came into view. She had taken the time to shave for him, she was thinking about it now. Knowing that she had purposefully done this just for him boosted his ego. He couldn't want to make her cum.

"Spread your legs for me, Brynn," he said, his deep tone like velvet. "I'm hungry."

Doing exactly as told, she parted her shaky thighs. Lifting her head from the mattress, she felt her heartbeat quicken as his head dipped between them. Freezing in anticipation, she whimpered when she felt his tongue give her wet pussy a single, agonizing slow lick.

Encouraging her to drape her toned legs over his broad shoulders, he wedged his hands under her hips. Placing a handful of hot kisses on her hairless cunt, he used the tip of his tongue to part her. Greedily tasting her arousal, he growled as the sweet liquid dripped down his chin. It tasted just as good as her blood. It made him realize that after this, he would always crave her.

Breathing hard, Brynn reached down to run her fingers through his dark locks. Instinctively moving her hips, she wordlessly pleaded for more of his wicked tongue. She had never been worshiped like this before, it was almost as if he wanted to make sure he tasted every single bit of her pussy.

Knowing she was good and ready, Nik focused on her readied clit. Wiggling his rough tongue between her slit, he easily found the hardened pearl. Gently placing it between his teeth, he lavished attention on the sensitive bud. Swirling his tongue counterclockwise over and over again, he groaned as he felt her thighs quake.

"Oh fuck! FUCK!" Brynn squealed, twisting and yanking on his disheveled hair.

Turning his narrowed eyes upwards, he watched mesmerized as she writhed her slim body. Taking interest in her pert tits, he memorized the way they moved with every quick rise and fall of her labored breath. She was stunning to look at, letting herself cave into her carnal lust. He couldn't wait to bury himself to the hilt inside her.

Swiping his tongue back and forth over her clit, he suckled on her pink flesh. Coaxing out a handful of high-pitched moans, he dipped into the edges of her mind. Not wanting the pleasure to end, she was forcing herself back from the edge each time she started to come undone. No man had done this to her, and she was afraid of never feeling this good again. It both excited and infuriated him. Instantly, he made a silent promise to give her pleasure whenever she wanted it.

Staring up at the sunlit ceiling, Brynn shivered as her body ramped up once more. Furrowing her brow, she ground her aching pussy against his mouth like a needy slut. Feeling his tongue flick over her buzzing clit, she lost more and more of her resolve. All she wanted to do was fall apart, she just needed a little push.

Knowing exactly what she needed, Nik bit down ever so gently on her clit. Sucking against it, he rapidly tapped his tongue. As with most Mortals, she just needed an edge of pain to completely fall apart.

Give in, he whispered into her mind. *Give in to me.*

Listening to the phantom voice as it echoed in her brain, she caved into her heady desire. Crying out into the cool air of the room, her overstimulated body seized as the sharp bolt of her release took over. Switching quickly from pain to bliss, she trembled as it shot from her core out through her limbs.

Holding onto her as she broke, Nik slowly eased her clit from his teeth. Keeping his mouth on her warm cunt until she fell limp on the bed, he gave her one last lick before lifting his face from between her parted thighs.

"Did that feel good?" he asked, knowing damn well the answer.

Trying to catch her breath, Brynn nodded her dizzy head. Swallowing hard, she looked at the confident man crawling up her thrumming body. Good wasn't exactly the word she would use.

"Oh my God," she whimpered, her eyes glassy and wide. "How did...I thought I heard...oh fuck that was amazing!"

Savoring the remnants of her essence from his lips, he gave her a knowing look. Lifting his hand, he skimmed his fingertips across her right nipple.

"I swear to you, Brynn...I will make you cum as often as you want for the rest of your life," he purred.

Lifting her head from the mattress, she met his intense gaze. Swallowing hard, she tried to process what he had just said. Unsure if she had heard him correctly, she simply nodded. Things between them just became serious insanely quick. Not that she was complaining.

"My turn," she said, already wanting more. "Lie down on your back and let me ride you."

Bending down to give her a swift kiss, Nik obliged her naughty request. Lying in the middle of the large bed, he pawed at his rigid cock. Watching her glide over him, he felt his lust bubble. With her hair wild and her eyes hungry, she was the most beautiful creature he had ever seen.

Straddling his hips, Brynn leaned forward as she reached between her legs for his thick cock. Playfully slapping his hand away, she tsked him with a click of her tongue.

"Do you know how many times I've thought about this for the past two days?" she asked, holding his cock steady at the base. "Just lie there."

Dropping his arms to the mattress, he gave her a devilish grin. Little did she know she would tire before he finished. He would let her have her fill and then take over.

"Yes, Ma'am," he replied.

With a wicked grin, she brought the tip of his hardened cock to her wet pussy. Running it along her slit, she made sure to coat his skin with her arousal. After making several passes, she brought her to her entrance. Inch by inch she slowly lowered herself onto him, squeezing her cunt to tease him until he was fully inside.

Moaning happily, she paused for a moment as her cunt adjusted to his size. Relishing the way he filled her, she wiggled her warm body.

"God, you feel good," she said, starting to move her hips. "So *fucking* good."

Suppressing a groan, he nodded in agreement. He had the exact same sentiment. Her pussy felt amazing wrapped around him, clenching his shaft in just the right way. Perhaps she would be the one to finally test his stamina. He was looking forward to finding out.

Encouraging her with a tiny lift of his hips, he brought his rough hands to the sides of her thighs. Gripping them tightly, he clenched his jaw as she began to work his thick cock.

Moving slowly at first, Brynn swayed her hips from front to back at a leisurely pace. Focusing her eyes on his face, she placed her hands on her firm tits. Cupping them in her hands, she toyed with them. Pinching and pulling in time with her lazy thrusts.

Roaming his gaze over her flushed face, he dropped down to her breasts and further to her cunt. Watching it as she sped her thrusts, it took all his willpower not to reach for her clit peeking between her pussy lips. Telling himself to give her time, he praised her with silken words.

"You're a Goddess, Brynn…yeah…just like that…*ahhh*…fuck…such a…*good* girl," he said, lovingly massaging her thighs.

Smiling down at him, she picked up the pace of her hips. Easily sliding over his shaft, she hummed as she heard the sound of her sopping pussy glide across his skin. The sounds and smells of sex were always such a turn on for her, they drove her crazy in the best way.

Speeding her thrusts, she used her knees as leverage. Lifting herself up and dropping down, again and again as she whimpered with need. With every slap of skin, every labored breath, she felt her need grow deep in her belly. Dropping her hands from her sensitive tits, she slapped them upon his chest.

"Oh, God," she spat, circling her hips for a handful of passes before bouncing on his cock. "I…I don't…wanna…cum…fast."

Arching a dark brow, Nik moved his touch from her thighs to her waist. Helping her fuck his throbbing cock, he growled as she squeezed her silken pussy around him.

"Why?" he asked.

"I don't…want this…to be over…so soon," she panted.

Laughing low, he released his right hand from her waist. Bringing it to his mouth, he sucked his thumb into his mouth. Coating it in his spit, he released it with a pop before maneuvering it to the apex between her thighs.

"Ohhhh…beautiful…you don't have to…worry about that," he purred, finding her perfect clit with the pad of his thumb.

Whimpering a series of curses, she swayed her hips from side to side before thrusting up and down. Digging her nails into the skin of his chest, she moved faster and faster, giving into white hot need.

"Ahhh…ahhhh!" she cried out, closing her eyes to focus.

Circling the tip of his thumb against her clit, Nik grunted as she worked him towards his own peak. Not quite ready to lose control, he forced himself to stay the course. With a hand on her waist, and his open palm spayed low on her belly, he held her securely as she lost control.

"That's it…yes…just…like *that*…good girl," he praised.

With the blood rushing in her ears, Brynn pushed herself to the point of no return. Hearing his honeyed voice, her release snuck up on her. Screaming in shocked pleasure, her body rocked as her second orgasm sliced through her body. Shaking uncontrollably, her eyes blew open wide as she rode out her bliss.

Feeling her pussy flutter over his cock, Nik barred his white teeth. Meeting her eyes, he watched as the fine features of her face tightened. Listening to her racing heartbeat, he waited for her to come down from her high. Making sure that her orgasm had subsided, he gently pulled her torso flat against his before rolling over.

"My turn," he said, recalling her words only minutes prior.

Still fully inside her pussy, Nik placed his hands on either side of her chest. Giving her a moment to adjust to this new position, he leaned in to kiss her open lips.

Returning the passionate kiss, Brynn squealed as he began to thrust his cock into her spent cunt. Wrapping her legs around him, she pushed him deeper and deeper. With every sharp slap, she lost more and more of her mind. *Holy fuck.* No man had ever lasted this long with her.

Arching his hips upwards with every push in, and downward with every push out, he alternated his speed. Trying to feel every part of her, he tipped his cock in just at the right angle. Having the warm friction he desperately needed, he found himself giving into his own burning need.

Abruptly ending the kiss, he rested his forehead against hers. Memorizing the look of euphoria in her hazel eyes, he raced towards his jagged pinnacle. Suddenly realizing something, he brought his lips to her ear so she could hear him.

"Can I cum…inside you?" he asked, growling with every quick thrust.

Furrowing her brow, it took a moment for Brynn to comprehend what he had asked. Shit. They should have talked about this beforehand.

"I…I'm not…on birth control," she replied.

Kissing the side of her face, he hummed. Being sterile, that wasn't an issue for him. He just wanted to have her permission. Some women just didn't like the sensation of cum dripping out of them.

"We don't have to worry about that," he said huskily.

Saying a silent oh, Brynn squeezed her legs around him tighter. He did say on his profile that kids weren't an option for him. Figuring he had taken his own precaution, she gave him the ok with a nod of her head.

"Good," she mewled. "Cum in me!"

Twisting his hips, he hissed as his release tickled his balls with every slap against her cunt. Wanting to hear her permission again, he demanded it from her one last time.

"Say it again!"

Breathing hard, Brynn purposefully clenched the walls of her cunt around him. She wanted to feel him fall apart, she wanted to milk him dry. "Please! *Please*…cum in me…cum in my pussy," she begged.

Listening to her strained voice, Nik let his release take over. Growling in her ear, his ecstasy washed over him, causing him to thrust one final time. Fully buried inside, his cock twitched as his clear cum spurted inside her waiting cunt.

Wrapping her arms around him, Brynn pulled him close as he broke at the seams. Savoring his masculine sounds, she turned her head to nuzzle the side of his jaw. Hearing such a strong man whimper and groan was music to her ears. She wanted to pat herself on the back for a job well done.

"Mmmm…good boy," she whispered.

Staying still as the last bit of his orgasm dissipated, Nik gave Brynn a loving kiss before slipping his spent cock from her cunt. Waiting until her arms and legs fell from his body, he rolled to the side. Reaching for her, he let out a contented sigh and she curled against him.

"Well. That was the best sex I've ever had," she admitted with a smile.

Kissing the crown of her head, his ego swelled. Wrapping an arm around her, he grazed his fingertips over her tanned skin. Absorbing the warmth of her body, he nodded his head. Sex was always infinitely better when you cared about the other person, and when you had an invested interest in their well-being.

"Me too," he said. "It just proves that we're destined, Brynn. We were meant to find each other."

Turning to look at his face, she eyed him for a long moment. His heavy comment caught her off guard, but she agreed with every word. She didn't know why, but she felt exactly the same.

"Stay with me," she said softly.

Meeting her eyes, he gave her a loving grin. He would stay with her until her heart stopped and she slipped away from this plane of existence. Although he couldn't promise her forever, she would have every broken and beautiful part of him until she took her last breath.

"I promise you Brynn Smith, from this moment on, I am your faithful servant…even Satan's demons couldn't rip me away from you," he vowed, ignoring the feeling of dread seeping into what was left of his damned soul.

CHAPTER NINE

Stretching her exhausted body, Brynn wiggled against the outdoor chaise. She had just awoken from her fifth much needed cat nap, this time under the awning protecting part of the master suite's patio. She and Nik had spent much of the day talking and laughing, bathing and relaxing, making love and fucking. She had never been so emotionally and physically satisfied.

Pulling her dark sunglasses from the top of her head, she fixed them onto her face. Glancing around the balcony, she wondered where Nik had run off to this time. Debating on whether she should go look for him, she quickly brushed the thought away. He would soon reappear, looking like the statuesque God he was. Ready to make her smile in any way he could.

He really was the most giving and attentive man she had ever known.

Over the course of the morning, he had told her more about his past, something he stressed to her that he rarely talked about. Only a handful of people truly knew him, and he wanted her to be one of the few. She felt honored to hold such precious information and promised to keep it safe.

His tale was one of heartache, to which she could relate. Born in a small town in Romania called Sighișoara, Nikolai had a relatively idyllic childhood. The only child to Marius and Iona, he was the apple of their eyes. They doted on him, giving him the best life and education they could. He couldn't have asked for better parents.

When he was twelve years old, however, his joyous life was shattered. While he was preparing with the choir for Sunday Mass, his parents were killed in a tragic and bizarre house fire. Suddenly orphaned, little Nikolai was forced to live with his only living relative. An alcoholic uncle in Bucharest named Boris.

Boris was a wealthy, morally corrupt man with ties to the underbelly of the city. It was a time where the law could be bought, and he owned much of the governing force. A sick and sadistic oligarch, he believed his duty was to prepare Nikolai to take over his wicked empire. Nik spent years well into adulthood forced to bend to his uncle's every dark whim. Carrying out unspeakable acts that he said had ultimately damned him for all of eternity.

Nik hadn't said much after that, no doubt not wanting to relive the various traumas he had clearly been through. She recognized that familiar pain and remorse when she saw them flash behind his green eyes. Although she desperately wanted to know more, she didn't press any further. He would share when he was ready.

Letting out a sigh, Brynn pushed their heavy conversations to the back of her mind. Looking around her million-dollar view, she turned her head when she heard the glass door slide open. A bright smile flashed over her face when she noticed Nik step into the light. Wearing black Wayfarer sunglasses, skintight boxer briefs, and carrying a large tray of brunch items, she felt her mouth water for more than one reason.

"Mmm...there you are," she said, fixing the tie of her white fluffy robe. "I was wondering where you had run off to."

"Hi, Sunshine...well, you were sleeping so peacefully, and I didn't want to wake you again. I had to take care of something, anyways...and I ordered some food from Freshly Laid," he said, lifting the tray.

Lifting a brow, she gave him a flirty look. "Freshly Laid, hmm? How appropriate...well thank you, I'm starving."

Snickering under his breath, he nodded his head. The double entendre was not lost on him. Walking over to the round patio table, he eased the tray onto the table. Pulling out a chair, he waited as she stood from the chaise and walked his way.

"I knew you would be...we've had quite the morning," he replied.

Taking a seat on the canvas lined chair, Brynn agreed with a small laugh. She was having probably the best day of her life; she didn't want it to end. Looking over the tray, she heard her stomach growl. Everything looked so incredibly decadent. She didn't know where to begin.

"Wow," she said, adjusting her sunglasses. "This looks amazing!"

Taking a seat next to her, Nik shrugged his broad shoulders. Basking in the heat as the harsh sun beat down upon his pale skin, he couldn't stop staring at the beauty beside him.

"I wasn't quite sure what you would be craving so I ordered a little bit of everything. There's orange juice, a vanilla cold brew…a jumbo cinnamon roll, avocado toast…some bacon…this breakfast sandwich they call the Walk of Shame. That sounded really delicious…oh and uh, sweet potato tots with marshmallow dipping sauce," he said, taking in her shocked face.

"Oh my God…thank you for getting all of this…but what about you? Aren't you going to have anything?" Brynn asked, popping a marshmallow dipped tot in her mouth.

Shaking his head, he leaned back in his chair. He hated that he still had to skirt these issues, it made him feel incredibly guilty. He would tell her everything soon, but not yet. Nothing was going to ruin their day.

"I ate while you were sleeping…I'm sorry, I know that's insanely rude, but you worked up my appetite," he said, selling his lie with a sly grin.

Giving him a cheeky smile, Brynn reached for the nearest plate. Lifting a messy breakfast sandwich, she thought about all of the fun they had had together over the past six hours. Her Benefactor had the most insane stamina. All she had to do was say the word more and he was ready to go.

"I'll forgive the rudeness this time…it's the least I can do for the what…*nine* orgasms you've given me, today?" she said, taking a very unladylike bite of the brioche sandwich.

Lifting a brow over the rim of his Ray-Bans, he leaned in towards her. "Let me know when you want me to start on the next nine," he said, his voice silken and deep.

Chewing on her huge mouthful, she felt her already warm cheeks flush scarlet. Truth be told, she was a little sore, but she'd be damned if she didn't want him to make good on that offer. Swallowing the delicious bite, she licked the sauce from her lips before replying.

"Mmm...maybe after I'm done eating? We haven't broken in the living room couch, yet," she said suggestively.

Reaching over, Nik brushed her long hair over her shoulder. With a confident nod, he felt his lust rise from the mere thought. He couldn't wait for her to finish her meal so he could enjoy his. She was a feast for him in more ways than one, and he was already dangerously addicted.

"I love that plan," he said, relaxing back against his chair.

"Good...I'll hurry," she said, taking another bite.

Clicking his tongue against his mouth, he encouraged her to slow down with a lift of his hand. He really didn't want her to choke on her food.

"No, Sunshine...take your time. I know I'm going to," he purred, folding his arms over his bare chest.

Feeling a shiver run down her spine, Brynn blinked at him through the dark lenses of her sunglasses. Oh God. He was so good at turning her knees to jelly.

"Yes, Sir," she said.

"Good girl," he praised lovingly.

Sitting in comfortable silence, Nik watched his beautiful brunette as she enjoyed her brunch. He hated how quickly the day was already passing. After spending centuries hiding from the sun, it was an indescribable feeling to have it beat upon his alabaster skin. Brynn had been so sweet, forcing him to let her slather SPF seventy-five sunscreen on his body. She was worried that with him being so white, the sun would burn him to a crisp. Of course, she was right, just not for the reason she imagined.

Relaxing in his chair, his thoughts slowly drifted towards Leona, with her wild copper curls and gentle face. He had only taken from her once while on the draining bed, weeks before she lost what was left of her sanity, and only upon her insistence. Her blood had neutralized the sun for seven full days. It was a beautiful gift that he didn't deserve. He still felt horrible that he couldn't save her.

Brynn's blood wouldn't sustain him for quite as long, of that he was sure. It wasn't as strong as Leona's, having been diluted through the generations. He hoped it would last until sundown the following day. He wasn't ready to say goodbye to witnessing firsthand how the sun made his new lover come to life.

Finishing her bacon and egg sandwich, Brynn picked up the glass of orange juice. Bringing it to her lips, she paused for a moment as she looked at Nik. He had been staring at her in quiet contemplation for what felt like an hour. She almost felt self-conscious. Was she eating too fast?

"Is everything ok?" she asked, drinking the tart juice.

Blinking himself back to reality, Nik hummed a reply. Nodding his head, he offered a small grin. He was thankful to be wearing the sunglasses.

"Yeah, of course it is...I was just admiring your beauty, that's all," he said.

Unable to stop herself from smiling, she dropped her covered eyes to her plate. Every time he said something sweet, she felt herself becoming more and more enamored with him. She had never been truly in love before, but she was almost certain she was on her way with him.

Pulling off a piece of the huge cinnamon roll, she wondered how soon it would be to tell him how she felt. Gathering the courage, she was stopped by the sound of the sliding glass opening. Confused as to who would be in the penthouse, she turned her head just in time to hear a woman shriek at the top of her lungs.

Dropping the dress bag draped over her crooked arm, Yetta dropped on the hard travertine as her hooded eyes fell on Nikolai. Crying out, she raised her gnarled hands in prayer. A miracle had happened, she thought to herself. *God had answered her!*

Instantly standing from his chair, Nik rushed to his assistant's side. Helping her from the floor, he looked her over for any injuries. He had told her to call him first before she came over so that he may warn her. He didn't know why he was surprised that she didn't do as she was ordered. Yetta was incredibly headstrong. It was something they had spent decades arguing about.

Startled by Yetta's fall, Brynn quickly followed Nik. Asking aloud if the older woman was alright, she realized her words were ignored in the chaos. Watching him as he helped the older woman, she caught them speaking to one other in a foreign language. She wished she had her new phone on her so she could decipher what they were saying. Whatever it was sounded serious, she hoped everything was ok.

Dropping his voice low, Nik explained the situation to Yetta using his native tongue. No, he hadn't been cured as she thought. It had the potential to be something better, though. Neither of them thought they would come across a Sun Walker. Yetta now understood why they needed to wipe Brynn from the program completely. The Clan could never know about this unexpected gift.

With her eyes welling with hot tears, Yetta took Nikolai's cold hands in hers. Bringing them to her lips, she kissed them soundly as he talked. She was stunned to see him in the light, he had never looked so handsome. It was a Divine miracle, just not the one she had prayed for decades to happen. Nikolai had been right all along; the girl was indeed special. She just didn't understand why he hadn't immediately hidden her from the others. Deleting her from the computer programs wouldn't be enough. The Elder's weren't imbeciles.

Turning her attention away from Nikolai, Yetta focused on the young deity to her side. Grabbing Brynn's hands, she kissed them as soundly as she had with Nik's. Saying an ancient prayer, she then wrapped her weakening arms around her in a warm embrace. She would insist to Nikolai that they leave to his safehouse in Norway. The sooner, the better.

Unsure as to what exactly was happening, Brynn gently hugged the petite woman back. Looking to Nik for an answer, she shrugged her shoulders. She honestly had no idea what was going on. The last time she saw Yetta she didn't know if she liked her or not, and now she was giving her a hug. *Huh?*

"She's just really happy…she didn't think she would ever see me fall in love," Nik said, coming up with the plausible truth.

Mouthing the words 'oh my God,' Brynn gave the older woman one more hug before letting her go. This was all so incredibly sweet, she hoped he wasn't just saying that. She wanted desperately to believe her feelings for Nik were reciprocated.

Nodding her head, Yetta patted Brynn's arm. "Yes. So happy."

"Well, good! That makes me happy too! But…what happened when she opened the door…why did she scream?" Brynn asked, half of her confusion hidden behind her sunglasses. "Is everything ok?"

Thinking on his toes, Nik pushed out a small laugh as he bent down to pick up the crumpled dress bag. "She only saw me from the waist up and thought I was completely naked…which then made her trip and fall, but she's ok. Aren't you, Yetta?"

"Yes. Good," Yetta replied, waving the comment away. "I ok…you see."

Furrowing her brow, Brynn glanced back and forth between the pair. Yetta was old enough to be Nik's grandmother, so she could understand why seeing him in the buff would be a little off putting. But still. Something seemed odd.

"Well, I'm glad you're ok," she said before motioning to the bag. "What's that?"

"Ok, yes…this. Well, I have a special date planned for us this evening. Yetta was so kind to swing by Neiman Marcus and pick up the order I placed for you," he said.

Dropping her mouth open in surprise, Brynn felt instantly giddy. A special date in which she didn't even have to plan her own outfit? She loved how he always thought of everything. He truly was the full package.

"Really? God, Nik…this is so amazing, thank you!" she said, clearing the steps between them to kiss his cheek. "You're the best."

Smiling at his lover, Nik mentally patted himself on the back. He had high hopes for the night. She needed to be secure in the knowledge of just how much he cared for her. He wanted it to negate any of the difficulties that no doubt was coming their way.

"I try…now if you'll excuse me, I'll go hang this up in the closet. I'm not quite ready for you to see this yet," he said, giving both ladies a quick nod before slipping through the sliding door.

Making sure Nikolai was out of immediate hearing range, Yetta stared at Brynn. With a somber look passing over her lined face, she once again grabbed her hands. She promised Nikolai she wouldn't say anything to the girl, but she didn't know when he would tell her the truth. She was far too valuable to the Elders. She needed to be warned, if only cryptically.

"You are special, Brynn Smith. You have fire in veins. Yes. Much power. There many…many monsters in this world. They no understand your power. Nikolai no understand. You no let monsters take that power when they come. Understand?" she said, tightly squeezing her hands. "Fight. Always fight! Use your fire!"

Scrunching her face, Brynn tried to make sense of Yetta's words. There was a good chance she didn't hear her correctly. Did she say she had fire in her veins? And what monsters should she fight? She had absolutely no clue what she was talking about. Not wanting to offend the petite woman, she nodded politely.

"Ok, yes…yes, I understand," she said with a forced grin.

Huffing in triumph, Yetta released Brynn's hand. Fully believing the girl already knew how to wield her innate power, she gave her a slow once over. When the monsters finally arrived on their doorstep, both she and Nikolai would be ready. Together, they would triumph. She felt it in her old bones.

"Remember. Cut off head. Stake through heart. Only way they die," she said before turning away from the girl standing with a befuddled look marring her features.

CHAPTER TEN

Securing her long curls with setting spray, Brynn coughed as she accidentally breathed in the fine mist. Shaking her head, she waved her hand in front of her face to fan away the chemicals. Settling down the hairspray on the bathroom countertop, she took a good look at herself in the framed mirror.

Donning a silver sequined Alexander McQueen mini-dress and Rene Caovilla satin stilettos, she marveled at her reflection. She had never looked this glamorous before. Wherever Nik was planning on taking her had to be spectacular. She couldn't wait to find out what this secret date entailed.

Leaning in, she ran the tip of her pinky along the edge of her berry-stained lower lip. Admiring her expertly applied makeup, she let out a happy sigh. She still had a hard time believing that this was her life. She had been saying that a lot lately, but it was the God's honest truth. Less than two weeks ago she was worried about having to live in a bedbug infested motel, and now she was wearing an outfit that cost more than a year's tuition.

Part of her was waiting for the other shoe to drop.

Suddenly reminded of Yetta's bizarre comments, Brynn frowned at her reflection. She still had no idea what the woman was talking about. After Yetta left, she casually mentioned the odd conversation to Nik. He quickly shrugged it off, saying that his assistant's age was beginning to take its toll. She often made weird remarks, it wasn't anything to worry about.

Only she couldn't shake the nagging feeling that it was.

Swearing under her breath, Brynn forced herself to ignore the tiny pit in her stomach. Focusing on the exciting night ahead, she did one last spin in front of the mirror before leaving the master bathroom. Barely crossing the threshold, she heard a low whistle come her way.

Turning towards the sound, Brynn smiled brightly as her eyes settled upon Nik as he sat on the edge of the messy bed. With his tailored navy suit and partially unbuttoned dress shirt, he looked like a Hollywood star on his way to some red-carpet event.

"Hey, handsome," she said.

Quickly standing from the bed, Nik cleared the space to his lover. Raking his green eyes over her from head to toe, he reached out to grasp her hand. Encouraging her to do a spin, he hummed in approval. He knew the McQueen dress would fit her perfectly.

"Mmm…you're stunning…absolutely stunning," he said, his tone thick with adoration.

Twirling carefully in her high heels, Brynn swallowed a squeal. Coming to a stop before him, she met his simmering gaze.

"Why thank you. You're looking quite delicious, yourself," she said, reaching up with her free hand to smooth her fingers over the fabric of his lapel. Drifting her eyes to the exposed skin of his chest, she lifted her sculpted brows. "That sunscreen really worked…you didn't even get a hint of a tan."

Closing his eyes for a moment, Nik felt his guilt creep back in. She was such a smart woman, no doubt her subconscious was already putting the pieces together, especially with the little stunt Yetta pulled. He knew he would have to come clean soon. He would be lying if he said he wasn't terrified.

"Well, it helped that you slathered me in it what…every half hour?" He replied with a smirk.

"I can't risk you getting sun cancer on me…besides, it gave me an excuse to touch you," she said.

Lifting his hand, Nik lightly brushed his knuckles over her painted cheek. Narrowing his eyes, he resisted the urge to smear her lipstick with a needy kiss.

"You never need an excuse to touch me, my beautiful Brynn," he purred.

"Hmm…I'll hold you to that when you're grumpy and annoyed with me," she said, lifting her lips into a tiny grin.

Dropping his hand, he took hers once again. Looking over her sweet face, he tried not to snicker. He couldn't imagine ever being sour to her.

"I don't think that will ever happen…but on the off chance it does, I give you full permission to do your worst to draw me out of my mood, hmm?" he said, gently squeezing her hand. "Well, Sunshine…we should head out. We don't want to be late."

Widening her eyes, Brynn quirked her head. She was both excited and incredibly nervous for their date. Judging by their outfits, they wouldn't be doing anything too physically strenuous. It was somewhat a relief after everything they had done. Perhaps he planned dinner and some stargazing? She always loved doing that. The night sky was particularly beautiful in the desert.

"After you, Mr. Draven," she replied.

. . .

Chewing on the inside of her cheek, Brynn relaxed as much as she could in the rear seat of the stretched limousine. Sitting in darkness due to the silken blindfold covering her eyes, she focused on the soft classical music filling the cab to pass the time. It was a good thing she didn't get carsick; the sudden wide turns of the limo were a doozy. She hoped they would arrive at their destination soon.

Sensing his lover's anxiety, Nik gently squeezed his fingers into her toned thigh. Turning his head, he leaned in to brush his lips against the shell of her ear.

"We're almost there...just try to relax and enjoy the air conditioning while we have it," he whispered before kissing her temple.

"While we have it?" Brynn asked, covering his large hand with hers. "So we're going to be outside, then?"

"Maybe...maybe not," he replied nonchalantly, not wanting to spoil the surprise.

"Tease," she said.

Answering with a small laugh, Nik nodded his head. She now knew firsthand how true that statement rang. Pulling his gaze from the blindfolded beauty, he moved his eyes to the tinted window. The sun was dipping below the horizon, casting a warm glow on the various buildings as they headed into downtown Phoenix. It wasn't an ideal way to watch what could be his last unguarded sunset, but it was still breathtaking.

"Thank you," he said without thinking.

Quirking her head towards his deep voice, Brynn furrowed her covered brow.

"For what?" she asked.

With a small smile, Nik looked at Brynn from the corner of his eyes. Studying her for a long moment, he gave her the honest truth.

"For giving me the best day of my life," he replied.

Instantly melting, it took everything she had not to rip the blindfold from her face. She should be the one thanking him for the exact same thing.

"It's not over yet," she said.

"You're right, it's going to get better," he said, perking a bit once the limo turned onto West Adams Street. "We're here, Sunshine."

Smiling brightly, Brynn fixed her seated posture. Feeling the limo slow to a stop, she tried to calm her racing heartbeat. She was on pins and needles to know what he had up his sleeve.

Waiting for the driver to open the limo door, Nik climbed out of the luxury vehicle first. Thanking the driver with a small wave, he leaned back in through the door to help Brynn from her seat. Urging her to be careful as she stepped onto the sidewalk, he held her steady as she stood to full height.

Making sure she was alright to stand by herself, he reached into the pocket of his navy-blue slacks. Pulling out a folded hundred-dollar bill, he handed it to the young driver.

"Thank you, we should be done by ten," he said.

Nodding a thanks, the driver quickly took his tip and stuffed it into his pocket. He wondered if he would get another Franklin after drop-off. He loved it when the uber rich tipped well.

"Thank you, Sir. I will be here waiting," the young man replied, taking his leave.

Maneuvering his lover closer towards the Spanish styled building, Nik made sure to center her so that her line of vision would be focused on the theater's marquee. Stepping behind her, he slowly untied the blindfold.

"Keep your eyes closed…you can open them on the count of three, ok?" he said.

Squeezing her eyes shut, Brynn kept her arms glued to her sides. Balling her hands into fists, she swallowed a nervous giggle. Listening to the surrounding sounds she surmised that they were in the hub of a city, no doubt Phoenix. Besides that, she was stumped. She couldn't wait to see what was before her.

"Ok!" She replied.

Paying no mind to the odd stares coming from pedestrians walking around them, he folded the piece of silk and put it in his back pocket. Leaning in, he slowly began his countdown.

"One…two…three," he said.

Opening her hazel eyes. Brynn blinked away at her blurry vision. Adjusting to the darkening light, she looked straight ahead. It took a few moments for her to realize where she was, and what she was looking at. She was pleasantly surprised to see the historic Orpheum Theater. Reading its large white marquee, she felt her adrenaline spike with excitement.

"Broadway's Pride and Prejudice…Private showing," she said.

Giving it a chance to sink in, Nik wrapped his arms around her. Pulling her flush against his body, he held her in a loving embrace.

"I know how much you love musicals…and how much you adore Pride and Prejudice. This is a brand-new Broadway show, they don't even open for another month. I rented out the entire theater and flew all the cast and crew out to perform a show just for you," he purred, dropping his voice low. "I hope you like it."

Dropping her mouth open in shock, Brynn openly scoffed. He had flown out an entire Broadway production from New York City just for her? She was gob smacked that he actually listened to her on their first date when she told him all of the things she loved. Nothing could ever top this. This was officially the best day of her life and would forever be.

"Oh my God, Nik…I can't believe you did this!" she said, her eyes welling with happy tears. "This is…oh, God…I…I don't…thank you. Thank you!"

Feeling triumphant, Nik placed a tender kiss upon the crown on the top of her head. Holding her for a handful of long seconds, he released his embrace before taking her hand.

"I'm so glad you like your gift...I've heard very good things about the show. We should head inside, hmm? I have a feeling there are a couple of seats in the balcony with our names on them," he said, leading her towards the entrance.

Carefully walking a step behind Nik, Brynn couldn't stop smiling. Keeping her eyes glued to his handsome face, she thanked the Universe for bringing him into her life. She was the luckiest girl in the entire world. Was this what falling in love felt like? Because she was almost positive that it was.

Reaching the metal handle, he paused a moment as the door to the Orpheum opened. Squeezing Brynn's hand, he grinned at the older gentleman who was encouraging them inside with a flick of his hand.

"Mister Draven, Miss Smith...please, come inside. We've been expecting you. My name is Bill, I'm the manager of the Orpheum...I spoke to you on the phone, Mister Draven," he said warmly.

Not wanting to let Brynn's hand go, Nik gave the man a friendly grin. He was incredibly thankful for Bill's flexibility; it had been somewhat of a logistical nightmare to get everything in place. But even still, nothing was impossible if you had enough money to spend. Nik knew the man would bend over backwards for the enormous payout. Humans were predictable that way.

"Ah, yes! Hi Bill, it's nice to meet you in person...thank you for making all this possible on such short notice," he said.

"Oh, it was no trouble at all, Mister Draven...no trouble at all!" Bill said, his crooked smile deepening the wrinkles around his brown eyes. "Now please, follow me...I'll take you to your seats!"

Following Bill and Nik, Brynn glanced around the opulent theater as they headed towards the rounded staircase. Her heart was still beating a million miles an hour from the excitement of everything. She had always wanted to see a play or comedy show in The Orpheum; it held such a rich history within its walls.

"This is beautiful," she remarked as they made their ascent to the second floor.

Leading her up the winding staircase, Nik squeezed her hand. He had the same wondrous look on his face when he had seen the theater for the first time in the nineteen thirties. It was a jewel in the desert at that time, part of the Orpheum circuit known for its vaudeville acts. He had laid his connections to the growing city during that fateful trip. Connections that continued to hold true. He would be forever thankful to The Orpheum for all the luck it gave to him.

"It pales in comparison to you, Sunshine," he said with a quick look over his shoulder.

Catching his gaze for a split second, Brynn sucked in a sharp breath. At this rate, she was sure she was getting a cavity from all the sweetness constantly thrown her way. Not that she was complaining.

Trying not to intrude in the private moment, Bill waited until everyone had reached the second floor to speak. Motioning towards the double doors, he gave them each a kind smile.

"The balcony is just behind those doors…I'll give you two some privacy. The lights will go down in about five minutes but please don't hesitate to let me know if you need anything…we hope you enjoy your show!" Bill said, bowing his head.

"Thank you, Bill," Nik said.

"Yes, thank you!" Brynn chirped.

Leaving the pair to it, Bill made his way back down the spiral staircase. He was crossing all his fingers and toes that they would have a wonderful time. This one night would keep the theater in the black for the next two years, he wanted to stay on Mister Draven's good side.

Leading her to the entrance of the balcony, Nik opened the heavy wooden door. Waiting for her to brush past him, he watched her like a hawk for her reaction to the decorated space.

Crossing the threshold onto the balcony, Brynn let out a loud gasp. Multiple, extravagant bouquets of peonies lined the area next to their front row seats, all in various shades of glorious pink. Too stunned to say anything, she turned towards him and wrapped her arms around his muscular torso. Squeezing him tightly, she fought to keep herself from crying.

Returning her joyful embrace, Nik lifted the corner of his lips into a pleased grin. Although it wasn't on the Benefactor questionnaire, he surmised that pink peonies were her favorite flowers after catching the image of her dancing with a handful of them in one of her dreams. He didn't know the significance of that particular flower, but the brain rarely lied when it came to mortals and their subconscious dreams.

"Do you like them?" he asked, his deep voice like velvet.

Resting her head against his chest, she nodded a reply. She couldn't believe he had done this; it was such a thoughtful and loving gesture. She had never mentioned peonies to him before, of that she was certain. Either he was a mind reader, or just took a wild and lucky guess. Either way she was shocked. Oh, she couldn't let him go now.

"I love them…they're my favorite, my absolute favorite…when I was seven, my foster family had these huge pink peony bushes that I just loved. My foster mother, Sherry, would let me go out every afternoon and cut a handful of peonies for the dinner table. They always had bugs in them, but I didn't care…they were too beautiful to care. Anyways, that summer with them was one of the happiest summers I ever had so peonies always bring me back to that bright spot," she said, looking up at his angular face. "How did you know they were so special to me?"

Shrugging his broad shoulders, he leaned down to place a soft kiss upon her forehead. Now that he understood why they were precious to her, he would make a point of giving them to her every chance he could. Leading her to her seat, he pulled a single stem from a bouquet and handed it to her.

"Honestly, I didn't," he said, taking his seat beside her. "They just called to me, something told me you would love them. I don't know how to explain this, but I'm connected to you in a way that I haven't been with anyone else in a very long time. Maybe your soul just happened to tell mine?"

Bringing the flower to her nose, Brynn breathed in its sweet perfume. Soaking in his romantic words, a look of total adoration passed over the fine features of her face. Admiring him for the man he was both inside and out, she made the instant decision to seize the perfect moment. Wanting to tell him exactly how she felt, she blurted out what had been weighing on her heart.

"I'm falling in love with you, Nikolai," she said, her voice not much louder than a whisper.

Stopping dead in his tracks, Nik roamed his gaze over her freckled face. Committing everything to memory, he lifted his hand to gently cup her flushed cheek. He was shocked that she had said it first, but he was thrilled that she had. Truth be told, he had been falling in love with her since the moment he first laid his eyes on her.

Leaning towards her, he brought his lips within an inch of hers.

"And I'm madly in love with you, my sweet Brynn. You have me…now and always," he replied, claiming her lips just as the lights in the theater dimmed.

CHAPTER ELEVEN

Dabbing the tears from her cheek with her fingertips, Brynn took in the last few seconds of the romantic musical. Melting at the sight of Elizabeth and Mr. Darcy kissing for the final time, she let out a happy sigh before glancing towards Nik. To her amazement, he was paying attention. It was the first time she hadn't caught him staring directly at her instead of the actors.

"Ugh...so good!" she exclaimed as the red velvet curtain fell. "That was amazing!"

Completely energized by the entertaining musical, she clapped her hands in gratitude. Smiling at her love as he joined in, she tried not to feel silly. The cast did a phenomenal job, they deserved so much more than the applause of an audience of two.

Watching as the curtain lifted to reveal the entire Pride and Prejudice cast, Nik rose from his seat. Standing at full height, he glanced at Brynn as she followed suit. He was pleased to see her so happy. It was a good production; he had spent his money well. There was no doubt that their stint on Broadway would be a success.

"Bravo! Bravo!" he yelled.

Continuing to clap as the actors took their final bows, Brynn felt a tiny bit of disappointment creep into her mind. Her perfect night was ending. She wasn't quite ready.

Almost on cue, Nik leaned in towards her. Moving his lips to the shell of her ear, he whispered. "Don't worry, my love. Your life will be filled with days and nights such as this. I promise you."

Closing her red rimmed eyes, Brynn hummed as she felt him kiss her cheek. Letting her applause trail away, she took in a breath before focusing on the handsome man standing beside her.

"I'm not sure if I deserve you, Nik," she said.

Nodding thanks to the actors as the lights in the theater went up simultaneously as the heavy curtain fell, he gave her a serious look. She had it all wrong, he was the one unfit to walk in her shadow.

"No. No...I don't deserve you, Brynn. You're everything good and decent in this miserable world. And you've allowed me...a broken, despicable sinner...the pleasure to fall at your feet. I hope you will grant me the opportunity to worship you until your last breath," he said, knowing full well how peculiar he sounded.

Giving him a curious look, she tried to make sense of his words. It was yet another odd conversation that left her puzzled.

Sensing her confusion, Nik reached for her hand. Lifting it to his lips, he brushed her knuckles with a kiss in hopes of distracting her. The last thing he needed right now was for her to fall down the rabbit hole.

"Come, let's go downstairs and meet the leads," he said, encouraging her to follow.

Glancing around at the lush bouquets of peonies, she hesitated for a moment. "But what about the flowers? Can we give them to the cast and crew?" she asked.

Leading her towards the circular staircase, he looked at her fondly. Her heart was too pure, too golden. He would do everything in his power to make sure it stayed that way.

"Of course, my love. I'll have Bill take care of that," he replied.

Smiling brightly, she was pleased that the beautiful flowers wouldn't go to waste. She would love to have them, but this made much more sense.

"Thank you," she said.

Walking behind Nik, she was careful to mind her steps as they made their descent. Her stilettos were beautiful to look at, but a pain to walk in. She shouldn't be complaining though, blisters and bruised heels were a small price to pay.

"Do you mind if I take off my shoes in the limo?" she asked.

Looking over his shoulder, he lifted the corner of his full lips into a sinful smirk. "Not at all…in fact, you could take off that little dress, too," he purred.

Gripping the brass banister, Brynn felt her knees turn to jelly. Now there was a thought. The limousine was pretty spacious.

"I think I'd like that…it is a little tight," she said, tugging on the short hem of the sequined dress with her free hand.

Reaching the landing, he gave her a knowing look. Opening his mouth to reply, he pushed out a sigh instead as he noticed Bill round the corner. Putting the bawdy image of Brynn splayed on the floor of the limo into the back of his mind, he reluctantly addressed the manager.

"That was wonderful, Bill…but we were wondering if you could grab Elizabeth and Darcy for us? Brynn would like to thank them," he said.

Immediately halting his steps, Bill nodded in agreement. Instantly turning on his heels, he waved his finger in the air as he walked towards the back of the theater.

"Of course! Not a problem! Be right back!" he replied loudly.

Clasping her hands in front of her, Brynn took in a cleansing breath. She didn't know why she was nervous all of the sudden, they were just actors. Actors that she wanted to make a good impression on. They would both be massive stars once the play opened. There was no doubt in her mind.

Hearing the subtle uptick in her heartbeat, Nik looked at his love. Staring at the space of her throat just below her jaw, he felt his mouth water. Her nerves were releasing bits of adrenaline into her bloodstream, making her already saccharine blood all the more divine. He had to distract the both of them, before his hunger became too great.

"Is all of your work finished for class tomorrow night?" he asked.

Blinking herself back to reality, she thought for a moment. Oh, school. She had honestly forgotten all about it. She was too busy living in a romantic dream. Thank goodness the semester was almost over. She was thankful that she would never have to take another night class ever again.

"Yeah...but do I really have to go? Finals are next week so it will just be a review," she asked.

Clicking the tongue against the roof of his mouth, he gave her a serious look. Even though her schooling would take a drastic turn in the next few weeks, he wanted her to finish strong with ASU. As far as she was concerned, nothing was amiss. She was just a normal coed. He would keep it that way for as long as possible.

"Yes, you absolutely do," he said sternly.

Letting out a dramatic sigh, she shrugged her shoulders. It was good that he actually cared. He really did love her.

"Fine...but do you mind if Jenni picks me up? She really wants to meet you," she said.

Meeting her hazel eyes, he nodded his head. *Ah, yes.* Jenni. The best friend. The one he should be thanking for bringing Brynn into his life.

"Yes, of course," he replied. "I'm looking forward to meeting her, too. I know just how important she is to you."

"Aww...yeah, she really is. And I know she's just going to adore you. She's already been talking about going on a double date with her and her boyfriend. He's ancient, though...I'm not sure you two would have anything in common. But it might be fun," she said, giving him a smile that crinkled the corners of her eyes.

Keeping in a laugh, he took a step closer. If she thought a man in his fifties was ancient, her mind was going to explode when she learned the truth about him.

"I'm sure we can make that happen," he said.

"Great! I'll let Jenni know!" she replied happily.

With a small grin on his face, Nik nodded. Suddenly hearing the door to the backstage open, he turned his attention towards Bill and the emerging actors. Instantly reading their auras, he didn't care for the busty brunette who played Elizabeth. Annoyance radiated off her in heavy waves, it put a bitter taste in his mouth.

Ushering the actors along, Bill called out to the pair.

"Mister Draven, Miss Smith…I'd like to introduce you to Matthew Lee and Lilly Fontaine," he said, standing off to the side of the foursome. "Matthew, Lilly, this is uh…Nikolai Draven and Brynn Smith."

Trying to contain the butterflies filling her belly, Brynn reached out to shake Matthew and Lilly's hands.

"It's so nice to meet you two! You guys did a phenomenal job…phenomenal!" she exclaimed. "Thank you so much for doing this! You've made my year, I swear!"

Giving both Nikolai and Brynn a warm smile, Matthew shook her hand. Noticing Nikolai's cool demeanor, he cleared his throat nervously. With all the money the guy plunked down to make this happen, he hoped he didn't hate the performance. At least his girlfriend seemed happy.

"It's nice to meet you, too! We're so glad you liked it, Miss Smith. This was all for you so…yeah, we're thrilled you liked it," he said, glancing at his moody costar. "Aren't we?"

Forcing a wide smile, Lilly nodded before reluctantly taking Brynn's hand. She was exhausted and just wanted to get back to the damn hotel room. She hated having to pretend to like pretentious, rich asshats. She couldn't care less how hot the prick was, or how much money he had spent. His kind was what was wrong with the world.

"Definitely! Sooo thrilled!" Lilly said, her voice too cheerful to sound sincere.

Pressing his lips into a thin line, Nik narrowed his green eyes. Remaining silent as Brynn excitedly conversed with the actors, he pushed his way into Lilly's mind. Not caring that his sudden intrusion would cause a painful migraine, he rustled around her thoughts.

Eat the rich. Eat the rich. She silently chanted. *Fuck her and fuck him. But especially her. God. What an annoying bitch. Ugly fucking whore.*

Ahh, he mused. Now it made sense. While he could sympathize with her hatred for the wealthy, he drew the line at her nastiness towards the woman he loved. The young actress needed to be careful, he had the ability to ruin her blossoming career with a single phone call.

Be respectful, Lilly. He spat into her head. *You are beneath Brynn Smith. Act like it.*

Immediately dropping her faux smile, Lilly blinked her dark brown eyes. Straightening her posture, a blank expression passed over her face as her brain rewired itself. After a handful of seconds, all her rude thoughts evaporated. Replaced with the feeling of inadequacy, and the painful edge of a searing headache.

Looking from Matthew to Lilly, Brynn was caught off guard by her abrupt change in demeanor. Lifting a sculpted brow, she addressed the beautiful actress.

"Are you ok?" she asked.

Shaking her head, Lilly snapped back into the present. Squinting as her eyes adjusted to the bright lights, she scrunched her face. Her head was beginning to pound, but she didn't want to disappoint Miss Smith. She was so lucky to be talking to her.

"Yeah, yeah…I'm fine I'm just…I'm just getting a little bit of a headache. It happens sometimes after a show. I was just so nervous about making sure my performance was good enough for you and I think my body is just like…crashing or something," Lilly replied with a giggle.

"Oh my gosh, you were nervous that I wouldn't think your performance was good enough? But I'm just a nobody, you totally didn't have to worry about that," Brynn said, surprise lifting the tone of her voice.

Scoffing, Lilly lifted her open hand and placed it upon her bosom. Like hell Brynn Smith was a nobody.

"You're so incredibly special, Brynn…I honestly can't believe I'm even talking to you right now! Thank you for letting me entertain you, I will remember this night for the rest of my life!" Lilly said.

Giving Lilly a curious look, Matthew didn't know what had gotten into her. He genuinely couldn't tell if she was being serious, or if she was having yet another bitchy moment.

"Umm…yeah," he said, stopping Lilly from saying anything further. "We're both incredibly grateful for this opportunity."

Glancing back and forth between Matthew and Lilly, Nik knew it was a great time to take their leave. Brynn was more than confused over Lilly's turnabout and he didn't want her to obsess over it for the rest of the night. Perhaps he shouldn't have laid on the demand so thick, but given her attitude, he expected her to have a much stronger will.

Interrupting the conversation, Nik took half a step into the space separating him and Brynn from the actors. Placing his hand on the small of her back, he addressed the pair.

"I'm sorry, but we really need to get going…once again, thank you very much for making this night magical for Brynn. I have no doubt that you two will both become huge stars," he said politely.

"Thank you, Mister Draven," Matthew said. "That really means a lot!"

"Uh, yeah…thank you, that's very kind of you to say," Lilly replied, wincing from the volume of her own voice.

Letting out a sigh, Brynn gave Matthew and Lilly a thankful smile. Nik was right, they were going to hit it big. She was excited for their adventure into stardom.

"Someday I'm going to brag about having a private performance from you two and no one is going to believe me! This really has been a wonderful night. Thank you for everything!" she said, letting Nik take her hand.

Not caring for the conversation to go any further, Nik gently led Brynn away. Turning his attention to Bill as they headed for the front door, he talked to the man while they walked.

"Bill, could you please make sure the flowers in the balcony are divided and given to the cast and crew?" he asked.

"Oh yes, of course Mister Draven!" Bill replied, quickly following them. "Again, thank you for all that you've done for the Orpheum. We really appreciate it and hope to see you back soon!"

Nodding a thanks, Nik opened the front door of the theater. Letting Brynn slip out into the warm night, he quickly stepped behind her. Wrapping his arms around her, he pulled her flush against him. Looking to the left, he noticed the limo driving down the street right on time.

"So…was the night a success, Sunshine?" he asked, nuzzling her crown.

Resting against him, Brynn closed her eyes. Humming a reply, she swayed with him from side to side.

"Definitely...thank you, Nik," she said.

"Mmm...you're very welcome my beautiful Brynn...oh, before I forget...there's one more thing I want to give you," he said, releasing her to dig his hand into his front pocket.

Turning on her heels to face him, she quirked her head to the side. Blown away that there was yet another surprise, she glanced down to his hand. Surely, he wasn't going to do something crazy, was he? A proposal would be insane. Right?

"Really? What is it?" she asked, her voice cracking slightly.

Lifting his large hand, he opened his fist to reveal his next gift. A bronze chain necklace with a large pendant attached. Obviously an antique by the presence of green patina, the pendant was that of a family crest. Worn down from years of handling, the image of a cross surrounded by a circle of thorned roses was still clearly visible. Despite his immeasurable wealth, the necklace was the most valuable thing he owned.

Looking at the necklace under the light of the bright marquee, Brynn's eyes widened. The vintage necklace was much better than a diamond ring. For now, at least.

"Oh, wow...this is beautiful, Nik," she said.

Making sure she got a good view of the pendant, he couldn't help but smile. He was glad that she liked it, it meant so much to him.

"This is my family's crest...it's been passed down through the generations. My great-grandfather gave it to my great-grandmother. My grandfather gave it to my grandmother. My father gave it to my mother...and now I'm giving it to you. Please wear it, it carries a great power and will protect you," he said, meeting her eyes.

Swallowing hard, she felt a shiver race down her spine. This felt more important than any ring could ever be. She was flabbergasted.

"I'll...I'll never take it off," she breathed. "It's gorgeous, thank you."

Moving behind her once again, he brought the opened necklace to her throat. Mindful of her long curls, he clasped the ancient chain closed. He was pleased that she genuinely loved it. Unlike the first woman he gave it to.

"It suits you, my love," he said.

Lifting her hand, she felt the cool metal with her fingertips. Tracing the outline of the cross, she spun around to face him. Studying his sharp features under the artificial lights, her heart swelled with a mixture of adoration and lust. God, she loved him so much.

"You're amazing, Mister Draven," she said.

Taking her hand, he gave her a wink as he walked her towards the parked limousine. Although he might not deserve it, he hoped she would always think of him in such a way.

"I know," he replied. "Now let's get you into this limo and out of those shoes."

"Mmm...and out of this dress," she said cheekily.

Stopping just before the limo, Nik gave her a hungry look. Raking his intense gaze over her from head to toe, he let out a low growl.

"And out of that tight, little dress," he said, leaning down to kiss her parted lips.

CHAPTER TWELVE

Raising her arms above her head, Brynn used her knees to steady herself on the narrow floor of the moving limousine. Kneeling before Nik's spread legs, she mumbled something intelligible as he helped her from her sequined dress. Her heart was racing a million beats per minute as they sped aimlessly along I-10. She couldn't believe she was finally acting out one of her favorite fantasies.

Freeing her of the designer gown, Nik flung the piece of fabric onto the row of leather seats to his left; joining the pile of his own clothes she had stripped him of half an hour before. Now they were both on an even playing field. He could finally retaliate against her for almost making him lose his mind with her devilish mouth on his cock.

"It's my turn, love," he purred. "Switch positions with me so I can lick that pretty little pussy of yours."

Shaking her head, she reached out to grasp the base of his thick cock. Leaning forward, she once again settled herself between his bent legs.

"But I'm not done, yet," she protested, moving her opened mouth closer to his dick.

"Brynn," he warned. "Brynn, don't you dare…it's my tu—"

Before he was able to finish his sentence, he was silenced by his hellion wrapping her lips around his aching cock. Hissing a dark curse, he grit his teeth in a mixture of pleasure and frustration. After already being edged a handful of times, he didn't know how much more of her delicious torture he could take.

"Fuck," he groaned, watching the shadows of the highway dance on her face.

Humming lightly, Brynn slowly bobbed her head. Taking more of his length into her warm mouth, she wiggled the flat of her tongue against his skin. Rhythmically sucking and relaxing, she held him firm at the base with her left hand. Glancing upwards, she relished his desperation. This was fun for her, to watch him twist and moan. It sharpened her own need, the wanting ache building in her cunt. She would let him cum this time. As a reward for not only him, but for herself.

Maintaining his heady eye contact, Brynn moved her mouth faster. Gripping him firmly in her hand, she worked the top half of his hardened length. Swirling her tongue in tight circles, she paused every time she reached his head. Keeping him between her lips, she flicked her tongue over his sensitive tip. Over and over, until she finally tasted the warning of his precum.

"Mmmmm," she moaned, savoring his clean taste.

Pulling his full lips back into a sneer, Nik hissed as his love expertly pulled the first few drops from his throbbing cock. With every deliberate pass of her tongue, he felt the string of his pleasure grow almost painfully taunt. Causing the muscles of his abdomen to flex as she inched him closer. It wouldn't be long before he broke.

"Brynn....my love...*fuck*...I can't...I can't," he groaned, reaching his hand to cup the back of her head. "Please...*please!*"

Feeling him twist his fingers in her locks, she shivered as she soaked in his pleas. It made her feel powerful to have him beg her like this. Halting her wicked movement, she suddenly pulled her mouth from his cock with a loud 'pop.' Breathing hard, she paused for a split second to gather her thoughts as her spit dripped down her chin.

"Cum in my mouth," she demanded.

Quirking his spinning head, Nik narrowed his eyes. It was the one thing he hadn't let himself do with her. It was dangerous to give her so much control over him. But it was far too late. She already owned every torrid part.

"Brynn," he breathed, not wanting to cave.

Toying with his cock with her hand, she used her spit as lubrication. Twisting her touch as she moved her fingers up and down, she shook her head.

"Nik...I said that I want you to cum in my mouth. Let me taste you...I know it won't ruin our night...you'll be rock hard right after...how the fuck is that possible, anyways?" she asked, huffing a small laugh.

Swallowing hard, he closed his eyes to delay his orgasm. Her hand was just as talented as her sinful mouth.

"It's a blessing...and a curse," he muttered, his voice shaking at the seams. "Brynn...please."

"Are you gonna cum in my mouth like a good boy?" she asked, loving the small bit of dominance she had over him. "Hmm?"

Opening his stormy eyes, Nik furrowed his brow. Twisting his fingers into her chestnut locks, he resisted the urge to pull her onto his lap. How the hell could he deny her? Or himself, for that matter.

"Yes," he replied.

Smiling triumphantly, Brynn pumped his rigid length. Steadying herself as the limousine sped down the highway, she dipped her head downwards.

"Such a good boy," she said, once again taking him within her wanting mouth.

Mindful of her teeth, she greedily suckled on his thick cock. Toying and teasing him with her needy tongue, she slowly bobbed her head. Relaxing her throat, she took him deeper and deeper until she heard the breathy grunt he always made right before he lost control.

Resting his head against the back of the leather seat, his muscles tensed as he felt the first spark of his release. Looking down at her beautiful face, he hissed a warning. She was driving him headlong into madness with every wanton lick. Her tongue was too demanding, her mouth too warm and sloppy with spit. It was all too much.

Growling into the dark cab of the limousine, Nik arched his hips. Holding her still with the hand gripping her hair, he seized as his orgasm roared to life. Closing his eyes, his body shook slightly after the first spurt of cum spilled from his cock. Instinctively pumping his cock into her mouth, he selfishly rode out the entirety of his release.

Eagerly swallowing his warm cum, Brynn squealed as he gently fucked her face. Relaxing as much as she could, she memorized the intensity of the moment. He looked absolutely feral, like a man possessed. It heightened her own arousal, making her cunt ache and her heart pound against her rib cage.

Slowly slipping back into reality, Nik eased his tight hold on her hair. Releasing her curls, he touched her reddened cheek as she let his spent cock fall from her mouth. Murmuring sweet words of reverence, he urged her to climb onto his lap.

"Come here…let me hold you, my love," he said, his voice deep and gravely.

Wiping her mouth with the back of her hand, Brynn nodded her head. Climbing onto him, she straddled his thighs as she soaked in his honeyed words. Snuggling against the crook of his neck, she savored the taste of him still on her tongue. It was sweet and clean, almost like sugar water. Unlike any cum she had tasted before.

"How do you taste so good?" she wondered aloud, cuddling his naked body.

Wrapping his arms around his love, he held her tightly as the limo changed lanes. It was a question he had been asked before but didn't have an answer to. The elders had refused to have their kind studied, so much of their physiology was still a mystery. He had always theorized that it was because the bitterness of his humanity had been removed. But he didn't know for sure.

"Well, you're welcome to do that again anytime you have a craving," he snickered.

"Oh yeah? So you liked it?" she asked, kissing his throat.

Nodding his head, he languidly ran his fingers over her tanned skin. Inhaling the intoxicating scent of her blood as it pumped through her veins, he closed his eyes to settle the part of him that wanted nothing more than to sink his teeth into her flesh.

"Mmm...very much so," he replied, forcing his bloodlust into sexual desire once more. "I don't mean to sound crass but fuck, Brynn. I swear I felt the back of your throat...do you not have a gag reflex?"

Lifting her face from his neck, she moved to look at him. Meeting his eyes, she shook her head.

"Nope. Sure don't," she said, giving him a cheeky grin.

Inching his face closer to hers, he hummed an approval. A Goddess without a gag reflex. He wondered what he had finally done right to receive such a wondrous gift.

"Mmm...well aren't I lucky," he purred.

Bracing her weight on her shaky knees, Brynn dipped her hand between their naked bodies. Touching his semi-hard cock with her fingertips, she arched a brow. Just as she suspected, he was almost ready to go again. He had the most insane stamina. It was almost as if he was some otherworldly, sex crazed beast.

"I'm pretty sure I'm the lucky one...do you think we have enough time for one more? I know it's all we've done today...but God...I need you again," she said, teasing his hardening length.

Sucking in a tight breath, Nik slowly dragged his hands down her back to her ass. Cupping her cheeks, he gave them a tight pinch. Of course they had time. He would make the driver drive all the way down to

Tucson and back again if he had to.

"I need you too…and don't worry, we have all the time in the world," he said, his razor-sharp desire building with every flick of her wrist. "Now be a good girl and fuck me."

Suppressing a squeal, she gently pumped her hand along his now rigid length. She marveled at his ability to sound so loving, while asserting his dominance. It instantly made her want to do anything he asked.

"Yes, Sir," she replied.

Raising herself on her knees, she lined the entrance of her wet pussy with the head of his cock. Slowly taking in every inch of him, she let out a moan as her cunt stretched around his thick girth. Pausing for a moment once he was fully inside, she moved her hands to his broad shoulders.

"Mmm…and how would you like me to fuck you, Mister Draven?" she asked, digging her manicured nails into his alabaster skin. "Fast? Slow?"

Gritting just teeth while his cock throbbed inside her warm pussy, Nik resisted the urge to slap her ass. Giving her firm cheeks another pinch instead, he dropped his eyes to look at the pendant between her firm breasts. Having the sudden need to watch it bounce against her body, he hissed a command.

"Fast and hard…and don't you dare stop until you cum. Do you understand?" he spat, his tone dangerously deep.

Widening her hazel eyes in excitement, she nodded her head. She was hoping he would say that. It was much easier to move at a quick pace while the limousine was moving. She also enjoyed it a hell of a lot more.

"Yes, Sir," she replied.

"Good girl," he praised, pulling his hands from her ass to her hips. "Now hurry, I want to feel you cum on my cock."

"Ooh...yes, Sir," she said.

Using her grip on his shoulders as leverage, Brynn began to rock her hips. Keeping him fully inside, she did exactly as she was told. Not bothering to ease herself into a gradual rhythm, she went straight for it. Moving back and forth, over and over in tight, quick thrusts that made her heart race.

Spitting an expletive, Nik dug his fingers into her slim hips. Dropping his gaze from her face, he stared unabashedly at her perfect tits. Watching her rosebud nipples pebble as she fucked him faster and faster, he felt his mouth water. He wished he could latch onto them with his teeth and tongue.

"Ahhh...yes...just...like that," he growled, enjoying the lewd sound of their lovemaking.

Switching the motion of her thrusts, she used her knees to lift herself ever so slightly before dropping back down on his dick. Again and again, whimpering with every pleasurable push. Ignoring the burning muscles of her thighs, she concentrated on the bliss building low in her belly.

"Ohhh...God...God!" she moaned.

Shaking his head, Nik pulled his right hand from her hip to the back of her head. Carefully grabbing a fistful of her long hair, he made her look him in the eyes.

"No...no...*no God*," he said in between grunts. "Only me...understand?"

Completely turned on by his words, Brynn nodded. *Holy shit*. That was probably the hottest thing anyone had ever said to her. And it was the truth. He was the one doing this to her.

"Yes!" she squealed.

Releasing his fist, he snaked his hand from her hair to her left breast. Palming it tightly, he leaned forward to claim her delicious lips.

Returning the kiss with fervor, she grazed her nails along his shoulders. Working his cock, she twisted her narrow hips from side to side as she rode him. Her release was bubbling just beneath the surface, teasing her with the promise of intense pleasure. But for whatever reason, she just couldn't break.

Distracting her with his tongue, Nik carefully brushed against the edges of her thoughts. Although her bliss was growing and she was thoroughly enjoying herself, she was becoming frustrated. Pressing a little further, he instantly realized the problem.

Neither of them could reach her little pink clit.

Calming his thoughts as best as he could, he ignored his own orgasm as it threatened to boil over. Wanting so badly for his love to fall apart, he went further into her chaotic mind. Physically grounding her with his demanding mouth and roaming hands, he planted a lewd suggestion into her consciousness.

Arch your back, Brynn. Let my cock hit that special little spot in your cunt. I'll make you cum so hard if you just do that.

Furrowing her brow, Brynn slowed her pace. Trying to make sense of Nik's words as they echoed in her mind, she began to pull away from the kiss. This has happened before, hearing his deep voice in her head during sex. She just didn't understand why.

Sensing her confusion, he pulled her back into the moment. Increasing the frequency of his otherworldly influence, he repeated his words. Going the extra mile to coat them in a burst of pleasure to make her fully accept them.

Arch your back, Brynn.

Once again melting into his kiss, she moaned as a tiny wave of bliss ebbed through her body. Savoring it before it melted away, she ground down wantonly on his cock. After a few quick heartbeats, she followed the silken voice in her head. Pressing her flushed torso against his, she lifted her ass to arch her back just as she was ordered to.

Needing to take control, Nik moved his hands to her waist. Stilling her hips, he suddenly broke the kiss. Moving his head, he nuzzled against her throat with his nose and mouth.

"I'm taking over," he growled, licking a bead of salty sweat from her skin.

Moaning a reply, she squeezed her eyes shut as he pumped his length in and out of her sopping pussy. With every rapid push, he hit her at an angle that made her see stars. Again and again the head of his cock grazed a hidden crevice, causing her orgasm to finally break free.

Kissing the soft skin of her neck, Nik lost a small bit of the control he was holding onto so dearly. With both his bloodlust and carnal lust filling his body, his fangs extended and his eyes turned black. Wildly fucking into her cunt, he pressed his teeth against her flesh. Just as he began to bite, he felt her pussy clench around him as her bliss consumed her.

It instantly stopped the monster trying desperately to escape.

Ripping his mouth from her neck, he closed his ebony eyes to hide his true nature from his love. Jerking as his own release snuck up on him, he snapped his mouth shut to suppress his elongated fangs. Writhing in a mixture of pleasure and anger, it took him a moment to realize his love had collapsed against him.

Laughing happily, Brynn snuggled against her lover. Feeling his muscular body shake, she smiled to herself. Apparently, she wasn't the only one who felt the Earth move.

"Mmm...that was probably the best one yet," she breathed, her mind completely glossing over the odd way she was able to cum.

Forcing the monster back in its cage, he wrapped his arms around her.

Holding her close, he chastised himself for losing the reins. He couldn't allow himself to do that ever again.

"Are you ok?" he asked, his handsome face twisting with concern.

Lifting her face from his chest, she gave him a full smile. Noticing his expression, that smile immediately fell to a frown. He looked incredibly worried. It made her suddenly perk.

"Of course...why? Did something happen? Are you ok?" she asked, her eyes widening.

Pausing for a moment, he kicked himself for alarming her. He didn't want to ruin her afterglow. It wasn't her fault that he was a blood sucking demon.

"Yeah...yeah, I'm ok. I was just making sure. You let out quite the scream, my love," he said, trying to sound lighthearted.

Humming low, she gave him a quick kiss on the cheek. She should be embarrassed for being so brazen, but she felt too good to care.

"Uh oh...think the driver heard me?" she asked, raising a brow.

Chuckling, Nik nodded his buzzing head. "Definitely...the cars around us probably heard you, too," he teased, massaging his fingertips over her back.

Shrugging her shoulders, she let out a tiny snort. Good. Let them hear. The man she was madly in love with had just given her the best orgasm of her life. Let them be jealous.

"So...do we need to get dressed or can we stay like this for a while?" she asked.

Kissing the top of her head, Nik forced himself to relax against the leather seat. At that moment, he honestly didn't want to move an inch. Not because he was too relaxed, but because he was too frightened.

"Why don't you take a nap, my love," he suggested, his eyes drifting towards the window of the limousine. "I think you've earned it…I'll wake you when we're almost home. We'll get dressed, then."

Letting out a yawn, Brynn got one more snuggle in before letting her eyes drift close. She was happy and satisfied, a nap on his lap would be the cherry on the top.

"Perfect," she said.

Pressing his lips into a fine line, he gently rubbed his hands over her skin. Listening to her heartbeat as it slowed to a comfortable rhythm, he felt instant relief as she fell asleep. Watching the nighttime traffic as it whizzed by, he replayed the moment over and over again. His feelings for her were too strong, and far too dangerous. He knew he had to tell her the truth before something like that happened again.

He just didn't know how he was going to do it.

CHAPTER THIRTEEN

Stuffing her laptop into her backpack, Brynn let out a long sigh. She was not looking forward to her night class, she was too worried about leaving Nik alone. He had woken up with a terrible migraine and spent much of the day tucked away in their darkened bedroom. He told her that these happened frequently, with clusters usually lasting weeks at a time. Apparently, the harsh desert sun was to blame. He said something about it triggering his migraines with its brightness and heat. It sounded odd to her, but what did she know? She wasn't a neurologist.

Perking as she heard soft footsteps walking down the hallway, she set her backpack down upon the dining room table. Walking towards the sound, she gave her love a sympathetic smile as he came into view. She was happy to see him out of bed and semi-dressed. Maybe he was finally feeling better?

"Hey, handsome...how are you feeling? How's your head?" she asked, closing the space between them.

Holding out his long arms, Nik pulled Brynn against his bare torso. Snuggling her close, he breathed in her intoxicating scent. He hated lying to her but felt the need to. The effects of her ambrosial blood didn't last as long as he had hoped for, and he just wasn't ready to tell her the truth.

"Better now that the sun has set...the pain is just a dull roar. I'm almost functional," he said, leaning in to kiss her forehead.

Easing out of the embrace, she gave him a look of relief. Humming lightly, she reached up to touch the side of his chiseled face. She was so glad to hear that. He did look better; he could actually open his green eyes all the way.

"Good...do you still want me to go to class? I can totally blow it off, it's just a review," she said, hoping he would say yes.

Shaking his head, he met her hazel eyes. She had been trying to wiggle out of class all day. He understood that she was in the beginning stages of love and only wanted to be with him and take care of him. He felt the exact same way. But she needed to do well on her exam. It might be the last one she took for a while.

"No, you totally *can't* blow it off, Brynn," he said sternly. "Besides, isn't Jenni almost here to pick you up?"

Scrunching the fine features of her face, she shrugged her shoulders. He was right, she should go. Jenni would be highly annoyed if she ditched, she was dying for Brynn to tell her all about her new dream lover.

"Yeah, she is…why don't you put on a shirt and some shoes and walk me out?" she asked, drifting her eyes over his muscular chest.

Suddenly very aware of his physical state, Nik nodded in agreement. "I'd love to…I'll be right back, Sunshine," he said with a wink before turning on his heels.

Watching him as he headed back towards the bedroom, she let her eyes take their fill. She never really understood the women that went feral whenever they saw a man wearing grey sweatpants with nothing on underneath.

Now she did.

Smacking back her lustful thoughts, she slowly walked to the dining room. Suddenly feeling a vibration on her thigh, she reached into her denim shorts for her cell. Seeing Jenni's name on the screen, she flashed a bright smile. Pressing the answer button, she brought the sleek phone to her ear.

"Hey, girl!" she said.

"Hey, bitch! I'm here, but I'm parked illegally so hurry up and get your ass down

here," Jenni said.

"I'll be right down, I'm just waiting for Nik to get some clothes on," Brynn replied.

"Wait...Nik is there?!" Jenni asked, her voice lifting in surprise. *"Holy shit does this mean I get to meet him?"*

"Yes, and yes and girl...I have so much to tell you. Like. Jesus you're gonna die," Brynn said, holding in a squeal.

"Fuck, I can't wait to hear all about it! But yeah, hurry...there's a guy walking to his Beamer giving me the stink eye right now. I might be blocking him. Meh...whatever. Just get your ass down here!" Jenni said.

"Ok! Ok! Be down in a sec. Bye," Brynn said.

"Bye, bitch!" Jenni replied, ending the call.

Laughing to herself, Brynn put her phone back into her pocket. God, she couldn't wait to spill the tea. So much had happened since the last time she had seen Jenni. Her best friend was going to lose her mind. Grabbing her black backpack, she threw it over one shoulder. Stepping towards the front door, called out to Nik.

"Hey, Nik? Jenni's here, are you almost done?"

Walking out of the master bedroom, Nik made his way down the long hallway. Pulling the hem of his black T-shirt down his torso, he hurried his steps. He really wanted to make a good first impression on Jenni, she meant so much to Brynn.

"Yes, love, I'm coming!" he replied.

Reaching the open concept living space, he walked towards Brynn at the door. Raking his eyes up and down her body, he regretted not driving her to her class, himself. She was too beautiful, and he didn't trust men, especially college aged men. If any of them so much as dared to touch her...

"Think you'll be warm enough? You said the lecture hall was usually freezing," he said, interrupting his own thoughts.

Glancing down at her outfit, she shrugged her shoulders. Sure, she was wearing shorts, but she did have on an oversized Sun Devils hoodie. She might be a little cold, but it would help her stay awake. Opening the door, she gave him a nod.

"Yeah, I'll be fine," she said.

Giving her a critical look, he took the door from her. Letting her cross the threshold into the hallway, he pushed out a tiny sigh before following her.

"Ok, but if it gets too cold during class let me know and I'll bring you a blanket," he said.

Giggling lightly, Brynn's mind went wild with that little scenario. She could just see him striding into the lecture hall with all the bravado in the world just to bring her a blanket because she might be a little chilly. She had no doubt that he really would do anything for her.

"Mmm...yes, Sir," she replied, hitting the call button for the elevator.

"Good girl," he praised, leaning over to kiss the side of her head.

Hearing the ding of the elevator, he gave her a sly smile before stepping inside the lift. Waiting until she had followed suit, he pressed the button to the ground floor. He couldn't believe he was starting to feel nervous. But that probably had more to do with the phone call he had to make than meeting Jenni. In a not so surprising turn of events, Ulysses was still upset with the loss of Mia, at least that's what he hoped the Elder wanted to discuss. Knowing his luck, the brute would bring up Brynn as well.

It worried him that he might have to take his love into hiding sooner than he anticipated. But he would cross that bridge when he got there.

Watching a blank, almost trance-like look form over Nik's handsome face, Brynn cleared her throat to gain his attention. Unable to get a response, she reached out to grab his hand. Clearly, he was thinking about something, and whatever it was had him worried. She could just tell.

"Hey…are you ok?" she asked, her eyes filled with concern.

With Brynn's voice cutting through his thoughts, Nik blinked his dark green eyes. Coming back to the present moment, he looked at her just as the elevator came to a stop.

"Hmm? Yeah…I'm fine, Sunshine. It's just this damn lingering migraine," he said, lifting her hand to kiss her knuckles.

Dropping the corner of her lips into a frown, she eyed him critically. She really hoped his migraine was the problem. Something nagging at her in the back of her mind told her otherwise.

"Are you sure you don't want me to stay home?" she asked.

Shaking his head, he led her from the elevator to the front door of the condo complex. Opening the hunk of metal, he held it for her so she could cross the threshold.

"No, you need to go…I'll be fine, I promise," he said.

"Hmm…well, ok. You should probably go back to bed and get some rest. I'll try not to wake you when I get home," she said.

Walking with his love down the sidewalk, he lifted the corner of his full lips into a sly grin.

"You'd better wake me up…it's been almost twenty hours since I've been inside that tight little cunt of yours…that's probably why I have this damn thing. I'm going through pussy withdrawal," he said with a wink.

With her knees instantly turning to jelly, Brynn accidentally stumbled.

Quickly catching herself before any damage was done, she laughed as her cheeks flushed red. *God.* Now that's all she would be thinking about for the next two and a half hours.

"Well, then...I will have to give you a good dose of medicine when I come home," she said.

"Mmm, I look forward to it, Nurse Brynn," he replied.

Raising his arm, he wrapped it around her shoulders. Holding in a chuckle, he walked side by side with her to the bright red G-Wagon parked in the no parking zone. The flashy car had to belong to Jenni. It was a car a typical Sugar Baby would drive.

"Well, that's my ride!" Brynn chirped.

Before Nik had a chance to respond, a cute little blonde jumped out of the Mercedes. With a sharp squeal, the young woman came running towards them with her arms open wide.

"Brynn!" she exclaimed, giving her a warm embrace.

Having his arm pushed away by Jenni's hug, Nik took a step backwards to let the girls have their moment. Reading the blonde's aura, he was surprised to see not one mean streak. Jenni was a genuinely sweet girl, and she loved Brynn dearly. It was bittersweet to see them so happy to see one another.

"Jenni, oh my God I feel like I haven't seen you in years," she said, pulling back from the bear hug. "Oh hey...I'd like you to meet Nik! Jenni, this is Nik...Nik, this is Jenni!"

Holding out his hand, Nik gave Jenni a warm smile. He was trying not to read her thoughts but couldn't help but catch a few bits and pieces. She was both thrilled for Brynn, and incredibly jealous. She wondered where he was when she had first downloaded the Benefactor app. It made him snicker internally.

"It's very nice to meet you, Jenni," he said.

Taking Nik's hand, Jenni gave him a firm handshake. She tried not to think about how small her hand was in comparison to his. Everything about the man was large and gorgeous. Holy fuck, she was so happy for her best friend.

"It's nice to meet you too, Nik!" she replied, her blue eyes wide with excitement. "And it's really good to know that you're real…I mean…I honestly thought Brynn was being catfished at first!"

Nodding his head, he gave her a knowing look.

"Although we try our hardest to vet the Benefactors, catfishing does happen on occasion, so your worry was valid but yes…I'm very real," he said, politely dropping her hand. "Thank you for taking Brynn to class with you, I really appreciate it."

"Oh, of course! And don't worry, I'll bring her home right after class, safe and sound," she said, glancing back and forth from Brynn to Nik.

"Wonderful, make sure that you do," he said, turning his attention to his love. "Good luck, my beautiful Brynn. Stay warm and pay attention."

Stopping herself from rolling her eyes, Brynn nodded her head instead. Turning her body, she cuddled herself close to him. "Yes, Sir…I love you," she said.

"I love you, too," he replied before giving her a tender kiss on the lips.

Humming softly to herself, Brynn reluctantly pulled away from Nik. Motioning towards the SUV with her hand, she painted a bright smile on her face.

"Alright, we should head to class, hmm?" she said.

Keeping her mouth closed from saying something that would only embarrass her friend, Jenni nodded. Walking back to the driver's side of the G-Wagon, she waved goodbye to Nik.

"Bye, Nik! I'll see you later," she said.

Lifting his hand, Nik returned the wave. He wished he could say the same. Unfortunately, the chances were high that their paths would never cross again.

"Take care, Jenni," he replied.

With one last look at her handsome lover, Brynn opened the passenger door of the Mercedes. Tossing her backpack to the floor, she hopped in and quickly settled herself. Blowing a kiss to Nik through the window, she urged Jenni to hurry. She was dying to talk to her.

"I'm going as fast as I can!" Jenni replied, ripping open her door.

Climbing into her seat, she closed the door behind her. Slapping on her seatbelt, she put her SUV into gear. Once again waving to her friend's handsome Benefactor, she carefully maneuvered out of the parking lot.

Waving to the girls, Nik let out a sigh. Watching them pull out onto the main road, he said a silent prayer for their safety. Stuffing his fists into the pockets of his sweatpants, he turned and headed back to the condo. Trying desperately to ignore the feeling of dread creeping over him.

. . .

"Holy shit, Brynn! *Holy shit!* Nik is HOT…like *super* hot…actually, he's like Super*man* hot! He's like the Wish version of Henry Cavill!" Jenni exclaimed, driving her G-Wagon on the side streets heading towards the 101.

"It's more like Henry Cavill is the Wish version of Nikolai Draven," Brynn replied with a snort. "But yeah, he's beautiful…it's like his body is carved out of marble. He's perfect…like every part. Inside and out! God…I'm so in love, Jenni! I am head over heels in love with that man!"

Furrowing her brow, Jenni slowed down for the red light. Clicking her turn signal, she stopped herself from saying something stupid. She had never seen Brynn this happy. Ever.

"Brynn…you're in love? But…babe…you've only just met," she said.

Taking in a deep breath, Brynn tried not to take offense with her critical tone. Yes, it was rash of her, but she couldn't help how she felt.

"I know…I know…but like, I just know that I love him. It's like that saying, 'you know when you know.' But maybe I should just start at the beginning? Yeah…ok. Well first off, I did sign an NDA but our relationship is no longer transactional, so I think that's null and void," she said with a wave of her hand. "But just in case…I'm not telling you any of this. Everything lives and dies here, ok?"

"Ok," Jenni replied. An NDA wasn't unusual, she had signed one with Don initially, too.

"Alright so…our first date went really well and we decided to move forward with the whole Benefactor, Sugar Baby thing. So, the next night he had a driver come pick me up and take me to The Soho. It's the most gorgeous condo I've ever seen in my entire life…and I'm walking through these rooms with my head exploding because it looks like a fucking Pottery Barn showroom, and it had these fantastic views and I'm just like…dying because he's following me around, giving me these looks like I'm the most gorgeous thing he's ever seen. Anyways…he asks me if I like the condo and I'm like…yeah, of course! And then he's like…well good, *because it's yours*. And I swear I had a stroke!"

"Holy shit!" Jenni exclaimed, getting onto the on-ramp.

"I know! Ok so…like…then he sets down his ground rules and I just say yes to everything because well…he's hot, I really liked him, and he was rescuing me from all my problems, you know? Plus, they weren't that bad. I just had to eat right, exercise, stay in school, spend time with him, give blood every two weeks—"

"Wait...what?" Jenni asked, interrupting her best friend. "You had to give blood?"

Shrugging her shoulders, Brynn looked at Jenni.

"Yeah, I know it sounds weird...but one of the organizations he owns supplies blood to like, third world countries and it's really important to him. He said everyone in his life has to do it, it's just something that's non-negotiable for him. It's not that big of a deal, I'm not afraid of needles or anything," she said nonchalantly.

"Umm...ok...*weird*, but if you're fine with it, I guess that's what matters," Jenni replied. "Ok so go on!"

"Right...ok...so I agree to it all and we start making out, things get really hot and heavy and then he gets a phone call. Something happened with a client or something, I'm not sure...but all of a sudden, he had to leave for LA. So, he left, and I was all alone in this massive condo. Anyways, the next day his assistant comes over. She's a sweet little old lady...but really curt and stern. I think that's just because she's from Eastern Europe, I donno. I thought it was weird that his assistant was old enough to be his grandma but apparently, she's incredibly loyal and he really trusts and respects her. Ok so anyways...Yetta...that's her name...she gives me a new phone, all these supplements, a fucking black American Express card...and I'm just freaking out. I felt like Cinderella or something...like, Jenni...my whole life completely changed in a blink of an eye. It's insane!" Brynn exclaimed.

Trying to wrap her head about Brynn's story, Jenni chewed on her bottom lip as they zipped down the interstate. This was all so incredible, but there were things that just seemed off. Especially the giving blood part. Maybe it was just her jealousy talking. After all, Don never gave her a black AMEX card.

"Well, you deserve it, bitch...you deserve it all," Jenni said.

"Mmm...thanks, girl...that really means a lot. So yeah...but oh my God, this is a little insane. We had sex twelve times yesterday!

TWELVE!"

Looking at Brynn out of the corner of her eyes, Jenni huffed in disbelief. There was no way, she had to be lying.

"Brynn...how is that even humanly possible?! There's no way! Wait...what kind of sex are we talking about? Like...did you guys have sex twice where he came twelve hours apart and then he got you off ten more times in between? By the way, that sounds crazy too...like is your clit still working?"

"Ha ha ha. Yes...it's still working. Quite well, thank you...but I know it sounds insane," Brynn agreed, holding in a laugh. "But I swear to you, we had sex where he physically came twelve times yesterday. And I don't know how he did it...all I know is that we would fuck, he would cum...and then like, ten minutes later, he would be hard again!"

"Holy shit...is he taking Viagra? Don has to take it sometimes, but the most I can get out of him is two rounds...twelve just sounds impossible. I mean...he is human, right?" Jenni joked.

"Definitely human...and I'm not sure about the Viagra. I mean, I didn't see him take anything, but I guess it's possible," Brynn said with a shrug. "But it wouldn't matter if he had taken a little blue pill...it was literally the best sex I've ever had in my entire life! He's so...attentive...and God his tongue is so talented. He just knew how to get me off every single time!"

Switching lanes, Jenni's mind was swimming. She still couldn't believe a man in his thirties could cum twelve times. Not that she didn't believe her best friend, it's just that she had never heard of such a thing. Nik needed to have his cock studied in the name of science.

"I'm so jealous, you have no idea...but girl, were you guys careful?" Jenni asked.

Shaking her head, Brynn winced slightly from the tongue lashing she knew she was about to receive.

"No…but…but…before you yell at me, he's sterile so. Yay!" she said.

"Girl!" Jenni hissed. "I don't care how in love you are…men can't be trusted! You know this!"

Sitting back against her chair, Brynn let out a sigh. Jenni was right, men couldn't be trusted. But Nik was different, he wasn't your typical man. She trusted him emphatically. She trusted him with her life.

"I know you won't believe me but…I trust him. I know he wouldn't lie to me. I just know it," she said confidently.

Staying quiet for a moment, Jenni concentrated on the road before her. Brynn was right, she didn't believe that Nik wouldn't lie to her. All men lied; it was in their DNA. But she loved her best friend so very much, and only wanted to see her happy. So, she would support her and her decisions, and be there for her when the shit hit the fan.

"If you trust him, then that's all that matters, Brynn. I love you, and I love seeing you like this…so I'm going to give Mister Draven a huge pass. But I swear to God, if he breaks your heart, I'm gonna hunt him down and break that movie star face of his," she said with a tiny grin.

With a laugh, Brynn nodded and turned to look at her. She would expect nothing less. God help Nik if he did end up hurting her. For being such a small thing, Jenni had a mean right hook.

"Thanks, girl…I love you," she said.

Giving Brynn a wink, Jenni put on her blinker to exit the interstate. Getting onto the off-ramp, she slowed down to merge onto the street headed for the University. She wanted to know more about this so-called perfect specimen of a man, but it would have to wait until after class.

"I love you too, bitch," she replied fondly, letting go of the steering wheel to grab Brynn's hand.

CHAPTER FOURTEEN

"Nikolai. I am not pleased," Ulysses spoke through the phone, his voice as hard as concrete.

Pacing down the hallway of the condo, Nik pressed the glass screen of the cell against his ear. Mouthing a silent expletive, he balled his free hand into a fist. The Elder wasn't telling him something he didn't already know. He fully understood how upset he was over Mia. His voice still worried him, nonetheless.

"And why is that, my Lord?" he asked, preparing to receive a tongue lashing over the drug addicted blonde.

Hearing an almost animalistic growl on the other end of the cell, Nik swallowed hard. He wished he could read Ulysses' thoughts. Unfortunately for him, the brute was exceptional at keeping his mind hidden.

"I am HUNGRY!"

Groaning internally, Nik halted his steps. Ulysses was a glutton, of course he was hungry. Between the fiasco with Mia and the complication with Brynn, Yetta had been delayed with coordinating the blood harvest in the Eastern Quadrant. It was a simple mistake. One he thought he had resolved quickly enough to not cause a disruption.

"My Lord…with all due respect…there is plenty of blood for you in the reserves…and the newly pulled batch should be arriving at the Manor by tomorrow. I apologize profusely for its delay, Mia tied me up for a few days. But this batch is from my girls in Japan, I know how much you enjoy them. I've made sure that they've feasted on Wagyu three times a week for the past month, so that will be reflected in their blood. I assure you, you will be quite satisfied with how savory and silky it will taste. It will be worth the wait," Nik replied.

"No. I don't want their blood, Nikolai. I want fresh blood. I want the blood from the new girl you promised me. The one from America...what the hell is that state called? Arizona? Yes. Her. My mouth has been watering since you sent me her pictures. I want her blood."

Swinging his balled fist into thin air, Nik's face twisted in anger. Ulysses' brain may be ancient, but it was still incredibly sharp. Why did he think wiping Brynn from the archives would solve his problem? His feelings for her were making him stupid and sloppy. He should have nipped this in the bud immediately.

"Ah. Yes...the Arizona State co-ed. I've been meaning to tell you...there was a problem with that particular candidate, my Lord," he replied, keeping his tone even and steady.

"Problem? What problem?"

Pausing for a scant moment, Nik froze to calm his body. He had gone over this conversation in his mind dozens of times. He had no doubt that he could sell his narrative. It wasn't a big deal. Women had left the program before.

It wasn't a big deal.

"She had second thoughts," he said simply.

"Second thoughts? Second thoughts?! That's why we have put you in charge of the program, Nikolai. You're supposed to Charm them so there are no second thoughts! What good are you and your talents if you refuse to use them, hmm?"

"Yes, well...there was a sudden death in her family, and she needed to go home for a few weeks," Nik said, confidently spitting out the lie. "She was incredibly unstable and distraught and unsure if she wanted to continue. Under the circumstances, I thought it would be best if we paused our agreement until her emotions aren't so raw. After all, stressed blood is bitter blood...and I know how much that disgusts you. But now that I know you're craving her, as soon as she comes back to Phoenix, I will Charm her to bring her back into the fold. You will taste her. I swear to you."

"A death in the family, hmm? I will never understand mortals and their grief. It's quite infantile," Ulysses said, pushing out an annoyed sigh. *"Be sure that you follow through with your promises, Nikolai. Until then, send me my portion of her initial pull."*

Physically taken aback, Nik stammered into the phone. Fuck. He thought he had taken care of that quickly enough.

"Initial pull, My Lord? I'm sorry, but I don't know what you're talking about…we never got that far with her," Nik said flatly.

"Why are you lying to me, Nikolai? I saw with my own two eyes that the nurse had logged her initial pull into the system. Per usual, you are supposed to send me half…and I still haven't received it. I want to taste her!"

"My Lord I'm sorry but you must be mistaken…there's no way you saw that because she was never put into the system. You can search for her right now and see that I'm right," Nik said, measuring himself. "She isn't there."

"I know what I saw, Nikolai. I don't like being lied to."

"I'm not lying to you, My Lord," Nik said, shifting his weight from one leg to the other. "But even if we did have an initial pull from her…if you haven't received it by now, it would be rancid. You wouldn't be able to drink it."

Waiting for a rebuff, Nik heard nothing but deafening silence. It wasn't a good sign; he could tell the Elder's wheels were churning. His lie was weak at best. With just a little digging Ulysses would see through it.

"I'm giving you one week to get me a sample from the girl, Nikolai. I don't care what you have to do to get it for me. I don't care if her blood is bitter. I want what is mine. Do you understand?"

"Yes, my Lord…I understand," Nik said, a deep frown on his handsome face.

"Good. One week, Nikolai. Tick tock," Ulysses said, ending the call.

Quietly seething, Nik threw his phone against the wall in a moment of rage, knocking a hole through the drywall into the belly of the guest bedroom. Closing his serpentine eyes, he tried to quell his anger. Breathing through the waves of bloodlust, he bit them back as they threatened to consume him.

This wasn't good. It wasn't good at all. Ulysses would think about their conversation repeatedly, finding micro inconsistencies each time. Soon he would send his Hounds to confirm his suspicions. They would quickly sniff out the truth about Brynn.

They had to be long gone before any of that happened. He had to warn Leonardo of the interrogation headed his way. They would seek him out first to grill him about the archives. He also had to tell Yetta to secure their secret travel plans, the sooner the better.

It didn't look like his love would be taking that final, after all.

. . .

Slouching in the hard plastic chair, Brynn tried her best to pay attention to her professor. Hovering her fingers over the keyboard of her laptop, she waited for the older gentleman to say something worth typing into her notes. She couldn't wait to finally be free of this particular class. Lucky for her, he was giving them the choice to take the final early. She hoped Nik would be ok with her taking it the following night. With him being so invested in her studies, she knew it wouldn't be a problem.

Moving her hand to her mouth, she let out a large yawn. Blinking her tired eyes back into focus, she suddenly felt a sharp jab to her side. Turning her head towards Jenni, she gave the blonde a semi-annoyed look. The girl had the boniest elbows, she wondered if she would get a bruise.

"What?" she whispered.

Licking her lips nervously, Jenni leaned in close to her best friend. Keeping her voice low, she kept her gaze on the professor as she talked.

"Ok...so...don't look...but there's a guy sitting in the top row to your right. He's been legit staring at us for like...twenty minutes now. Just fucking staring," she said.

Furrowing her brow, Brynn forced herself not to look at the man in question. Honestly, it wasn't unusual for guys to gawk at Jenni. She didn't know why she sounded so freaked out.

"Did Don's son wander into our class by mistake?" she joked.

"Ha ha...very funny...and no, Landon is at GCU. Anyways...I've never seen this guy before, he's giving me the major ick," she replied.

"Why? What's wrong with him?" Brynn asked.

"Remember that really old movie from the eighties? The one with all the vampires? God...what the hell was that called? It was about a gang of vampires that looked like they belonged in like a motorcycle club or something?" Jenni said.

Scrunching her face, Brynn tried to think of an answer to Jenni's question. She was pretty sure she knew what movie her friend was talking about. The older brother that was turned into a vampire was incredibly attractive, he kind of reminded her of Nik in a way.

"Um...do you mean The Lost Boys?" Brynn replied.

"Yes!" Jenni exclaimed, trying so hard to keep her voice no more than a whisper. "Yes, exactly! He looks like he is one of those vampires! The crazy eighties hair, the black leather jacket, everything. I've never seen him before, I don't think he's in this fucking class. He just won't stop staring! It's like his eyes are almost black or something...serious ick vibe!"

"What?!" Brynn hissed.

"Shhh! Just be chill...but yeah, look at him, but don't make it obvious...God he's creepy," Jenni said, glancing at the man from the corners of her blue eyes. "Who even wears a studded leather jacket when it's like, eighty degrees outside? Freaking weirdo."

Having her interest thoroughly piqued, Brynn straightened her posture in her chair. Not caring to be as inconspicuous as her friend, she turned her head to look at the creeper in question. It didn't take long to find him; he stuck out like a sore thumb. He looked exactly as Jenni described, she almost laughed out loud at the absurdity.

He really did look like a punk rock vampire.

Boldly meeting the man's dark brown eyes, she scrunched her nose as if she had just smelled something foul. To her surprise he didn't budge an inch at her rudeness. Quite the contrary, she felt the heat of his otherworldly gaze intensifying. Within the span of a handful of heartbeats she felt the room and its occupants melt away, replaced by an inky black void and a masculine voice breathing into her ear.

Hello little lamb.

Unable to turn away, she swallowed hard as his voice echoed in her mind. His words sounded ominous; she didn't like the way they bounced around her skull. Attempting to speak, she found herself sufficiently silenced. It was as if her jaw had been sutured together with sharp wire.

Shhh...don't worry about the pain. You won't remember it. You won't remember any of this. Fortunately for you, I can't rummage through your mind like Nikolai. That's not my talent...but I can do this, and it's enough for now. Until it isn't. You see, Nikolai has been hiding you. The Elders don't like that...they don't like it at all...and so they've sent me. But I can't do anything until my orders are handed to me. So, I will just sit back and silently observe until then. And I do like watching you...I like watching you very much. I can see why Nikolai wants to keep you all to himself.

Brynn whimpered, tears welling in her eyes. As the dark voice continued, the pain in her jaw swelled to a dizzying level. She didn't know how much more torture she could take.

But that's not how things are done. You are to be shared like the other lambs in our flock. What makes you special? Hmm? Well. We're about to find out. Until then, take care Brynn. I'm looking forward to our next meeting.

Feeling an intense, phantom punch to her jaw, Brynn's world went dark. Swimming in a sea of black water, she lingered in the void while her memory was wiped clean of the wicked psychic encounter.

Satisfied with his little cat and mouse game, the stranger pushed Brynn towards consciousness. It didn't matter to him that she wouldn't remember their special moment together. He did this for his own sick pleasure. It made the wait more palatable, though he hoped the Elders wouldn't keep him waiting too long.

Next time, he would make sure she would remember the pain.

Suddenly thrust into reality, Brynn blinked her hazel eyes. Looking around her surroundings, she turned her head towards Jenni. Her friend had the oddest look on her face, it made the hair on the back of her next stand up on end.

"What? What's wrong?" she whispered.

Swallowing hard, Jenni kept her gaze on where the creeper had been only seconds ago. Now his chair was completely empty. How had he left so easily? The doors to the lecture hall were heavy and loud. She would have heard him leave, she was sure of it.

"Where the hell did he go?" Jenni asked, her azure eyes widening in fright.

Glancing over to where Jenni was looking, Brynn shrugged her shoulders. She had absolutely no idea who she was talking about.

"Where the hell did *who* go?" she said, keeping her voice low.

"The creeper! The weird biker vampire!" Jenni quietly exclaimed. "We were just talking about him…I know you saw him!"

Giving the blonde a curious look, Brynn didn't know what to say. She hadn't seen any weird biker vampire. She had absolutely no idea what Jenni was talking about.

"Girl…did you take shrooms this afternoon or something? I didn't see any weirdo. Well, besides the ones we always see," she said.

Huffing in annoyance, Jenni rolled her eyes. No, she hadn't taken any drugs. It pissed her off that Brynn was being so dismissive. She had seen him, she was sure of it!

"Never mind," she hissed bitterly, turning her attention back to their professor. "It doesn't matter."

Furrowing her brow, Brynn frowned at Jenni's sudden attitude. She didn't understand why she was so upset. It wasn't her fault she didn't see whatever ghost she was talking about.

Knowing the best way for Jenni to cool off was to let her stew, she let out a small sigh. Looking over her shoulder one last time, she eyed the spot where the supposed creeper had been.

She wished she knew what the hell was going on.

CHAPTER FIFTEEN

Breathing in the warm night's air, Brynn turned her head to look at her love. Once again, he was staring into nothing, the look of worry lining the masculine features of his face. She had caught him this way a handful of times since she returned home from class almost twenty-four hours prior. She had no idea what happened while she was at her review. He refused to admit that anything was wrong.

"Are you sure you don't mind me taking my exam tonight? I mean...I can wait until next week, it's not a big deal," she said, closing the gap between their bodies as they waited for the car service on the sidewalk.

Lifting his arm, Nik brought Brynn in close. Holding her against his side, he pushed his fears to the back of his mind. While he was slightly uneasy letting her out of his sight, her absence worked in his favor as he finalized their preparations with Yetta. He knew how slowly the Elders moved. They hadn't even checked in with Leonardo, yet.

He was confident that Brynn would be safe. At least for the night.

"No, I don't mind at all Sunshine...I'm extremely proud of you for taking the initiative to take your exam early. You've been studying all day and I know you're ready...you're going to ace it," he said, giving her a warm smile.

Looking up at her handsome man, she beamed at his words. Although she felt awful that he had spent the day nursing another migraine, it allowed her the opportunity to study. She felt like she knew the coursework inside and out. She was more than ready to take the exam. Still, she felt uneasy about leaving him. Though she didn't know exactly why.

"I'll try to be as quick as possible...then maybe I can give you another dose of medicine for your migraine," she said suggestively.

Dancing his fingertips along her bare arm, he nodded his head. He couldn't think of a more perfect way to end a rather stressful night than between her thighs.

"I'd like that very much, Nurse Brynn," he said, his voice silky and deep. "But don't rush…there will be plenty of time for us when you come home."

Humming happily, her thoughts turned to the previous night. It was the first time in her life where she had actually made love. It was slow and tender, intense and incredibly passionate. She felt as if he was purposefully going above and beyond to prove to her just how much he loved her. She would remember it for the rest of her life.

"Mmm…yes, Sir," she said.

"Good girl," he replied, kissing the crown of her head.

Glancing towards his right, he watched as a pair of headlights moved down the road towards them. He had specifically requested that the car service use their Rolls-Royce Phantom to take Brynn to and from campus. He wanted to spoil her as much as possible while he could. He hoped she liked her luxurious chariot. Clearing his throat, he gave her one more squeeze before motioning to the car with a lift of his chin.

"I think that's your ride, my beautiful Brynn," he said.

Following his line of vision, she squinted her eyes in the moonlight. Catching the vehicle as it passed under a series of streetlights, she audibly gasped. Holy shit! Was that what she thought it was? She had only ever seen them on tv or in movies, never in real life.

"Nikolai!" she exclaimed, shock lifting the tone of her voice. "Are you serious?"

Grinning at the sound of her saying his full name, he mentally patted himself on the back. Her excitement pleased him to no end. It was always so genuine, so pure. Sometimes he felt like he was experiencing things for the first time through her.

"It will bring you luck, my love," he replied. "Not that you need it but...yeah, I just thought you deserved it for finishing this class so strong."

Clapping her hands happily, Brynn eyed the black Phantom as it came to a stop in front of them. Turning back to Nik, she leaned up to kiss his cheek. She was about to have the most comfortable ride to campus; too bad the commute was short.

"Thank you, handsome," she said.

"You're more than welcome," he replied.

Waving to the driver, Nik urged him to stay behind the wheel. Opening the door himself, he helped his love into the Rolls-Royce. Watching her as she took a seat, he let his dark green eyes take their fill of his family crest as it bounced against her chest. The necklace suited her, he was thrilled that he finally found someone worthy to wear it.

Climbing into the Phantom, Brynn dropped her backpack to the floor. Settling into the leather seat, she marveled at the interior. Not only did it look amazing, but it smelled incredible too. Like the new car smell on steroids. She couldn't believe how incredibly lucky she was.

Leaning into the imported vehicle, he pulled the seatbelt down and secured it over her. Making sure it was tightly buckled, he lovingly brushed his full lips over hers.

Returning the gentle kiss, she hummed against his mouth. Reluctantly pulling away, she met his hungry eyes. How did he always have the ability to turn her into a puddle with a simple look? It wasn't fair.

"I love you," she said.

"I love you too, Sunshine. Text me when you get there and when you're done," he said.

"I will," she replied.

"Good girl," he praised before turning his attention to the driver. "Thank you for taking her to campus…please stay until she's done with her exam."

Looking over his shoulder, the young driver nodded a reply. He had been told that Mister Draven was an excellent tipper. He had no qualms about staying in a parked Rolls-Royce for an hour or two if that's what he wanted.

"Yes, Sir," he said.

"Thank you," Nik said.

Giving his love one last look, he offered her a wink. Mouthing the words 'good luck,' he closed the door to the Phantom. Lightly tapping the roof of the car with his open hand, he took a step back onto the sidewalk. Watching it as it pulled onto the road, he frowned slightly as he felt a twinge of anxiety run down his spine.

Stuffing his hands into the pockets of his navy slacks, he chewed on the inside of his cheek. Standing quietly for a moment, he talked himself out of his sudden reservation over letting her leave. Of course he was anxious, their lives were about to change forever in just two nights time. But that wasn't something he could dwell on.

With a long sigh, Nik started to head back to the condo complex. He only made it a handful of steps before he heard a familiar voice shout out from behind him.

"Nikolai! Stop! Help," Yetta sniped, hobbling her way towards him with a large tote bag on her gnarled arm. "I have mail and all you need for Norway!"

Turning towards his faithful assistant, he strode quickly towards her. Reaching out with his long arm, he took the canvas bag. Shaking his head as he felt its weight, he clicked his tongue against the roof of his mouth. She was far too delicate to be carrying around so much. It really was time she retired.

"Yetta…from now on, I'm going to make you take it easy," he tisked, taking her hand to help her walk.

Waving away his concerns, Yetta pushed out a disbelieving laugh. He and the Sun Walker had just put a kibosh on her ever having an easy life. Not that she would have it any other way. She had vowed to serve them both until she took her final breath.

"Nonsense, Nikolai…now come. Much to discuss," she said sternly, hurrying her hobbled steps.

. . .

Plopping a large manila envelope on the dining room table, Yetta pointed at it with her arthritic finger. Its contents included the beginnings of Nikolai's new life with Brynn Smith. A life she had been silently mapping out for decades just in case he ever needed a clean slate. There was a time, when she was young and beautiful, that she had hoped it would include her.

But as her grandmother always said, things happen as they should. And now she understood why they were never meant to be.

"Here. Open, Nikolai. Everything there," she said, choosing not to use their native tongue. "I take care of everything."

Grinning warmly at his faithful assistant, he picked up the yellow envelope. Pulling it open, he took a quick look inside. He didn't know how he would ever repay her for her lifelong commitment to serving him. He would miss her dearly when her time came.

"Thank you, Yetta," he said, removing its contents bit by bit until it was empty.

Looking down at the table, his serpentine eyes scanned over the various documents. She had secured Norwegian Passports, identification cards, birth certificates, bank cards with account information, even a deed and keys to a row house overlooking the fjord. Everything that he and Brynn needed to begin a new life.

Watching him look over her work, Yetta started her explanation of each piece. It was a little difficult altering her information so that it matched Brynn's, but thankfully Leonardo stepped in to help. She hoped he would be the one to come out of all this unscathed. He was such a nice young man.

"You now Erik Magnus Larsen. Brynn now Emilie Astrid Larsen. Live in Bergen," she said.

"Bergen," he interrupted, picking up the passports. "I should have known."

Dropping her old eyes, Yetta lifted her lips into a wistful smile. The rainy Norwegian town is where they had first met when she was only nineteen. She had fled to the Netherlands for what she hoped would be a better life. One night while fetching milk for the family she nannied for, she was attacked by a group of thugs hellbent on raping and killing her. By the grace of God, Nikolai had heard her cries and ran to her rescue. He dispatched the men one by one in the most terrifying of ways, saving her life in the process. Nikolai had always seen himself as a monster, but to her he was her angel. She had faith that someday he would see himself as she did.

"Yes, Bergen," she replied. "Good memories."

Nodding his head, he reached out to take her hand in his. Giving it a small squeeze, he moved his gaze towards her still beautiful face.

"Very good memories," he said fondly.

Meeting his intense eyes, she allowed herself to dip into those memories for a few precious moments before shaking them away. Dropping his hand, she blinked back tears. She was glad he had found love with the Sun Walker. He deserved to have true love. Even if it wasn't with her.

"Yes. Yes. Ok. Move on. Next. Bank Norwegian checking. Twenty-five million Krone," she said, motioning to the bank cards.

Arching a dark brow, Nik gave her a quizzical look. He was absolutely blown away by the amount. He was expecting a few thousand, maybe. Twenty-five million? How the hell was she able to do that?

"Twenty-five million Krone, Yetta? How?" he asked.

Chuckling under her breath, she shrugged her hunched shoulders. It was a secret she had been keeping for years. She was still shocked that she had never been caught.

"I embezzle from Elders. Small amount over time add up. Twenty-five million for you, twenty-five million for me. Not much, but enough," she said proudly.

Widening his eyes, he joined in on her laugh. He had absolutely no idea she was doing anything of the sort. They had an understanding that he wouldn't use his powers against her, so this information was surprising to say the least.

"I'm so proud of you, Yetta...you're such a smart woman. Thank you for doing this," he said.

Waving off his sweet compliment, she mumbled something unintelligible. She secretly loved it when he praised her. He would never know that, though.

"Yes. Yes...now house. Blue row house. Two bedroom, very small but enough. You own outright. Right near water. You love it, I know," she said.

"Yes, I have no doubt that we will...you have impeccable taste," he replied. "So what are the travel plans?"

Pulling out a dining room chair, Yetta carefully took a seat. Resting her old bones, she took a sharp breath before relaying their itinerary.

"Leave Friday night. We fly private from Phoenix to JFK. JFK to Flesland Airport. Use new names. All private. New pilot, new carrier. Elders never know," she said confidently.

Nodding while he listened, he ignored the part of him that said this plan was too simple, that it wouldn't work. He was banking on the Elders being too inept with technology to find their virtual trail. Everything was a risk, but it was a risk they needed to take.

"Thank you for coming along…I need to make sure you're safe, too," he said, looking down at her.

"Yes. I stay little while," she said, grabbing her tote bag from the floor. "Oh, I have mail for you."

Quirking his head, he watched her curiously as she pulled a large white envelope from her bag. It was odd that she had physical mail for him. He couldn't remember the last time that had happened.

"Hmm…is that so," he said.

Handing him the oversized envelope, Yetta pressed her lined lips together. She thought it was just as weird. Perhaps she should have given it to him first.

"No return address," she muttered.

Matching her frown, Nik tore into the piece of mail. Tossing the ripped paper to the table, he reached inside and pulled out a series of eight by ten photographs. Scanning his eyes over the first one, he spat a harsh expletive that made Yetta perk. Quickly flipping through the photographs, he felt his adrenaline spike higher and higher with every image.

"What? What wrong, Nikolai?" Yetta asked.

Dropping the full colored photographs in front of her, he let out an angry growl. Somehow, someone had gotten ahold of images from the security system he had installed on the patio attached to the master suite. Each of the large photographs held an image of him and Brynn enjoying each other's company.

Enjoying each other's company in broad daylight.

The realization of the moment hit him like a sledgehammer. Instantly reeling from the implications, his mind whirled in a mixture of fear and rage. He never should have let Brynn out of his sight. Unbeknownst to her, she was in serious danger, and he wasn't there to protect her.

"They know Yetta...they already fucking know!" he yelled, his voice dripping with acute anger. "I need to get to get to her...I have to get to Brynn before they do!"

CHAPTER SIXTEEN

Waving thanks to the driver as he pulled away, Brynn adjusted her nearly empty backpack on her shoulder. Taking her cell from the pocket of her shorts, she quickly turned on her Spotify playlist. Smiling to herself as the first few riffs of "Personal Jesus" played through her AirPods, she began her walk towards the Lecture Hall.

Keeping her phone in her hand, she glanced around the dark campus. She had to admit, she enjoyed Arizona State this way, when it was quiet and almost deserted. The crowds during the day always rubbed her the wrong way. There were too many dudebros, too many influencer wannabes. The students at night were generally serious about their education. It was refreshing.

Lip syncing to the lyrics, she got lost in the consuming beat of the song. It reminded her of Nik, but then again almost everything did. Letting her thoughts drift towards her handsome lover, she let out a shrill shriek as she felt someone run up behind her and tap her shoulder.

Spinning around in surprise, she immediately silenced her Spotify app. Yanking out an AirPod, she looked at the stranger with wide eyes. He was tall, almost as tall as Nik. Wearing a spiked leather jacket and ripped concert tee, he reminded her of the description of the invisible man that Jenni swore she saw.

He gave her the ick.

Holding his hands up to show he meant no harm, the man gave the brunette a lopsided grin. She was even cuter up close. From a physical standpoint he could see why Nikolai wanted to keep her all to himself. She was definitely his type. His type too, if he was being honest.

"Hey, sorry…I didn't mean to scare you," he said.

Laughing nervously, Brynn shrugged her shoulders. Meeting his brown eyes, she felt her heart race. He was objectively handsome, even with a mop of unkempt bleached blonde hair, but his creep factor was off the charts.

"Uh, oh…that's ok," she replied, trying her best to be polite. "Is there…uh…is there something I can help you with?"

Hearing the rush of her blood as it pumped through her veins, he felt his mouth water. She was afraid. *Good.* He hoped that when her fight or flight response kicked in that she would fight. Things were always more fun that way.

"Uh, yeah! I just transferred from the U of A down in Tucson and I'm still trying to learn where everything is on campus. I'm supposed to meet up with a couple of people…we're doing this group project thing. Anyway, could you tell me where the Library of Music is?" He asked, trying to look as non-threatening as possible.

Shifting her weight from one foot to another, Brynn scrunched her face. Wanting to give him a quick answer, she pointed to the building to their left.

"Uh, yeah…it's actually right there, can't miss it," she said.

Turning his head towards where she was pointing, he pretended to look surprised. Looking back at Brynn, he softened his features. "Hey, thanks…I really appreciate it…I'm sorry, I didn't catch your name," he said.

"Because I didn't throw it," she replied, huffing under her breath. "But it's uh…it's Brynn."

Quirking his head, he slowly said her name aloud, purposefully rolling it off his tongue. Letting his eyes fall from her freckled face, he paused for a split second as he noticed her gaudy necklace. Fuck. Nikolai had claimed her, she was under his protection. It pissed him off to no end that he wouldn't be able to carry out his orders as planned. The Elders would be furious.

Quickly thinking on his toes, he came up with an alternate plan. Something that would give the Elders the confirmation they needed until Natalia could step in to finish the job.

"That's a really pretty name...Brynn. Well, Brynn...I'm Anton, it's nice to meet you," he said, hoping she would remember his name. "Could I...could I walk you to your class? It's the least I can do and it's so dark out. A girl like you shouldn't be walking alone."

Noticing a familiar uneasy feeling settling in the pit of her stomach, Brynn shook her head. A little voice in her head was screaming at her to get away from Anton. The sooner, the better.

"Oh no, that's totally ok...the Lecture Hall is literally right across the courtyard," she said, motioning towards the large building. "I'm ok, but thanks for the offer, I uh...I hope everything goes well with your project."

Lifting his calloused hand, he reached up to take her by the elbow. Looking her dead in the eyes, he hardened his sharp features.

"No, really...I must insist," he said, his tone low and menacing.

Jerking her arm away from the creeper, a panicked look fell across her face. Needing to create some distance, she took a shaky step backwards.

"No, I'm fine! Really!" she said, taking another step.

Letting out a long sigh, Anton looked around their immediate vicinity. Noticing that they were completely alone, he shrugged his heavy shoulders. He was going to be nice and leave her on the grassy knoll, but if she wanted to bite the pavement, who was he to say no?

"Fine...we'll just do this here, then," he said flatly.

Swallowing hard, Brynn felt her body tense in fright. Unable to move an inch, she glanced down at the phone still in her hand. Trying desperately to get her fingers to work to call for help, the blood drained from her face when they refused to budge. Suddenly feeling like a deer caught in headlights, she said a silent prayer for God to protect her. She knew in her bones that Anton was about to do something horrific.

"Please...don't," She whispered.

Lifting the corner of his lips into an evil grin, Anton pulled his muscular arm back. Within the span of a single heartbeat, he unleashed his pent-up aggression. Throwing a strong right hook, his closed fist made contact with her jaw with a sickening smack. Instantly knocking her out cold and fading her world to black.

. . .

Racing down the interstate in a stolen Ford Bronco, Nik clenched his jaw in anger. He couldn't believe he was stupid enough to think they had time. They should have left days ago. He would never forgive himself if anything happened to her.

Pressing harder on the gas pedal, he glanced over to Yetta in the passenger seat. She looked as worried as he felt as she spat orders into her phone, her voice gruff and low using their native tongue. She was securing their jet out of Scottsdale, needing to get to Norway as soon as possible.

They were both banking on the protection his crest afforded Brynn. Although he didn't have permission from Ulysses to give it, the rule still held true. While she wore it, she was untouchable to their kind. She was essentially his property, and his alone.

Gritting his white teeth, he pulled onto the off-ramp. Flying down the street towards campus, he blew through every red light. He knew the Elders had sent Anton to do their dirty work, as they always did. He and the rabid dog had a very contemptuous relationship. Sired only a year apart, they were often pitted against one another for entertainment. Over the centuries they had had many altercations, most of them resulting in Anton nursing his wounds with his tail between his legs.

He worried that Anton would use this opportunity to get a lick in. He was one to always skirt the rules, bending them just enough where he wouldn't be severely punished. There was no doubt in his mind that Anton would bend them with Brynn.

Abruptly ending her call, Yetta stuffed her phone into her tote bag along with all their documents. Wincing as a car almost sideswiped the SUV, she stopped herself from criticizing Nik's driving abilities. She couldn't fault him for wanting to get to the Sun Walker as quickly as possible.

"Everything set. We get Brynn, we go Scottsdale Airport…jet ready," she said, ignoring the loud car horn behind them.

Nodding his head, Nik sped the Bronco onto campus. Heading directly towards the Lecture Hall, he calmed his mind to tap into his sixth sense. Scanning through invisible wavelengths, he searched desperately for his love. Driving closer to the Hall, he let out a sigh of relief as he came across her heartbeat. It was slow and faint, but there.

Brynn was alive.

"I have her heartbeat!" he exclaimed.

Making the motion of a cross, Yetta kissed her fingertips in relief. Saying a silent prayer, she reached over to pat his extended forearm. A heartbeat was good, very good. A body could be repaired, but not a silent heart.

Taking solace in Yetta's touch, Nik followed the alternating rhythm of Brynn's heart. The closer they got, the louder it became, drawing him towards a parking lot flanking two large buildings.

Driving into the nearly empty lot, he drove towards the front row. Putting the Bronco into park, he jumped out of the running vehicle. Stepping onto the pavement, he immediately caught the unmistakable scent of spilled blood.

Scanning his eyes in the darkness, he ran towards the sweet scent of Brynn's ambrosial blood. Frantically searching with his heightened eyesight, he pushed out a low growl as he found her splayed on the sidewalk connecting the parking lot to the courtyard. She had been viciously beaten, her broken and bloodied body discarded like trash.

It filled him with rage.

Running to his love, he spanned a hundred yards in less than a second. Kneeling beside her, he lifted his hand to gently caress her swollen face. With the scent of her blood filling his nostrils, he stole a long moment to force his bloodlust back. Now was not the time to let the monster go free.

Looking over her face, he made note of her injuries. Her left eye was black and blue, her right swollen shut. Blood was dripping from her nose and split bottom lip. An odd protrusion threatened to break through the skin near her rounded chin, a clear indication of a broken jaw. Moving his serpentine eyes lower, he bristled as he saw bruises in the shape of fingertips marring the skin of her throat. The bastard had strangled her. Not to kill her, but to torture her.

Looking closer, he was shocked to see the bruises were the only injuries to her neck. There were no bite marks, no tearing of her flesh. With all the damage inflicted, he was surprised that Anton hadn't taken from her. He had already broken the rules of protection, what had stopped him from crossing that line?

Visually scanning the rest of her body, he hardened his features as he noted more injuries. Her right wrist was broken, her left leg twisted at an unnatural angle. Although not visible, he could sense multiple ribs were bruised and split. Her pelvis was cracked in more than one place, most likely from a few rapid kicks of a steel toed boot.

Anton had treated her like a toy doll. He could almost feel the fucker's giddy excitement as she crumbled under his fists. He would kill him, slow and painfully. He didn't care that it was a mortal sin for their kind. Anton would die by his hands.

Gritting his teeth, he made note of her wounds once again. Noticing a trickle of crimson blood dripping from the crook of her left arm, he leaned in closer to inspect the injury. It was a puncture wound, clearly from a large surgical needle. The asshole had taken from her after all, just not in the way Nik expected. Now it all made sense.

Anton couldn't physically take Brynn, but he could take a sample of her blood for confirmation. Soon the Elders would know her truth, and no amount of running would ever make her safe. He had failed her in so many ways.

Whispering apologies again and again, he barely heard Yetta as she stumbled behind him. Glancing over his shoulder, he blinked back livid tears.

"She's breathing…but barely," he said.

Hobbling to Nik's side, Yetta mumbled a heated phrase under her breath. Drifting her hooded eyes over the Sun Walker's badly injured body, she turned to him with an urgent look over her lined face.

"Heal her! Now!" she exclaimed.

Lifting his gaze to hers, he met her wild eyes. Healing Brynn without the consent of the Elders carried heavy consequences. There were core laws in place, and he had followed them religiously for centuries. Healing a mortal without permission was strictly forbidden. It had the possibility to link them together until her last breath. It was a liability that his Clan never took.

"Yetta," he said, pain saturating his voice.

Knowing the source of his hesitation, Yetta knelt her old bones down beside him. Reaching to grab his bicep, she squeezed his arm as hard as she could. The Elders be damned, he had to save the Sun Walker.

"Heal her now! Or she die, Nikolai!" Yetta shrieked.

With a sharp growl, Nik nodded once. Yetta was right, he couldn't let her die. In that moment, he couldn't care less about the consequences. The Elders would want his head either way. Brynn was the only thing that mattered to him. She would understand.

Bringing his right wrist to his lips, he gave into the monster begging to be freed. Within an instant his eyes turned black, and his sharp fangs emerged. Changing his usually handsome face into something evil and grotesque. A lowly demon unworthy of the Goddess before him.

Biting into his alabaster flesh, he hissed as his supernatural blood spilled from the wound. Reaching down with his free hand, he tenderly moved Brynn's marred face upwards. Mindful of her jaw, he opened her injured mouth with his thumb. Dropping his wrist, he hovered his broken flesh over her mouth. Watching her intently, he let his blood spill into her mouth.

Drop by drop his dark scarlet blood fell past her lips, filling her with his otherworldly magic. Though unconscious, she instinctively swallowed once, then twice. Eagerly taking more and more of his essence.

Fully placing his opened wrist to her mouth, he raked his ebony eyes over her. As the hollow seconds ticked by, he heard her heartbeat grow stronger as her body absorbed his blood. Before his worried gaze, her shattered bones healed first. Followed by torn muscles and ripped ligaments. Soon after her skin followed suit, erasing her bruises, stitching her cuts, and soothing her swollen features.

Satisfied with the restoration of her body, Nik eased his wrist from her lips. Bringing it to his own, he gave the wound a slow lick of his tongue. Swallowing the taste of his ancient blood, his self-inflicted wound healed almost instantaneously. Closing his eyes, he pushed out a cleansing sigh as the monster withdrew back to its cage.

Watching Nikolai silently, Yetta hummed in approval as his features changed from demonic to angelic. She was proud of him for following his heart. He would always harbor guilt over this attack, but maybe he would grant himself grace for saving her.

"Good job, Nikolai. Very proud," Yetta said, patting him on the shoulder. "Very proud."

Taking Yetta's words to heart, Nik looked at her from the corner of his eyes. Muttering a loving phrase in Romanian, he gave her a tiny grin. He owed her so much, he wished she would reconsider his long-standing offer.

Hearing a sudden whimper, he turned his attention back to Brynn. She was regaining consciousness and in a considerable amount of pain. She would stay that way until her mind realized her body had been healed. The brain usually had to play catch-up, having no understanding of the otherworldly miracles.

Leaning down towards her furrowed face, he psychically brushed against her vivid aura. Not wanting to scare her, he whispered a command.

Sleep now, my love. Just sleep.

Latching onto his suggestion, Brynn slipped into the warm embrace of slumber. She gave a contented sigh as her pain evaporated into a cotton candy hue.

"Good girl," Nik praised before addressing Yetta. "Could you gather her things please, Yetta? I will carry her to the car and we'll head to the airport. I'll wake her when we're in the air."

"Yes. And you tell her the truth, Nikolai. Tell her everything," Yetta said curtly.

Gathering his love into his arms, he stood from the sidewalk. Holding her close against his torso in a bridal carry, he watched her smile in her sleep. She was so pure, so incredibly sweet. He was terrified to tell her the truth. He didn't want her to hate him. He didn't know what he would do if she did.

"Yes, Yetta...I will tell her everything," he said, leaning down to kiss Brynn's forehead.

CHAPTER SEVENTEEN

Cradling Brynn securely against his torso, Nik studied her as she slept. They had been in the air for nearly an hour, and he knew he would have to wake her up soon. To say that he was dreading it was an understatement. He didn't know what he would do if she hated him for thrusting her into this new life. One in which she would always be living in fear. A life where she would always be looking over her shoulder, terrified that mythical beasts and monsters were around every corner waiting to kill her.

It certainly wasn't the life she had signed up for.

Drifting his eyes over her face, he felt a phantom hand squeeze around his heart. Even with her skin smeared with dried blood, she looked so angelic, so pure. He had wanted to clean her of the remnants of the attack, but Yetta had talked him out of it. Saying that Brynn needed to know that what happened was real. That it would somehow soften the mental blow of learning the truth about him and his kind.

He hoped that she was right.

Bringing a glass of merlot to her thin lips, Yetta took a large sip. Watching Nik's face twist as he held the Sun Walker, she took pity on him for the first time in their sixty years of knowing each other. He was making himself sick with worry, she hated seeing him this way. It was time for him to tear off the bandage.

"Nikolai," she began, adjusting herself in the oversized airline recliner. "Take her back to bed. Wake her up. Tell her what happen. I give you privacy."

Shifting his gaze to his assistant, he gave her a single nod in response. Yes, it was time. He could do this. Brynn would understand why he had kept the truth from her. She had to.

Carefully lifting her in his arms, he stood to full height from his comfortable seat. Steadying himself as the private jet hit a pocket of air, he let out a long sigh. Turning to his left, he headed for the very small sleeping quarters located in the back of the plane.

Sliding the lacquered door open, he carefully crossed the threshold while carrying his love. Closing the door behind them, he glanced around the narrow space. All the shades of the portholes had been drawn before they boarded, per Yetta's request. Two modern wall sconces flanked the full-sized bed in the center, their dimmed LED's casting a comfortable light. One that wouldn't jar her when she came out of her blissful dream.

Taking a step to the bed, he eased her down onto the firm mattress. Making sure her head was nestled on the down pillow, he took a seat next to her on the edge. He wished he could lay next to her and curl his large body against hers. Unfortunately, there wasn't enough room. This particular space was meant for single, high-powered executives, not the warm embrace of lovers. Perhaps it was better this way.

Reaching for her hand, he took it in his and gave it a gentle squeeze. Closing his eyes, he focused on the sound of her unique heartbeat. Finding comfort in its strong and steady rhythm, he switched his attention to her consciousness.

Brushing the edges of her colorful thoughts, he smiled to himself as he caught a glimpse of her dream. They were on the beach of some tropical island, laughing and kissing while dancing on the pristine white sands. It was the happiest he had ever seen her in her dreams. He hated to steal her away.

Brynn, wake up my love, he said softly into her mind. *Wake up and be with me.*

Resisting her lover's initial command, Brynn whimpered in protest as she heard his voice interrupting her vivid dream. With his singsong tone nudging her for a second and then a third time, she finally caved. Following his invisible lead, she groaned as she reluctantly left the safety of her fantasy.

Slowly lifting her eyelids, she danced her gaze around the tiny cabin. She had no idea where she was, or how she got there. The last thing she remembered was Anton choking her before she passed out for a second time. With the memory of the terrifying moment flashing in her mind's eye, she began to panic. Instinctively reaching for her throat, she gasped for much needed air.

Realizing she was reliving her attack, Nik leaned over her prone body. Making her wild eyes meet his, he lovingly shushed her as his hands gently pulled hers from her throat. Whispering words to calm and soothe, he waited patiently for her anxiety to subside.

"You're ok, Sunshine…you're ok…you're safe…come back to me," he said, brushing her dirty locks from her face.

Pushing the traumatic event to the back of her mind, Brynn took in a cleansing breath as her lover's words took hold. Looking at him with her eyes wide, she hoisted herself into a seated position.

"Nik?" she asked, reaching out to touch his chest to make sure he wasn't a figment of her imagination. "What's…what's going on?! Where are we?!"

Lifting his large hands, he cupped the sides of her freckled face. Forcing her to keep her hazel eyes secured on his, he inched himself closer. Using his otherworldly influence, he tempered her anxiety until she was as calm as a kitten fat on cream.

"You're safe, my beautiful Brynn. You're safe with me…we're on a private jet, far away from what happened. Now…can you tell me what he did to you? What he said? I need to know everything, my love," he said, his voice buttery and warm.

Melting into his touch, she felt her heart slow to a peaceful rhythm. Coached into using her rational brain instead of her erratic emotions, she calmly answered his questions.

"Well…it's a little fuzzy but I was walking towards the courtyard to get to the Lecture Hall and I was listening to some music. Which was really dumb because it distracted me…and I know better than that. But, uh…yeah so I was walking up the sidewalk and all of the sudden I felt this tap on my shoulder…so I jumped and turned around and this guy…this guy was staring at me and he freaked me out, Nik. He looked wrong, you know? I didn't like him…I…I…don't know how to explain it…I just knew he didn't belong there," she said, her voice rising as her anxiety crept back in. "He was so creepy…he had this awful studded black leather jacket and this bleached blonde hair. And…and he was pale…really pale. Kinda like you."

Holding her face steady, Nik pressed his lips into a fine line. His anger was rising with every uptick in her heart. He was right, Anton was the fucker who attacked her. He hoped the prick knew he had signed his own death warrant. He didn't care that it would be a mortal sin. He would be the one to send Anton to hell for once and for all.

Smelling the unmistakable scent of adrenaline, he focused on Brynn as she began to stammer. Her mind was trying so desperately to put the pieces together. Not only of her attack, but of the oddness surrounding him. He didn't care for how upset she was becoming. Wanting to keep her placid, he used his supernatural talent once again.

"Shhh, my love…it's ok…just take a deep breath and continue," he said aloud.

Following his command, Brynn took in a handful of cleansing breaths. With his silken voice repeating, her chaotic emotions stilled. Allowing her to continue with her recounting of events.

"So…yeah, I didn't like him. Anyways, he asked me where the Library of Music was and I wanted to be polite so I pointed him to it. He thanked me and asked if he could walk me to class. I refused. I just wanted to get away from him as fast as I could…but then he said something like *'fine, we'll just do this here, then.'* And I knew he was going to hurt me…I just knew it. I tried to run…I tried to scream…but I couldn't move. It was like I was frozen. I could not move. So I just prayed. And I prayed and prayed…and then I saw him raise his fist. He punched me in the jaw…he hit me hard and I blacked out. I…I don't know how long I was out for...but I came to and he was strangling me. I was in so much pain...my whole body hurt, I felt like every bone in my body was broken. I know I was bleeding...I thought I was dying...and then...I think...he said *'you're lucky you're wearing that necklace, bitch. But don't worry, I'll see you again. Nikolai won't be able to save you next time,'* she said, her eyes widening as she realized the implications of that moment.

"Nikolai won't be able to save you next time," she repeated.

Knowing she was just a hair's breadth away from solving the puzzle, Nik suddenly pushed his influence onto her. He didn't want her to find out like this. She was too upset. It didn't bode well for either of them with his blood still coursing through her veins.

Calm down, my love. Just calm do—

"NO!" Brynn screamed, her face twisting as she rejected his mind trick.

Stilling in shock, Nik furrowed his brow. This had never happened before. Looking at her with a stunned expression, he tried once again to regain control.

Brynn...listen to me...cal—

"I SAID NO!" she screamed, this time forcibly pushing him away with a ball of pent-up fury.

Thrown from the bed by Brynn's sudden strength, Nik slammed into the wall of the small cabin. Falling to the carpeted floor with a heavy thud, he watched her with a mixture of awe and panic. She shouldn't be this powerful, he thought to himself. What had he unleashed?

Blinking her eyes into focus, Brynn watched Nik as she stood back to full height. In an instant, her rage evaporated just as quickly as it appeared. Replaced by confusion and fear. She didn't know what was going on. Her mind was racing. Trying to make sense of it all.

"He knew you...he knew you, Nik," she found herself saying.

Unsure of how he should handle the situation, he simply nodded.

"How...why...does this have something to do with your money?" she asked.

Taking a step towards the bed, he softened his body language as best as he could. He didn't want to provoke her. Until his undead blood wore off, she had the potential to be dangerous.

"His name is Anton. Anton Petrov. We've known each other for many, many years," he began, boldly taking a seat on the mattress.

"You have? Did you piss him off or something? Why...why would he want to hurt me?" she asked, a deep frown on her face.

Keeping a blank look on his face, he paused for a long moment. What hadn't he done to piss Anton off? They had over three hundred years of history with one another. Most of it unpleasant. Anton was probably chomping at the bit to do this little errand.

"Things between Anton and I are...complicated to say the least. But no, he didn't do this because I pissed him off. He did this because he was tasked with it," he said plainly.

Lifting a brow, Brynn felt the hair of the back of her neck stand up on end. She didn't like the sound of that. Was this a failed Mafia hit?

"Tasked with it...what do you mean? Like...are you in the Mob or something? Hmm? Is that how you're so rich?" she asked.

Scooting closer to her on the bed, he reached out to take her hand. Giving it a small squeeze, he did a quick mental prep. This was it. There was no going back.

"No, I'm not in the Mob or Mafia as you know it...but I am a part of an ancient and clandestine society. One that has ties to every facet of your modern world as you know it," he said.

"What…like…the Freemasons?" she asked.

Holding in a laugh, Nik kept his face neutral. The Freemasons were created as a direct result of his kind trying to interfere with the ways humans worshiped what they believed were Gods. They were a joke, essentially. But as humans normally did, they took what should have been a detriment and turned it into something powerful. They were fascinating creatures that way.

"No. We are more influential than the Freemasons will ever be. In fact, they work for us," he said.

Staring at her lover, Brynn became more and more confused. What could be bigger than the Mafia or Freemasons? The Knights Templar?

"Ok…please, just spit it out, Nik. What is this secret society you belong to?" she asked, her tone dripping in annoyance.

"Brynn…what I'm about to tell you. It's going to change everything…but I need you to know just how much I love you. How madly in love I am with you," he said, squeezing her hand. "You need to know and believe that."

Looking into his eyes, she felt her breath hitch in her throat. She had no idea what he was talking about, but she could tell he was nervous. Still, he didn't have anything to worry about. She was just as in love with him. Whatever he was about to tell her wouldn't change that fact.

Nothing would.

"I do know that, and I believe it, Nik…I believe it in my soul…now please, just tell me," she said.

Licking his lips nervously, he gathered his courage. Not giving himself time to think and craft a lie, he blurted out the ugly truth.

"I'm a Vampire," he said.

CHAPTER EIGHTEEN

Letting out a disbelieving laugh, Brynn gave Nik an incredulous look. Had she heard him right? Did he really say that he was a Vampire? What in the ever-loving fuck?

"A Vampire?" she asked.

Nodding his head, Nik remained as calm and serious as possible. It was normal for humans to reject the truth at first. He only hoped that she would jump to acceptance sooner, rather than later. He needed her to.

"Yes," he replied flatly.

Huffing under her breath, her mind raced to different scenarios where him being a Vampire could make sense. She had seen TikTok's of people claiming to be Vampires, usually to prey on the sexual kinks of others willing to send them Cash App's for racy videos. Maybe he meant that?

"As in like...a kink?" she asked, raising a brow.

"No...not a kink. I don't dress in old Victorian garb and wear fake canines to get laid," he said, guessing where her mind was at. "I'm an actual Vampire. I require the blood of others to sustain myself."

Furrowing her brow, Brynn felt a shiver run down her spine. Her automatic response was to reject what he was saying. He was lying. He had to be. Vampires weren't real. They were simply a fantasy designed by overactive minds for entertainment. Like Unicorns or Bigfoot.

"Ha ha. Very funny, Nik," she said, rolling her eyes.

Squeezing her hand, he forced her to look at him. Narrowing his green eyes, he leaned in closer. It would be easy for him to use his powers on her, but he wanted her to understand and trust him on her own. It would be better for both of them that way.

"Brynn, my love...I know this is hard to process...hard to understand...but I'm telling you the truth. I have been undead for three hundred and fifty-eight years. If you take a moment to think, I think you'll find that I really am telling you the truth," he said, lifting her hand to kiss her knuckles. "Just think."

Opening her mouth to speak, Brynn wanted to protest. To tell him to knock it off, that this wasn't funny. But something nagged at her, telling her to listen to him. Why would he joke about this?

Reluctantly following his request, she stilled her chaotic mind. Taking in a breath, she allowed herself to re-examine all the odd inconsistencies she had excused away. His billionaire status. The fact that he was always cold to the touch, that she never really felt his heartbeat when pressed against him. That he never ate or drank around her. His odd migraines triggered by sunlight. The way he was able to have sex again and again without his body giving out.

His requirement of her donating blood every two weeks to his highly important organization.

"Holy shit," she whispered.

Watching the lightbulb flicker to life behind her eyes, Nik let out a small chuckle. She had figured it out faster than he thought. He didn't know why he was surprised; she was so very intelligent.

"Holy shit, indeed," he said.

Staring at him, she was initially stunned by the realization that he was an actual Vampire. That feeling was short-lived, however. Within a split second, it was replaced by anger.

"You lied to me," she said through gritted teeth.

Softening his masculine features, Nik cleared his throat. Oh, he didn't need her to go down this path right now.

"Yes, yes I did," he admitted.

Trying not to let her anger swallow her whole, Brynn stayed quiet for a long moment. Her adrenaline was spiking, her mind spinning in a million different directions. She had so many questions for him, she didn't know where to begin.

"Were you ever going to tell me the truth?" she finally asked.

"Initially, no. I was not," he replied truthfully.

"Why?" Brynn asked.

Pushing out a sigh, Nik shrugged his broad shoulders. She couldn't be mad at him over this. They both had ulterior motives in the beginning.

"There wasn't a need…we had a contractual relationship…but then everything changed. I fell in love with you, Brynn. I was planning on telling y—"

"When?" Brynn interrupted.

"Friday," he said without skipping a beat.

Quirking her head, she eyed him critically. She expected him to say something like 'when the time was right.' She didn't understand why he had set an actual date.

"Why were you going to wait?" she asked. "What's so special about Friday?"

Knowing that there really was no turning back, he prepared himself for the floodgates. She wasn't prepared to learn the truth about herself, but it was already too late. There wasn't any going back.

"I had everything prepared for us to make our escape on Friday…for us to start a new life. Which is what we're doing now. We had to bump up the timeline after your attack," he replied.

Thoroughly confused, Brynn stammered as she tried to make sense of what he had just said. He was planning an escape? Planning a new life? What else was he hiding?

"Why…what…what the fuck are you talking about, Nik?" she asked.

Gently releasing her hand, he lifted his to her face. Cradling her flushed cheek, he made himself comfort her with his touch instead of his otherworldly persuasion.

"You're incredibly special, Brynn. You just don't know it…and what I'm about to say to you is going to sound almost as unbelievable as me being a Vampire…but you must believe me. It's the reason why your life is in danger, and why I will do everything in my power to protect you from my kind," he said.

Scrunching her features, she met his searing gaze. She knew he meant to soothe her, but he was inadvertently scaring her instead. Why was he speaking in riddles? She wished he would just spit everything out.

"Okay…please, just come out with it Nik," she said.

Dropping his hand from her face, he nodded his head. "You're not just a mortal, Brynn. You're what my kind calls a Sun Walker," he said.

"A what walker?" she asked, straightening her posture. "A Sun Walker? What the hell does that even mean?"

"Your blood is special, Brynn. It allows my kind to walk unprotected in daylight," he said, trying to be as direct as possible.

Holding up her hands, Brynn visibly scoffed. God, this was so weird. "Wait…wait…wait…ok. So, you're saying that if your kind…meaning Vampires…drink my blood then you guys can just…walk around in the sun? Which is a big deal because what…you Vampires can only come out at night, right? Like in the movies?" she asked.

Nodding once, Nik kept his eyes glued to hers. He knew it sounded ridiculous, but she had to know that this was a serious situation. Her life was on the line, here.

"Yes. Exactly. Now…Sun Walkers are extremely rare. I've only come across one other one…and I know firsthand what my Clan did to her. I won't allow that to happen to you, Brynn," he said, his voice dipping dangerously low.

Sucking in a breath, Brynn swiped her eyes across his face. He was being genuine with her; she could feel it in her soul.

"What…what did they do to her?" she asked.

Letting his gaze fall to the mattress, he caught a glimpse of Leona in his mind. She was so vibrant and dynamic when Christos first ensnared her. By the time they were done with her, she was just a hollow shell, and then became something vile. He wouldn't let them do that to his beautiful Brynn.

"They tied her down to a table and bled her…again and again for years. By the end of it, her blood had become so weak that it was no longer useful…and she had gone mad. So, Christos…he's one of the three Elders…he wanted to conduct an experiment. He turned her into one of us. She…well, she was completely feral. A killing machine that hunted during the day, and well into the night. They used her for sport for a while. It was entertainment for them…but then she threatened some long-standing treaties we held in Europe. The Elders didn't want the liability, so they destroyed her. Like she was nothing," he said.

Swallowing hard, Brynn suddenly became icy cold. If all of this was true, she definitely didn't want to have the same fate as that poor woman.

"And you think that they will do that to me?" she asked.

"I *know* they will," he replied, once again lifting his green eyes to hers.

Humming low, Brynn sat with her thoughts. Little by little she was slowly accepting his truth. She still had so many unanswered questions, though. She needed more from him.

"How…how did you know I was a Sun Walker, Nik? You've never bitten me…at least I don't think you have?" she asked.

"No…I haven't taken from you directly, but I have tasted your blood. When the nurse took your first blood donation…I took one sip, and I just knew. Once you've had Sun Walker blood, it's unmistakable," he said.

"And is that why you wanted me? Is that why you say you're in love with me? Is it because of my magical blood?" she asked.

Immediately taken aback, Nik gawked at her. He didn't know why her questions surprised him. With her history it made sense that she would automatically jump to that conclusion. Still, it stung to know there was a small part of her that didn't truly believe in his love.

"No…no…I *wanted* you from the moment my eyes laid on your profile. I *lusted* after you when I saw you in the flesh…and I fell in *love* with you after you shared your heart and mind with me. After I tasted your blood, I did feel the need to protect you but no…that had zero influence over my feelings towards you, Brynn," he replied, reaching to touch her thigh. "I mean it when I say that I love you…and I mean it when I say that I will do everything in my power to protect you from them."

Covering his hand with hers, she exhaled the breath she had been holding. And just like that, all the anger and doubt surrounding his intentions evaporated into thin air. She believed him. It might come back to bite her in the ass, but what was the alternative?

"But how are you going to protect me from them? Hmm? I mean…that asshole…what was his name? Anton? He almost killed me, Nik…and I still don't know how I'm sitting here, completely ok. How the fuck did that happen?" she asked.

"Well…ok. I'll try to make this as concise as I can. The necklace you're wearing was supposed to protect you, Brynn. When I gave you my crest, I marked you as my Mate. It should have made you untouchable to my kind. And it did in that he wasn't able to abduct you…however, Anton skirted the rules by hurting you…as he always does. And he will pay for that…trust me. But he was banking on me finding you before you died. He knew I would save you," he said, gently squeezing her blood-stained thigh.

Lifting her free hand, Brynn toyed with the copper medallion hanging from her neck. She had no idea that it was more than just a family heirloom. Now she wouldn't ever take it off, not even in the shower. She no longer cared that it would turn her skin green.

"And how did you save me?" she asked.

"I gave you a small amount of my blood," he replied.

"And how did you do that?" she asked.

"Well…I broke the skin of my wrist and let my blood trickle into your mouth. You instinctively swallowed it," he said matter-of-factly. "It wasn't much…just enough to heal you."

"That didn't make me a Vampire?" she asked, raising a brow.

Shaking his head, he swallowed a laugh. The process of Turning was much more complex than simply letting a mortal drink a few sips of undead blood.

"No. It didn't," he said.

"Well, what if I want to be one?" she asked, not really thinking before speaking.

Immediately frowning, Nik narrowed his eyes. This was a topic he would never budge on. Brynn would never become one of his kind. She would live a full mortal life.

"No. Absolutely not, I will not allow you to become a monster like me," he said, his voice steady and deep.

Imitating his serious face, Brynn straightened her shoulders. It annoyed her that he would refer to himself like that. He was a good man. The best one she had ever known.

"The man I love isn't a monster. Don't you dare call yourself that!" she chastised.

Instantly touched by her words, he couldn't help but grin. He wanted so badly to believe that he wasn't. Perhaps it was enough for the woman he cared so deeply for to believe it for him.

"I do love you, my beautiful Brynn," he said.

"And I love you, my handsome Vampire Nikolai," she replied with a smirk. "So now what? Hmm?"

Letting his eyes get their fill of the dried blood painting her face and limbs, he debated his options. They still had much more to discuss, but everything would come out in due time. For now, he just wanted the evidence of Anton's attack gone.

"Can I help you clean yourself off? There's a small bathroom across the hall. I wanted to wipe the blood from your skin before you woke up...but Yetta thought I should leave you be," he said.

Looking surprised, Brynn sat up straight. "Yetta is here?" she asked.

"Yes, she's in the lounge," he replied. "And yes...she knows everything."

Blinking her hazel eyes, she mouthed a silent 'oh.' Of course Yetta knew everything. It was almost comforting that she did.

"I'd like to talk to her after I get cleaned up," she said.

With a nod, he eased his hand from her thigh. He surmised that talking to Yetta would be a good thing. She might need a different perspective on him and his kind.

"Yes, yes of course," he said.

"Good...but um...no, I can clean myself. Thank you for the offer...I just...I just need a few minutes by myself, is that ok?" she asked.

Giving her an understanding smile, he took his cue. Standing from the small bed, he found his balance in the moving jet.

"There's a towel and robe hanging in the bathroom. We will be landing at JFK to refuel in a couple of hours. Yetta has already placed an order for you for some clothes, they will deliver it to us then...the bathroom is small, and the water will run cold sooner rather than later but you'll have a proper bath once we get to Norway," he said.

Watching Nik as he took a few steps to the door, Brynn quirked her head. Norway? Why the hell were they going there?

"What's in Norway?" she asked.

"I'll let you know before we get there...for now, I just need you to get cleaned up. I'll make sure the attendant has some hot food ready for you," he said, giving her a look of adoration.

Studying his chiseled face, she memorized the odd moment. She felt like she was just bobbing in the sea with nothing to cling to. She hoped the feeling would subside after getting more answers.

"Ok...thank you," she said, her voice soft and small.

Dipping his head in reverence, he opened the lacquered door. Stepping over the threshold, he kept his attention on her. He wasn't sure if leaving her was the smartest move.

"Are you sure I can't help you clean up?" he asked.

Shaking her head, she waved off his concern. Truth be told, she did want him to stay. But her pride was getting the best of her. She didn't want him to watch her fall apart. Not yet at least.

"I'm sure, Nik…I'll just be a little while," she replied.

"Ok…well, let me know if you need anything. My will is to serve you, Brynn. Always remember that," he said before slipping out of the tiny room.

Watching her love as he closed the door behind him, Brynn's face fell as a wave of emotion suddenly crashed into her. Dropping her eyes to her lap, she furrowed her brow as she noticed bold splotches and swipes of dried blood caking her legs. It anchored the night's events, making them entirely too real.

Finding herself unable to move off the firm mattress, she lifted her shaky hands to her face. Having the urge to hide, she covered herself as best she could with her palms and fingers. Realizing the gravity of the situation, she began to sob. To her dismay, her life wasn't ever going to be the same.

Nothing would ever be the same.

CHAPTER NINETEEN

Tightening the knot on her fluffy black robe, Brynn took a quick look at herself in the anti-fog mirror. Her eyes were swollen from crying, her skin pink from being rubbed raw. As Nik predicted, the hot water hadn't lasted long. It didn't matter to her, though. She was too preoccupied with cleaning herself to care. She just wanted the evidence of her attack gone. If only she could scrub her memory just as easily as her skin.

Lifting her hand, she swiped an errant tear from her cheek. Feeling a sudden burst of turbulence, she let out a gasp. Holding out her arms, she braced herself against the walls of the tiny bathroom. She had almost forgotten she was on a jet zipping through the sky.

"Fucking hell," she muttered under her breath.

Waiting until the plane stabilized, she dropped her hands from the damp walls. Wiping them on her robe, she took in a cleansing breath. She wished she could stay in there until her eyes weren't so puffy. She hated it when people knew she had been crying.

Slipping on her dirty sandals, she gave herself another once over before unlocking the door. Opening it with a flick of her wrist, she stepped into the small walk though. Hearing the murmur of conversation, she turned her head. Off in the near distance Nik and Yetta were huddled over a small table, speaking in a language she didn't understand. She hated to interrupt them. Whatever they were talking about seemed serious.

As if that was a surprise.

Walking towards the pair, her stomach began to growl as she breathed in the scent of savory food. Suddenly, she was famished. She felt like she hadn't eaten in ages. Being on death's door sure had a way of working up one's appetite.

Knowing his love was only a few feet behind him, Nik let his words trail off. He and Yetta would continue their debate another time. Turning his torso, he gave Brynn a genuine smile.

"Hi, Sunshine…I hope you're hungry, the attendant just dropped these off for you and Yetta," he said, motioning to the plates on the table before him. "I hope it's something you're in the mood for."

Humming a reply, Brynn looked over the spread for her and Yetta. Steak with lobster tails, warm bread and butter, steamed asparagus. Who knew you could have fine dining at forty-one thousand feet in the air?

"Wow, this looks amazing…thank you," she replied.

Standing from his seat, Nik nodded his head. Moving his large body out of the way, he urged Brynn to take his place.

"You're welcome, my love…now please, sit down and enjoy. I'll head back to the sleeping cabin so you and Yetta can have some privacy to talk about…things. Hmm?" he said.

Giving Yetta a small smile, she turned her attention towards Nik. Although he was doing his best to mask it, she could see a flash of concern behind his green eyes. She hated that he was worried. He didn't have any reason to be, she had already made the decision that she wasn't going to run away from this.

"Ok…I only have a few questions, I don't think it will take very long," she said.

Leaning down, Nik placed a tender kiss on her damp forehead. Stepping aside so she could take her seat, he looked at the women that he held so dear. Yetta would be brutally honest; he knew that for a fact. He only hoped Brynn wouldn't take offense to anything she said.

"Ok…just let me know when you're done," he said, giving a quick bow of his head before heading towards the back of the jet.

Picking up her third glass of red wine, Yetta watched Nik take his leave. Making sure he was fully inside the bedroom, she arched a gray brow at Brynn.

"Ok, Sun Walker. How you feel?" she asked, taking a sip.

Settling against the leather seat, Brynn let out a large sigh. What a loaded question. She wasn't quite sure how to answer it, or how to take being called a Sun Walker.

"Not great," she replied honestly, picking up her silver fork and knife.

Nodding an acknowledgement, Yetta hummed low. She knew the feeling of whiplash very well. It was something she had become quite accustomed to over the decades. Brynn would learn, too. Eventually.

"You be ok. You strong," she said.

Slicing into her steak, Brynn huffed lightly. "Well, I definitely don't feel like I am," she said, shoving a large bite into her mouth.

Shrugging her hunched shoulders, Yetta set down her wine. Picking up a soft dinner roll, she tore it into two with her arthritic hands.

"It will come. Now. What question you have?" she asked, biting into her roll.

Swallowing her perfectly seared steak, Brynn paused for a moment. A million things were swirling around her brain, she wasn't sure where to begin.

"Hmm…well…I guess…uh, how long have you known Nik?" she asked.

"Sixty years. Met when I was nineteen," Yetta replied without skipping a beat.

Widening her hazel eyes, Brynn tried her best not to look shocked.

"And uh…how did you two meet?" she asked.

Dropping the other half of the roll onto her plate, Yetta cleared her throat. She hated talking about that moment in her life, but she knew it would be good for Brynn to know she wasn't the only one that had lived through trauma.

"Group of men attack me, almost kill me. But Nikolai save me. He kill them instead," she replied.

Cutting an asparagus spear into two, Brynn took in a sharp breath. She could see Nik saving a young Yetta. It was who he was. He might not believe it, but he truly wasn't a monster.

"That must have been terrifying," she said.

"Yes. Terrifying for them. Nikolai drink their blood, rip them apart. But they deserve what Nikolai did. They deserve it all. He think he devil, but he angel," she said with a nod.

Soaking in her broken words, Brynn's mind came up with her version of what that must have looked like. She was still having a hard time getting her head wrapped around Nik being a Vampire. She wondered if he turned into some sort of beast like they do in movies. Even still, he would never be grotesque in her eyes.

"I'm so glad he saved you…is that why you've been his assistant for so long?" she asked.

"Yes. He save my life, I give him mine. Life for life," she said.

Stabbing her asparagus, Brynn brought it to her mouth. She understood wanting to repay the man that saved you, but dedicating your entire life to him? There had to be something more to it.

"Didn't you ever want to move on? Do something different with your life? Maybe have a family?" she asked.

Shaking her head, Yetta dismissed that thought with a wave of her gnarled hand. She never once felt deprived of never having a husband or children. For all intents and purposes, Nikolai was her family.

"No. No. I love to serve Nikolai. Hard work but good work. I have fulfilled life. And now I serve you too," she said.

"You serve me?" Brynn asked, surprise lifting her features. "Why?"

"Yes. You are Goddess. The Vampire no understand what you are. Not even Nikolai," Yetta said.

Dropping her fork on her plate, Brynn gave Yetta an incredulous look. There was no way that she was a Goddess. Just how many glasses of wine had the older woman had?

"I'm not a Goddess," she said with a huff.

"Yes. Yes you are. In my country we have old tale. Two God rule Earth. Night God and Sun God. Always at war. Night God create army to fight to take over Earth. He create Vampire. After time they grow strong. So strong they walk in daylight. Sun God create Sun Walker in return. Sun Walker had power of sun in blood. This fire kill Vampire. After many battles, Night God concede. Make treaty with Sun God. His army stay in darkness. Sun God made Sun Walker mortal. Over time, no need for Sun Walker. Mortal forget, but power of sun still in blood," Yetta said.

Thoroughly confused, Brynn told herself to take everything with a grain of salt. What Yetta was saying made zero sense. Why would Vampires still be allowed to roam the earth while Sun Walkers were essentially thrown away?

"This sounds so weird, Yetta…Nik said that if his kind drinks my blood, that they can walk in the sun. Why would this Sun God allow that? It makes no sense," Brynn said with a sigh.

Shrugging her shoulders, Yetta stared Brynn dead in her eyes. Some things were just not meant to have an answer. The Gods knew more than they did.

"Never question God. But, yes. Your blood valuable to Vampire. But you have power to kill them," she said.

"Well…but what about Leona? She was a Sun Walker…don't you think she would have killed the Vampires that tortured her if she could?" Brynn asked.

Grabbing her wine glass, Yetta took another healthy drink. Swallowing the robust liquid down, she held the glass to her chest to keep it stable. Leona was way before her time. She had no idea why she allowed the Vampires to do what they did.

"Maybe. Maybe she no understand how to use power," she replied simply.

"And I do?" Brynn said with a laugh.

"Well…you know you have it. If Vampire attack you again, listen to soul. It will speak," Yetta replied with certainty. "But no say anything to Nikolai or to any Vampire. Keep this secret."

Pressing her lips together, Brynn nodded her head. Sitting quietly for a handful of long seconds, she suddenly felt mentally drained. Everything sounded so insanely ridiculous, and nothing made sense. But maybe it wasn't supposed to. When had anything in her life truly made sense?

Picking at her food, she decided to ask another question while she still had Yetta's attention. Lifting her eyes to the elderly woman's serious face, she pressed on.

"What are they like? The other Vampires?" she asked.

Making a disgusted sound, Yetta resisted the urge to spit. Nikolai's Clan made her skin crawl. She hated having to deal with them on a nearly daily basis.

"Awful. Terrible. Beautiful on outside, disgusting on inside. Keep distance. Trust only Nikolai and Helen," she said.

"Helen? Who is that?" Brynn asked.

Thinking of her pseudo-grandmother, Yetta couldn't help but grin. There was a period of seven years when she lived full-time with Helen in her estate on the island of Capri. It was right after she and Nikolai had agreed to end their romantic relationship, when they both needed space from one another. The Sun Walker didn't need to know that, though. What was in the past was in the past. And Brynn was Nikolai's future.

"Helen is Elder. But no live with Clan in Romania. She good like Nikolai. Beautiful. Strong. Smart. You meet her, someday. I know she like you," she said.

Taking a bite of lobster tail, Brynn took note of the third Elder. It was a good sign that Yetta thought Helen would like her. Especially considering it seemed like the other two wanted to drain her dry. Perhaps she would be an ally? They would probably need a few.

Opening her mouth to say something, Brynn stopped herself when she heard a door opening behind her. Turning her head, she smiled when she saw Nik's head peeking out from the small bedroom.

"Hey, handsome," she said.

Glancing back and forth between Yetta and Brynn, Nik lifted a dark brow. He had been purposefully ignoring their conversation and emotions. He fully expected Brynn to be in some sort of distress, but to his relief, she seemed relatively even keeled. It was a very good sign.

"Do you need more time to talk?" he asked.

Shaking her head, Brynn lifted her hand to call Nik into the belly of the jet. Just seeing his face made her feel instantly better about the whole situation.

"I think we're ok for now," she said.

"Yes, Nikolai. Come, join," Yetta said.

Clearing the space towards the women, Nik eyed their plates. He didn't expect Yetta to eat much, but he was surprised to see that Brynn had barely touched hers. Gently intruding into her thoughts, he let out a small sigh. Her worry had canceled out her hunger. Although he couldn't blame her, it was a problem that couldn't continue.

"Would you like me to ask the attendant if she could make you something else, Brynn? Maybe some dessert?" he asked.

Shaking her head, Brynn brushed his offer away. "Oh, no…I'm fine for right now. Maybe after we refuel in New York," she said.

Grunting in disapproval, Nik took a seat in a chair opposite the women. Leaning against its high back, he flicked his dark hair from his eyes.

"I'll hold you to that," he said, his voice deep and velvety. "I need you strong from here on out."

Turning her chair towards Nik's, Brynn quirked her head. She wasn't sure if she liked the sound of that.

"Why? What's the plan? Are we going to be running for the rest of our lives?" she asked.

Letting out a small cough, Yetta set down her wine glass. Carefully standing from her chair, she looked back and forth between Brynn and Nikolai. She was too old and not nearly drunk enough to deal with the bickering that was sure to come.

"I too tired to talk. Nikolai, you tell her plan, I take nap," Yetta muttered.

Softening his facial expression, Nik stood from his seat. Offering his assistant his hand, he waited patiently for her to soothe her aching joints.

"I'll walk you," he said.

Shaking her head, Yetta gently smacked his hand away. She may be old, but she was perfectly fine to walk ten feet unassisted.

"No. No. I can walk," she said, stepping away from the table.

Watching Yetta as she slowly moved past, Nik bowed his head. It had been a bittersweet experience to watch her age. Her stubbornness had grown in leaps and bounds over the decades. It was both endearing and incredibly annoying.

"Sleep well, Yetta," he said.

Muttering under her breath, the elderly woman hobbled towards the sleeping quarters. She was hoping she would be able to sleep through the refueling. The sooner they arrived in Norway, the better.

Making sure Yetta had entered the bedroom, Nik moved towards her now empty seat. Sitting down, he looked at his love from across the table. He didn't care for the apprehension plastered on her beautiful face.

"To get back to your question... *no*, we won't be running for the rest of your life. But we will be hiding for the foreseeable future," he said.

"In Norway of all places?" Brynn asked, picking up her carton of water.

"Yes... I know it seems odd my love, but it's the safest place right now. We... meaning my Clan... have treaties with almost every single organized government on the planet. Except for Norway... so we have that working for us. But also... Norway has the most Hunters per capita of any country on Earth," he said, relaxing into his leather chair. "My Clan avoids Norway like the plague. It really is the perfect place."

Swallowing a mouthful of water, Brynn coughed as some of it went down the wrong tube. It's great that his Clan wouldn't be on their doorstep but he kind of glossed over a huge problem.

"Wait…what? Hunters? I'm assuming *Vampire* Hunters, right? How is being in a country that refuses to harbor your kind and also hunts your kind, safer for us?" she asked.

"Not us. *You*. This is the safest place for you, Brynn. That's all I care about…but the Hunters are never a problem. I've lived in Bergen off and on for centuries and haven't had an issue, yet," Nik replied.

With her hazel eyes open wide, Brynn scoffed at his answer. "Yet," she said.

Meeting her disbelieving gaze, he leaned forward in his seat. He understood her reservation. It was going to take time for her to fully trust him again, but he was sure about this. Hunters were nothing more than a nuisance.

"Everything will be fine, my love. Most of them don't even know how to properly kill my kind," he said.

"Hmm…and how do you properly kill your kind?" Brynn asked flippantly.

"Sever the head, stake the heart, and burn the body," he said matter-of-factly. "Would you like me to find you a sword and a stake so you could give it a go on me?"

Blinking at him, she shook her head. She hated that she couldn't tell if he was being serious or not.

"No…of course not," she said with a frown. "I love you too much to ever do that to you."

Keeping his eyes on her freckled face, Nik breathed an internal sigh of relief. It felt so good to hear her say that. He hadn't prayed to God since he was Turned, but he had found himself praying twice in the span of three hours. Once when he found her mangled body, and another while in the sleeping cabin. To his amazement, both prayers seemed to have been answered.

"Still? After everything you've learned?" he asked, his voice suddenly soft.

Taking in a shaky breath, Brynn nodded. It might be foolish, but she loved him wholeheartedly. Man, or Vampire, it didn't matter. It would never matter. He was the keeper of her heart. Now and forever.

"You have all of me, Nikolai…just as I have all of you. Now let's plan our happily ever after in Norway, hmm?" she said, giving him a flirty wink.

CHAPTER TWENTY

Crossing the threshold to his office, Ulysses let out a low growl as his brown eyes happened upon Anton sitting behind his desk. It was about time the rabid dog graced the Manor with his presence. He had been waiting two long nights for him to deliver his beautiful present.

In his humble opinion, it was two nights too long.

"Move," he ordered with a flick of his head. "And where's the girl? Is she upstairs with Serena?"

Reluctantly standing from the black leather chair, Anton let out a sigh. Trying to look as nonchalant as possible, he shrugged his spiked shoulders. It was best not to show any weakness around Ulysses. The former Roman general outranked his Sire, giving him carte blanche to dole out punishment as he deemed fit. He really didn't want a lashing over this.

"I had to leave her...for now. It seems as if Nikolai has marked her as his Mate," he said.

Stopping dead in his heavy tracks, Ulysses glared at Anton. With his rage instantly bubbling to the surface, he bared his sharp teeth.

"He did what?!" he bellowed.

Visibly wincing, Anton stood painfully still. Making sure not to meet Ulysses' wild eyes, he cleared his throat.

"She was wearing his crest. I was bound by our laws...but I did make them both suffer for Nikolai's little show of rebellion, Sir," he said.

Narrowing his dark eyes, Ulysses balled his hands into tight fists at his side. He was really regretting his decision to send Anton. Knowing the youngling's handiwork, there was a good chance that the girl would be permanently damaged if Nikolai hadn't gotten to her in time. He should have made the confirmation himself.

"Did you make her useless to us?" he asked, clearing the opulent room.

Straightening his posture as the Elder entered his personal space, Anton shook his head. Staring down at the wooden floor, he swallowed hard. It was entirely possible that he had done more harm than he meant to. The smell of her blood had sent him into a small frenzy.

"No, Sir...I assure you, she's alive and well," he said, having no real clue if that was true.

Glaring down at Anton, Ulysses plastered a sour look on his face. He was lucky that Christos enjoyed his company so much. It was the only thing saving his garish ass.

"Hmmm...and did you taste her?" he asked, his voice low and gravely.

Shaking his head, Anton lifted his hand to his chest. Reaching inside his leather jacket, he grabbed a hold of a child's sized thermos hidden in his inside pocket. Pulling it from its confines, he boldly met Ulysses' eyes.

"No, Sir. I will let you have that honor," he said, handing him the warm metal container.

Taking the dented thermos, the ancient Vampire gave it a critical once over. Unscrewing the top, he brought the small cylinder to his nose. Breathing in its delicious aroma, he hummed low. It wasn't much, perhaps a mouthful or two, but it was enough.

"How did you get this?" he asked curiously.

"Don't worry, I didn't use my teeth, the blood isn't tainted. I had a needle and syringe in my pocket left over from my last party...it was clean, still in its package. As was the thermos. I'm not a total heathen. It's pure blood...pure Brynn Smith," Anton answered.

Pleased by his answer, Ulysses gave a curt nod. Placing the rim of the thermos against his bottom lip, he tipped it back. Greedily taking all of its contents, he held the thick liquid in his mouth. Letting the heady blood roll over his tongue, he savored it; allowing it to dance over his taste buds before swallowing it down.

Moving his gaze back and forth from the floor to Ulysses, Anton bit back his own hunger. Staying silent, he waited patiently for the Elder to give his assessment.

Closing his eyes, a sly smile curled the corners of Ulysses' lips. Anton was right, the blood was incredibly pure. Delicate and intoxicating, saccharine and otherworldly, it was unmistakably Sun Walker. It made him crave the nightly goblets he drank from Leona, along with the power they afforded him.

"Mmm…a blood so sweet," he said in an almost groan. "She is indeed a Sun Walker."

Arching a brow, Anton couldn't help but grin. This was great news. Surely the Elders would share her just as they had the previous Sun Walker. He couldn't wait to take Sara to the Amalfi coast, where they could lounge and fuck on the sun-drenched beaches.

"Sir, what are we going to do about Nikolai?" he asked.

Licking his lips, Ulysses pulled away from Anton. Stepping towards the fireplace on the opposite side of the room, he basked in the tingling effect Brynn's crimson blood had on him. It mimicked the tickle before an orgasm, skirting the edge of annoyance and bliss. He would be damned if he allowed a gnat like Nikolai to deny him his full pleasure.

"Fetch Natalia for me, she's out in the garden," he said, glancing at Anton. "I have an errand for her."

Bowing his head in reverence, Anton silently cackled. Ooh. This was going to be good.

"Yes, Sir," he replied.

Knowing it was best not to keep the Elder waiting, Anton left the office in an almost half run. Skirting down the long hallway, he headed towards the ornate garden just outside the Manor's back door. He knew exactly what Ulysses' little errand entailed. He could visualize the pained look on Nikolai's face when he realized there was nothing he could do to save his precious Mate. It made him insanely giddy.

CHAPTER TWENTY-ONE

Folding her arms over her chest, Brynn slowly looked around the living room of her new home. Turning in a lazy circle, she let out a tiny sigh. It was cozy and warm, with an overstuffed couch and two mismatched armchairs facing a roaring fireplace. Paintings of frozen fjords and woodland scenes hung from plastered walls next to bookcases full of thick novels. Dark wooden beams lined the uneven ceiling. It reminded her of a fairytale cottage.

She definitely wasn't in Arizona, anymore.

Hugging her cardigan closer, she stepped towards the stoked fireplace. Closing her eyes, she enjoyed the heat as it kissed her face. She was surprised at how cold and wet Bergen was, the climate was eerily similar to her home city of Tacoma. It was the only thing she wasn't too thrilled about. Well, that and the threat of Nik's Clan or Vampire Hunters knocking at their door.

Shaking away her frightening thoughts, she stood in comfortable silence as she waited for her love. They had arrived only two hours prior, right after dusk had settled. Surrounded by water and mountains, the city was beautiful at night. She knew it would be even more spectacular during the day, even if it was raining. She hoped Nik would agree to take her sightseeing under the sun.

Suddenly hearing the sound of footsteps creaking the floorboards above her, Brynn opened her eyes. Turning her gaze towards the ceiling, she grinned as she heard Nik wish Yetta a good night. The walls were thin in their small row house, it was something she needed to keep in mind. She didn't want to make Yetta feel uncomfortable in any way.

Listening to the footsteps as they headed for the staircase, she counted the heavy thuds as he made his way down to the first floor. He was moving quickly. Good, she thought. The night was young and she still had so many unanswered questions.

Reaching the main floor of the quaint house, Nik rounded the corner. Catching Brynn as she stood by the fire, he couldn't help but smile. The light of a fire flattered her.

"Staying warm?" he asked, walking over to her.

Nodding her head, Brynn hummed as Nik wrapped his arms around her. Melting into his embrace, she nuzzled against his torso.

"Mmm...yes...I always forget how good an old-fashioned fire can feel," she replied.

Chuckling to himself, he leaned down to kiss the top of her head. An old-fashioned fire was once the only way you could stay warm on a chilly night.

"Well, we do have a fireplace in our bedroom...I'll build you a fire anytime you want," he purred.

Instantly perking, Brynn pulled away to look up at his face. "Wait...we do?" she asked, her voice lifting in excitement.

Meeting her eyes, he curled his full lips into a sly grin. He could think of nothing better than throwing down a blanket in front of the fireplace and making love to her as the night slipped by.

"Mmmhmm...would you like to go take a look?" he asked, lifting a dark brow.

"Yes, very much so...but, uh...do you think we could talk for a little bit, first? I know that's all we've been doing but I, uh...I still have a few questions," she said.

Easing his embrace, Nik ran his hands along her back. Giving her an assuring look, he motioned towards the couch with a lift of his chin. He had all the time in the world for whatever else she wanted to know.

"Yeah, of course…let's sit down, hmm?" he said, moving his hand to take hers.

Leading her towards the brown sofa, he waited for her to take a seat. Sitting down next to her, he turned his body ever so slightly.

"Ok…fire away," he said.

Wiggling against the back of the couch, Brynn cleared her throat. Mimicking his body language, she looked up at his handsome face. It was still hard for her to wrap her brain around him being a Vampire. To her he was still just a man.

"So…you mentioned Vampires had special attributes. What did you mean by that?" she asked.

Lifting his arm, Nik casually draped it over the back of the sofa. Ah. Yes. He had glossed over that when they had landed in New York.

"Well, when a mortal is turned into a Vampire, they are given a special gift or two by the Night God. At least that's what we've been taught…but you never know what your talent will be until you have been successfully turned. There doesn't seem to be any rhyme or reason to it," he said with a shrug.

"And what is your special gift?" Brynn asked.

"I was given the gift of Charm," he replied.

"And what does that mean?" she asked.

Keeping his green eyes locked on hers, he softened his features. This was about to become uncomfortable. No matter how badly he wanted to, he couldn't lie.

"I have the ability to read minds and emotions…the ability to influence people," he said.

Furrowing her brow, her smile immediately fell. She honestly wasn't expecting that. She thought that maybe he could fly like she had seen in movies. Something supernatural in a cliche way. But this? This carried implications she didn't think she was quite prepared for.

"Have you...have you done any of this to me?" she asked.

"Yes," he replied honestly. "But before you overthink this Brynn, please let me explain."

Swallowing hard, she nodded once. Her thoughts were already running away with her. Was this the reason he so enamored her? Had he twisted her emotions to suit his needs?

"I have never, and I repeat *never*, used my abilities to influence your feelings towards me. What we have," he said, motioning with his hands. "This is real. I promise you...your love for me is through your own volition. Now I did read your mind on our first date...and have felt your emotions every now and then. But nothing detrimental to you. Your actions...your feelings...their *yours*, Brynn."

Giving herself a moment to think, she gave him a curious look. She was suddenly reminded of a moment that seemed very out of place. "Wait...there was one time where we were having sex and I heard you in my head...that really happened, didn't it?" she asked.

Groaning internally, Nik pushed out a sigh. He had forgotten about that. "Yes, that did happen...I shouldn't have done that, but you were so close to having that orgasm and your body just wasn't letting you...so yes, I did give you a little push, but that's it," he said.

Mulling over his answer, she felt the need to let that one slide. How could she really be mad about that? It was one hell of an orgasm.

"Ok...but Nik...I don't want you to invade my thoughts or emotions from now on, ok?" She said, her tone firm.

Staying quiet for a moment, he hummed low. He was fine agreeing to that up to a point. If he needed to use his gifts in an emergency, he would.

"Ok," he finally said. "There is a way for you to shield yourself from me, would you like me to teach you how?"

"Yeah…not that I don't believe you or that I want to like…keep things from you…I just want our relationship to be as…I donno…pure? Yeah…as pure as possible," she said.

Understanding what she meant, Nik gave her a knowing grin. If that is what she wanted, he would oblige.

"Sure, ok…first, relax yourself as much as possible and think of something embarrassing. Something you would hate for me to know," he said.

Closing her eyes, Brynn took in a cleansing breath. It didn't take her very long to think of something she would turn scarlet over.

"Ok," she said.

Fully turning towards her on the couch, he leaned in close. Dancing his eyes over her serene face, he resisted the urge to kiss her.

"Ok, good…now build a mental wall around it. I know that sounds odd but…just try to barricade it any way you can," he said softly.

Scrunching her face, she wondered how she could accomplish that task. Deciding to just give it a go, she imagined a large wooden box. Slipping the embarrassing thought inside, she sealed it with phantom nails.

Watching her face twitch in thought, Nik waited until she fully relaxed her brow. Certain that she had completed her task, he whispered low to not break her concentration.

"Ready?" he asked.

"Mmmhmm," she replied.

Closing his own eyes, he let his otherworldly talent take hold. Brushing against her consciousness, he couldn't help but smile as he was met with nothing but an empty void. Pushing a little further, he rooted around for a handful of seconds before he found a large box. Pressing upon it with his phantom hands, he was easily able to find a tiny crack. It was small, but not small enough. Reaching through the opening, he pulled the thought from the box. Chuckling lightly, he opened his eyes. Of all the things she could have chosen…

"I already know you pass gas when you're sleeping, Brynn…but for the record, it's nothing to be embarrassed about. It's completely mortal of you and I happen to think it's adorable so…yeah, don't be worried about that," he said, lifting his hand to touch her face.

Letting out a full belly laugh, Brynn opened her eyes. Playfully slapping his hand from her face, she shook her head. She should have thought of something else for her first go. Something not as cringeworthy. Suddenly remembering Yetta, she clamped her hand over her mouth. Quieting her laugh, she felt her cheeks flush from embarrassment.

Smirking at his love, Nik waved off her worries. There was no need to be quiet, nor was there a need for her to feel ashamed.

"It's ok…Yetta is a sound sleeper. Nothing short of a sonic boom will wake her…and seriously, I think it's cute. I love all your human quirks, they're very endearing to me," he assured her.

"Oh, God…well…I'm glad that you think it's adorable," she said, catching her breath.

"Very much so…ok, let's try again, hmm? This time, try to visualize something that terrifies you. And try to feel me as I push past your defenses. It will probably feel a small tickle near your temples. When you feel that, hide your fear deeper…and keep hiding it until I yield, ok?" he said.

Pulling her bottom lip between her teeth, she instantly thought of something that scared her to the core. A few weeks ago, it was the fear of being murdered. But now? Now it was the fear of losing him in any way, shape, or form. Having to live life without him was a fate worse than death.

"Alright," she said, once again closing her eyes.

Placing the fear at the end of a winding maze, she darkened the imaginary world around it. Barricading everything with a layer of brick, then steel, then concrete, she hid it in the upper corner of her mind. Thinking of the sound of white noise and visual static, she straightened her posture.

"Ok, I'm ready," she said.

Keeping his eyes open this time, Nik quickly dipped into her thoughts. Momentarily caught off guard by her initial defenses, he grunted an approval. It was very clever of her to do that, it made him wonder how she had known about that little trick.

"Good girl," he whispered.

Pushing further, he swirled through her consciousness. Poking and prodding, he moved through the opaque reaches of her mind until he found a shadow in light grey.

Feeling a sharp prick at her temples, Brynn whimpered. It wasn't the harmless tickle he had mentioned, this was sharp and uncomfortable. Angry from the pain, she slid the phantom fortress to the opposite side of her mind.

Knowing he was causing discomfort, he pressed on. Becoming bolder in his search, he carefully sliced through the recesses of her brain again and again. Pushing and pulling against wisps of memories until he heard a soft hiss escape her lips.

Not wanting to cause her any additional pain, he withdrew his phantom advances. Trying to be as gentle as possible, he healed the precise cuts left in his wake. Chastising himself, he did his best to soothe her migraine. He shouldn't have been so rough, but she truly needed this lesson.

"I'm sorry, my love...but I'm proud of you. So very proud, you did beautifully," he praised.

Slowly opening her eyes, Brynn winced as she registered the flickering light of the fire. There was a light pounding at her temples that she found incredibly annoying. It almost overshadowed the pride she felt for keeping her fear safe. Almost.

"Mmm...thank you, handsome. That wasn't so bad, ya know," she said.

Lifting a brow, he swiped his gaze across her freckled face. "Hmm...are you sure? Would you like me to fetch you some acetaminophen?" he asked.

Shaking her head, she did her best to ignore the dull headache. The pain wasn't enough to warrant medicine. However, she wouldn't turn down a good orgasm. That was how she usually dealt with a pounding head.

"No...no, I don't need any Tylenol, thank you. But I wouldn't mind us having a bit of fun after you take me to bed," she said suggestively.

With a devilish grin, Nik leaned in closer. Ah. Yes. He wouldn't mind that, either.

"Oh...I'll give you all of the fun you can handle, Sunshine...just let me know when you're ready to turn in," he said, his voice deep and silken.

"I will...soon, very soon. I just have a few more questions," she said.

Dipping his head, Nik relaxed against the sofa. Ignoring the image of them breaking in their new-to-them bed, he switched gears. He wanted to make sure she was satisfied mentally before being satisfied physically.

"Ok, my love...what else do you have for me?" he asked.

"Well...are you the only one in your Clan with this gift?" she asked.

Shaking his head, he let out a sigh. Unfortunately, he was not. And he would do everything he could to keep Brynn away from her.

"No. There is another...her name is Sara. She's quite young. Anton Sired her in I believe nineteen eighty-six. I've tried to help her hone her power, teach her how to use it properly. But she's refused every single time. She will only listen to Anton and the Elders. Anyone else can piss off. But yeah...I compare our styles like this. I try to go in with a surgical scalpel...I try to make things as clean and precise as I can. She goes in with a chainsaw, decimating more than she retrieves. It's quite terrifying to watch her, honestly," he said.

Feeling a shiver run down her spine, Brynn's eyes widened. She never wanted to run into Sara. Or Anton again, for that matter.

"That sounds awful," she murmured.

"Yeah, it is," Nik agreed with a nod of his head. "That's why the Elders have always used me to do the brunt of the mental work. They only call upon her when they want to inflict excruciating pain. But now that they don't have my gifts...I do wonder what will happen."

Furrowing her brow, she tilted her head. Wonder what will happen? To what?

"What do you mean?" she asked.

Softening his masculine features, Nik gave a tiny shrug. There was no need for Brynn to know about the Benefactor Program at that moment. It was a can of worms not worth opening.

"Well, my Clan has business deals all over the world. Deals that I have been the one to facilitate and conduct because of my Gift. Those are now in jeopardy...which will affect my Clan's revenue. Sara doesn't have the capacity to save those deals," he said.

"Ahh...I gotcha," Brynn said with a knowing look. "So there goes the Clan's money, hmm?"

Keeping his body language neutral, Nik allowed her to believe she was right. Money was just a small fraction of what was at stake, here. Without the steady supply of blood from his now former girls, members of the Clan would break the treaties he worked so hard to create. Mortals were once again in serious danger. It left him with a sour taste in his mouth.

"Correct," he said.

"Hmm...well...that is a shame. No one likes poor Vampires," she said jokingly.

"Oh, I know...how gross, hmm?" he said with a playful smile. "A broke bloodsucker? Ugh."

Laughing lightly, she inched closer to her love. Although he hadn't said anything about their finances, she knew things had definitely changed. Not that it mattered. The broke bloodsucker before her was still the most delicious man she had ever met.

"Ok, so...what other powers do some of the other members of your Clan have?" she asked.

"Well...some have incredible strength. Some are insanely fast. Others can hypnotize, which sounds similar to what I can do, but it is vastly different. One has telekinesis and teleportation Gifts," he said, his face and body automatically hardening.

Noticing a distinct change in Nik, Brynn straightened her back. Arching a brow, she gave him a curious look.

"Wait. Who has those Gifts...the telekinesis and teleportation?" she asked.

Pressing his lips into a fine line, he debated on how much information he needed to divulge. He really didn't want to talk about his former

Mate. Especially to his new one.

"Natalia," he said simply.

"Natalia," she replied, rolling the name on her tongue. "God...why do Vampires have such sexy names?"

Giving her a tiny grin, he groaned internally. Natalia's name was the only sexy thing about her. Everything about her paled in comparison to Brynn.

"Yes...well...I'm sure it's a requirement somewhere," he said with a wave of his hand.

"Oh, I'm sure," Brynn agreed. "Well, those are some pretty serious Gifts, I would imagine?"

Nodding a reply, he did his best to look as nonchalant as possible. He didn't want to scare her, but Natalia's Gifts were very dangerous. The only reason he felt even remotely safe from his Sire was the fact that there was a Hunter currently living right down the street. One whose wife and infant son she had killed.

"They are," he said, not realizing he had a sudden scowl on his face.

Suddenly wanting to change the subject, Brynn cleared her throat. Her questions about specific members of his Clan could wait.

"Ok...so. I know this is kinda off the wall...but what does my blood taste like? It's different from regular blood, right?" she asked.

Giving her a curious look, Nik hummed low. He wasn't quite sure why she had asked that question, but it was a harmless one to answer. The mere thought of it made his mouth water, and his cock ache. Within an instant, the lust for both her body and her blood took hold.

"It is the most delicious thing I've ever tasted. Next to your cunt, that is," he said huskily.

Lifting the corners of her lips into a flirty grin, Brynn met his sinful eyes. She suddenly wanted to know what it felt like to have his teeth pierce her skin. What it felt like to give him complete control over her.

"Mmm…well, take me to bed Nikolai and you can have both," she said.

CHAPTER TWENTY-TWO

Shaking his head, Nik automatically declined her invitation. She didn't understand what she was offering him. He couldn't take from her. It was wrong on a multitude of levels.

"No. I won't drink from you," he said.

Huffing a sharp breath, Brynn gave him an incredulous look. What was the big deal? Why was he being so weird about this?

"Why?" she asked.

Clenching just jaw, he stared into her wondering eyes. He was on the precipice of a slippery slope. One he wasn't sure he was strong enough to avoid.

"Because I'll crave you for all of eternity," he replied.

Lifting the corner of her lips into a smirk, she stopped herself from laughing. Boldly slinking her body onto his, she straddled his hips. Draping her arms around his neck, she leaned in close to his face.

"Mmm...but don't you already?" she asked, arching a brow.

Grunting low, Nik placed his hands on her narrow waist. Giving her a gentle squeeze, he savored the feeling of her lightly grinding onto his hardening cock. She wasn't wrong about that. But his craving could turn into one for something more. There would come a time when he would have the all-consuming need to Sire her. He absolutely couldn't let that happen.

"You know that I do," he replied.

Tilting her head, she quietly studied his expression. He was battling something; she could tell by the way the green in his eyes was wavering between tones. She didn't understand why this was causing him some sort of internal conflict.

"Then what's the problem, Nikolai?" she asked.

"I don't want to weaken you," he said in a half-truth.

Narrowing her eyes, she gave a tiny shrug of her shoulders. She didn't understand why that was a problem. "But blood is regenerative…so I'll be a little sleepy for a bit, big deal," she said.

Shaking his head, he moved his right hand from her waist to her cheek. Touching her reverently, he let out a small sigh.

"I just don't want what happened to Leona to happen to you. I want you to keep your magic," he said.

Leaning into his touch, she stopped herself from rolling her eyes. His excuses were weak at best. This was a discussion that she wasn't going to let him win.

"What happened to Lenona won't happen to me because you won't use me as some sort of Sun Walker juice box like they did. One time won't hurt me, Nik…*you* won't hurt me. I know you won't. Besides…I need you to show me around Bergen. I want to see it in the daylight with you," she said, purposefully pouting her lips. "Please? Pretty please? Just this once?"

Spitting an expletive, Nik felt his steadfast resolve slip away. The thought of basking in the sun with her was massively appealing. If he did take her up on her offer, it would just be the one time.

"Brynn, I—"

"Shhh," she interrupted. "Please, Nik. I want to know what it's like…I want to know what it's like to be loved and needed by a Vampire."

"But you already know," he replied, giving her a small grin.

Unable to stop herself this time, Brynn rolled her eyes. *Ugh,* she thought. He knew exactly what she was talking about. She would just have to be direct, then.

"I want to know what it feels like to have you bite into my neck at the same time you're fucking my cunt," she purred.

Instantly dropping his hand from her face, Nik gently wrapped his hand around her perfect throat. Feeling her heartbeat quicken under his touch, he played out the lurid fantasy in his mind. He could taste her saccharine blood on his tongue as he slid in and out of her wet cunt; hearing her soft moans as they both rode out their linked pleasure. It stoked his need like nothing had before.

"Just this once," he said, his voice low and strained.

Humming happily, Brynn gave him a wicked grin. Sure. Just this once. Although she knew for damn sure that neither of them could stick to that.

"Take me to bed, Nikolai," she said.

Not needing to be told again, he eased his grip from her throat. Moving his hands to her ass, he leaned forward. Making sure he had a good hold on her, he stood from the couch in a single, fluid motion.

Laughing lightly, she wrapped her legs around him as he carried her through the living room to the staircase. Hugging his neck, she pressed a sprinkling of hot kisses along his jaw. She prayed to God that Yetta was not a light sleeper. She had a feeling she wouldn't be able to stay quiet.

Lightly stomping up the creaky staircase, Nik groaned as Brynn's lips danced across his alabaster skin. Reaching the top of the stairs, he dug his fingers into her denim covered ass. Turning the corner into the narrow hallway, he walked to the second door on the left. Removing his hand to grab the doorknob, he paused for a brief second.

"Are you sure, Brynn?" he asked, his deep voice nothing more than a whisper.

Nodding her head, she eagerly wiggled her body against him. Pulling her head away, she found his gaze in the dim light.

"One hundred percent," she replied softly.

Turning the metal knob, he opened the door to their bedroom. Crossing the threshold, he gently closed it shut using his foot. Clearing the modest space to the full-sized bed, he bent down to place her upon the quilt covered mattress.

Releasing her arms and legs from his body, Brynn immediately began to remove her clothes. Ripping the cardigan from her torso, she tossed it to the floor. Moments like these she wished she were a nudist. Clothes could be such a nuisance.

Watching his love as she tore off her tank top and jeans, he quickly followed suit. Taking off his shirt and slacks, his eyes never left her. How did a sinner like him become so lucky? He didn't deserve the ethereal woman before him.

Scooting to the edge of the bed, Brynn wriggled out of her lace panties. Looking at the naked planes of his body, she swallowed hard. The shadows of the room combined with city lights cracking through the curtains cast an otherworldly glow on his pale skin. He reminded her of a Greek God in a Renaissance painting.

"You really are a beautiful man, Nikolai," she said, drifting her gaze to take in every delicious inch.

Dropping to his knees on the wooden floor, Nik grinned from the compliment. Lifting his large hands to her knees, he gently parted her legs. Moving between them, he traced phantom lines over her skin from her thighs to her pert tits.

"Thank you for seeing me as just a man," he replied huskily, leaning in to kiss her left nipple.

Taking in a sharp breath, Brynn lifted her hand to his mop of dark locks. Twisting her fingers, she closed her eyes as he took her breast into his mouth.

"Mmmm...I'll make sure that you eventually see yourself as one too," she promised.

Grunting a reply, he greedily suckled her firm tit. Pulling her rosebud nipple between his teeth, he lazily swirled the tip of his tongue across it. Again, and again until he heard her breath hitch.

"Ahhh...that feels so good," Brynn whispered.

Spurned by her words, Nik snaked one arm around her. Raising his free hand, he palmed her right breast. Holding her firmly in place, he lavished his attention on her tanned skin. Sucking and licking, pinching and biting. He savored every lewd, feminine moan.

Opening her glassy eyes, Brynn focused her gaze on her lover. Watching his lips move over her skin, she bit down on her lower lip to keep herself from crying out. With every graze of his teeth, her sharp need for him grew. She wondered if he could take blood from other places on her body.

Gripping her nipple between his middle finger and thumb, he gently rolled it in time with his tongue. Toying with her, he purposefully withdrew from her brightening aura. It would be difficult to stay away, but it was a promise he wanted to keep. He would have to read her using her body alone. It was something he hadn't done in centuries.

Whimpering from the mixture of pleasure and pain, she arched against his mouth. Tugging on his hair, she begged him to move his touch lower. The ache in her cunt was almost too much to bear.

"Please," she breathed. "You're making me so wet."

Growling against her tit, he gave her nipple one last flick of his tongue before pulling away. Licking his lips, he moved his touch from her breast to the medallion of her necklace. Glancing up at her, he felt his hunger spike. Her words were music to his ears.

"Mmm…is that right? Well then, I think I need a taste," he said, trailing his fingertips from his family crest down her belly. "Lie back, beautiful. Show me that pretty pussy of yours."

Gasping in excitement, Brynn immediately did as she was told. Flopping back onto the bed, she wiggled her ass to the edge of the mattress, giving Nik full access to her shaven cunt.

Taking his fill of the splayed goddess before him, Nik helped to drape her legs over his broad shoulders. Pulling her thin form closer to him, he dipped his head to her inner thigh. Using his tongue, he drew invisible symbols of protection used by his kind. Although most likely useless, it certainly didn't hurt. The intention was there.

Laughing softly as his tongue and lips tickled her sensitive skin, she reached for her breasts. Roughly squeezing them in her hands, she pleaded for more.

Obliging his love, Nik moved his attention to her perfect cunt. Hovering his mouth over her, he gave her soft flesh an agonizing slow lick. Savoring her arousal as it met his tongue, he groaned in approval. Next to her blood, it was the most divine thing he had ever tasted.

Hissing an expletive, she pinched her hardened nipples between her fingers. Lifting her head from the mattress, she glanced down at the man between her thighs. Watching mesmerized as he teased her aching pussy, she felt her heart flutter wildly against her rib cage.

"Ahhh…God…yes…please," she moaned wantonly.

Turning his eyes upwards, he smiled wickedly against her cunt. She looked so desperate, so needy. It made him swell with pride to know he had such an effect on her. Caving into her desire, he pushed the tip of his tongue past her slit. Slowly swirling upwards, he easily found her waiting clit.

"Ohhh, fuck!" Brynn cried, arching sharply.

Moving his hands to the side of her hips, he stopped her from moving another inch. Holding her tightly, he parted her cunt with his lips. Using the flat of his tongue, he lapped at her reddened clit. Slowly at first, lazy but deliberate. He wanted to turn her into a whimpering mess before letting her cum.

Releasing her right tit, Brynn reached down to her lover's head as he worshiped her with his tongue. Threading her fingers into his dark hair, she twisted and pulled with every warm press.

"More…more," she panted.

Easing her clit between his teeth, Nik sucked on the delicate bud. Circling the tip of his tongue clockwise, he paused every few passes to tap it. Over and over again until he felt her thighs tremble over his shoulders. Looking up at her writhing body, he savored the lewd sight of her dancing towards the edge of her bliss.

Reminding herself to keep quiet, she pressed her lips together. Only allowing herself to make muffled moans, she sharply pinched her nipple. Mimicking the movements of his expert tongue, she rolled it between her fingertips, squeezing it with each completed circle on her clit.

Listening to her rapid breaths, he ramped up the speed of his administration. Changing the direction of his tongue, he crossed tiny hatch marks across her clit. Making a low humming sound, he used the vibration to take her closer and closer.

Hearing her blood rush through her veins with every rapid pump of her heart, his own desire begged to take over. Wanting her to break before he did, he encouraged her to give into her pleasure by tightening his grip on her hips.

Tugging on his locks, Brynn instinctively ground her pussy against his sinful mouth. Unable to hear anything but her deafening heartbeat, she focused on the ball of pleasure behind her public bone. Between the swipes of her lover's tongue and the vibration of his voice she felt herself splitting at the seams.

Shutting her eyes closed, she found herself unable to hold onto the reins a moment longer. Squealing into the air of the small bedroom, she jerked violently as her orgasm crashed against her. Sending torrents of decadent pleasure though the muscles of her thrumming body.

Tasting a tiny gush of arousal as she came around him, Nik greedily lapped it up. Allowing her to make a mess of him, he patiently waited for her to still. Giving her sopping cunt one last kiss, he stood from the floor. Leaning over her, he brought his face to hers.

"Taste yourself on my lips," he said, his voice deep with want. "Taste just how good you are."

Breathing hard, Brynn blinked her eyes into focus. Giving him a cheeky smile, she took him up on his offer. Lifting her head, she licked her essence from his chin and lips. Swallowing it down, she moaned before claiming his mouth in a desperate kiss.

Matching her passion, he slid his large hands under her. Gathering her in his arms, he helped to reposition her on the bed. Placing her head on the pillow by the headboard, he moved between her spread legs. Gently pulling away from her lips, he rested his forehead upon hers.

"Are you *absolutely sure* you want me to take from you? Now is the time to say no…I won't…I won't be able to stop myself once I'm inside of you," he husked.

Pausing for a moment, Brynn met his searing gaze. A shiver of anticipation ran down her spine as she gave his words another thought. She didn't have to think for long. For her, there was no going back. She wanted this just as badly as he did.

"I'm sure," she replied, lifting her hands to cradle the sides of his handsome face. "Now fuck me and bite me…I want to be yours."

Spitting a dark curse, he kissed her hard. Reaching his hand between their naked bodies, he grabbed onto his thick cock. Pumping his length, he pressed the head of his dick against her wet pussy. Not able to hold back, he entered her with a single press of his hips.

Reveling in the way he filled her so completely, she whimpered into his needy kiss. Bending her legs towards her torso, she gave him complete access to her body. She knew this would be all consuming now that he had permission. She couldn't remember the last time she had been so excited.

Placing his hands under her shoulders, he began to thrust within her warm cunt. Slow and deep, he groaned as she squeezed around him. Breaking the kiss, he pulled away to watch her beautiful face as he fucked her.

"You're...perfect," he praised lovingly.

Dropping her hands, Brynn let her arms fall to the bed. Furrowing her brow as he moved within her, she relinquished all control. She wanted him to take his pleasure any way he wished.

Speeding his thrusts, Nik placed a series of hot kisses along her rounded jaw. Pressing and pulling, he rocked his hips faster and faster. Slamming into her sopping cunt again and again, he allowed his lust to take over.

Burrowing his face into the crook of her exposed neck, he licked the salty sweat from her skin. With the rushing sound of her blood enticing him, he easily found her carotid artery. Kissing her throat reverently, he felt the monster take over.

Crying out with each quick press of his cock, Brynn leaned her head to give him better access to her neck. Shivering with sudden apprehension, she reminded herself that this is what she wanted. The first time for everything was nerve wracking. This would be something she remembered for the rest of her life.

Relaxing her body and mind, she wrapped her arms and legs around him. Closing her eyes, she focused on his lips as she suckled on her neck. This was it, she thought to herself. There was no going back.

Growling like a possessed animal, Nik's serpentine eyes turned black. Pulling his full lips back, his sharp fangs extended. With his ecstasy threatening to boil over, he bit into her neck with a hunger he hadn't felt in centuries.

Opening her mouth to scream, Brynn found herself unable to make a single sound. Her lover's bite was initially painful, slicing through skin and muscle to get to her artery. After the shock of acute pain, she found a sudden euphoria as her blood spilled. Constant and steady, the pleasure filled every fiber of her being. It melted any fear she had left.

Swallowing mouthful after mouthful of her saccharine blood, Nik felt his body shudder as his release snuck up on him. Cumming into her pussy he grunted as his body absorbed the remnants of his orgasm along with her blood. Gripping tightly onto her, he selfishly took all he could. Swallowing more and more as he spent his cock inside of her. It wasn't until he heard the sudden drop in her heartbeat that he forced himself to stop.

Letting the last warm mouthful slide down his throat, Nik pressed the flat of his tongue over the pierced wounds caused by his fangs. Holding still, he closed his ebony eyes as his innate magic set to work. Sealing her internal and external wounds, he made sure she was fully healed before pulling away. Pushing the monster back in its cage, he licked her crimson blood from his lips.

With her eyes open wide, Brynn tried in vain to catch her breath. Slowly her pleasure dissipated, replaced by utter and complete exhaustion. She felt like she hadn't slept in weeks.

"Oh my God," she whispered, letting her heavy legs and arms fall from him.

With the overwhelming intoxication of her blood coursing through his body, Nik shivered as he moved to look at her face. Suddenly noticing her shallow breaths, he forced himself to ignore his own afterglow.

"Brynn? Are you ok?" he asked, a look of concern painting his masculine features.

Meeting his worried eyes, she gave him a small laugh. "I don't know…I mean…yeah, I'm ok…it's just…*holy fuck* that was intense, Nik…I'm like, so tired right now. But God did that feel good," she replied.

Cursing himself internally, he lifted her torso to his. Rolling their bodies over the full-sized bed, he held her on top of his naked form.

"Ohhh…my beautiful Brynn…I'm so sorry. I didn't mean to take so much," he said, kissing her cheek. "I wish you knew just how amazing you taste. I haven't felt this fantastic in a lifetime…you're magic, my love. Pure magic."

Nuzzling his bare chest, Brynn paid no mind to the few drops of blood he hadn't licked from her neck. Relishing her sleepiness, she let out a yawn.

"Mmm…am I? Well, good. I'm glad you enjoyed my gifts…I know I certainly enjoyed yours," she said, lifting her head to rest her chin on his pec. "So, this means you'll take me sightseeing tomorrow?"

Relaxing against the pillow, Nik gave her a satisfied smile. Of course he would. He was chomping at the bit to see her in the sunlight again.

"I'll wake you at dawn so we can watch the Sunrise together…and then I'll take you to this little cafe for coffee and pannekaker. How does that sound?" he asked.

"I have no clue what pannekaker is, but that all sounds wonderful," she said softly, her eyelids fluttering down halfway.

Raising his hand, he brushed a strand of chestnut hair from her face. Looking at her tired eyes, he suddenly felt very guilty for taking so much. She would be anemic for the next couple of days. Possibly more. He would have to make sure she ate well and rested as much as possible.

"It's a Norwegian pancake. I've been told they're delicious…I'm sure you'll love them," he replied, studying her as she drifted off. "Sleep well, my beloved."

Muttering a 'good night,' Brynn went limp as she gave into her exhaustion. Her last coherent thought was that of a wish. A wish that she would be able to spend the rest of eternity by his side.

CHAPTER TWENTY-THREE

Adjusting herself on Nik's lap, Brynn brought her third glass of orange juice to her lips. Taking in a hearty gulp, she looked over the overcast fjord from the comfort of the small porch of their new home. She had to admit, the sunrise itself was underwhelming at best. The clouds and mist had snuffed the sun, dulling the painted sky into a muted gray with only hints of aubergine at the seams.

Not that she should be complaining. She was able to enjoy a full day with her love. A less than stellar sunrise was a tiny price to pay.

Playing with the end of her long braid, Nik leaned back in the wooden lawn chair. Absorbing the filtered light, he kept his gaze on the side of her face. Her skin looked pale and dull, the hint of exhaustion still smudging dark rings under her hazel eyes. It caused a pit of remorse to lodge in his stomach. He had taken far too much from her.

"How are you feeling?" he asked softly.

Glancing at him from the corners of her eyes, she let out a tiny sigh. It was the fifth time he had asked her that. Sure, she was a little tired but that had more to do with what she had been through over the last few days than him taking a few mouthfuls of her blood.

"Nikolai…I'm ok. Please believe me," she said, turning on his lap to face him. "The sugar from all the oj you've been giving me is starting to kick in. I'm feeling really good."

Lifting a brow, he couldn't stop himself from frowning. He didn't have to read her thoughts to know that she wasn't telling him the truth.

"Brynn—"

"Shhh, Nik," she interrupted, leaning in to press a quick kiss on his disbelieving lips. "I'm thrilled that I get to enjoy the day with you…so stop worrying, ok? Let's just have fun. Would you like to go on a little walk before the rain comes?"

Softening his hard features, he gave her a nod. It was important for her to learn her way around her new home. There would be times where she had to leave during the day without him. Whether that was to pick up groceries, or to see a doctor. Tiny mortal nuisances that he didn't miss one bit.

"I would love to…why don't I go grab your jacket and then we can go?" he said.

"Perfect," she replied, standing from his lap.

Watching him as he stood to full height, she handed him her glass. He looked so good wearing a cable neck sweater and jeans. Although she couldn't help but think that they would look better on the floor of their tiny bedroom.

"Don't be too long," she said.

"Yes, Ma'am," he said before leaning down to kiss her forehead.

Clearing the small space to their front door, he turned the metal knob and stepped inside. Leaving the door ajar behind him, he walked towards the kitchen. Finding Yetta grabbing an apple from the fruit basket sitting on the windowsill, he offered her a smile.

"Good morning, Yetta. How did you sleep?" he asked, setting down the glass of orange juice on the counter.

Pushing out an exasperated sigh, Yetta lifted her free hand to rub her hooded eyes. "Long night," she replied.

Feeling instantly guilty, he visibly winced. He honestly thought she had been fast asleep for most of the night. He hoped it wasn't too awkward for her. It would be for him if the roles were reversed.

"I'm sorry if we…well, if we were too loud," he said.

Brushing him off with a wave of her hand, she tutted under her breath. She couldn't care less about him and the Sun Walker giving into the temptations of the flesh. It wasn't her business.

"No. No. Not you. I talk to Helen. Big fight between Elders. Ulysses and Christos hiding something from her. No talk to her for one week," she said, taking a bite of her apple.

Instantly perking, Nik narrowed his eyes. Helen hadn't lived in the Manor in over a century but had religiously stayed in daily contact with her counterparts. The fact that Ulysses and Christos hadn't spoken to her in a week was odd. And alarming.

"What do you think is going on?" he asked.

Swallowing her bite, Yetta shrugged her hunched shoulders. It could be anything knowing those two. They were always jealous of Helen and her power over the Clan. But their sudden silence was suspicious, given the attack on the Sun Walker.

"I no know. But I leave today for Capri. Helen ask me to come. Leonardo there now. She want us both to see if electric problem. She no like computer," she said.

Shaking his head, he folded his arms over his chest. He highly doubted that it was a problem relating to Helen's computers or her internet.

"No. This isn't an electronics issue. Those bastards are planning something…something that they know Helen would object to. Did you happen to tell her that we were back in Norway?" he asked.

"No. No. I no tell. And my phone tracker off. If they listen, they no know where we are," she said, looking at his concerned face. "You and Sun Walker safe here. I safe with Helen. We find out what wrong and I be back in one week. Maybe two. No worry."

"I really don't like you leaving, Yetta," he said sternly.

Placing her bitten apple back in the basket, she clapped her gnarled hands together. She was traveling during the day. The members of the Clan hadn't been blessed by Brynn's blood like Nikolai. She really didn't have anything to worry about. Neither did he.

"I be fine, Nikolai. No worry. Ulysses and Christos too chicken to go to Capri. Too scared to come here. You enjoy time with Brynn. Have sort of honeymoon," she said with a full smile.

Opening his mouth to reply, he sighed instead as he heard Brynn's soft footsteps walking up behind him. Turning his head, he painted on a forced grin.

"Hey Sunshine…sorry, Yetta and I were just talking," he said, holding out his hand. "She has to go to Capri for a little bit."

Taking his hand, Brynn gave him an odd look before turning her attention to Yetta. Italy? Now? She definitely wasn't expecting that.

"Capri? Really? But we just got here," she said.

Shuffling her feet, Yetta stepped towards the pair. She didn't care for the look of concern on Nikolai's face. He knew damn well that she had learned how to take care of herself.

"Helen need me," she said simply.

Furrowing her brow, Brynn quirked her head. She didn't even want to pretend like she understood the Clan's hierarchy, but she could guess that if the Matriarch of the Clan said jump, you would ask 'how high?'

"Oh. Ok. Well, we will miss you," Brynn said, looking to Nik. "Won't we?"

"Yes…yes, of course. I just want to make sure you're being smart about this, Yetta," Nik said, pressing his lips into a fine line.

Rolling her brown eyes, the older woman flicked away his comment like she was shooing an insect. Nikolai worried far too much. Always had, always would.

"Of course. Very smart. Now, I must pack. Go. Have fun. I will text when I see Helen. No worry. I explain all to her. Will be good to have her as ally," she said.

Squeezing Brynn's hand, Nick stayed quiet for a moment. His faithful assistant was right, if they had Helen in their pocket then there was potential for Brynn to be safe. She always did have a soft spot for Yetta, but he knew that there were no guarantees.

"You're right, Yetta. We need her…text me as soon as you get to her Villa," he said.

"Yes. Yes. I text. I call. No worry," Yetta replied, walking past the pair to exit the kitchen. "I see you soon."

"Bye, Yetta. Safe travels," Brynn said.

"Goodbye Sun Walker," Yetta said over her shoulder as she headed to the staircase. "Remember. You have power! Use it if have to!"

Arching a brow, Nik gave Brynn a curious look. The way Yetta said that made it sound like they had a secret between them.

Giving Nik a small grin, Brynn blinked her eyes in feigned innocence. "What? I do have power in my veins…as you well know…and I did use it, didn't I?" she said.

Humming low, Nik lifted her hand to his lips. Placing a soft kiss upon her knuckles, he decided to drop it. She and Yetta could keep whatever it was for themselves. It was actually a good thing that his confidant had taken to his new love the way she had.

"Mmm…that you did, my love. Now let's enjoy some of the power you shared with me and go on that walk," he said, leading her from the kitchen.

. . .

Holding Nik's hand as they stepped down the city's sidewalk, Brynn glanced around with wide eyes. Bergen was unlike anything she had ever seen. It was what she would categorize as being distinctly Nordic, with its charming buildings that reminded her of gingerbread houses and old-world cobblestone lined roads. It was such a stark contrast to the American Southwest she loved so much. Not that she was complaining. Far from it. She was enjoying every second of this grand tour. She could see her and Nik living quite comfortably here. Creating a life together that lasted not only just a few decades, but centuries.

She only needed him to see it, too.

"Hey, Nik?" she said, deciding to brave the subject once more.

"Yes, my love?" Nik replied, making sure they sidestepped a young gentleman walking past while yelling into his cellphone.

"I want you to Sire me," she said nonchalantly.

Immediately halting his steps, he stood ramrod straight. Looking around to make sure no one was noticing them, he pulled her to the side of a white plastered building. Caging her against the wall, he bit back his instant annoyance. She had totally caught him off guard.

"No. No you don't, Brynn," he said, his voice deep and flat.

Meeting his green eyes, Brynn squared her shoulders. She didn't understand why he was so adamantly against the proposition. It was perfectly logical in her mind.

"Oh, I absolutely do Nik...what we have...our love...I know that I want to be with you forever," she said.

Letting out a sigh, Nik softened his features. All of this was still so new for her, she didn't understand the implications of what forever entailed.

"Brynn…it's not that simple. You'd be giving up more than you would be gaining. Being a Vampire it's not…it's not glamorous like it is in the movies," he said.

Holding back a laugh, she took half a step away from the cold wall. That was a lie, she knew firsthand just how glamorous his life as a Vampire was. Money. Power. Influence. Insane sex appeal?

No. Not glamorous at all.

"Sure it is…I mean…just look at you. You're a walking billboard for a hot Dracula reboot or something. But like…even if it was dark and gritty, I would still want it because I want *you*. All of you, for all of eternity," she said, lifting her hands to grab the lapel of his navy pea coat.

Pausing for a long moment, he resisted the urge to kiss her repeatedly until she couldn't remember what she was asking of him. He had said the exact same thing to his own Sire. Now he couldn't even stand the sight of her.

"You may feel differently about that after a few centuries…and then you'd be stuck. Tied to me until the end of time. I assure you…that is a worse fate than growing old and passing away naturally," he said, leaning in towards her beautiful face.

Blinking up at him, she lightly tugged on his coat. She couldn't ever see herself feeling differently about him. And even if she did, she didn't understand why she would be stuck.

"That doesn't sound so bad," she said with a small grin.

"Trust me, Brynn. It is…maybe I should explain to you the bond between a Sire and their Novice," he replied.

"Please do," she said.

Looking to his right and left, Nik took stock of the nearly deserted street. Now was as good of a time to talk about this as any. The morning had barely broken, most of the businesses were still closed. They would be able to talk openly for a little while.

"There isn't a relationship as unbreakable as one between a Sire and their Novice. It transcends everything. To a Novice, a Sire is essentially a God. *Their* God. There is no such thing as free will when it comes to your Sire. You're at their every beck and call…you have to fulfill any and all of their wishes. The word *no* doesn't exist," he said, keeping his voice low.

Raising her shoulders in a tiny shrug, she lifted the corners of her lips into a grin. "I'd be ok with that," she replied.

"Well…maybe now…but what happens if we begin to feel differently about one another? Hmm? What if we decide we don't want to be with each other? We would still tied to one another…I could still be your puppeteer," he said.

"Well…I know you…I know you wouldn't do anything to hurt me," she said.

Tutting under his breath, he lifted his hand to the side of her face. Brushing the pad of his thumb over her cheek, he couldn't stop himself from frowning.

"You know the Nikolai that's madly, deeply, *passionately* in love with you. But that could change. My kind…we may not change physically, but we grow mentally and emotionally just as mortals do. There may come a time…let's say, hundreds of years from now…where you fall in love with another. If you betrayed me, Brynn? If you told me that you didn't want me anymore…that you loved another…oh. You would see the other side of me. The one I keep on a tight leash. You have no idea how vengeful I can be…how *inherently evil*. If I was your Sire, I would have carte blanche to make your life hell. And here's the worst part of it…*I would*."

Swallowing hard, Brynn shook her head. She didn't believe that for a second.

"You wouldn't...I know you," she whispered.

"Oh, but I would, Brynn," he replied, his voice taking on an edge of darkness. "I told you that I'm a monster, and I meant that. I would make it my mission to make your eternity as horrible and painful as I could."

Staring into his eyes, she caught a hint of something past the sudden anger. Fear. Worry. Hurt. He was speaking from his own experience, she realized. Projecting his pain and using it as an excuse as to why they couldn't be together until the end of time.

"Just what did your Sire do to you, Nikolai?" she asked softly.

Letting out an unintended growl, he dropped his hand from her flushed cheek. He didn't want to talk about Natalia. Not here. Not now.

Not ever.

"Enough," he said, his tone strained. "She did enough...and I won't let history repeat itself. I can't Sire you, Brynn. I won't. So please, don't ask me again," he replied.

Sighing softly, she reluctantly nodded. She knew that it was best if she dropped the subject. She honestly didn't want to ruin their day together. This conversation was far from over, though. She would bring it up again and again until he caved.

She was persistent and hardheaded like that.

"Ok...I'm sorry, Nik," she said.

Leaning in, he placed a tender kiss on her forehead. He didn't mean to get upset with her; she didn't know it was such a touchy subject. Even though he didn't want to, he would probably have to tell her more about Natalia. Just not now. Not when there were fresh Norwegian pancakes to be had.

"No…don't apologize, Brynn. I should be the one apologizing. I didn't mean to snap at you…let's have a good day, hmm? I still owe you a coffee and pannekaker," he said, once again taking her hand.

Humming lightly, she followed him as he led her down the rustic sidewalk. Hugging his arm against her torso, she felt her stomach growl. He had fetched her eggs and sausage before they watched the sunrise, but she found herself starving again.

"Does it ever make you feel weird…watching me eat?" she asked curiously.

"No…not at all. I love it, actually…it gives me pleasure to watch you enjoy something that I can't," he said, navigating her around a broken cobblestone.

"Oh…well I hope you're ready for a show. I'm famished," she said with a small laugh.

"I'm looking forward to it," he said.

Glancing at her from the corners of his eyes, Nik smiled warmly. Motioning with his freehand which way to turn, he took a shortcut to the small cafe by the University. He hoped that one day Brynn would learn Norwegian fluently and continue her studies there. But that was a dream years down the line.

Winking at her love, she looked at the buildings as they headed down the new street. She wished she understood what the various signs said. Pointing to a random piece of painted wood hanging from the roof overhang, she cleared her throat.

"What does that say?" she asked.

Following her finger, Nik gave her a quick answer. He knew he was about to open a can of worms.

"That's The Metro…it's a nightclub," he said.

Gasping lightly, Brynn stopped walking. Holding onto his arm to make sure he stopped too, she smiled brightly. It had been weeks since she had gone dancing. It was one of her favorite ways to blow off steam.

"Oh my God…Nik…can you take me there?" she asked excitedly.

Groaning internally, he found himself nodding. He hated Norwegian electronic music, but he loved her more.

"Sure, my love," he replied.

"Yeah? Tonight?! How about tonight? I mean…it *is* Friday," she said.

"I don't know, Sunshine…we've only just arrived," he said.

Fully turning towards him, she gave him puppy dog eyes. She knew he was powerless against them. "Please? Pretty please? Pretty please with *me* on top?" she asked cheekily.

Lifting a dark brow, he curled his lips into a sly grin. He rather liked hearing beg, especially when it included a delicious innuendo.

"With you on top?" he asked.

Nodding her head, she leaned in close. Meeting his eyes, she made a point of licking her lips.

"Mmmhmm…take me to the club tonight and when we get home, I'll ride you until you can't even remember your own name," she promised.

Spitting an expletive, Nik felt a shiver run down his spine. A few hours of hell listening to blaring music was well worth that reward.

"Deal," he said.

Smiling in triumph, she gave him a kiss on the cheek. Not only was she going to have the best day with her love, but also the best night. She didn't know how she became so lucky.

"Yay! Good...ok...so...breakfast...then the fjord before the rain comes...and then tonight, The Metro!" she said excitedly. "Gah...we're going to have the best time, I just know it!"

Nodding in agreement, Nik had to chuckle at her enthusiasm. He was sure that she was right. After everything that had just happened, they were due this little bit of happiness.

"Yes we will, my love," he said, leading her down the sidewalk once again. "Yes we will."

CHAPTER TWENTY-FOUR

Pulling her white tank top down her torso, Brynn let out a happy sigh. She had just had the most perfect day with her lover and was excited to see what the night would bring. She had absolutely no idea what a Norwegian nightclub was like but was dying to find out. It would be a good distraction from everything going on in the background.

Leaning towards the bathroom mirror, she wiped a smudge of mascara from under her hazel eyes. Hearing a soft knock on the door, she looked towards its reflection.

"Come in, it's unlocked," she said.

Opening the creaky door to the bathroom, Nik stood in the threshold. Leaning against the door jamb, he raked his gaze over her from head to toe. He needed to thank his assistant for making sure she had black leggings in the clothing order they picked up in New York. They hugged her perfectly.

"Hi, beautiful...are you almost ready?" he asked.

Nodding her head, she grabbed a hair tie from the edge of the sink. Securing it on her wrist, she turned around to face him. She was beyond ready. She couldn't wait to lose herself in electronic music for a few hours.

"Yep," she said, taking her fill of his body filling the doorway. "Mmm...you look good in all black. If I didn't know any better, I'd swear you were a Vampire."

Chuckling under his breath, he righted his posture. Taking a couple of steps towards her, he shrugged his broad shoulders.

"Should I go grab my cape? Really dial it up?" he asked.

Widening her eyes, she gave him a cheeky smile. She suddenly wanted to see what he looked like in full Hollywood Vampire regalia.

"Mmm...and don't forget the top hat and gloves," she said.

"Of course...can't forget those," he replied, giving her a wink. "Oh...I have something to show you before we leave."

Reaching into the back pocket of his jeans, he pulled out a passport. Clearing his throat, he handed her the new identification. He should have had this conversation with her while they were still on the plane, but time had run away with them.

"I should have gone over this with you way before now but...here's your new Norwegian passport. They will check it at the door," he said.

Taking the red booklet, Brynn quickly opened it. Looking over the information page, she lifted her brows in surprise. She didn't know how he was able to procure it, but it definitely looked official. Glancing over the stats, she hummed when she found her name.

"Emilie Astrid Larsen?" she asked.

Nodding his head, Nik nonchalantly reached back into his pocket. "For as long as we live in Norway, this is your new name. Everything you do from now on will be under Emilie. You're Emilie Larsen and I'm Erik Larsen. They're clean identities...we shouldn't have any issues with the Kingdom of Norway sending out their Hunters," he said.

Licking her lips nervously, she met his serious gaze. Not noticing what he had pulled from his pocket, she gave him a curious look.

"So, we're both Larsens? I'm assuming we aren't brother and sister, hmm?" she asked, setting down her passport onto the edge of the sink.

"Definitely not brother and sister...no. As far as the Kingdom is concerned, we are husband and wife," he replied, lifting a two-karat diamond solitaire ring held between his index finger and thumb. "I know this isn't romantic in the least...but if you'll have me, maybe one day Nikolai and Brynn will be married as well."

Looking at the platinum ring, Brynn's eyes widened in shock. Feeling an instant lump in her throat, she stammered for a moment before being able to speak.

"Are you...are you *proposing* right now?" she wondered, her voice breaking.

Hit with a burst of excitement radiating from her aura, Nik spat an internal curse. Fuck. That wasn't his intention. He should have worded that differently. Much differently.

"No...uh, not yet at least. I was just testing the water. Seeing if that was something you might be interested in down the road," he replied.

Visibly disappointed, she let out a sigh. Of course he wasn't proposing. They were standing in a freaking bathroom for God's sake. She shouldn't have tried to put the cart before the horse.

"Oh...well yes. Yes, that is something I would be *very* interested in," she said, glancing back at the ring. "So, I'm taking that this ring is a ring that Erik is giving Emilie?"

Nodding his head, he lifted his lips into an apologetic grin. He really felt like a heel but would make it up to her. Sooner rather than later. Now that he knew that she was open to the idea of getting married.

"Yes...the ring Nikolai gives Brynn will be much more spectacular, I promise," he said.

Taking the platinum band, she slipped it onto the ring finger on her left hand. Holding it up closer to the light, she audibly scoffed. The oval shaped diamond looked flawless; she couldn't imagine a more perfect ring.

"More spectacular than this?" she asked, meeting his dark green eyes. "Wow...well, hell...now I'll really be on pins and needles waiting for Nik to propose properly."

Taking her hand, he brought it to his lips. Kissing her knuckle next to the ring, he made a mental note to find a jeweler as soon as possible. He would normally give a task such as this to Yetta, but it was best if he left her alone until they figured out what was going on with the Elders.

"You won't have to wait long, my love," he promised.

With a pleased smile, she gently squeezed his hand. She could tell by the gleam in his eye that he wasn't lying. But she had a feeling that this would be the longest wait of her life.

"I'd better not be," she teased. "So…does Erik have a ring as well, hmm?"

"Of course he does," he replied, lifting his left hand.

Glancing at his hand, Brynn hummed an approval. It was a thick band of platinum, matching her ring perfectly. The wedding band suited him. Even if it was a ruse.

"Mmm…very nice. Well, Erik, shall we go?" she asked, picking up her passport from the vanity.

Giving her a nod, he motioned to the door with a flick of his chin. Was he looking forward to being in a packed nightclub with young mortals unable to contain their emotions? No. But was he looking forward to the look of pure joy on his love's face as she released pent up fear and frustration? Very much so.

"Yes, my darling Emilie…let's go dance the night away," he replied.

. . .

Walking down the rain slicked sidewalk, Nik gave a quick look at Brynn. She was fiercely typing away on her phone, completely oblivious to the hazards of the uneven path. It was a good thing she was wearing sneakers. Had she gone with the high heels he would be a nervous wreck right now.

"It amazes me that you can text while walking," he said.

Laughing lightly, Brynn finished her rambling sentence. Sending the text with a press of her thumb, she turned her head to look at him.

"And it amazes me that you can't…you old man," she said with a wink.

Chuckling under his breath, he lifted his long arm. Gently draping it over her shoulder, he brought her in close. He really didn't have a comeback for that. But truth be told, he rather liked her little jabs.

"Very funny, my love…how's Jenni?" he asked.

Wrapping her right arm around his waist, she sighed a reply. Even though it was necessary, she felt awful lying to her best friend. She only hoped that one day she would be able to see her again.

"She's better now that I've texted her. She thought I was dead or something…but I told her that you've taken me on an amazing vacation touring Europe this summer for finishing the semester with straight A's. Don is taking her to Ibiza as we speak so she totally bought it…she's hoping that maybe we can meet them in Monaco before the season is over…but I told her that I didn't know what our schedule looks like. Anyways…she knows in alive and happy, so…I donno. I'll miss her, ya know?" she said, frowning slightly.

Brushing his open hand along her upper arm, he nodded his head. He intimately understood how hard it was to lose loved ones. Not due to death, but circumstance. Perhaps there would come a time where they would be able to make that trip to Monaco.

"I know…and I am very sorry…but as long as the security on our phones hold, at least you'll still be able to text and call her…I know it's not the same, but it's something." he said.

"Yeah…yeah, you're right. Although I don't know what I'm going to tell her when the fall semester comes," she replied with a sigh. "Oh, hey…could you hold my phone for me? I don't have a purse."

"Yes, of course," he said, taking her phone and slipping it into the front pocket of his jeans. "And don't worry, we'll come up with something."

Staying quiet for a long moment, she turned her attention to the city street ahead. She really didn't want this to ruin her night. Nik was right, at least she could text and call Jenni. That would have to be enough.

Leading her down the road, Nik felt her suddenly shiver under his touch. Holding her closer, he cursed himself for not suggesting that she wear a jacket. The night air was too cold to be walking around in a thin tank top. Fortunately, the nightclub was dead ahead. No doubt she would warm up on the dance floor.

"We're almost there, my love…it's just the next street over," he said.

"Oh, good," she replied, following him as he picked up the pace. "I hope I can get used to cooler weather, again. This frigid weather is brutal! It's damn near summer, for crying out loud!"

"Don't worry…I'll find ways to keep you warm," he said.

"Mmmm…I do like the sound of that," she replied, wiggling her body suggestively.

Curling his lips into a sly grin, he motioned to the opposite side of the street. Helping her cross the cracked pavement, his mind swirled with a handful of torrid ideas. His fantasies were short lived, however, the moment he caught the line of people huddled in front of the club.

"I think all of Bergen decided to come here, tonight," he said with an internal groan.

Shrugging her shoulders, she looked up at his semi-annoyed face. The thought of standing in line didn't sound so great to her, either. Lucky for them, they didn't necessarily have to.

"I'm sure you could get us right in, hmm?" she said, arching a brow.

Smirking at her, he nodded in agreement. He was glad she had suggested it. This would be the first time she got to witness his Charm in action. Well, this would be the first time where she actually knew he was using it.

"I sure can, Sunshine," he said.

Removing his arm from her shoulder, Nik gently took her hand in his. Leading her to the front entrance of The Metro, he headed straight towards the meathead bouncer guarding the door.

"Just smile and look confident, my love," he whispered to her.

Doing as she was told, Brynn righted her posture and painted a small smile on her face. Toggling her gaze between Nik and the bald bouncer, she tried to pay the other patrons no mind. It was easier said than done, however. She could almost feel them boring holes in the back of her head.

Relaxing his facial features, Nik leaned in close to the muscular man. It wouldn't take much to sway him, he could easily read from the edges of his thoughts that the bouncer couldn't care less about his job. Reaching into the back pocket of his jeans, he pulled out the passports for him to record.

Watching her love intently, Brynn stayed silent as he worked his otherworldly magic. Unable to decipher the Norwegian volleying back and forth, made a mental note to learn the language as quickly as possible. Within a handful of seconds, the bouncer's mood changed from sullen to almost cheerful. Sharing a laugh with Nik, he took a quick look at their passports before jotting down what she could only assume was their passport number on a small tablet.

Taking their identifications from the muscular brute, Nik slipped them back into his pocket. Saying a heartfelt thanks, he squeezed Brynn's hand. Giving her a quick wink, he waited for the bouncer to open the door.

"Ok, we're in my love," he said, lifting his voice above the boom of music slicing through the night's cool air.

'Thank you,' she mouthed silently.

Nodding to both Brynn and the bouncer, Nik helped her through the door of the loud club. Letting out a cleansing sigh, he filtered as much of the radiating energy as he could. Focusing on the rhythmic deep basslines, he snaked her through to the dance floor.

Looking around with wide eyes, Brynn took everything in. The nightclub was pitch black save for a dozen or so LED tube lights crisscrossing the walls. Red and blue in color, they bathed the undulating crowd in ethereal light. At the head of the dance floor stood the DJ. Completely lost in the music, the young man worked the dancers into a frenzy as he brought the crescendo closer.

Gripping her hand tighter, he took her to the center of the floor. Looking around to the frantic dancers flanking them, he gently pushed into their consciousness to give them a small bit of space. Satisfied that he and his love had enough room to move, he couldn't help but smile as he watched her immediately throw herself into a dance.

Still holding onto his hand, Brynn twisted and bounced along to the foreign music. Moving in a half circle to face him, she found his intense eyes in the artificial light.

"Come on! Dance with me!" she yelled.

Reluctantly caving to her demand, Nik followed suit. Slinking to the beat, he abruptly released her hand. Grabbing her by the waist, he pulled her tightly against him. Synchronizing their bodies to the beat, he absorbed some of the maddening energy surrounding them. Using it to clear his mind of everything but the beautiful woman dancing suggestively against him.

Closing her eyes, Brynn threw her head backwards. Becoming lost in the beat, she moaned silently as she felt her lover's hands eagerly roam her body. As the song moved on, his touch grew more and more demanding. With his fingers tugging on her clothes and his nails grazing her exposed skin, an all too familiar ache settled between her thighs.

Bringing his face within a few inches of hers, Nik debated on whether he should creep into her mind. He so desperately wanted to talk to her, to ask her if she wanted him to use his phantom touch to make her cum right then and there. It wouldn't take much. He could tell from her heartbeat that she was already working herself into a frenzy. Deciding to take his chances, he skirted the edges of her mind. Just enough for her to hear him over the music.

Should I make you mine right here?

Suddenly opening her eyes, she met his hungry gaze. Swallowing hard, she blinked up at him with a confused look. *Holy fuck*. Was that really him, or just her overactive imagination?

Lifting his hands to the sides of her flushed face, he stilled both of their bodies. Paying no mind to the chaos writhing around them, he pushed a little deeper into her thoughts.

I can make you cum like this…with just my voice in your head…I did it before…would you like me to do it again?

Spitting a lewd curse, Brynn's knees turn to jelly. Between the heat of his stare and the constant pulse of the music, she was wound incredibly tight. Nodding her head, she happily gave him permission to use his Vampiric talent.

With a sly grin, Nik broke eye contact with his love for a handful of seconds. Glancing around to the dancers surrounding them, he forced them to ignore everything but the animated DJ.

Turning his attention back to her, he cradled her face in his hands. Peering into her eyes, he flirted with her thoughts, bringing up obscene images of what he wanted to do to her once they got home.

Gasping lightly, Brynn's skin pebbled in anticipation. Closing her eyes tightly, her want grew with every lewd scene that slipped into her mind. On the floor, in bed, and in the shower. He fucked her like a wild animal, taking her in positions that made her head spin. Moaning and begging for more aloud, she melted as she felt him press his forehead to hers.

Oh…you like that, don't you? He mentally purred. *I bet you're so wet right now…mmmm…I can't wait to taste you when we get home.*

Purposefully holding her in sensory overload, Nik set to work. Not giving her time to process his words, he slinked deeper into her thoughts. Slowing down the racy visions, he allowed her to latch onto her favorite one.

Whimpering loudly, Brynn lifted her hands to grasp his wrists. Using them to ground herself, she mentally slipped into the racy scene. After a few quick seconds the chaotic world around her fell away. Leaving her a squirming mess on the floor of their tiny kitchen.

Keeping her locked in her dream, he used his supernatural touch to mimic what was happening in the fantasy. Sending a wave of pleasure towards her clit, he quickly withdrew it. Again and again, in time with her dream Nikolai's cock.

Such a good girl, he praised, using his energy to relentlessly toy with her, blurring her line between dream and reality.

Writhing on the uneven wood planks in her mind, she squealed as her phantom lover pounded into her pussy. Wrapping her arms around him, she clawed her nails into his back. Getting lost in the hazy moment, she wantonly begged for more. The pleasure building within her cunt felt incredible. She was afraid that he would stop.

No, don't worry, he said, reading every single thought. *I won't stop until you break for me.*

Watching her face twist with each imaginary flick of her clit, Nik ignored his own lust begging for release. Reminding himself that he would have his way once they returned home, he focused everything he had on the mewling woman before him.

Do you want more? he teased, his voice deep with need.

Unable to reply, Brynn nodded her head. Before she realized what was happening, a sharp vibration centered over her pink clit. Working in tandem with her dream lover's thick cock as it slammed in and out of her wet pussy, she lost all semblance of control. Falling over the edge of her release, she cried out from the intense pleasure as it coursed through her body.

Turned on by the sight of her cumming from nothing more than his suggestion, Nik leaned in possessively. Claiming her lips in a hungry kiss, he rode out her orgasm with her. To his shock, her intensity spilled over, causing him to suddenly cum in his jeans.

Growling against her lips, he eased her back into the present. Dropping his hands from her face, he wrapped his arms around her waist and held her close. Listening to her heartbeat as it began to settle, he shivered as his own release flatlined. He had never experienced anything like that before, it filled him with awe.

Holy fuck, Brynn…that was beautiful…you're so fucking beautiful, he praised, not willing to break his mental connection just yet.

Returning his desperate kiss, Brynn wrapped her arms around his neck. Slowly her fantasy evaporated, and the nightclub returned. Suddenly *very* aware of where they were, she pulled away from his lips. Looking around, it took her a few seconds to realize that no one was looking at them. She wondered if it was another one of his dream worlds.

Oh, this is real, Brynn…don't worry, I had them look away. No one knows what just happened. It's our little secret.

Blinking at him, she mouthed an 'oh.' She was grateful that he had done that. She probably looked ridiculous just shaking and screaming for no apparent reason.

Paying no mind to the music as it swelled, Nik continued to hold her in his arms. Placing his mouth to the shell of her ear, he finally spoke to her using his real voice.

"How do you feel?" he asked, lifting his voice so she could hear him.

Pulling back to look at his handsome face, Brynn gave him a satisfied smile. "Amazing!" she yelled, exaggerating her mouth to make sure he understood. "And thirsty! Oh…so damn thirsty!"

Nodding his head, Nik set her feet down upon the ground. He had a feeling that she would be. He could feel her temperature rising with every rapid breath. Motioning to the bar at the back of the club, he met her glassy eyes.

"Let's get you some water," he said.

Only hearing the word 'water,' Brynn gave him an enthusiastic thumbs up. Taking his outstretched hand, she let him lead her through the packed dance floor. With her body still buzzing and her thoughts filled with nothing but the images of refreshing water, she was completely oblivious to the pair of ice blue eyes that had been watching her and her lover the entire time.

CHAPTER TWENTY-FIVE

Muffling her laugh as best as she could, Brynn hugged Nik's arm as they headed home. It was early in the morning, nearing three o'clock. They had stayed at the nightclub until closing, then she had talked him into going to a bar near the University for a drink. One nightcap had turned into two. Two into four. She was about to order a fifth when he had rightfully put his foot down.

Suffice it to say, she was a wee bit intoxicated. Hovering in that sweet spot where she felt invincible and free. She couldn't wait to get home and physically do all the things Nik had mentally done to her on the dance floor. She had been thinking about it nonstop all night.

"Fuck…I'm…I'm gonna…ride you sooooo hard when we get homeee," she said, her words slurring at the seams.

Chuckling under his breath, Nik carefully led her down the final street to their row house. As much as he wanted to believe her, he had a feeling that she would be spending most of the day either passed out in bed or hugging the toilet. She wouldn't be riding his cock anytime soon. He shouldn't have let her have those last couple shots of akvavit.

"Let's just get you home, my love. I'm very glad you had such a good night," he said, keeping his voice low.

Stumbling slightly, she squeezed his arm for leverage. Recovering quickly, she giggled at her clumsiness. It was a good thing she was wearing sneakers. She would've broken her ankle five times over by now had she gone with the high heels.

Slowing his steps, Nik looked at her with concern as she righted herself. He had wanted to carry her home, but she had stubbornly refused. He really wished he hadn't listened to her protests.

"Are you ok?" he asked.

Nodding her head, she attempted to focus her eyes on his face. Although it took a few seconds, she was finally able to force her double vision into one. He was so cute when he was concerned. No one had ever cared about her the way he did.

God. She really loved him.

"Mmm…yess…of course I'm ok. Neverrrr better…are we…are we almost homeee?" she asked with a small hiccup.

Humming lightly, he lifted his free hand to point towards the end of the street. Their little blue house wasn't far, perhaps ninety meters away.

"We are, it's just right down the road…another minute or two and we'll be home safe," he said with a grin.

Furrowing her brow, she mumbled an unintelligible reply. Something about needing to get inside to get away from the Hunter. She thought she might have seen one at the nightclub, but Nik wasn't concerned in the least. She brushed the fear away after that. If he wasn't scared, then she didn't have a reason to be either. Still, she would feel much better once they were tucked away in their little love nest.

Not understanding a word of her drunken gibberish, Nik debated on whether he should skim into her thoughts. But there really wasn't any point. He could tell just from the look on her face that her mind was spinning.

"Alright…just a few more steps, my love," he assured.

Being as careful as her heavy legs allowed, she followed his lead down the last handful of yards. Turning onto the stone path leading to their front door, she let out a happy sigh once they reached their modest porch.

"Mmm…home sweettt homee," she muttered, releasing the hold on his arm.

Leaning in towards her, Nik gave her a quick kiss on the forehead before dipping into his front pocket for the keys. Home sweet home, indeed.

Smiling from the sweet gesture, Brynn watched him intently as he fished for the keys. Suddenly very jealous, she let out a loud snort.

"It's not fair! Why do men have the best pocketsss? Hmm? Look! You've got our keysss…our passportsss…our phonesss…hell, even my chapstick!" she exclaimed, roughly patting her own thighs. "What do I have…hmm? Nothing. It'sss not fair!"

Pulling the keys from his denim jeans, he gave her a sympathetic look. She wasn't wrong. Modern pockets were a marvelous thing, they shouldn't only be reserved for men's garments. Like most things in the mortal world, it wasn't fair.

"I know, my beautiful Brynn…I know," he replied, unlocking the wooden door and helping her inside. "If you want, I can find a tailor here who can modify your pants to give you some extra pockets…how does that sound?"

Gasping lightly, she turned her wobbly body towards him as she shut the door behind them. Ugh, he was just the sweetest. She couldn't stand it. It was such a turn-on.

Raising her arms, she placed her open hands on his chest. Pushing against him, she pressed him against the plastered wall. Running her touch over his torso, she batted her eyelashes in an attempt to flirt.

"You're sooooo fucking hottt, do you know that?" she asked.

Tilting his head, Nik couldn't help but smirk. He hadn't ever seen her quite this drunk. He knew he probably shouldn't be thinking it, but she was quite adorable.

"Oh yeah?" he replied cheekily, enjoying the way her fingers roamed over his chest.

"Mmmhmmm," she replied.

Not wanting to waste any more time, Brynn pressed her body to his. Dancing her hands upwards, she wrapped her arms around his neck. Steadying her wobbly movements, she leaned up to press her lips to his in an eager kiss.

Grinning against her lips, he laughed internally. She was sloppy and clumsy, all tongue and teeth. He loved her excitement, but knew she needed to calm herself before she became sick. Gently grabbing her waist, he returned her kiss. Softly and tenderly, guiding her into a simple game of give and take meant to calm her dizzy head.

Moaning lightly, she melted against him. Loving every swipe of his tongue and press of his full lips, she felt her need spike once again. Kissing him again and again, she felt a sudden pain in her lower abdomen. Furrowing her brow as her lips moved with his, it took her a long moment to realize the source of her ache wasn't radiating from her cunt. Pulling away abruptly, she took in a large breath.

"I'm sooo sorry...I gotta pee," she said.

Giving her a knowing look, Nik dropped his hands from her waist. Of course she had to use the bathroom, she hadn't gone all night. It was another facet of mortality that he didn't miss one single bit.

"Do you need me to walk you?" he asked.

Releasing her hold on his neck, she shook her head. She was quite capable of walking to the bathroom by herself. Her feet still worked just fine.

"No...no...stayyyy here...I'll be right back...thennn...then you can fuck me against that wall...like you sh...showed me inn the club," she replied.

With a nod, he looked at her fondly. She was in no condition to be fucked against the wall, but he would wait for her to return. A few more minutes of light passion and she would be ready to pass out.

They could carry out that particular fantasy when the alcohol had worn off.

"Ok, my love…I'll stay right here," he said.

"Good boyyy!" she praised, turning towards the hallway. "I'll be backkk in a sec!"

Watching her as she stumbled towards the bathroom, Nik brushed his dark hair from his eyes. Taking the time to still his own lust, he instantly froze as a familiar laugh echoed through his mind. It was sultry and dark, full of luscious sin and vicious intent. A sound he once thought he would never tire of hearing.

Looking at the door, he felt a phantom dagger slice through his heart. The sudden realization of who was on their porch slapped him across the face. It wasn't a Hunter Brynn had seen in the nightclub. What she had seen was far, far worse. Why the fuck hadn't he felt her before now?

Hearing a light rap at the door, Nik swallowed hard. With his entire body tensing, his mind raced as to what he should do. Not that it would matter. He was essentially powerless. How could he have been so foolish as to think she wouldn't come? Once again, he had failed to keep his love safe from the monsters he vowed to protect her from.

"Nikolai…open the door," the feminine voice purred.

Unable to disobey the command, he reluctantly inched forward. His brain was screaming, trying desperately to break the invisible bond tethering him to the woman behind the wooden door. It was all for naught, however. Fighting her was futile.

Grabbing the brass knob, he twisted his wrist harshly. Yanking open the carved door, he winced slightly as his serpentine eyes settled upon the raven haired beauty before him. Seeing her in the flesh took his breath away and filled him with utter contempt. He wasn't prepared for what was about to happen. Neither was Brynn.

"Natalia…don't you dare," he warned, his voice gruff with pain.

Letting her eyes roam up and down her Novice's body, Natalia slowly brought her gaze to his chiseled face. Clicking her tongue against the roof of her mouth, she leaned in towards him. After all their years together, he knew better than to try to assert any type of dominance over her.

"Niky," she tisked, narrowing her light blue eyes. "We've been apart for far too long. It seems as if you've forgotten who is in charge. Now be a good boy and invite me in."

Baring his sharp teeth, he let out an angry hiss. It was a childish display, the Vampire equivalent to a pout against their Sire. But it was the only way he could show his displeasure over her sudden appearance.

Rolling her kohl rimmed eyes, Natalia placed her hands upon her curvy hips. It was good to see that he was still a pissy little thing in need of training. She would gladly reteach him, once everything was said and done.

"Yes…yes…I know…now let me in before I get upset and take my frustration out on your new toy," she warned, dropping her voice low.

Knowing full well that the bitch wouldn't think twice about hurting Brynn out of spite, Nik instantly caved. It was imperative that he watch himself from here on out. He was intimately aware of how his Sire operated. One wrong move and she would snap.

"Natalia. Please come in," he said curtly, moving to the side of the door to give her room.

Letting out an exasperated sigh, Natalia crossed the threshold of her Novice's quaint little home. Brushing past him in a flourish of crimson satin and lace, she glided into the center of the narrow foyer. Facing him as he closed the door behind her, she clapped her manicured hands together.

"Wonderful. So… I assume you know why I'm here?" she asked

nonchalantly.

Taking a step towards his Sire, Nik twisted his hardened face into a snarl. It had been careless of him to think they were safe in Bergen. He had made so many mistakes, and Brynn would be paying for them all.

"Don't do this, Natalia…please," he said.

"Aww, Niky…now as much as I love to hear you beg…you know I have to do this. Ulysses ordered me to bring her back to the Manor. I must do his bidding just as you have to do mine. It's all one insane circle jerk, hmm? Meh…no matter. I would have done this without his orders. How *dare* you hide her from us…after everything we have done for you!" she chided.

"I hid her because I know what you animals will do to her!" he growled angrily.

With a wicked laugh, she folded her arms over her ample chest. My, how self-righteous he had become. As if he was any different. No matter how hard he tried to deny it, they were all cut from the same demonic cloth.

"No…you hid her because you wanted to keep her all to yourself, Nikolai," she replied, matching the venom in his voice. "I can *smell* her blood in your veins…you want her magic all to yourself. You selfish bastard!"

Shaking his head, he balled his hands into tight fists at his sides. She didn't have a clue what she was talking about.

"I hid her because I love her…and I'll be damned if the Clan tears her apart the way they did Leona," he spat bitterly.

Huffing incredulously, Natalia took half a step closer to him. Plastering a disgusted look on her beautiful face, she couldn't help but bristle. He was such a foolish fop.

"You love her? Nikolai! You barely know her! Admit it, she meant *nothing* to you until you tasted her and found out what she was...and instead of sharing her with us...*your family,* you took it upon yourself to hide her from us! You've always wanted to be more than your station allowed and this was your chance! You wanted her power all for yourself!" she hissed.

Clearing the space to his Sire, he leaned down to look her in her eyes. Wanting so desperately to wrap his hands around her neck, he forced himself to contain his anger as best as he could.

"That's not true! You know noth—," he said, stopping mid-sentence as he heard Brynn emerge from the bathroom.

"Fuck," he whispered.

Perking at the sound of the Sun Walker's shuffled footsteps, Natalia whipped around to face the hallway. It was a good thing the girl was so drunk, she wouldn't be able to put up much of an initial fight. Not that being sober would've made a lick of difference, but she really wanted to get back to the Manor as quickly as possible.

Stumbling down the hall, Brynn braced her hand upon the wall as she walked. She thought she had heard another voice alongside Nik's, but that was impossible. Brushing it off as a figment of her imagination, she rounded the corner into the foyer. Opening her mouth to say something sexy, she let out a gasp instead as she noticed a gorgeous woman next to her love.

"What the hell?" she said softly.

"Hello, Brynn," Natalia said sweetly. "It's so good to finally meet you."

Moving her blurry gaze back and forth between the mystery woman and Nik, Brynn felt all the blood drain from her face. She had never seen him look more livid, or more terrified.

It instantly sobered her up.

"Who...who are you?" she asked nervously, her voice audibly shaking.

Unfolding her arms, Natalia slinked over to the terrified girl. Fully aware of Nikolai following, she paid him no mind. He couldn't stop what was about to happen even if he tried.

"Who am I? Why…my name is Natalia. I'm sure Nikolai has told you about me. Hasn't he? I mean…I am his former wife and Sire, after all…I made him what he is, today," she said, reaching out to brush a damp lock of hair from Brynn's startled face. "You're welcome, by the way."

Silenced by fear, Brynn felt a painful lump in her throat. Trembling as Natalia continued to play with her hair, she looked at Nik with pleading eyes. Within seconds she felt the edge of a panic attack starting to take root. With her heart racing and her breath hitching, her body went into a fawn trauma response. Much like it had during Anton's assault.

Hearing the Sun Walker's blood rush through her veins, Natalia gave her a satisfied grin. The girl's reaction gave her a boost of confidence. The poor thing was incredibly frightened, there was no doubt that Nikolai had told her stories. It was clear that she was still lodged under her Novice's skin. Perhaps there was hope for them yet.

"Mmm…I knew it. Well, I assure you…everything he has told you about me and our Clan is true," she said, her voice warm and sultry.

"Natalia," Nik hissed in warning.

Glancing over her shoulder, she gave him a scathing look. "What, Nikolai? What are you going to do? Oh, that's right…nothing. Now keep your mouth shut, my dear boy…I'm trying to have a conversation with your newest little slut," she said.

Sneering at his Sire, Nik was forced to bite his tongue. Brynn wanted him to save her, he didn't have to read her thoughts to know. It was written on her face as plain as day. It tore him to pieces that he couldn't. He hated feeling so powerless.

Willing her sluggish legs to move, Brynn's frustration bubbled as she was barely able to scoot an inch. Toggling her gaze between Nik and Natalia, she was at a loss as to what she should do. Not that there was anything for her to do.

"Why...why are...you here?" she asked, somehow able to squeak out a question.

"Ah...well, I'm positive you already know why I'm here, Brynn...but I'll oblige you with an answer. I'm here to collect you and bring you back to the Manor to meet our Clan. Now...Nikolai has probably told you stories about Leona, our other Sun Walker, and how we tortured her into madness...blah, blah, blah," she said, waving her hand in the air. "And while all of that is true...Ulysses and Christos want to do something a little different with you."

Moving his intense stare from Brynn to Natalia, Nik clenched his jaw. He didn't like the sound of that.

"You see...we haven't had any excitement within the Clan for a very, very long time. The Elders are bored...they see this as a perfect opportunity to liven things up, so to speak. So...there's to be a Hunt!" she said excitedly, glancing at her Novice. "Remember our Hunts, Niky? Mmm...we made some fond memories during those Hunts, didn't we? Well...I'm looking forward to making more with this one. The reward will be so much sweeter...instead of the restoring blood of a pure and innocent virgin, the winning pair will enjoy the magical blood of a Sun Walker! Isn't that a wonderful prize? And of course...I plan on being on that winning team, don't you worry."

"Helen forbade us from carrying out Hunts over a century ago," Nik said, narrowing his eyes.

Shrugging her shoulders, Natalia placed a hand on her hip. "Ulysses and Christos haven't been able to contact Helen...they presume that she's dead. As such, her rules over our Clan no longer apply," she said simply.

Knowing that Natalia had been given false information, Nik felt the tiniest glimmer of hope. If Ulysses and Christos upheld the rules of past Hunts to this one, there was a chance he could save Brynn. It was small, but there.

Her fate was no longer so bleak.

Pausing for a moment before continuing, Natalia reached out to touch Brynn's freckled cheek. She hated to admit that she could see why Nikolai was attracted to her. She fit the new, modern standard of beauty. It made her jealousy spike.

"So that's why I'm here, sweet Sun Walker...and I'm wasting precious time. Let's get on with this, shall we?" she asked, dropping her hand to point at the familiar necklace gracing Brynn's neck. "Take that off, Nikolai. She is no longer your *Mate* and no longer under your protection."

With a pained look on his face, Nik waited until his Sire had moved to the side. Unable to override her command, he walked to his love. Brushing her wavy hair over her shoulders, he went to unclasp his necklace. Locking eyes with her, he tried his best to soothe her fears. Her alarmed pleas were a million knives to the heart.

"It will be ok," he whispered, slowing his fingers to buy him time to talk. "I will come for you...I promise."

With tears welling in her eyes, Brynn whimpered in agony. She wanted to believe him but the alcohol still in her system was filling her with doubt. He hadn't saved her from Anton and now Natalia. He wouldn't be able to save her from his entire Clan.

"I promise. I will come for you," he repeated softly, pocketing his family crest.

Rolling her blue eyes, Natalia stomped her heeled boot onto the wooden floor. His empty, albeit romantic, words were sickening at best. Though it was nice to know that Nikolai was still all talk. Very rarely was he able to keep his word, but it would be fun if Brynn believed his brave declaration.

"Ugh…enough already. Put her to sleep, Nikolai. Time is short and Ulysses is an impatient man," she said.

Reluctantly lifting his hands, Nik cradled Brynn's face just as he had a hundred times before. Although physically silent, her mind was screaming, begging him not to let her go. Over and over again, causing him to shake with a burning rage. Snaking into his love's consciousness, he forced himself to calm his emotions. He couldn't add to her pain.

'Shhh…don't cry. Everything is going to be ok,' he whispered into her thoughts. 'You won't be afraid when you wake up…you'll be filled with anger and hatred. I need you to take my gifted fire and fight with it, Brynn. Fight with everything you have. Don't give up. I will come for you. I love you more than you know. Nothing will stop me from saving you. Satan could unleash all his demons and even they wouldn't stop me. Believe me…believe me. I love you.'

Lulled by his otherworldly gifts, Brynn let out a sigh. After a handful of heartbeats, she felt a wave of exhaustion crash into her. Closing her red rimmed eyes, she faded into a colorful dreamland. One filled with serenity and peace, erasing all her harbored fears.

Watching her as she slipped into a blissful sleep, Nik caught her before her body fell to the ground. Tenderly hugging her against his torso, he pressed a handful of kisses against her temple. With contempt etching deep lines on his otherwise handsome face, he spit a dark vow into the heavy air.

"I *will* find a way to kill you," he growled, turning to face his Sire. "I will kill all of you."

Smirking at her former husband, Natalia waved off his idle threat. He was nothing more than an annoying puppy. All bark and no bite.

"Promises, promises Nikolai…now hand her to me," she said, reaching out her arms.

Giving Brynn one last kiss, Nik leaned down and eased her into

Natalia's arms. Frowning as his Sire immediately threw her over her shoulder like a sack of potatoes, he once again bared his sharp teeth.

"You will regret this, Natalia," he spat.

Meeting his livid gaze, Natalia gave Brynn a firm slap on the ass for his insolence. She wouldn't regret a damn thing. Once she had a good dose of Sun Walker blood, Nikolai would be the one lamenting over his threats. Although it was forbidden for a Sire to destroy their Novice, she had a feeling Ulysses would be more than willing to look the other way.

Hell, he might even help her.

"You know, Nikolai...if you truly loved her, you would've turned her when you had the chance," she said.

Leaving him with that parting thought, Natalia raised her free hand. Snapping her fingers together, she used her demonic gift to tear an interdimensional rift into the air behind her. Falling backwards into the abyss, it swallowed her and the Sun Walker whole. Leaving Nikolai completely alone with only his regrets to wallow in.

CHAPTER TWENTY-SIX

Groaning as the last tendrils of her dream slipped away, Brynn slowly opened her eyes. Lifting her buzzing head from the satin pillowcase, she glanced around her new surroundings in a small panic. The room was large and windowless, its darkly painted walls draped with heavy tapestries. Each depicting demonic creatures in various woodland settings. Chasing mythical unicorns and naked damsels.

Separating each medieval tapestry were golden wall sconces, holding a trio of pillar candles. Their flickering flames bathed the room in an eerie light that made the hair on the back of her neck stand up on end. She suddenly felt as if she was in the middle of some gothic horror story. Just waiting for the monsters to come and tear her apart.

Swallowing hard, she hesitantly wiggled her body over the soft mattress of the four-poster bed. Tucked inside a velvet comforter, she was shocked to find that she was completely free of any restraints. She didn't know why she wasn't tied to a gurney, like Leona had been. As far as she could tell, her accommodation was luxurious. Not the hellish dungeon Nik had warned her about. Why was she being treated better than the previous Sun Walker?

The question left her with a sour taste in her mouth.

Watching Brynn from the corner of the room, Natalia let out an annoyed sigh. Continuing to file her nails into sharp points, she adjusted herself in the oversized armchair. *Finally,* she thought. She was beginning to think Nikolai had put her in a coma.

"Good morning, sleeping beauty," she said, her tone thick and condescending. "It's about time you woke up. I've been waiting for nearly twenty-four bloody hours. Do you know how boring it is to watch a mortal sleep? Especially one that's sleeping off alcohol? Ugh…and the snoring! My God! Did you know that you sound like a pregnant sow when you snore? Hmm?"

Immediately pulling herself into a seated position, Brynn looked towards Natalia. Focusing her eyes on her, she felt a mixture of fear and anger gnaw at her stomach. She hated the woman. She wanted nothing more than to hurl an insult right back at her but knew it wouldn't be wise.

"Where am I?" she asked instead.

Finishing the nail of her index finger, Natalia dropped the glass emery board on the side table beside her. Waving at the room with her hands, she lifted a dark brow.

"Isn't it obvious? You're in our guest suite," she answered.

"Oh. So, I'm a guest, then?" Brynn asked flippantly.

Chuckling under her breath, Natalia stood from the armchair. Slowly walking towards the bed, she made a point to click her heels with every deliberate step.

"No...I wouldn't call you that. I voted to throw you in the cellar with all the other vermin. Lucky for you, the majority of the Clan didn't feel the same...Christos seems to believe your blood will taste sweeter if you're treated well," she said with a shrug.

Inching backwards towards the mahogany headboard, Brynn tensed as Natalia stalked closer. She wished she had something to defend herself with. She didn't like the look behind the Vampire's pale blue eyes.

"And you don't buy into that belief?" she asked.

Taking a seat on the edge of the bed, Natalia ran the palm of her hand over the velvet comforter. Shaking her head, she lifted her red lips into a half grin.

"I couldn't care less what your blood tastes like, dear Sun Walker...I only care about the power it allows. *That*...is what I want. I am very much looking forward to it," she replied.

Gasping lightly as Natalia grazed her calf with her touch, Brynn instinctively brought her legs to her chest. Wrapping her arms around them, she dared her anger to surpass her fear. Nik wouldn't want her to be afraid. He wanted her to fight. At least that's what she thought she remembered him saying.

"And what makes you so sure you'll get it?" she asked, lifting her chin in defiance.

Smirking at the girl before her, Natalia scooted her body closer. Catching a sharp uptick in her heartbeat, she felt her hunger spike.

"Mmmm...well...probably the fact that I've won the last thirteen Hunts we've had. Well...technically Nikolai and I won them together but...eh...I can Hunt just as well solo, so I'm not concerned," she said.

Furrowing her brow, Brynn felt an ice-cold shiver run down her spine. "Nik...he...he participated in the Hunts?" she asked, her voice shaking slightly.

Nodding her head, a pleased look passed over her face. Although Nikolai now thought of himself as somehow superior, there was a time where he was just as evil and depraved as she. Brynn really had no clue what kind of demon she had let into her bed.

"Of course he did! He was the one who lured the girls to us...how could they resist his Charm, hmm? So yes...we hunted together and won together...and then we would take their innocence and their blood together...there really is nothing like virgin cunt and virgin blood," she said, smiling wistfully. "Mmm...those were the years we were truly happy. Sometimes I miss them."

Twisting her features in disgust, Brynn fought back a wave of nausea. She didn't want to believe that the man she loved was capable of something so vile. Not once had he ever been anything less than a gentleman. Natalia was simply lying to get under her skin. She had to be.

"He hates you," she spat.

"Yeah? Well...there's a very fine line between love and hate. He'll come around...eventually," Natalia replied.

Pressing her lips together, Brynn began to seethe. No way in hell would Nik ever crawl back to the bitch sitting next to her.

"Over my dead body," she found herself saying.

Letting out a small snicker, Natalia lifted her index finger to her nose. Giving it a gentle tap with her nail, she then pointed to Brynn.

"Yes, exactly...over your dead body, Brynn. You see...sooner or later...and I'm betting on sooner...you will die. And I'll be there to soothe his poor broken heart," she said.

Narrowing her eyes, Brynn shook her head in disbelief. Nik wouldn't crawl back to his Sire if she was the last woman on earth.

"You can shake your head all you want, Sun Walker...but I've known Nikolai since he was a mortal of sixteen. I made him a man...and then I made him immortal. I am his God. Naturally, I want him to come back to me on his own accord but...seeing how angry this is making you? Mmm...I'm halfway tempted to drag his ass back here and make him fuck me while you watch," she said.

Clenching her jaw, Brynn stopped herself from screaming at the smug bitch. She knew that Natalia had the power to follow through with her little threat. There had to be a way to break Nik's bond to her. Yetta said it was possible to kill Vampires. What did she have to do? Cut off the head, stake the heart, burn the body? She could do that.

Yes. She could do that.

Staring at the Sun Walker, Natalia studied the girl's freckled face. She could tell she was stewing. The small twitch in the corner of her right eye gave her away. It was good of her to keep her mouth shut. She had promised the Elders not to lay a finger on her, but the temptation to break her word was growing stronger by the minute.

"Yes...I think I will do that. After Ulysses and I have won you in the Hunt. What a wonderful reward that will be. It'll feel so good to break you...to break *both* of you. And then...once we've all had our fill of your blood and you begin to wither...I'll have Nikolai rip your pretty little head from your neck," she purred, lifting her crimson lips into a shit eating grin.

"Just as I made him do to Leona."

Instantly stunned, Brynn's hazel eyes open wide. She had forced Nik to kill Leona? Now it all made sense why he harbored such guilt, such self-hatred. Not just over ending Leona's suffering, but of every heinous act done under her influence. Natalia was the true monster, not him.

"You're disgusting," Brynn hissed.

Nodding in agreement, Natalia took the compliment to her black heart. Wanting to make a witty retort, she pushed out a sigh instead as she felt a familiar presence outside the chamber door. Reluctantly standing from the bed, she addressed the girl one last time.

"We'll continue this after the Hunt, hmm? Then I can show you just how disgusting I can be," she said, annoyed that their time together had come to an end.

Looking from Natalia to the door, Brynn suddenly tensed. Squeezing her legs to her chest, she held her breath as the door slowly opened. Within a split second the outline of two tall silhouettes came into view. Although she had never met the pair, she instinctively knew who they were by the way Natalia curtseyed herself all the way to the floor.

"Ulysses, Christos...I have done what you have asked of me," Natalia said softly.

Gliding into the room first, Christos clapped his hands in approval.

Waiting for a moment for Ulysses to follow, he headed straight towards the girls with a bounce in his step.

"We knew you would be successful, Natalia," he said, helping her stand to full height. "We're so proud of you, aren't we Ulysses?"

Nodding curtly, Ulysses hummed low. Moving to stand beside her, he lifted his hand to touch her rounded cheek. Reverently caressing her skin, he met her eyes. There was never any doubt that his gorgeous Novice would be successful. Not once in nearly six centuries had she ever let him down.

"Good girl…now go wait for me in my chambers, Talia. I just received your gift for a job well done. Your new Shenzhen Nongke Orchid will look stunning in your collection," he said.

Gasping audibly, a genuine smile lit up Natalia's face. She had been begging her Sire to make the Shenzhen Nongke Group cultivate a Shenzhen Nongke Orchid for her for years. It made her giddy to know she finally had one of the beautiful blooms.

"Ah! Thank you, Sire! Thank you!" she squealed, turning her head to kiss his fingers.

"You're very welcome, my Child. Now go. Enjoy your reward. I'll join you shortly," he said.

Nodding her head, Natalia gave him a loving look before glancing at Christos. Bowing her head to the other Elder, she quickly took her leave. Not bothering to say anything to Brynn, she all but danced towards the door. Leaving the trio alone to discuss the Hunt in privacy.

Wincing slightly as the door closed behind Natalia, Brynn nervously glanced back and forth between Ulysses and Christos. Breathing hard, her anxiety came back with a vengeance. They both looked like they wanted to devour her.

Tossing his sandy blonde hair over his shoulder, Christos raked his honey-colored eyes over the frightened Sun Walker. Wanting to soothe

the girl, he gingerly climbed into the bed next to her. There was plenty of time for her to worry later.

"Shhh...don't be frightened. We aren't here to hurt you...we just want to talk," he said, moving his lithe body under the covers. "Now where are our manners? Hello, I'm Christos and this is Ulysses. We're the Elders of our Clan. We've been so looking forward to meeting you."

Momentarily freezing as Christos snaked his arm around her, Brynn began to dissociate. Mentally slipping into another world, she was yanked back by Nik's words echoing in her head. With her fear turning to sharp anger, she pushed the Vampire off her. Using her closed fists, she landed a few quick punches against his stone-like torso.

"GET OFF OF ME!" she screamed.

Giggling at her weak attempt, Christos gave a quick nod to Ulysses.

Taking his permission, Ulysses lunged towards the girl with a cat-like grace. Finding her throat with his open hand, he slammed her against the wooden headboard. Purposefully squeezing the wind from her, he leaned in close, forcing her to meet his dark eyes.

"Careful girl...how you behave now determines how I treat you after the Hunt," he warned.

Baring her teeth at the ancient Vampire, Brynn continued to fight. Squirming under his strong hand, she clawed at his arm. Scratching at any bit of alabaster skin as she could. His physical and verbal threats didn't scare her in the least.

Growling at the hellcat, Ulysses flashed his own sharp teeth. Shaking his head in warning, he boxed in his rising lust. As laughable as her little display was, he always loved it when they fought back. He couldn't wait to savor her blood as it passed over his greedy tongue.

Not caring for how red Brynn's face was becoming, Christos huffed critically under his breath. Reaching for Ulysses' wrist, he urged him to ease his hold. While he adored his Roman lover's confidence that he would be the winner, he simply wasn't correct. Natalia didn't have a chance against his Anton. The Sun Walker was as good as his.

"Not to worry, dear Brynn...*I* will be the first one to taste you. But Ulysses is right...you *must* calm down. We will get nowhere if you don't. Now...he's going to let you go and you're going to be as sweet to us as can be, hmm?" he said, his tone surprisingly gentle.

Blinking back warm tears, Brynn was only able to whimper a reply. She hated feeling so helpless, but what other choice did she have? She was truly at their mercy.

"Mmm...good girl," Christos praised, cuddling his body against hers. "Now let go, Ulysses."

Giving her neck one last squeeze for good measure, Ulysses obliged his other half. Releasing his hold, he stood to full height beside the bed. A dark smirk lifting his thin lips.

Gasping for much needed air, Brynn closed her bloodshot eyes. Lifting a shaky hand, she brushed her fingertips over her bruised neck. She was trying so hard not to cry. She didn't want to give them the satisfaction.

"Ohhh...there, there beautiful girl," Christos said, effortlessly pulling her onto his lap. "I'm so sorry we had to do that...but you left us with no choice, hmm? So, really...that was your fault. But I'm sure you won't let it happen again, will you?"

Remaining silent, Brynn shivered as he cradled her body against his. Slowly opening her eyes, she looked upwards. She wanted so desperately to spit in his angelic face but valued her life more. She wished she had some way to defend herself. Why the hell hadn't Nik turned her?

"Mmmhmm," she replied.

Holding her in faux reverence, Christos rocked her as a mother rocks their child.

"You're very valuable to us, Brynn...I hope you know that," he said, brushing his glazed lips over the crown of her head. "And yes...I know the Hunt sounds scary, but I assure you, it will be great fun! But we will discuss all of that tomorrow at the Gathering."

"The Gathering?" Brynn asked, her voice hoarse and strained.

Nodding his head, he nuzzled her once again. Breathing in her intoxicating scent, he locked his bright eyes on the statuesque man before them. Sending him a mental image of the lascivious way he intended on taking the Sun Walker once he won her.

"Mmmm...yes, the Gathering," he purred, taking pride in the way Ulysses' face hardened. "We've summoned all our Children back to the Manor to meet you. They will be here tomorrow night and they're all very excited...but don't you worry that pretty little head of yours, you'll be the guest of honor...no one will touch you. Except for Ulysses and me, of course."

Scrunching her face, Brynn tried in vain not to let her fear get the best of her. She was about to be surrounded by God knows how many Vampires, all of whom wanted to make her their very own personal juice box. How could she not worry?

"It's then that we will go over the rules for the Hunt...they're pretty simple...straightforward. Just a game of cat and mouse, really. I actually have an inkling that you'll like it," Christos continued.

Letting out a sigh, Ulysses moved his gaze from the Sun Walker to his counterpart. Per usual, Christos was talking too much. They had seen her, instilled a little bit of fear. Their task for the night was complete. It was time they retired to their chambers. Quickly. Before the morning broke.

"Christos," he said flatly.

Narrowing his eyes, Christos gave him an annoyed look. He knew it was time to leave, but she felt so good in his arms. Reminding himself that he would get his fill of her in two nights' time, he begrudgingly removed her from his lap.

"Ugh. Fine," he said, gracefully pulling her from his lap and climbing out of the bed. "Well, precious Sun Walker...it's time that we say goodnight. We'll come back at sundown. There is water and some biscuits on the table by the chair...there's a chamber pot under the bed. Although you will try, you'll find it unable to break the lock on the door. Our advice to you is to just rest. Conserve your energy. You'll need it."

Scooting towards the middle of the mattress, Brynn eyed the Vampires as they walked towards the door. Watching them leave filled her with instant relief. It wasn't much of a reprieve, perhaps ten hours at the most, but it was something. It would give her just enough time to mentally prepare herself for what was to come.

Opening the heavy wooden door, Ulysses allowed Christos to walk ahead. Glancing over his shoulder at Brynn, he lifted a black brow. He didn't know why Nikolai hadn't turned her; he would've had an unstoppable weapon at his disposal. His loss was their gain, though. He would thank the poor bastard the next time he saw him.

"Welcome home, beautiful Brynn," he said, purposefully using the pet name he heard Nikolai call her multiple times on the security footage. "You will learn to appreciate our love...it's so much more than what Nikolai was able to give you."

CHAPTER TWENTY-SEVEN

Pacing back and forth at the foot of her bed, Brynn toyed with the diamond ring on her finger. She didn't understand why she had been allowed to keep it, but was thankful, nonetheless. She had lost all semblance of time and was starting to feel like she was losing her mind. Touching the ring helped to keep her grounded in a way that nothing else had.

It reminded her of Nik and the promises he made. He loved her and he was coming for her. He wasn't going to let anything horrible happen. At least that's what she thought she remembered him saying. She didn't know when, or how, but he would. She only hoped it would be before Ulysses or Christos tore into her flesh.

Shivering at the thought, she lifted her hand to swipe her fingers across her swollen eyes. Trying not to dwell on her fear, she continued her steps. She wondered when her captors would come back to claim her. Not because she was anxious to see any of the disgusting bloodsuckers, but because she was starving. She had polished off the water and biscuits ages ago. What she wouldn't give for a giant slice of chocolate cake.

Almost on cue, she heard a rustling outside her chamber door. Immediately halting, she braced herself for whatever was to come. Forcing a blank look on her face, she straightened her posture. She couldn't let her captors know how scared she truly was. They didn't deserve the satisfaction.

Opening the heavy door wide, Natalia let out a loud sigh. Giving Brynn a critical once over in the dying candlelight, she placed a hand upon her rounded hip. It was good that Ulysses had made her draw the Sun Walker a bath. Her mortal stench was overpowering. She reeked of sweat and tears. And something else that would soon throw everyone into a tizzy.

"Good evening, Brynn…come…follow me," she ordered.

Hesitating for a moment, Brynn swallowed hard. "Where are we going? Is it time for the Gathering?" she asked.

Folding her arms over her chest, Natalia quirked her head. She wanted to say something absurd to get a rise out of her. Knowing her Sire wouldn't approve, she reluctantly told the truth.

"I've drawn you a bath. The Elders want you clean for the Gathering. My Brothers and Sisters will be here soon so...let's be quick, hmm?" she said.

Widening her eyes at the mention of a bath, Brynn walked to the bedroom door. Crossing the threshold into a dark hallway, she followed Natalia. While she was dreading the Gathering, the idea of soaking in warm water for a moment or two made her almost giddy.

"How long do I have?" she asked.

Winding the Sun Walker through the East Wing of the Manor, Natalia glanced over her shoulder. "Twenty minutes. Just long enough for you to wash your bits. We will give you a proper cleanse after the Hunt," she replied, a smirk lifting her burgundy painted lips.

Frowning at the back of Natalia's head, Brynn continued to follow in the bitch's footsteps. *Yay,* she thought. Something else to look forward to.

Stopping in front of Christos' chamber door, Natalia grabbed the golden doorknob. Giving it a sharp twist, she opened the door. Walking into the opulent space, she motioned for Brynn to hurry.

"Just this way...Christos has been kind enough to let you use his bath...he has the best bathtub in the whole Manor. It holds seven...but don't worry, it will just be you this time," she said, leading her towards the en suite.

Gawking at the large bedroom as she walked, Brynn held in a disbelieving laugh. It was probably the most garish bedroom she had ever seen. Three large crystal chandeliers hung from a gold leafed ceiling, bathing the room in artificial light she was not afforded. Hand painted murals of angels and cherubs graced every wall, something sinister and wicked hiding behind their beautiful faces. Along the opposite side of the room was a carved four poster bed, its heavy red velvet curtains suspiciously drawn. Staring at it as she neared the bathroom, she could've sworn she heard a breathy moan from behind the fabric.

The sound instantly made her skin crawl.

Opening the door to the newly renovated en suite, Natasha allowed Brynn to enter first. Giving the bed a swift glance, she couldn't help but roll her pale blue eyes. She had a feeling Anton would be there, the little prick. This was the fourth time this week that he had serviced his Sire. It was clear that he really wanted to secure his Proxy status. Not that she had any room to talk. She had done the exact same with her own Sire.

Waiting until Brynn was fully inside, she stepped into the bathroom behind her. Purposefully slamming the door, she snickered as she watched the Sun Walker jump.

"Whoops," she said with a shrug. "Better get in…the water should still be quite warm."

Taking in a calming breath, Brynn tried to settle her anxious stomach. Turning to Natalia, she gave her an odd look. Was she really just going to stand there and watch?

"Can't I have a little bit of privacy?" she asked.

Huffing under her breath, Natalia sauntered over to the marble vanity next to the large bathtub. Taking a seat on the cool slab, she raised a sharp brow.

"Why? You don't have anything I haven't seen before, Brynn," she replied.

Pressing her lips into a fine line, Brynn screamed internally. She wanted nothing more than to slap the smugness from her pretty face.

"Fine," she whispered.

Turning her back to Natalia, she began to strip her clothes from her body. Letting each piece fall to the floor, she got her first full look at the square bathtub. It was the largest one she had ever seen, it reminded her of a hotel hot tub. There was no doubt in her mind that it could hold at least ten people. Just how many orgies had this sucker held?

"Uh…what's in the water?" she asked, suddenly thrown by its cloudy white color.

"Goats milk and rose water…they're very good for the skin…and they have restorative properties. When you get out, you'll essentially be a virgin. I'm sure it sounds ridiculous to your modern sensibilities, but this is how it has been done for centuries. The Elders want to present you to the Clan in your purest form…you should take it as a compliment," Natalia replied.

Mouthing the words 'what the fuck,' Brynn climbed into the bathtub. Lowering herself into the warm mixture of milk and rose water, she closed her eyes for a long moment. Although laughable, if they thought this would restore her purity, then so be it. It felt too good for her to really care.

Opening the drawer to the vanity, Natalia reached inside. Pulling out a boar bristle hairbrush and white ribbon, she stood from the marble. Walking to the soaking Sun Walker, she knelt next to her. Raising the brush, she began the process of freeing the tangles from Brynn's hair. Being unusually gentle, she gave herself a pat in the back when she felt the girl stiffen.

"Don't worry. I'm not planning on ripping your hair out…we simply don't have the time to wash it so I'm just going to braid it for you," she said.

"Oh," Brynn replied, relaxing a tiny bit.

Resisting the urge to tug on a particularly bad tangle, Natalia breathed in Brynn's changing scent. Humming lightly, she was pleased that it was no longer vile. Though it highlighted something that was sure to become potent.

"When are you going to bleed?" she asked.

Furrowing her brow, Brynn stammered for a second. How the fuck would she know? She assumed shortly after there was a winner in the sadistic Hunt.

"I guess whenever one of you bloodsuckers sinks your teeth into me," she replied flippantly.

Shaking her head, Natalia whacked Brynn on the back of the head with the brush. Not hard, just enough to show her annoyance.

"No...your monthly bleed. Your woman's curse. I know you're going to start soon. I can smell it," she said.

Reaching up from the water to rub her head, Brynn groaned aloud. Fuck. She had forgotten about that. Doing a quick calculation in her mind, she felt her anxiety spike all over again. What perfect timing to be surrounded by bloodthirsty Vampires.

"Two...three days, maybe," she said, her voice shaking slightly.

"Ahh...so after the Hunt. Well, that bodes well for you...Ulysses will tie you to the bed and lap at your cunt until you run clear. He's no Nikolai but you'll enjoy it just the same," she said, sighing wistfully. "Mmm...Nikolai is pretty talented with that tongue of his, isn't he? You're welcome, by the way. I taught that man everything he knows."

Scrunching her face in disgust, Brynn bit back then bile rising in her throat. She felt like she had been punched in the gut. Twice. First with the knowledge that a rape was eminent and then again with the mental image of Nik between Natalia's thighs. It was almost too much.

Sensing Brynn's discomfort, Natalia let out a wicked laugh.

"You know his little trick where he will pull your clit between his teeth and just hold it there while his tongue wiggles against it? Hmm? Yeah...that was all me. Well, actually...I suppose Viktor taught him how to do that. But I made him watch so...I think that counts," she said, beginning to plait Brynn's chestnut locks.

"Wait...you made Nik watch as another man performed oral sex on you? God...you really are the worst," Brynn spat.

"Oh? And you think you're any better for him?" Natalia said, finishing her simple braid.

"I know I am!" Brynn hissed, looking over her shoulder to glare at the bitch.

Meeting Brynn's livid eyes, Natalia flashed her a sly smile. Tying her braid off with the white ribbon, she stood from the marble floor. Smoothing her hands over her royal blue dress, she went to grab a towel from the second vanity.

"Well...then I suppose it's too bad that you'll never be with him again," she said, fluffing out the thick towel.

"What? Of course I will be," Brynn said defiantly.

"Oh...dear sweet child. The Elders are going to put a Mark out on Nikolai's head," she purred, stepping towards the bathtub.

Staring at the Vampire with wide eyes, Brynn felt the blood drain from her face. Shaking her head, she straightened her posture in the water. *No,* she thought. No, no, no.

"Why? I...I'm here...they...they got what they wanted!" she exclaimed.

Shrugging her shoulders, Natalia motioned for Brynn to stand. She loved the look of sheer panic on her freckled face. Truthfully, she didn't know if the Elders really would place a bounty on Nikolai's head, but it was fun to watch the Sun Walker squirm.

"Now I'm just as devastated as you…but he did do something egregious and made them look like fools. As his Sire, it would only be right if I was the one to find him and dole out his punishment. But don't worry, I'll make it quick…well…quick-ish," she replied.

Darting her hazel eyes around the room, Brynn began to breathe hard. There had to be a way for her to warn him. Or maybe she could somehow persuade the Elders to spare him. Yes. That was her best bet. She would let them do whatever they wanted to her, just as long as they let Nik live.

Smelling Brynn's adrenaline, Natalia looked at her with faux sympathy. She could see her gears turning, she was obviously forming a plan. The poor thing truly thought she could save Nikolai. What a poor little lovesick trollop.

"Aww, don't worry Sun Walker…nothing will happen tonight so…just put your worries into the back of your mind and enjoy the night, hmm? Now come on and stand up…it's time to get out," she ordered.

Consumed by her thoughts, Brynn stared into the milky water. It wasn't until Natalia screamed her name for a second, and then a third time, did she react. Blinking her eyes, Nik's face disappeared into the abyss. God, she felt so sick.

"Ok! Ok!" she yelled back.

Standing from the warm bath, she climbed out of the massive tub. Mindful of the slippery marble floor, she grabbed the towel from Natalia. Noticing the Vampire staring unabashedly at her naked body, she shot her an angry glare.

"Should I put on my old clothes? Or do the Elders have something else for me to wear?" she asked, drying herself off with the white towel.

Folding her arms over her chest, Natalia shook her head. Looking like a cat that had just caught a bird, she took half a step closer.

"Your purity has been restored…you have no need for clothes," she replied.

Blinking at the bitch before her, Brynn huffed in disbelief. She didn't know why this tidbit of information shocked her so much. Things had been insane up to this point. It was par of the course, really. But it still irked her.

"You've gotta be fucking kidding me," she said flatly.

Shrugging her shoulders, Natalia kept her painted mouth closed. Watching Brynn wrap the towel around her body in defiance, she debated on whether she should warn her that Christos was heading their way. Deciding against it, she merely waited. This wasn't her circus, and Brynn wasn't her monkey. Not yet at least.

Securing the towel with a tight roll of the fabric, Brynn continued to eye Natalia. Wondering how long their standoff would be, her attention was suddenly pulled to the door of the bathroom. Holding her breath as it opened, she winced slightly as Christos sauntered into view.

"Mmm…there are my girls!" Christos quipped, pulling his black and gold embroidered robe over his shoulders.

Turning towards the Elder, Natalia softened her features. Moving her gaze up and down his thin form, she hid a smirk when she noticed red claw marks striping his chest. Judging by his languid movements and satisfied smile, Anton had done his job. And done it well.

"I'm sorry if we bothered you, Christos," she said, performing a curtsy as he came close.

Waving off her concern, the Elder shook his head. He honestly didn't even know Natalia had already brought Brynn in for her bath until a minute prior. Time had gotten away with him.

"Nonsense...Anton and I were just having a quaint discussion over the terms of Sara taking over the Benefactor Program," he said.

Lifting a brow, Natalia held in a laugh. Anton had been trying to up his Novice's position within the Clan for decades. It wasn't a surprise that he would try to use this situation to her advantage. But there was no way the idiot could fill Nikolai's shoes. Did he suck out Christos' brain instead of his cum?

"Sara...*Anton's* Sara is taking over the Benefactor Program? Really?" she asked, her voice lifting slightly.

Tossing his sandy blonde hair over his shoulder, Christos met her gaze. He didn't care for her questioning his judgment. "Of course she is...she's the only one that has Charm. Nikolai's abandoned lambs are starting to make a fuss...Sarah will appease them. We still need their blood...the machine must continue," he replied.

Toggling her attention back and forth between Natalia and Christos, Brynn became entirely confused. The Benefactor Program? Nikolai's abandoned lambs? They still needed their blood? What the hell did he mean? She wanted so desperately to interrupt and ask questions, but knew it wasn't the time. Tucking them into the back of her mind, she forced herself to remain quiet.

Snorting a little, Natalia caught a mental glimpse at Sara trying, and failing, to use her Charm on Nikolai's whores. Quickly reminding herself to behave, she dropped her amused expression. Christos took a great deal of pride in his lineage. She really didn't need to piss him off tonight.

"Yes, Sir...you're absolutely right. Sara will do a magnificent job. The Program Girls are lucky to have her as their new Benefactor," she said, obediently dropping her eyes to the floor.

Nodding his head, Christos turned his honey-colored eyes to Brynn. Taking in a whiff of her purified scent, he moaned lightly.

"Mmm...and speaking of our Program Girls...my sweet Brynn, you smell divine...but why are you wrapped in the towel, hmm?" he asked, reaching for the white fabric and yanking it from her body. "It's a sin to cover something so clean."

Gasping loudly, a look of mortification passed over her face. Instinctively covering her breasts and cunt with her arms and hands, she looked at Christos with wide eyes.

Clicking his tongue against the roof of his mouth, Christos shook his head. Modesty had no place here. She shouldn't be ashamed of what the Sun God had given her.

"No no no, my dear," he chastised, throwing the towel on the floor. "Don't you be ashamed. You're exquisite...it's a good thing I'm already spent. I'd be tempted to throw you into my bed and ravage you!"

Licking her lips nervously, Brynn felt her cheeks flush crimson. Standing awkwardly, she stayed silent as the Elder took his fill with his demonic eyes. She didn't understand why it was essential for her to be paraded around the Gathering completely naked. This would no doubt be one of the longest nights of her life.

Reaching towards Brynn, Christos brushed her thick braid over her shoulder. Letting his fingers dance over her tanned skin, he raised a brow as he audibly heard her stomach growl.

"Oh my...someone's hungry. Forgive us, we should have prepared some food for you...hmm, Natalia? Be a good girl and run to the village before the tavern closes for the night. Get the Sun Walker something good to eat...something hearty. She will need to be well fed for tomorrow night," he said, snapping his fingers.

Grumbling internally, Natalia bowed her head. She hated being the errand girl, but this would give her the opportunity to work some magic on the new bartender. She was such an adorable little thing. It might take some time, but she was confident that she would have her.

"Yes, Christos," she replied.

Calling upon her otherworldly ability, she raised her hands. Tearing a rift in their reality with a flick of her wrists, she gave Brynn one last annoyed glance before disappearing into the darkness.

Clenching her jaw as Natalia seemingly evaporated into thin air, Brynn stared at where she once stood for a handful of seconds. The Vampire's ability to transport herself was jarring. She wondered if she would ever get used to being around supernatural beings.

Clearing his throat to gain Brynn's attention, Christos closed the space between them. Wrapping his arm around her shoulder, he motioned her to move with his free hand.

"Let's get you to the ballroom, hmm?" he said, his tone unusually warm.

Following his lead, she padded her bare feet over the marble tile. Crossing into the bedroom, she saw someone from the corner of her eyes perched on the bed. Giving them a glance, she froze for a second as she noticed Anton lacing up his heavy black boots.

"Good evening, Sun Walker," Anton said, meeting her eyes. "Mmm…don't you look delicious…you're making my mouth water!"

Instantly filled with a mixture of terror and rage, Brynn balled her hands into tight fists at her sides. Getting ready to pounce towards him, she was quickly stopped by Christos, moving his arm from her shoulder to her waist.

"Calm down, Brynn," he warned, squeezing her against him as they continued their way to the door. "He isn't going to touch you tonight. None of our Children will. I promise."

Chuckling at the nude hellcat, Anton kissed the air as they walked past. After the way he had left her, it was nice to see her with some spunk. He hoped she kept it. It would make hunting her down all the more fun.

"Stay the fuck away from me!" she hissed, looking over her shoulder at Anton.

Rolling his eyes, Christos all but pushed Brynn out of the bedroom. Paying no mind to his laughing Novice, he shut the door behind them.

"Once you're mine, you will have to play nice, Sweetling," he tisked, ushering her down the hallway. "We're all one big happy family."

Huffing under her breath, she kept her eyes straight ahead. One big happy family. Uh huh. She believed that statement just as much as she believed in Santa.

"So, what's going to happen tonight?" she asked, changing the subject.

Winding her though the East Wing towards the belly of the Manor, Christos casually shrugged his shoulders. The Gathering wouldn't be too incredibly formal. It was a chance for the Clan to come together and see the Sun Walker with their own eyes. Oh, and to discuss the Hunt of course. He knew the new rules would ruffle some feathers but couldn't care less.

"This is your coming out party, so to speak...the Clan is very eager to meet you. But there will be music and dancing...perhaps some stolen kisses and egregious lapses of judgment. You'll have a grand time, don't worry," he replied, taking her closer to their destination.

Humming low, Brynn shivered as Christos opened the door before them. It was just a party. Sure. A party filled with Vampires just dying for a taste of her magical blood. With her walking around naked and completely vulnerable. What could possibly go wrong?

Encouraged to enter the room by a squeeze on her hip, she stepped into the massive ballroom. Looking around the brightly lit space, she gasped in complete awe. She felt as if she had just stepped into a Victorian castle.

"Beautiful, isn't it?" Christos said, his voice low and soft.

Nodding her head in agreement, she scanned over the ornate room. It was incredibly decadent, much like his bedroom. With scarlet painted walls laced in gold filigree and five heavy candle chandeliers hanging from the ceiling, it was obscenely grandiose. Along the far side of the room stood a raised platform with two large carved thrones placed atop it. In between them, a seemingly out of place golden cage.

One suspiciously large enough to hold a human.

Noticing a flash of confusion behind her hazel eyes, Christos couldn't help but grin. He enjoyed keeping people on their toes, the Sun Walker was no exception. Taking her by the elbow, he began to walk her towards the checkerboard stage.

"Our Children will be here any moment now…it's best if we get you safely tucked away into your cage like a good little pet," he purred.

CHAPTER TWENTY-EIGHT

Turning to face the Elder as he locked the metal door behind her, Brynn met his sparkling eyes. He looked quite pleased with himself. She wondered what other sick games he had in store for her.

"Is this really necessary?" she asked.

Nodding his head, Christos secured the heart shaped padlock. The tiniest bit of fear in her voice made him ache with want. He was so looking forward to swallowing her screams.

"Of course it is…you look so beautiful caged in gold. You really should take this as a compliment, Brynn…only the ones we truly care about are given such loving treatment. Now…just sit tight. I must go and fetch Ulysses," he replied.

Grabbing onto the golden bars, she gave them a harsh shake. Hearing him laugh as he walked away, she growled an expletive. Her assertiveness was quickly met with a phantom slap of her cheek. Immediately shocked, she winced as the sting radiated over the right side of her face.

"Careful, Sweetling…that was only a warning," he yelled over his shoulder. "I've been extremely patient with you, but my patience is wearing thin. Now just stand there and think long and hard about how you want to proceed from here on out!"

Glaring at him as he sauntered out of the ballroom, she clenched her jaw in frustration. She was in between a rock and a hard place. Fuck, she hated him. She hated them all.

Stewing in her bitter anger, she didn't notice Natalia suddenly appear out of thin air at her side. Catching a glimpse of the blue fabric of the Vampire's dress from the corner of her eyes, she jumped in surprise.

"Oh, fucking hell!" she exclaimed, placing an open hand over her heart.

Stepping up to the cage, Natalia laughed at her reaction. Giving herself a pat on the back for scaring the Sun Walker, she lifted her lips into a wicked grin.

"Ohh…poor *bebeluş*. I didn't mean to get your heart racing," she said, raising a paper bag for Brynn to see. "I've fetched some food for you. Do you want it?"

Locking her eyes on the bag, Brynn felt her stomach instantly rumble. Oh, food. Finally. She felt like she hadn't eaten in years. Sticking her arm through the bars, she attempted to grab it.

Yanking back the bag, Natalia clicked her tongue against the roof of her mouth. Shaking her head, she lifted a sculpted brow. "Where are your manners, Sun Walker? What do you say?" she asked.

Narrowing her eyes, Brynn stopped herself from replying with something rude. At that moment, having a full belly was more important than showing her displeasure. There would be plenty of time for that after she had her dinner.

"Please, Natalia…may I have the bag?" she asked, her voice laced with annoyance.

Feeling unusually generous, Natalia nodded once. Handing her the paper sack, she let out a small sigh. She really ought to make her beg, but she knew Christos would want her fed before the Gathering began. Watching a Sun Walker eat would only rile up her younger Brothers and Sisters.

"Yes, you may…I hope you like what I've brought," she replied.

All but tearing into the bag, Brynn peered inside at its contents. Held within were two white boxes and a black plastic fork. Shaking with hunger, she sat down upon the metal floor of the cage. Paying no mind to how cold it was against her bare skin.

"And just what did you bring?" she asked, pulling out the boxes.

Shrugging her shoulders, Natalia nonchalantly grabbed onto one of the golden bars. Looking down at the famished girl, she hummed softly. She wanted to give the mortal the vilest tripe stew she could find. The thought was short lived however, knowing it would somehow backfire.

A steak sandwich with fried potatoes…and a slice of amandină," she said, pointing to the smaller box with her free hand.

"Amandina? What's that?" Brynn asked, opening the small box.

"It's a chocolate cake…I've never actually had chocolate before, but…I've heard that modern women like to eat it around their bleed. I thought you might like it," she said.

Looking at the slice of cake, Brynn's stomach roared to life. The squared slice was thick and decadent. With layers of chocolate sponge and frosting, topped with what seemed like a glossy ganache. It smelled heavenly, making her mouth water in anticipation. But she was almost afraid to touch it. She didn't know what Natalia's ulterior motive was.

Sensing Brynn's hesitation, Natalia rolled her blue eyes. God. The Sun Walker was annoying in every sense of the word.

"I didn't poison it. It was freshly baked this afternoon. Sweets sweeten the blood…and I want to make sure yours is as sugary as possible when I drink it from you. Now eat," she purred.

With a sour look on her face, Brynn stabbed the cake with her fork and shoved a large bite into her mouth. The Vampire's answer was completely on trend. She loathed how confident she was. Come hell or high water, Natalia would never get a single drop of her blood.

"Is it good?" Natalia asked, bringing her face close to the bars.

Reluctantly nodding her head, Brynn scooped another forkful into her mouth. Truth be told, it was the best cake she had ever had. Not only did it have the most luscious chocolate, but rum and caramel too. She wished Natalia had brought her the whole damn thing. Not that she would ever admit it.

"It's alright," she said, her mouth full.

Frowning at the naked girl, Natalia merely watched as she ate her rich dessert. It was a little off putting that she was eating so much, so quickly. She was worse than a damn horse. How could Nikolai possibly be attracted to such a slovenly creature?

Finishing the last bit of cake, Brynn ripped open the second box. Licking the remnants of chocolate from her lips, she reached in to grab the steak sandwich. Still consumed by her hunger, she brought it up to her mouth and took two large bites of the meaty roll.

"Mmmm," she said, not caring about the drips of gravy running down her chin.

Making a disgusted face, Natalia took half a step away from the cage. Brynn wasn't worse than a horse, she was worse than a bloody Werewolf. They were the only other creature she had seen eat with such ferocity.

"Careful not to choke," she warned.

Looking upwards at the bitch, Brynn made a show of carefully chewing and swallowing her bites of food. Staring at her in uncomfortable silence, she finished the savory sandwich before moving to the fried potatoes.

"When will everyone get here?" she asked, using her fork to spear chunks of pan-fried potato.

Folding her arms over her chest, Natalia glanced at the door of the ballroom. It was hours past sunset. She thought everyone would've been here by now. Sometimes she really hated being the punctual one in the Clan.

"Soon. Ulysses is probably waiting on Christos to finish getting dressed…he's such a diva," she said with a sigh.

Chewing quietly, Brynn took a small solace in knowing she still had some time before the Monsters rolled in. She didn't like being alone with Natalia, but perhaps it was a good thing. It gave her a chance to ask her something that was nagging at her.

"What did Christos mean when he was talking about the Program Girls?" she wondered.

Widening her blue eyes in surprise, Natalia looked down at the Sun Walker. So, Nikolai hadn't been forthcoming with his little toy? She knew he wasn't truly in love with her.

"You don't know?" she asked.

Shaking her head, Brynn pressed her lips into a fine line. She didn't care for the Vampire's smug face. She was probably going to regret asking her that question.

Clearing her throat, Natalia began to slowly circle the golden cage. Keeping her narrowed eyes on Brynn, she let out a wicked laugh. *Oh.* This was going to be fun.

"I suppose I'll start at the beginning, hmm? Over the centuries, we have made deals if you will with various countries," she began, weaving her tale with her hands. "We won't actively hunt and kill their mortal citizens if they allow us to operate our little business. It's changed over the years…we once operated brothels and opium dens…health resorts with healing springs and even finishing schools where girls were taught how to be proper ladies. Although our businesses have changed, the core of what we offer stays the same. We give mortals something they want, and they give us what we want."

Watching Natalia as she stepped around her, Brynn felt her stomach tighten. She could see where this was heading. *Oh God,* she thought. How could she have been so dumb?

"Nikolai has been instrumental in getting these *businesses* off the ground, so to speak. His Charm gets the ball rolling. And he's one of the few of us that changes with the times…he stays grounded somehow. He's able to learn and grow with modern society. It's much harder than you would think…well. For a few decades now, he's tapped into the business of matching powerful, rich men with not so fortunate women. Is this starting to sound familiar?" she asked with another laugh.

Halting her steps directly in front Brynn, she carefully bent down. Making sure not to wrinkle her expensive gown, she got on her eye level.

"So, he created the Benefactor Program. It's a legitimate business, we do match the wealthy with the destitute, and we make a lot of money in doing so. But we need more than money, don't we? It only made sense that he brought our specific need into this particular business," she said.

Swallowing hard, the pit in the bottom of Brynn's stomach grew. When she learned that Nik was a Vampire, she just assumed that she was his only Beneficiary. She had it somehow twisted in her mind that every Vampire had their own. But now things were falling into place. It was stupid of her to be so naive. Of course there were others. And he probably used his abilities to make them all feel the exact same way he made her feel.

It was all a fucking trick.

"How many girls are in the Program?" she asked, the stress making her voice crack.

Leaning in towards the bars, Natalia couldn't help but smile. Now the fun was really beginning. "I think right now we have a little over three hundred lambs all across the globe," she replied.

Visibly taken aback, Brynn choked on her own spit. Three hundred? Holy shit. She was going to be sick.

Loving the way Brynn physically recoiled with her newfound information, Natalia continued. "So, no. You aren't the only one. That stings, hmm? Honestly there was nothing special about you when he brought you on. You were just one little cow added to the herd. He probably wouldn't even have remembered your name if it wasn't for that magical blood of yours. And he selfishly wanted to keep it all to himself…that's what he *truly* loves, Brynn. He loves your blood and the power it affords him."

Shaking her head, Brynn felt her heartbeat quicken. Her mind was racing at a million miles a minute. Her emotions whipping back and forth so fast it made her lose her breath. He loved her. Only he didn't. He wanted her. But only for her blood. He branded her as his Mate. Because his greedy ass didn't want to share.

And just like that, all the hope she had that he would save her evaporated. She truly was fucked.

Smiling brightly, Natalia felt the urge to dig the knife in a little more. Dashing all the Sun Walker's hopes and dreams was making her almost giddy. It had been far too long since she had felt so amazing.

"If Nikolai truly loved you, Brynn. He would have turned you. Then you would have been protected from us. He would have been your Sire, we wouldn't have been able to touch you. But he doesn't love you," she repeated, pressing her face against the metal bars. "That's why he kept you mortal. Because if he turned you, your magical blood would no longer be useful to him. Nikolai is greedy and selfish. And in the end, he will *always* choose what is best for Nikolai."

Narrowing her watery eyes, Brynn bared her teeth in a frustrated snarl. Everything was crumbling around her. And she had no one to blame but herself. She wished she had never downloaded the damn Benefactor app onto her phone. What she wouldn't give to rewind the last month of her life. Sleeping on the streets of Phoenix would've been a much kinder fate than this.

Basking in the Sun Walker's existential crisis, Natalia slowly stood to full height. Brushing her hands down the front of her torso, she pushed out a satisfied hum. The poor, mousy girl before her looked so defeated. So incredibly heartbroken. Her silent sobs were music to her ears.

With hot tears dripping down her face, Brynn dropped her gaze to her lap. Shivering in a mixture of anger and panic, she held back the scream threatening to claw from her throat. She felt utterly and completely hopeless. There was no escaping the terrifying fate before her.

Eyeing the crying girl, Natalia gave herself a mental pat on the back. Opening her mouth to say something, she paused for a moment as she heard the door to the ballroom open. Giving a quick glance over her shoulder, she offered Brynn some words of encouragement.

"Aww…please don't cry, dear Brynn…we will love you in the ways Nikolai couldn't. I promise," she said with a devilish grin. "Now pull yourself together. The Gathering is about to begin."

CHAPTER TWENTY-NINE

Shifting her weight from her right foot to her left, Brynn looked through the golden bars of her cage. Before her, dozens of Vampires danced in intricate circles. Twirling in time with the music of a phantom string quartet. They were all so beautiful in their designer gowns and tailored suits, but equally just as terrifying. Eyeing her with hungry glances as they danced, they licked at the corner of their lips in a brazen display. There was no mistaking their intentions.

She was thankful to be locked away in her tiny, gilded prison.

Swallowing the bile rising in her throat, she wrapped her arms over her bare chest. Hugging herself tightly, she attempted to calm her racing heart. She still couldn't believe that all of this was happening. It felt surreal. She wished she could just disappear into the air like Natalia.

"Fucking hell," she whispered, her gaze toggling between the Elders flanking her sides.

Watching the members of the Clan enjoy themselves, Christos soaked in the vibrant energy of the room. It had been far too long since their Children had come home. He felt like a proud Papa on Christmas morning about to hand out the most precious of gifts. Sighing happily, he looked to his counterpart.

"We should do this more often…I have missed them," he said, lifting his voice above the strings.

Nodding in agreement, Ulysses curled his hand over the edge of the throne's armrest. This was the first night in years where he wasn't filled with dull boredom. He was looking forward to the excitement the Sun Walker's presence would bring. It wouldn't last long, perhaps a decade, but it would be a welcome distraction.

"An Annual Bleed would do us all some good," he replied darkly.

"After the Allotment of Spoils, of course."

"Oh, of course darling," Christos purred, fully convinced of his forthcoming victory. "Of course."

Adjusting his rigid posture, Ulysses caught the heat of Brynn's glare boring into the side of his face. Hardening his masculine features, he turned his head towards her. She was lucky he had had his fill of both blood and flesh. Even still, he was tempted to pull her from the cage and onto his lap. He was counting the hours until he could ravage her.

"Your bratty behavior is really starting to annoy me, Brynn Smith. All of this…it's for you, and you alone. I should make you fall on your knees and thank me for doing this properly instead of simply taking what Nikolai promised me," he said, his gravelly voice booming over the classical melody.

Shivering from the implications of his words, Brynn swallowed hard. She didn't know exactly what Nikolai had promised, but her mind was running wild with a million possibilities. Perhaps Natalia was right, it really seemed that he would always do what was best for him.

Brushing his long hair over his shoulder, Christos let out a sigh. As much as he loved watching his Children play, he had a feeling Ulysses' mood would continue to sour because of Brynn's ungrateful attitude. They might as well get to the heart of matter. The party could resume after she was taken back to her room.

"I think it's time for us to begin, Ulysses," he said, waving his hand in the air.

Almost on cue, the invisible string quartet stilled, leaving the ballroom with a deafening silence. Halting their fluid movements, the Vampires turned their bodies in unison towards the stage. Although a handful were annoyed at the sudden intrusion, the majority seemed most pleased. Gleeful, even. They were ready to have their promised taste.

Moving his honeyed gaze over their Children, Christos curved his glossed lips into a smile. Waiting until he had everyone's attention, he began his planned speech.

"Hello darling Children...we are so pleased to see you. As you know, we've called you back home because we've found something special," he said, motioning to Brynn in the cage. "We've found another Sun Walker!"

Hearing heady gasps and excited murmurs coming from the crowd, Brynn's eyes widened. In an instant the feeling of the room changed. Now there was a collective feeling of almost desperation directed towards her. It made her tremble in fear.

"Yes, yes...I know, I know," Christos said, giving a wink to Anton in the front row as he stood with Sara. "Ulysses and I are just as thrilled...but...we will be doing things a little differently this time around."

Holding her breath, Brynn made herself focus on Christos. She still had no idea what was really in store for her. It was imperative that she paid attention.

"There is to be a Hunt!" Christos exclaimed; his announcement met with cheers. "However...and please listen to me...not all of you will be able to compete."

Almost immediately, jeers and harsh curses rang out amongst the Vampires. Causing Ulysses to give a strong warning with an animalistic snarl. Insolence wouldn't be tolerated tonight.

"QUIET!" he yelled.

Snapping their mouths shut, they collectively bowed their heads. All except for Natalia, who simply gave her Sire a knowing look.

Pausing until both his counterpart and Children had simmered down, Christos cleared his throat.

"Thank you, Ulysses...now as I was saying. We are doing things with this Sun Walker a little differently. We want her magic to stay potent a little while longer than poor Leona's did," Christos said, giving a mock pout before quickly moving on. "Tomorrow night, there will be a Hunt in the Maze of Hoia Baciu. Now we haven't used the Maze in a very long time…but it's appropriate for the changes we have made. There will be two Proxies. *Only two*. One Hunting for myself, and one Hunting for Ulysses. The one that finds the Sun Walker *first* wins. The Sun Walker will belong to the winning Elder and Proxy for the next five years. After that, she will belong to the entire Clan for the next five years. So yes, you will all get to enjoy her gifts…and really, what is five years, hmm? It will be worth the wait. *She* will be worth the wait."

With the room suddenly spinning, Brynn unfolded her arms to grip the bars of her cage. Leaning forward, she pressed her forehead against the cold metal. Ten years. She would be essentially their slave for the next ten years. Forced to let them use her in any way they pleased.

"What happens after ten years?" she found herself asking aloud.

Surprised to hear her voice, both Elders turned their heads. Looking at her for a long moment, they turned their attention to each other. With a smirk lifting Christos' lips, Ulysses chuckled under his breath.

"Well from our experience, around ten years is when your body will begin to give out. And then well…I suppose your final fate is up to you, my darling Brynn," Christos replied. "If you behave and do everything we say…we may grow fond of you. If we do, then you will be turned. But if you continue to act like a petulant child…well, then…we will kill you."

Closing her eyes, Brynn held onto the cage for balance. Fighting to keep herself from crumbling to the ground, she listened to the Vampires as they laughed at her reaction. Neither option was viable for her. She would find a way to end her suffering long before the ten years were through.

"Who are the Proxies!?" asked an unfamiliar voice.

Switching his attention back to the Clan, Christos clapped his hands. Casually crossing his legs, he let out a loud sigh.

"I'm so glad you asked that, Simon! We've thought long and hard about this...please know that we love each and every one of you, but we had to make a choice. *My* Proxy will be Anton!" he exclaimed, motioning to his beautiful Novice.

Bowing his head in reverence, Anton smiled as his fellow Vampires gave him a round of applause. Feeling Sara squeeze his side, he turned and gathered the dazzling brunette in his arms. Giving her a quick twirl, he kissed her soundly. He couldn't wait to secretly share his spoils with his love.

Opening her red rimmed eyes, Brynn latched onto the image of Anton enthralled with a woman she didn't know but hated just the same. She hadn't noticed him earlier amongst the flurry of whirling monsters. The sight of him looking so happy filled her with instant rage.

"Fucker!" she hissed, banging her open hand against the bar.

Narrowing his dark eyes, Ulysses shot Brynn a dirty look. "Careful," he growled, his deep voice carrying above Anton's laughter. "Or I'll let Sara have some fun with you."

Glaring at Ulysses, Brynn pressed her lips into a fine line. Putting two and two together she told herself to keep quiet. Sara was the only other Vampire that had Charm. Only according to Nik, she didn't know how to use it properly. She needed to keep her distance from Anton's insane lover. Trying her best to ignore the amused stares being thrown her way, she kept her hazel eyes on Ulysses. Watching him as he silenced the Clan with a lift of his hand, she anxiously waited for his answer.

Looking towards the corner of the ballroom, the ancient General found his stunning Novice. Giving her a wicked grin, he leaned forward in his throne. There wasn't any doubt in his mind that she would be the Victor.

"And as for mine...*I* have chosen Natalia to be my Proxy," he said.

Shuddering from the announcement, Brynn felt her stomach twist into sharp knots. She didn't know why she was surprised. Of course Ulysses would choose her. The thought of Natalia hunting her down terrified her to the core. At least with Anton, she knew exactly what he was capable of.

Dipping into a low curtsy, Natalia beamed with excitement. Slowly standing to full height, she smiled at her Brothers and Sisters as they gathered around her. She was incredibly relieved that all her hard work tending to Ulysses' every need was all for naught.

Giving Natalia a slow clap, Christos rolled his eyes at Ulysses' smug face. Natalia was a fine Hunter, but his Anton was superior in every way. She simply didn't have his physical strength to deal with the hidden traps of the Maze. The Sun Walker was as good as his.

"Yes, yes…well, there you have it, Children!" Christos said, lifting his voice high. "Anton and Natalia will be competing in the Hunt! Let's all have a round of applause for them, hmm?"

Following the Elder's order, the members of the Clan clapped their hands in celebration. Although many were disappointed, this was the biggest thing to have happened in over a century. Exclaiming words of encouragement to the Proxies, a loud gasp was suddenly heard by all. Followed by a surprised shout of a name that made the Elders all but jump from their thrones.

Gawking at the party crasher as she fully entered the ballroom, Christos stammered nervously. What the hell was she doing there? He thought she had been taken care of.

"Helen!?" he yelped.

Blinking her eyes in disbelief, Brynn watched in stunned silence as the third Elder came into view. With shoulder length silver hair and violet eyes that seemed to glow, she had a physical maturity that the other Vampires didn't possess. Age had touched her, she realized. Ethereal and poised, Helen was quite possibly the most beautiful woman she had ever seen.

Gliding her way towards the stage, Helen eyed the spawns of Christos and Ulysses as they parted a path for her. Ignoring their hushed whispers, she gave the naked girl in the cage a quick glance before turning her attention to her counterparts.

"What's this I hear about a Hunt?" she asked, biting back her anger.

Smoothing his hands over the lapel of his black velvet jacket, Ulysses lifted his squared chin. Like a human staring down a black bear, he didn't want to show any sign of weakness. Standing confidently before her, he looked her dead in the eyes.

"Helen, it's good to see you…you look as lovely as ever," he said, his tone icy and flat.

Placing her hands upon her silk covered hips, Helen scoffed at his poor attempt at flattery. She wanted to take him by the scruff of his neck and throw him to the checkered floor. However, she had made a promise that she would carry out this little plan. It was the only way for her to reassert her dominance over the Clan.

"Let's cut through the shit, hmm?" she said, slowly dragging her gaze from Ulysses to Christos. "Because I *love* you two so much, I'm willing to look past the fact that none of my Novices or I were invited to this little Gathering."

"It was just a slight oversight on our part," Christos said, his face looking uncharacteristically apologetic. "We truly meant nothing by it, Helen!"

Giving her blonde counterpart a full-on death stare, Helen forced herself to stay the course. There was a method to this madness.

"Yes, I'm positive my invite was lost in the post," she replied dryly. "I'm sure that the fact that I banned Hunts years ago had absolutely *nothing* to do with it."

Squeezing the golden bars of her cage, Brynn listened to the exchange. For a brief second, she had a glimmer of hope that Helen would put a stop to everything. It was short lived, however.

"Now this one," Helen continued, lifting a hand to point at Brynn. "Has something that I want just as badly…so I'm willing to look past everything. I will be joining this Hunt."

Glancing quickly at Ulysses, Christos carefully weighed their options. He didn't trust the bitch. It would be so easy for them to destroy her right then and there, but the fallout would be too great. Her otherworldly alliances overshadowed theirs. They would certainly be crushed in the ensuing war.

"Of course," he said, mentally bending the knee. "Feel free to choose anyone in this room as your Proxy, Helen…they would be delighted at the chance to serve you."

Lifting her red lips into a sly smile, Helen shook her head. As if she would choose any of their spawn. They were all snakes. Cut from the same cloth as their imbecile Sires.

"Thank you, Christos, but I have to respectfully decline. You see, I've brought my own Proxy with me," she replied, turning towards the ballroom door.

A hush fell over the grand space as every pair of evil eyes looked towards the newcomer. Once the recognition amongst the Vampires set in, another set of curses and gasps filled the space. As well as a feminine hiss escaping the lips of one very pissed off Proxy.

Stomping into the ballroom, the Vampire strode towards Helen. With a look of utter rage and disgust twisting his handsome features, his eyes narrowed as they fell upon the Sun Walker. Her physical state made him seethe, causing his bloodlust to spike throughout his body. Unable to control his need for revenge, his green eyes turned inky black, his sharp fangs extending like a poisonous serpent ready to strike.

Frozen in a state of shock and confusion, Brynn could only stare with wide eyes at the Monster as he advanced. She wasn't sure if this was all a figment of her imagination. Whispering a single word, she prayed to

God that her mind wasn't playing some sort of dirty trick.

"Nik."

CHAPTER THIRTY

Placing her arm in Nikolai's way, Helen halted his predatorial advance. She had warned him to keep a tight rein on his emotions. His love for the Sun Walker had once again blinded him. They were alone in a viper's den. She wanted her revenge just as badly as he did. But they had to play the game.

"Nikolai," she warned, her voice so low only he could hear. "Careful."

Calling for Natalia with a snap of his fingers, Ulysses motioned for her to move closer to Nikolai with a flick of his head. He had never seen him look quite so feral. She would keep her Novice in line if need be.

"Nikolai," he spat, taking a step to the edge of the stage. "Well, well, well. I'm surprised you have the bollocks to show your face here…especially after breaking rule after cardinal rule. You're lucky Helen has named you!"

"Honestly, Nikolai," Christos joined in. "We should have Natalia rip you limb from limb!"

Ignoring both Elders as they took turns chiding him, Nik took in a cleansing breath. Closing his black eyes for a long moment, he reluctantly forced the monster back into his cage. With his bloodlust sedated, he opened his green eyes. Immediately fixing his gaze upon Brynn's shocked face, he eased his way into her mind.

Are you alright, Sunshine?

Hearing Nik's warm voice in her head, it took Brynn a second to realize what was happening. It was only after the question was asked a second time did she react. Shaking her head, she shrugged her bare shoulders at the same time. No. She definitely was not alright, but what could either of them do?

Feeling her intense hopelessness, Nik wrapped her head to toe in a phantom blanket of warmth meant to comfort and soothe. Watching her relax against the barbaric cage, he spoke to her once more.

We have a fight ahead of us…but we will win, my love. I just need you to believe me.

Looking between the golden bars, Brynn focused on Nik's handsome face. Surrounded by Vampires that wanted nothing more than to destroy him, she realized that he was in a cage of his very own. She wanted so desperately to believe him, but how could they possibly win? Whimpering lightly, she dropped her hazel eyes to the floor in defeat.

Brynn…listen to me, he continued, using his otherworldly gift to force her to look at him. *It will all be alright. I promise you. Now stay strong. Don't show these fuckers an ounce of weakness.*

Lifting her eyes from the floor, Brynn met Nik's intense gaze. Emboldened by a sudden sense of strength, she straightened her posture. Lifting her chin, she gripped the bars as the Elders continued with their petty insults and idle threats.

Yes. That's it. Good girl, Nik purred before easing from her mind.

Glaring at Christos and Ulysses, he clenched his jaw. He hadn't heard a word either Elder had said and didn't care. As far as he was concerned, he was no longer part of the Clan. Their rules, their commands, their punishments no longer applied to him.

Growing tired of the childish tongue lashing, Helen stomped her booted foot against the ballroom floor. Giving Natalia a look of warning as she continued to inch closer, she stepped in front of her Proxy to command her counterparts' attention.

"No one here is innocent! Either one you would have done the same as Nikolai so quit the harping…it's tiresome…and the night grows old. But there is something we must discuss before we move any further. Clearly, my Proxy is at a disadvantage when it comes to yours, Ulysses," she said, eyeing Natalia up and down. "Call her off until after the Hunt."

Scrunching her face in protest, Natalia turned towards her Sire. Losing her power over Nikolai would put her at a great disadvantage in this Hunt. It would be stupid to agree to such a ridiculous request.

"Ulysses," she whined.

"Do it, Ulysses!" Helen interrupted, taking a step closer to the stage.

With a deep frown on his face, Ulysses silenced Natalia with a lift of his finger. He hated that the old bitch had the upper hand, but it was of no consequence. His Proxy would just have to work a little harder. He was still confident in his win.

Looking towards Natalia, Nikolai gave his former lover a slow once over. Ulysses wasn't an imbecile; he would cave to Helen's demand. He was looking forward to being free of her hellish leash. Permanently.

Knowing he was between a rock and a hard place, Ulysses relented. Meeting Natalia's ice blue eyes, he handed in his order.

"Natalia…your ties to Nikolai are severed until the Hunt is through. You cannot use your influence over him as his Sire in any way, shape, or form," he said, his voice incredibly hard and cold. "Of this I command you."

Gritting her teeth, Natalia gave a curt nod. A shiver ran down her spine as his words took effect. For the first time in over three centuries, the invisible tie to her Nikolai evaporated. Leaving her with a hollow ache that made her uncharacteristically forlorn.

All but moaning as he was engulfed by a pleasurable wave, Nik couldn't help but smile. It had been far too long since the last time he had felt true freedom. It was pure bliss to not be weighed down by Natalia's chains. And in that moment, he vowed to never be under her spell ever again.

Moving her attention from Nik to Natalia, Brynn smirked from behind the cage. She thoroughly enjoyed watching her otherwise beautiful face twist with heartbreak. Her pain made her laugh. As far as she was concerned, the bitch deserved every ounce of whatever it was that was making her so upset.

"Aww. Boo hoo, you whore," she said, louder than she meant to.

Catching the Sun Walker's words, Anton let out a deep chuckle. The sudden sound caused his surrounding Brothers and Sisters to join in. Soon the ballroom erupted in snickers and mocking jabs being thrown Natalia's way. Much to the dismay of the Elders.

"SILENCE!" Ulysses bellowed.

Pulling her painted lips back into a snarl, Natalia raced towards the stage. Hissing in anger, she morphed into something sinister and grotesque. With her sharp claws out, she set her sights on the pathetic mortal in the cage.

No longer bound to his Sire, Nikolai jumped out from behind Helen's shadow. Grabbing a handful of Natalia's dark locks as she rushed past, he roughly yanked her backwards. Pulling her against his torso, he wrapped his free arm around her. Holding her uncomfortably tight, he growled into her ear.

"Save it for the Hunt, Tali. I need to kill you properly," he spat, his embrace threatening to break the bones of her ribcage.

Thrashing against Nikolai, Natalia screamed in frustration. She had never tasted the heat of his wrath before. It shocked her just as much as it riled her. She had never once wished true harm against him, but now? Now she wanted to shred every bit of the body she loved so much.

"Fuck you, Nik!" she squeaked, managing to somehow free her arm.

With her crimson claws extended, she reached back towards her former lover. Catching Nik's cheek, she scratched his flesh with a wicked slash. Splitting his skin and spilling his dark blood.

Growling in a mixture of annoyance and anger, Nik grabbed her thin wrist. Quickly regaining control, he squeezed his arm around her before she had a chance to do it again. Holding her as she bucked, he winced as the sting of the healing process began.

Feeling the sudden need to insert himself, Anton laughed like a jackal as he moved closer to the grappling pair. Paying no mind to Sara as she followed him like a lost puppy, he gave them a round of applause. He always wondered what would happen if Nik could ever fight back against the biggest cunt in the Clan.

"That's it...yes...*please* kill each other! It would save me some trouble! I'll gladly take Miss Smith back to my bed and enjoy your forfeited Spoils. I have been dreaming of holding her again...she broke so beautifully in my hands last time" he said smugly, unable to resist poking the agitated bear. "I wonder what sounds she will make when both my fangs and cock are sinking deep inside of her?"

Instantly enraged by the crass comment, Nikolai moved his narrowed gaze to Anton. "What the fuck did you just say?!" he shouted.

Throwing Natalia to the floor without a second thought, Nik lunged towards Anton. Spitting out a series of dark curses, he attacked him with decades' worth of pent-up frustration. Pulling his arm back, he let his closed fist fly. Punching him with enough force to knock the blonde Vampire flat on his back.

Stunned by Nikolai's aggression, Anton immediately tried to roll away. His attempt was thwarted by Nikolai jumping onto his torso. Unable to move, he simply laughed as Nik landed blow after vicious blow. He knew full well it would get under his alabaster skin.

Screaming for Nikolai to stop, Sara looked towards the Elders with pleading eyes. Cringing as the checkerboard tile broke under Anton's head with every hit from Nikolai's fists, she stumbled towards the stage.

"Christos! Ulysses! End this!" she yelled over the chaos of the room.

"Quick! Before Anton is seriously hurt!"

Completely annoyed by the petty display of aggression, Christos gave Ulysses a knowing look. Taking the lead, he cleared the space between him and the cage. Although he hated to admit it, Anton's insane toy was right. This schoolyard fight needed to end. His Proxy had to be in top physical shape for the Hunt.

Reaching through the bars, he grabbed Brynn by the neck. Yanking her towards him, he forcibly pressed her naked body against the cold metal of the cage. Leaning in close, he pulled back his lips to show the Sun Walker a glimpse of his sharp teeth.

"Scream, girl!" he hissed, digging his long, manicured nails into the skin of her throat.

Whimpering as an acute pain shook through her body, Brynn moved her watery eyes from Christos to Nikolai. Watching in shock as her lover pummeled Anton, she let out a broken scream. Not immediately gaining his attention, she felt her skin tear and her muscles strain as the Elder dug his nails in. Screaming louder, she prayed he would hear before her body broke against the cage.

"NIKOLAI!" she cried. "NIK!"

Consumed by his rage, Nikolai slammed his fists again and again against Anton's bleeding, smug face. Damage was slow due to the strength of his unnatural body, but that mattered not. He was getting the best of the prick in front of the entire Clan, inciting terrible damage to his pride. That was more than enough.

Lifting his arm to swing again, he was suddenly stopped by the sound of a feminine scream. Instantly recognizing it, he whipped his head towards the stage. Jumping from Anton's prone body, he pushed through the crowd that had gathered.

"GET OFF OF HER!" he bellowed.

Lifting his free hand, Christos created an invisible barrier between

Nikolai and the stage. Shaking his head at the insolent twerp, he allowed his counterpart to step in to deal with the rest. Easing his grip on the Sun Walker's neck, he kept her still against the cage.

"Quiet, Nikolai! Or I might accidentally graze her artery," he warned, dragging the nail of his thumb towards her carotid.

With his fists balled at his sides, Nik forced himself to still for the sake of his beloved. Growling low, he focused on Brynn as she disassociated. How could he have allowed Anton to goad him into doing something so stupid? He continued to fail his love. He had to make this right. He had to make everything he had put her through right.

"I'm sorry," he physically mouthed to her.

Confident that Christos had Nikolai under control, Ulysses stormed off the stage. Hunching his broad shoulders, the ancient general stomped towards the still hollering crowd.

"ENOUGH! ALL OF YOU!" he yelled, his words commanding every Vampire in the ballroom to fall silent.

Looking at his Children with disgust and disappointment, Ulysses paced back and forth before them. Waiting for both Anton and Natalia to rise from the floor, he silently talked himself out of throwing each and every one of them into the dungeons.

Rolling her violet eyes at Ulysses and his weak display, Helen stepped towards Nikolai. Moving to stand by his side, she pushed out a sigh as her counterpart went about chiding the youngsters. The night hadn't gone exactly to plan, but when did it ever?

"Let go of her Christos," she said flatly. "Harm her before the Hunt and I'll be forced to call Rikard's Pack."

Widening his honey-colored eyes, Christos openly scoffed. Quickly realizing that Helen was deadly serious, he begrudgingly released his hold on the Sun Walker. Dealing with a mob of rabid Werewolves was not how he wanted to spend the rest of the evening.

"Fine," he said.

Wrapping her arms around the bars of the cage, Brynn held on as her legs threatened to collapse out from under her. Gasping for air, she blinked her eyes as she came back to reality. Looking at Nik and then Helen, she felt a surge of relief fall over her. She was so thankful that they had the Elder in their corner. For now, at least.

Glowering at Christos before turning her attention towards Ulysses, Helen placed her hands upon her narrow hips. Waiting until he had quieted the Clan, she commanded everyone's attention with a sharp whistle that made everyone wince.

"The sun will be rising in a few hours. I think it's time the Sun Walker and Proxies retire for the day," she said, giving each Proxy a stern look. "It seems as if they all need some extra time to prepare themselves for the Hunt."

Wiping a trickle of dark blood from his split lip, Anton rolled his swollen eyes. Admittedly, Nikolai had gotten in a few good licks, but he felt completely fine. Now Natalia on the other hand, she looked like a bitch who had just been kicked by her master. He had never seen her so miserable. He hoped she stayed that way.

Stepping back to Christos, Ulysses raised an eyebrow. He would leave it up to his counterpart to make the decision. It didn't matter to him one way or the other. He was too annoyed at that moment to care.

Lifting his chin, Christos let his eyes glide over the guilty faces of his Children. Settling his gaze on his beaten Proxy, he hummed low. Yes, Anton needed time to recover. He would be getting a deep tongue lashing as soon as the Gathering was over.

"Anton…Natalia…Nikolai," he began, giving each Proxy a stern look. "Back to your rooms…and you are to stay there for the rest of the night and day, hmm? Your respected Elders will join you once we are done with our little party. Now…off you go."

Almost in unison, Anton and Natalia bowed their heads. Making their way towards the ballroom door, they eyed each other as they kept their distance. Allowing the bitch to leave first, Anton gave a quick glance over his shoulder to Sara. Kissing the air, he bid his love farewell before slipping from the room.

"Nikolai," Christos tisked.

Staring unabashedly at Brynn, Nik skirted into her thoughts. Giving her a soft kiss on her cheek, he spoke to her using his otherworldly gift.

I'll come to you as soon as the sun rises, my love. The sunlight still can't touch me because of your blood. But they don't know that. Not even Helen. Wait for me. I love you.

Swallowing hard, Brynn barely nodded her head. His silken words filled her with true hope. Perhaps he had a plan for them to escape before the Hunt. Yes, of course he did.

"I love you, too," she replied aloud.

Tired of waiting, Ulysses snapped his fingers at Nikolai. Motioning to the door with a flick of his head, he pushed out a loud growl. He wished Natalia had never begged to turn him. Clearly, he was unfit for the Clan.

"Leave, Nikolai!" he shouted.

Not giving two shits about Ulysses or Christos, Nik instead looked at Helen. Bowing before her, he ignored the hushed whispers of his former Brothers and Sisters. Looking longingly at Brynn one more time, he left her with another dose of confidence and hatred. Positive that they would keep her safe until the morning came.

CHAPTER THIRTY-ONE

Wrapping the knitted blanket around her bare shoulders, Brynn scooted closer to the edge of the bed. Starting at the wooden door of her room, she all but willed it to open. She had been waiting for Nik for what felt like an eternity. She wondered if he was actually coming.

One thing was for sure, she was tired of waiting. It seemed as if that's all she had been doing since Natalia kidnapped her. She just wanted to be done with it. Whatever it was. She still had no clue what was going to happen. That was truly the worst part.

Lifting her hand, she brushed her fingertips across her freckled cheek. Closing her eyes, she shuddered as she remembered the kisses the Elders had left. Like everything else, it was a surreal moment. After being taken back to her room, Christos and Ulysses had each given a little speech. Thinly veiled threats of what would happen once they had won her, sealed with cold peck that made her skin crawl.

When it was her turn, Helen had chosen to remain silent. Only giving her a warm look of love and compassion. One she imagined a grandmother would give their frightened grandchild. Instead of a kiss, she had wrapped her arms around her and pulled her in for a gentle embrace. Whispering into her ear that Nikolai loved her dearly and to trust him with everything she had.

She had taken Helen's hushed words to heart. They helped to soften the mental blows Natalia had dealt. Trusting Nik was something she simply had to do. *No.* Trusting him was something that she wanted to do. For better or for worse, he was her destiny. She felt it with every fiber of her being.

Letting her mind drift to Nik, she caught the image of his shocking entrance at the Gathering. She had never seen him physically change, not even when he had taken blood from her back in Norway. Movie Vampires had nothing on the real thing. He was feral, and lethal. An animal designed to hunt and kill.

She should have been terrified, only she wasn't. On the contrary, seeing the monster within excited her. She hated that he seemed almost ashamed of what he was. She would have to change his mind.

Hugging the blanket tighter against her body, she suddenly perked as she heard someone toy with the lock on the door. Jumping from the bed, she raced towards the entrance to her room. She couldn't wait to see her love.

Stopping herself just before the door, she waited impatiently as he worked the lock. In an instant, her heart was in her throat, her stomach tied in knots. And all her fears melted away.

"Nik?" she whispered as the doorknob turned.

Opening the bedroom door, Nik stuffed the skeleton key into the back pocket of his jeans. Pushing his body through the small opening, he scanned the dimly lit room. Finding Brynn standing before him, he couldn't help but smile. She looked like a goddess bathed in the candlelight of the windowless room.

"Brynn...my beautiful Brynn," he breathed.

Reaching for her, he gathered her in his strong arms. Lifting her from the ground, relief flooded his body as his eager lips found hers. Hungry and desperate, his kiss relayed everything he had been feeling since the last moment he saw her. He was so thankful to have her back where she belonged.

Dropping the blanket to the floor, Brynn wrapped her arms around his neck. Wantonly moving her lips and tongue over his, she moaned softly as his hands cradled her naked body. Forgetting the world around them, she selfishly enjoyed every second of their heady reunion.

Kicking the door closed with the heel of his boot, Nik turned towards the wall along his left-hand side. Carrying her the handful of steps, he pressed her against the painted plaster. Teasing and tasting, he forced himself to stay with her lips. As much as he wanted more, now was not the time.

Squeezing her legs around his waist, she lifted her hands to his dark hair. Twisting her fingers into his locks, she playfully nipped at his tongue. Hearing him chuckle, she smiled against the kiss. Oh, how she had missed that sound.

Getting lost in the warmth of his love, Nik wished they could spend the rest of the day just like this. Wanting nothing more to make her body sing again and again, the nagging reality of the situation continued to poke at him. Reluctantly ending the kiss, he rested his forehead against hers.

"Mmm...Gods, I have missed you," he said, letting out a sigh.

Idly playing with his hair, Bynn hummed a reply. Trying to calm her racing heart, she licked the remnants of their kiss from her lips.

"I missed you too...I thought I'd never see you again," she confessed.

Pulling his head back, he stared her dead in the eyes. Furrowing his brow, a look of concern passed over the features of his face. Hearing her admission was a knife to the heart. Just what had they filled her head with?

"Nothing could keep me from you Brynn...*nothing*. Please believe that," he said, his tone deep and sincere.

Looking over his handsome face, Brynn gave a tiny nod of her head. She did. She believed him. But for whatever reason, she couldn't stop her brain from repeating what Natalia had said.

"I do, Nik...but...I...I have to ask you this, and please tell me the truth. Is the reason why you came...the reason why you want to fight for me...is it because of my blood?" she asked.

Not entirely surprised by the question, Nik instantly shook his head.

Silently cursing his bitch of a Sire, he tried to look as serious as possible. He knew Natalia would try to poison Brynn with her lies. It was probably killing her that she no longer had a hold over him.

"No, Brynn," he answered, softening his voice. "I'm here because I love you. You are the only thing that matters to me now…and I will risk my life to protect you from them," he replied, leaning in close. "And I hate that I wasn't here sooner…that I wasn't here to shield you from the humiliation and pain that they caused. But we needed Helen's help. What we're doing…what we're about to do…it's going to start a war."

Instantly tensing, Brynn stared at him with wide eyes. "War? Start a war? What the hell are you talking about?" she asked.

Pushing out a sigh, he lifted her away from the wall. Holding her tightly in his arms, he carefully stepped towards the bed.

"Let's sit down, there's quite a few things we need to discuss," he replied.

Not liking the sound of that, she scrunched her face in thought. A million questions were racing through her mind, causing the anxious boulder in her stomach to grow. Why couldn't things just be easy? Why was everything in her life always a fight?

Setting her down upon the bed, he pulled the halfway tucked in comforter free from the mattress. Wrapping it around her naked body, he took a seat next to her. Sensing her fear, he brushed across her heavy thoughts. She wanted to run. She honestly thought they could spend the rest of her life on the run.

"We can't, my love," he said, reaching to cup the side of her flushed face. "Running just isn't an option."

"Why? Why isn't it?" Brynn asked, her voice lifting. "Wasn't that the original plan? Weren't we just going to run and hide from Ulysses and Christos? Why isn't that still an option?"

Rubbing the pad of his thumb across her cheekbone, he met her hazel eyes. He didn't care for what he was forced to do, but his hands were tied.

"Everyone knows about us now, and they know about the power running through your veins. There's nowhere for us to run. We need Helen...we need her lineage...we need her alliances. And in order to secure her help, I had to make a bargain," he said.

"Bargain? What kind of bargain?" she asked.

Pausing for a moment, he clenched his jaw. Readying himself, he dropped his hand from her worried face.

"Helen knows that her power within the Clan is fading. Ulysses and Christos have undermined her authority with this Hunt, and there are whispers of them planning a coup. And we have a feeling that they intend on using *you* as their weapon to overthrow her. Helen needs to send a message to Ulysses and Christos that they've fucked with the wrong woman...and she needs me to do it," he said flatly.

"And just how are you going to do it?" Brynn asked, arching a brow.

"I'm going to kill Anton and Natalia," he replied.

Giving him an odd look, Brynn all but scoffed. If that was the message he needed to send, why wait?

"Well...why not do that now? You know exactly where they are, they're useless in the daylight, it would be like shooting fish in a barrel...why go through with this Hunt? I don't get it," she said.

Nodding once, he took a deep breath. Oh. If only it were that simple.

"We aren't the only Clan in the world, Brynn. If I killed Anton and Natalia now, without provocation...I would be a wanted man. Every Clan would be hunting me...not just my Brothers and Sisters. I wouldn't survive even a night, and neither would you. But...rules are different during a true Hunt. Accidents happen when we Vampires are consumed by our bloodlust. I can kill both Anton and Natalia without any true consequences," he said confidently, tilting his head. "It will be a huge blow to both Ulysses and Christos to lose their most beloved Novices…and, as an added bonus…with Natalia gone…I will be free."

Blinking at her lover, she mulled over his words. The thought of more Clans being out in the world was terrifying to say the least. It was best for them to do things the correct way, and the thought of him being free of the whore was music to her ears. But they would still be in harm's way during the Hunt. She knew firsthand just how strong Anton was, and Natalia was just as formidable.

"This is so risky, Nik," she said, a frown ticking at the corners of her mouth as she remembered something. "But wait…earlier you said that what we're doing is going to start a war. How could that be if they're killed in a sanctioned way?"

"Ahh…yes, there's the rub. Ulysses and Christos will want their revenge and will appeal to the different Clans for their help. Now most of them will turn them away…but there are a few that will join them. Some out of boredom, others because they too hate Helen. But Helen's alliances are strong. So even though they will declare a war, we will ultimately win," he replied.

Closing her eyes, she gave herself time to let everything sink in. There really was no easy way out of this situation. They were fucked in so many ways. It was maddening.

"Are you sure we can't just run?" she asked, opening her eyes.

Grinning softly, Nik huffed under his breath. He wanted nothing more than for that to be their best option.

"I've given my word to Helen…but even if we tried, we'd never get past Rikard's dogs, my love. No…unfortunately, we must go through with the Hunt. But afterwards, we will go back to Capri with Helen and Yetta and wait in luxury for the war to come to us," he said, leaning in close. "But we will be *together*. We will win the Hunt and whatever else will come our way *together*. Nothing is going to tear me away from you ever again."

Nodding her head, Brynn matched his grin. Waiting in luxury on the island of Capri didn't sound so bad. If he was by her side, she felt like they could take on anything.

"Wait…Yetta…is she ok?" she asked suddenly.

"She is, don't worry…she's currently in the forest with Clara leaving you clues. They will be heading back to Capri before the sun sets. She will stay safe, Clara will guard her with her life," he replied.

Stammering for a second, she tried to wrap her head around all the information that had been thrown her way thus far. She was very glad to hear that Yetta was safe and protected, but *huh?*

"Forest? Clues? Clara? I'm getting so confused, Nik," she said, visibly wincing.

Lifting his hand, Nik brushed an errand strand of hair from her eyes. Giving her a sympathetic look, he reminded himself to speak plainly. A headache was the last thing she needed right now.

"I'm sorry, Sunshine…I don't mean to overload you. Tonight, the Elders will have Simon and Michael take you to the center of the Hoia Baciu Forest. I don't want to alarm you, but it's quite haunted…but there are also other things that call it home than ghosts," he said.

"Things? What kind of things?" she asked.

"Well, it's home to Fae, Trolls, Harpies…and now Werewolves," he replied plainly.

Swallowing hard, Brynn shivered at the thought of these terrifying, mythical creatures being real. Now she had to worry about being hunted by other monsters, not just Vampires? Wonderful.

"But don't worry, my love…that's why Clara is there right now. She's a High Priestess of White Magik and she owes Helen a huge favor. She's striking deals with the creatures of the forest right now. Nothing will touch you, I swear it...and if Clara can entice them enough, they may even help you. Which is what I'm banking on...but if on the off chance they wash their hands of this whole situation, Yetta is leaving you clues to follow. They will take you somewhere safe until I can get to you," he said.

"What kind of clues? What should I be looking for?" she asked.

Quirking his head, Nik gave a slight shrug of his broad shoulders. He had to skirt a fine line between telling her too much, and not enough.

"They will be obvious to you...but I can't tell you exactly what they are. There's a chance that if you focus too much on trying to remember the clues, your thoughts will be so loud that both Anton and Natalia could easily pick up on them. Just keep your eyes peeled and you'll spot them," he said.

"Hmm...okay," she said, her frown etching deep. "I'm going to trust that they're so obvious that I will see them. But like...I completely ignored every red flag that you were a Vampire, so."

Chuckling low, Nik leaned in close. With much needed humor on his face, he brushed the tip of his nose over hers. "I suppose that's true...but I have to thank you for ignoring them," he said softly.

"Why? Do you think I would've gone running for the hills or something?" she asked curiously.

"Something like that, yeah," he replied.

Shaking her head, Brynn gently brushed her lips across his. Giving him a chaste kiss, she hummed as she thought about the first time she laid her eyes upon him.

"No...I knew I had to be with you after that first night. Finding out what you were wouldn't have stopped me," she breathed. "Even now, after everything I've been through...even with what's about to happen.

I wouldn't change a damn thing. I know I've said this before...but I want to be with you forever, Nikolai."

Holding her warm gaze, Nik lifted his lips into the smallest of smiles. In that moment, he realized that that was what he wanted too. The thought of watching her whither and disappearing from his world was just too great to bear. He couldn't lose her. He wanted nothing more than to fall on his knees and worship her every single night for all eternity.

"Let's discuss this back in Capri...but for now, you should get some rest, my love. You have a big night ahead of you," he said, his voice deep and silky.

Shrugging the soft comforter from her shoulders, Brynn reached up to hold his handsome face in her hands. It excited her to no end that he was at least willing to talk about their future. Between that and her fears over the Hunt, getting rest was the last thing on her mind.

"Mmm...I think my body has rested enough," she purred. "But my mind is still racing...maybe you could do something to stop me from overthinking?"

With a devilish grin, Nik moved his hands to the sides of her ribcage. Inching his fingers upwards, he grazed his rough touch over her tanned skin. Making love to her probably wasn't the smartest idea, but how could he say no? He wanted her to go into the Hunt knowing with every drop of her soul that he was hers.

"I think I can come up with something, Sun Walker," he said, hungrily claiming her lips.

CHAPTER THIRTY-TWO

Stripping the last bit of clothing from her lover, Brynn tossed it to the floor beside the bed. Climbing over his chiseled body, she leaned down to give him a kiss. Warm and tender at first, it quickly built in intensity. Becoming more needy and desperate with every pass of lips and swipe of tongue. She prayed this wouldn't be the last time she would feel his carnal embrace.

Lifting his hands, Nik held the side of her flushed face. Returning her feverish kiss, he groaned as he felt her straddle his hips. He loved how wanton she was, how she never thought twice about giving into her desire. It continually surprised him.

Holding her with a gentle touch, he nipped at her lips before pulling away. Meeting her lustful gaze, he grinned as she grazed her nails across his bare chest. He wished they had time for more foreplay, but morning was drawing closer.

"I want you to get on all fours," he said, his voice deep and sultry.

Arching a brow, she gave him a flirty smirk. He didn't have to tell her twice. It was one of her favorite ways for them to fuck. He was always able to get so deep.

"Mmm...yes, Sir," she replied.

Moving from his lap, Brynn scooted to the center of the four-poster bed. Getting down on her hands and knees as ordered, she turned her head to watch Nik as he maneuvered behind her. Anticipation made her skin pebble and her breath hitch. He looked like a hungry lion wanting to devour her.

Sitting up on his knees, Nik grabbed his hardened cock. Giving it a few lazy pumps, he watched the candlelight dance across her back. Pushing out a huff as his desire grew, he inched closer.

"You always make me cum so fast when we're like this…you should get a head start. Touch yourself and I'll start fucking you right before break so you can cum on my cock," he said, pawing at himself.

Swallowing hard, she nodded her head as his strained voice replayed in her head. She loved it when he was like this. Assertive and needy. They had been kissing and touching for hours, edging each other again and again with him in various stages of undress. She knew she wasn't the only one hanging on by a thread.

"Yes, Sir," she breathed.

Reaching between her parted thighs, she dipped the tip of her middle finger into her wet pussy. Soaking it with her heady arousal, she moaned as a shock of excitement ran down her spine.

Leaning back on his heels, Nik gave himself a full view of her beautiful cunt. Touching his length, he kept himself from groaning as she toyed with herself. He could watch her do this a million times and never grow tired of it.

"Good girl," he praised, his voice growing strained. "Now play with that little clit."

Grinning wide, she savored his delicious command. Her body was begging to begin. "Yes, Sir," she replied.

Taking in a shallow breath, she swiped her finger across her pink clit. Once. Twice. And then a third time. Arching sharply as a jolt of pleasure rocked her core.

"Ooh…does that feel good, beautiful?" Nik asked, lifting his free hand to palm her firm ass cheek.

"Yes," she mewled.

Giving her skin a firm pinch, he hummed a pleased response. Watching intently as her finger flicked over her sensitive clit, he slid his hand up and down his aching dick. Moving faster and faster, he worked himself to near madness.

"Gods that's a pretty cunt...and who does it belong to, Brynn?" he asked.

Moaning loudly, Brynn closed her eyes as her pleasure took her higher and higher. Swirling her touch around her clit, she didn't hesitate to answer.

"You, Nikolai," she whimpered.

Patting her ass lovingly, he nodded his head. Grazing his fingers over the tip of his cock, he used the beads of precum to lubricate his skin while he gripped himself harder. She was his. Totally and completely. For all of eternity.

"That's right...it's mine," he growled. "You are mine. Now...forever!"

Shivering as her needy touch took her closer to the edge, she gripped the sheets with the hand supporting her torso. Alternating the speed of her finger, she lost herself in the thought of being with her lover until the end of time. There was nothing she wanted more. Well, besides cumming, that was.

"Close," she squeaked. "I'm...I'm...so close."

Smirking to himself, he positioned himself directly behind her. Inching closer, he dragged the head of his cock across her folds. Back and forth, up and down. Drenching himself in her silky arousal.

"Don't cum until I'm inside you," he ordered.

Pushing out a strained moan, Brynn wiggled her ass impatiently. She was dancing on the knife's edge; it was unfair of him to make her wait.

"Hurry up and fuck me!" she cried, turning her head to look over her shoulder.

Meeting her eyes in the dim light, Nik clicked his tongue against the roof of his mouth. Playfully chiding her, he slowly entered her warm cunt. Stopping halfway, he moved his large hands to either side of her hips.

"Mmm...be careful what you ask for," he replied.

Grabbing her hips, he arched into her. Burying his thick cock to the hilt in a single thrust, his eyes rolled in acute pleasure. Feeling her perfect pussy wrap around him, he forced himself not to spill his seed. He would never tire of this, he said to himself. *Never.*

Squealing as his cock filled her cunt, her nimble fingers brought her to the edge. Tapping on her clit over and over, she trembled as her orgasm began.

"I'm cumming!" she yelled.

Holding her steady with the grip on her hips, Nik absorbed the intensity of her bliss as it radiated from her aura. With her cunt fluttering around his cock, he spit out a dark curse to keep himself from moving. Savoring every ebb and flow, he watched her in awe as she fell apart. He couldn't remember the last time she looked so beautiful.

"That's it...that's my good girl," he purred.

Dropping her shaking torso to the mattress, Brynn gasped for much needed air. With the last bit of her release evaporating from her body, she couldn't help but giggle. Having him stay so still inside of her was a million times better than she thought it would be. But she was antsy for him to give into his own lust.

Giving herself a moment to catch her breath and calm her heart, she readied herself for the fun ahead. Using her arm, she pushed herself upwards. Looking over her shoulder, she found his hungry eyes.

"Your turn," she said with a sassy wink.

Licking his lips, Nik narrowed his green eyes. Not needing to be told twice, he growled a low warning. He wouldn't be slow and gentle. No, not this time. Not with the pent-up anguish of almost losing her.

Digging his fingertips into the skin of her hips, he began to thrust inside her silken cunt. Short and quick at first, he barely left her pussy. With the sound of their hurried coupling filling the room, he grunted in approval as she purposefully squeezed around him.

"Gods!" he groaned. "Keep…doing…that!"

Happily obliging his request, Brynn teased his cock with her little trick. Clawing at the bed sheets, she whimpered as he slammed into her. Keeping her eyes on his face, she studied it as it twisted with need. She loved having this power over him. She loved being the only one who had this power over him.

"Yes…yes!" she squealed. "Fuck me…fill me!"

Gritting his teeth, he changed the angle of his thick cock. Arching upwards, he sheathed himself as deeply as he could. Frantic and wild, he hissed as his body warned him of his impending orgasm. For a split second he thought he should stop, to draw their lovemaking out. But she was too wet and felt way too damn good to stop.

Pushing back against every thrust, Brynn smiled as she noticed the tiny change in his rhythm. He was so close to shattering. He just needed a little encouragement. Knowing exactly what would break him, she opened her dirty little mouth.

"Cum in me…claim this…pussy as yours!" she ordered.

Yelling an expletive, Nik lost all semblance of control from her wicked words. Fucking into her a handful of thrusts, he closed his eyes as he slipped over the edge of his delicious release. Stilling in her perfect little cunt, he groaned as he spilled his seed. Shaking with every hot spurt, he tossed his head back.

"Mine…mine," he growled.

Nodding her head, Brynn gave his spent cock another squeeze before it slipped from her pussy. Feeling his cum drip from her cunt, she hummed happily.

"Yes, yours…only yours," she said softly.

Taking in a large breath, Nik collapsed on the mattress next to his love. With a pleased smile on his face, he wrapped his arm around her as she moved to snuggle against him.

"I love you so much…Gods I don't want this day to end," he said, kissing her forehead.

Letting out a sigh, she nuzzled his bare chest with her lips. She didn't want the day to end, either. Being with him was a wonderful distraction. But now that it was over, she was suddenly slapped with their stark reality.

"Are you sure we can't run?" she asked again.

Holding her close, he couldn't stop himself from frowning. He truly wished that they could, but running just wasn't in the cards. He hated how terrified she was. Perhaps there was something he could do to ease her fear. Even if just a little.

"I want to give you some of my power," he said abruptly.

Furrowing her brow, Brynn lifted her head from his chest. What the hell was he talking about? Surely, he didn't want to turn her now. It would screw up everything with the Hunt.

"I thought we were going to talk about turning me when we get to Capri?" she asked.

Giving her a small grin, he absently played with her hair. "Well…yes, we will have many lengthy conversations in Capri but that's not what I'm talking about. Remember how I healed your body after Anton's attack?" he asked, his voice smooth like vintaged wine.

Placing her head back down upon his chest, she took in a sharp breath. Yes, of course she remembered. She didn't think she would ever forget that surreal moment on the plane.

"Yes," she replied softly.

"Good...well, my blood can do amazing things to a healed and healthy body. It can give you physical strength...make your senses sharpen," he said, stroking her chestnut locks.

Lifting a brow, Brynn audibly scoffed. Seriously? "And you're just bringing this up now?" she asked, her tone sharp.

Shrugging his broad shoulders against the mattress, Nik glanced down at her. He understood her annoyance, but it truly was unwarranted.

"Honestly, Brynn...when was there time for me to bring this up? Should I have given you a dram of blood back in Norway? Perhaps. Yes. But I didn't know Natalia was anywhere near us...I still don't understand how I wasn't able to sense her. That has been eating away at me," he confessed before regaining his focus. "But hindsight is always twenty-twenty. The point is I can give you an advantage going into the Hunt. You won't be completely helpless...but there is a small catch."

"What kind of small catch?" she asked.

"Well, there's a chance that it could create a tether between you and me, and then we would be connected for the rest of eternity. Now it didn't happen the first time you drank my blood, but the chance is greater the second time around," he replied.

Narrowing her hazel eyes, she snuggled her body closer. Why was this a catch? It was going to happen eventually. So their connection would form a few months early, what was the big deal?

"Um...won't that happen when you turn me, anyways?" she asked.

"Turn you?" he asked, scrunching the masculine features. "Who said I was going to be your Sire?"

Lifting her head from his chest once again, she looked up at his face. She was instantly confused. It had never occurred to her that she would have another Sire other than him. She didn't want to be tied to someone else. That would be asinine.

"Well, who the hell else is there!?" she spat.

Sensing a shift in her attitude, Nik bit his tongue for a long moment. Arguing was the last thing he wanted to do, and time was of the essence. The discussion over who would Sire her was an adventure for another day.

"You're right, my love…and I'm sorry," he said, wanting to quickly smooth everything over. "So…may I give you some of my power?"

Pausing for a handful of seconds, Brynn allowed her annoyance to pass. She honestly didn't want to ruin their last few moments. It would be stupid of her to refuse his offer.

"Yes, please," she replied.

Taking in a breath, he helped both himself and his love into a seated position. Bringing his left wrist to his lips, he met her eyes in the candlelight. Silently holding her gaze, he let the monster partially out of his cage. With his canines extending and the entirety of his eyes turning ebony, he bit into his flesh.

Shivering with a small bit of excitement, she instinctively opened her mouth as he offered her his wrist. Taking hold of his hand and arm, she leaned in to look at his handiwork. His oozing blood was ink in color, and thick like old molasses. Not what she was expecting.

"Drink, my love," Nik encouraged.

Nodding her head, Brynn brought his wrist to her lips. Covering the bite, she closed her eyes as her tongue lapped his otherworldly blood.

To her surprise, it tasted like tart blackberries. Almost like the ones she would pick from the wild vines when she was a child.

Pushing out a long sigh, he relaxed his shoulders as she took his gift. Praising her as she suckled his torn skin, he committed the moment to memory. It was probably the most intimate act he had ever shared with someone. She truly was his Mate, in every sense of the word.

"That's it, Sunshine…just a little more," he purred.

Moaning softly against his wrist, she swallowed mouthful after mouthful of his cool blood. With every strong heartbeat, she felt a strange energy grow within her. It flowed across her skin like an overly warm blanket. Giving her the sensation of a spiking fever.

Closing his onyx eyes, Nik pushed the monster back into the inner recesses of his consciousness. Wincing as his teeth retracted, he focused on the pleasurable feeling of his love taking his essence. He was letting her drink more than he should, there was no doubt in his mind that they would surely be linked. It was a blessing and a curse.

"Ok…that's enough my beautiful Brynn," he said. "That should be enough to help you through the Hunt."

Swallowing one last gulp, she reluctantly pulled away from his wrist. Licking the remnants from her lips, she shuddered as the pseudo fever built in intensity. It gave her the most intense adrenaline spike as it danced through her body. Like a wildfire raging its way through an old-growth forest.

"Oh my God," she whispered.

Bringing his wrist to his own mouth, Nik gave the wound a swipe of his tongue. Instantly healing the bite, he tilted his head as he watched her. He didn't have to read her thoughts or emotions to know that it had worked. He could feel a curious heat radiating from her. Perhaps they had gone too far.

"How do you feel?" he asked, his deep voice raising ever so slightly.

Blinking once, Brynn focused on his handsome face. Every second that passed her vision sharpened. Lifting the darkness of the windowless room and revealing him as if he was in the light of day.

"Invincible," she replied.

With a single nod, Nik lifted his hand to touch her rosy cheek. Yes, they had gone too far. But thankfully, her newfound power was only temporary. He prayed her confidence would last until the Hunt was through.

"Good," he said, knowing their stolen time together was coming to an end. "Now let's get this Hunt over with, shall we?"

CHAPTER THIRTY-THREE

Sauntering into the dining hall of the Manor, Christos immediately looked at the wall on his right. Gone were the intricate tapestries he loved so dearly, replaced by row after row of flat screen TVs. As much as he hated technology, the mere sight of the sleek screens made him giddy. For the very first time, they would witness a Hunt in real time in every angle possible. He couldn't wait to see the Sun Walker's face the moment his Anton captured her.

Letting out a small sigh, he all but danced towards the center of the large room. Sitting behind a mahogany table facing the TVs sat a svelte man, his fingers frantically typing away on a keyboard. Gaining the man's attention with a single snap, Christos gave him a critical onceover before motioning towards the wall.

"Leonardo...I trust that everything has been set up properly?" he asked, lifting a blonde brow.

Adjusting his useless black rimmed glasses, Leonardo cleared his throat. Nodding an answer, he glanced back and forth between the TVs and the Elder. He had gone over the connections of every camera and drone dozens of times. He was finally confident that everything was in place.

"Yes, Sire...everything's ready," he replied.

"Good...and are all of the Clans tuned on or...whatever it's called?" Christos asked.

Gliding his fingertips over the keyboard, Leonardo eyed the bottom left-hand screen. Pulling up the official roll call, he said a silent thanks to the Night God. He was instantly relieved to see that all the eighteen Clans the Elders had invited were logged onto the live feed.

"Yes, Sire...they're all waiting," he replied, pointing to the TV.

Scanning his honey-colored eyes over the various Clan insignias, Christos crossed his arms over his chest. *Good,* he thought. He knew everyone would be chomping at the bit to watch history in the making. Two of the Ancient Families had already reached out to both he and Ulysses to strike a deal. One night with the Sun Walker in exchange for enough money to keep the Benefactor program going for at least another decade. They would be fools not to take it.

"And are they betting?" Christos asked, shifting his weight from one heeled foot to the other.

"They are, Sire…our Broker in Monte Carlo is quite pleased," Leonardo said.

"Mmm…and just who are they betting on?" Christos inquired.

Sucking in a breath, Leonardo groaned internally. Why did he have to be the bearer of this news? The Elder would no doubt take it personally that his Proxy currently held the worst odds. Not that it should be that much of a surprise. Many of the Clans harbored ill will towards Anton for fucking up their alliances with the Werewolves.

"Nikolai," he said simply.

Darting his gaze to Leonardo, Christos couldn't help but scowl. He didn't think he could hold any more hatred in his black heart for Natalia's pathetic spawn than he already did.

"Well, we will just have to make sure he loses tonight," he hissed.

Answering with a curt nod, Leonardo kept his mouth shut. He cared for Nikolai and didn't want to see anything egregious happen to him. Christos and Ulysses always played dirty, though. It was something he was intimately aware of.

Silently seething in place, Christos studied each of the screens. Three of the twenty-six screens were black and would remain that way until everyone was in place. Seven screens showed the feeds of drone cameras. Their infrared images were amazingly clear as the tiny robots flew through the gnarled trees and dense fog of the forest. The last sixteen screens held static night vision images of the Maze. While cameras were no match for Vampiric eyesight, he was pleased by what he saw.

"What time is it?" he asked.

Looking at the Swiss watch gracing his wrist, Leonardo winced ever so slightly. The countdown was officially on. He suddenly felt nauseous.

"Quarter to eleven. Everyone should be moving into place. Their cameras will automatically turn on in ten minutes, Sire," he answered.

"Splendid," Christos replied.

Reaching upwards to his ear, he turned on the earpiece that audibly connected him to his Proxy. Momentarily distracted by the sound of electrical snow, he perked as he saw Leonardo straighten his posture. Glancing to his left and right, he took notice of both Ulysses and Helen as they entered the hall from opposite ends. They both looked incredibly smug in their business attire. It made him chuckle.

"Well, well, well…it's so good for you two to finally make your appearance," he offered, thankful to be wearing his silk pajamas.

Adjusting the blazer of her form fitting suit, Helen slowly walked towards Christos. Ignoring his comment, she replayed her conversation between her and Nikolai in her mind. Although it broke their laws, it was wise of him to let the Sun Walker drink from him. Between that and what Yetta and Clara were able to accomplish, there was no doubt that she would be the ultimate Victor.

"Is everything ready?" she asked, halting her steps a meter away from her counterparts.

"Mmmhmm, we're just waiting for everyone to get into position," Christos replied.

Taking his place beside Christos, Ulysses grunted his approval. Standing confidently, he clenched his jaw as he turned on his earpiece. With the melodic hum of his Proxy filling his ear, he visualized her moving towards the second quadrant. He was glad she had pulled that particular card. It was a part of the Maze she knew extremely well.

"Natalia," he said, his voice all but a low whisper. "Can you hear me?"

'Yes, Sire.'

"Good. Make this quick, hmm? I want to taste both of you before sunrise," he barked.

'Yes, Sire.'

Catching Ulysses' portion of the conversation, Helen couldn't help but make a disgusted face. She and Nikolai were honestly doing Natalia a favor with what they had planned. Luckily for the trollop, she wouldn't have to worry about being her Sire's plaything ever again.

Noticing the old hag's sour demeanor, Christos let out a small sigh. Inching ever so closer, he forced himself to look at her ancient face.

"Helen, are you sure you don't need one of these?" he asked, pointing to his earpiece.

Dragging her violet gaze from Ulysses to Christos, Helen shook her head. Nikolai had requested that they not use them, and she had agreed. There really wasn't any point, her Proxy knew exactly what he was doing.

"Nikolai is capable of handling himself without my interference. Unlike your two toddlers," she replied, her tone dripping with annoyance.

Shrugging to look unbothered, Christos pursed his glossy lips together. It took a considerable amount of self-control not to say something flippant in return. *Fuck,* she was such a bitch. He didn't give two shits one way or another. He had only asked to seem polite.

"Fine," he said, pulling his attention back to the screens. "Leonardo...turn on the last of the cameras. We're ready to start the Hunt."

. . .

Lifting her chin defiantly, Brynn stepped through a pile of mud as her chaperones weaved her through the foreboding forest. Kicking the hem of the white cotton nightgown she was forced to wear, she huffed under her breath. They had been walking for what seemed like miles. She just wanted to get to wherever they were going. Her nervous anticipation was eating her alive.

"Where exactly are you dumbasses taking me?" she asked, dropping her gaze to the sharp rope restraining her wrists.

Tugging the Sun Walker forward with a harsh yank of the rope, Michael looked over his muscular shoulder. Narrowing his brown eyes, he gave a quick glance to Simon before glaring at Brynn. She sure was a mouthy little thing. He was growing tired of listening to her constantly bitch and moan.

"The Witch's Spire," he replied, his voice cold and gruff. "It's just up ahead. Now shut your mouth before I fucking shut it for you!"

Laughing lightly, Brynn rolled her eyes. Michael had been threatening her from the moment they had left the Manor. She knew that he was all bark and no bite.

"I'd love to see you try," she said flippantly.

Stopping dead in his tracks, Michael whirled around to face Brynn. Balling his fist, he instinctively pulled back his heavy arm. Barring his sharp teeth, he hissed a warning.

"When it's my turn to have you, you prissy little bitch...I'll make sure it's extra painful," he vowed.

Tilting her head, Brynn physically bristled. As if the fifth tiered Vampire would ever get the chance, she thought.

Opening her mouth to spit a response, she suddenly felt a phantom hand gently muzzle her. Instantly she knew it was Nikolai. Their connection wasn't quite what she expected. For whatever reason, it seemed one-sided; with him being able to read her from afar and send his influence. Not that she was complaining. His invisible presence was comforting.

"Ok, ok...I'll be good," she said, her words directed at her love.

"That's what I thought," Michael sneered, meeting Simon's knowing face before resuming his steps. "Now hurry!"

Stumbling slightly as the brute quickened his feet, Brynn growled an expletive as Simon pushed her forward. Out of the two, she was more afraid of the Vampire nipping at her heels. He was far too quiet for her liking.

"I'm going! I'm going!" she exclaimed.

Roughly pulling her around a dead stump, Michael felt a surge of relief when the Spire came into view. Once a lush Downy Oak tree, it now stood a shadow of its former glory. Fossilized by the spirits of the forest, its black trunk and bent limbs marked the very center of the Maze. Every mortal they had used as prey in the Hunts had been tied to it for the first five minutes. The Sun Walker would be no different.

Reaching back, he grabbed onto her upper arm and dragged her the last few steps. Paying no mind to her pathetic protests, he slammed her back against the unyielding trunk. Feeling his phone vibrate a warning in the back pocket of his jeans, he looked at his partner. The Proxies would be free to Hunt in five minutes. It was time to get the bitch into place.

"Tie her down, Simon," he ordered.

Taking the length of rope from Michael, Simon did as he was told. Halfway up the tree above the Sun Walker's head was a hook made of iron, nailed into the tree a century prior. Tossing the rope around the hook a handful of times, he used his weight to pull it taunt. Causing the Sun Walker to outstretch her arms over her head, he gave her a wicked smile as she winced and whimpered from the pain of having her limbs stretched.

"That's it, beautiful Brynn, cry for the camera," he said.

Recoiling from his words, Brynn's heart began to race. She didn't know how the Vampire knew Nik's pet name for her, but it made her skin crawl, nonetheless.

"Camera?" she asked, her mind registering the last bit of his sentence. "Wait...what fucking camera?"

Almost on cue, a white drone zoomed by the Spire. Circling the trio, it came to static hover right before her. Aiming the camera lens directly at her, it gave all the Vampires watching a clear view of her shocked face.

"Shit," she whispered.

Snickering at the Sun Walker, Simon gave the rope another tug to make sure it was secure. He hoped to watch a replay of the moment, the look on her face was beyond priceless. She was the epitome of what mortals called a 'deer caught in the headlights.'

Thoroughly amused, he reached into the back pocket of his leather pants. Pulling out a modest switchblade, he placed it in her right hand. She didn't realize how blessed she was. There was once a time where the prey was forced to break their limbs in order to free themselves. The Elders were being unusually kind.

"Good luck, Sun Walker," he said curtly, motioning to Michael with a flick of his bearded chin. "Let's go."

Gripping onto the sheathed weapon, Brynn widened her hazel eyes.

Trying her best to ignore the drone, she glanced back and forth at the amused Vampires as they began to walk away.

"Wait! Wait! What…what do I do?!" she yelled, standing on her tiptoes to elevate some of the pressure from her wrists. "What do I do?!"

Shrugging his shoulders, Simon followed Michael through the layer of thick fog before them. Not bothering to look back, he shouted an answer. "Cut yourself down! I'd hurry if I was you…the rabid bats are coming!"

Scrunching her face, Brynn wondered if she had heard him correctly. Bats? Did he say rabid bats? What in the ever-loving fuck?

"RABID BATS?!" she screamed.

No longer able to see the two Vampires in the swirling mist, she heard only their dark laughter as it echoed against the surrounding trees. Swallowing the bile rising in her throat, she looked with nervous eyes at the drone. This Hunt was more than just her being chased by bloodthirsty Vampires, she realized. It was a full-blown spectacle that no doubt included mental and physical torture.

"You fucking assholes!" she growled at the blinking red light of the camera.

Watching the nearly silent drone as it came closer, she pictured Ulysses and Christos mocking her on the other end of the wireless connection. Not wanting to give them the satisfaction of her distress, she hardened her features. Pushing the smooth button of the switchblade, the blade unsheathed from its hilt. It wasn't much. Perhaps only three inches long, but it would have to do.

Unsure of how much time she had, Brynn set to work. Placing the edge of the blade against the rope, she tried her best to saw into it. She was clumsy and slow, often missing due to the way her hands were bound. Growling and spitting in frustration, she lifted herself higher on her tiptoes.

Hovering a foot away, the drone swirled back and forth in the air trying to get the best angle. Whirling its tiny propellers, it reminded Brynn of an annoying gnat.

"I'm going to fucking destroy you!" she yelled at the robot.

Growing angrier by the second, she felt her blood boil as she barely made any progress. Stilling her hand, she gulped in mouthfuls of air. Silently cursing everything around her, she jumped slightly as she heard an odd whooshing noise off in the distance.

Looking around the forest with her enhanced vision, her heart began to pound against her ribcage. Second by second the sound grew louder, frightening her to the core. It reminded her like a swarm of pissed off hornets.

Or perhaps a swarm of rabid bats.

Swallowing hard, Brynn looked upwards at the rope. To her dismay, the majority was still intact. She would never be able to cut through it before the disgusting flying rats made it to her.

"Fuck! Fuck!" she exclaimed.

Panicking over what to do, she swung her body back and forth in desperation. Spitting and swearing, she began to tug on the damaged rope. Over and over again, until she heard a deep voice break through her jumbled thoughts.

Harder, Brynn! Harder!

Nodding her head, she followed Nik's supernatural command. Sheathing the switchblade, she pulled and yanked as hard as she could. Every sharp tug caused the hook to creak, loosening the metal from the Spire.

"C'MON! C'MON!" she screamed as the bats flew closer, their screeches filling the night air.

Gliding backwards, the drone widened its camera's shot. Moving around the Spire in a series of tight spins, it recorded every moment of Brynn's plight in glorious HD. Much to the excitement of the Vampires watching.

Jumping up and down, she used her weight to loosen the hook. After a handful of jumps she realized that Nik's blood truly did give her a boost in physical strength. Using that knowledge, she grit her teeth and pulled as hard as she could. Once. Twice. And then a third time, which tore the iron from the petrified Spire.

Squealing as the hook whizzed by her head, Brynn caught herself before she fell to the ground. Freezing for only a second, she knelt before the hunk of dark metal. Using her still bound wrists, she quickly worked the rope free.

Gathering the length of rope against her chest, she stood to full height. Breathing hard as the adrenaline ran through her veins, she wondered what she should do. Her repeated question was met with a single answer in her frightened mind.

RUN, BRYNN. JUST RUN.

CHAPTER THIRTY-FOUR

Holding the rope against her chest, Brynn ran as fast as her legs would carry. Stumbling every few steps from her cumbersome nightgown, she yelled in frustration. Of course they would put her in something so ridiculous. For a split second, she wished she was naked again.

Looking over her shoulder, her eyes widened as she noticed a black swarm slicing through the trees. Catching the leading bat with her enhanced sight, she let out a sharp gasp. These weren't normal bats, she realized. They were the size of barn owls, hissing and screeching at the top of their lungs. With large, pointed ears and fangs that dripped with saliva. They terrified her with their thunderous approach.

Swallowing a scream, she mentally begged her legs to move faster. Too focused on the demonic creatures as they flew closer, she didn't notice the small commotion ten yards ahead. Nor did she see the thorned vine pulled taut directly in her path.

Shaking her wild locks from her face, she continued to fight with the fabric slowing her steps. Tugging at the cotton with her full, and still bound hands, she spit an angry curse.

Noticing something white out of the corner of her eyes, she jumped as she ran. The damn drone was flying to her left, weaving effortlessly through the dead branches of the forest. Recording every frantic step to its Vampiric audience.

Distracted by the hissing bats and whirling drone, Brynn let out a strangled yelp as her shin hit the wicked vine. Caught totally off guard, she fell forward face first. Hitting the ground so hard that it knocked all the wind from her lungs.

Rolling onto her back, Brynn winced in acute pain. Gasping and coughing, she felt time slow. Blinking the stars from her eyes, she gulped in mouthfuls of much needed air. Dazed and confused, she barely registered the two child sized silhouettes closing in. Within a split second, the shadowy creatures were at her feet, but Brynn couldn't take her eyes off the approaching swarm.

Keenly aware of the dangers flying towards them, the larger of the two moss covered figures leaned in. With stoic features and a body carved from granite, he gave the Sun Walker an assuring grin. Without saying a word, he motioned to his partner to attack. Waving his small hands in the air, he called upon a blanket of mythic protection. The low-lying mist around them swirled as if moved by a gust of wind. Covering them all in a spell that made them invisible to the flying beasts, both organic and robotic.

Lifting a heavy rock from the muddy ground, the female troll narrowed her beady little eyes. Watching the drone as it zig zagged around them, she pulled back her arm. Lofting the rock as hard as she could throw, she yelled in triumph as it knocked the drone from the air. Shattering it into tiny pieces that rained down upon the forest floor.

"Bravo!" gruffed the husband. "Now tend to the Sun Walker, I'll hold the spell until they pass!"

"Aye," replied the wife, stepping to Brynn's side.

Groaning low, Brynn furrowed her brow as she looked at the stone skinned creature leaning over her. Not understanding what the hell was happening, she merely stared at the odd-looking thing.

"Ye poor thing! But...why are ye still in these nasty binds? Hmm? The magic in your blood is so much stronger than these ropes! Eh, no matter! Just lay there 'an catch yer breath...I'll take care of them for ye!"

Taking the switchblade from Brynn's hand, she pressed the release button. Unsheathing the blade, she cut through the rope tethering her hands. Freeing the Sun Walker from her restraints, she then moved to her long nightgown. Cutting the fabric to mid-thigh, she tore a circlet in the cotton.

"There!" she exclaimed, pushing the rope and fabric to the side. "Much better!"

Nodding an approval to his wife, the husband motioned towards the raging bats. "Here they come, Winnie!"

Glaring at the beasts, Winnie gently covered her tiny hand over the Sun Walker's mouth. Speaking to her in a hushed voice, she tried to maintain a calm demeanor.

"Quiet now, dearie...just until the devil spawn have passed," she said.

Doing as the creature said, Brynn stayed as quiet as her lungs would allow. Breathing hard through her nose, her heart raced as the bats came closer. She had no idea who her guardians were but remembered Nik telling her about Clara making deals with the forest folk. She was so very thankful they had come to her aid.

Outstretching his arms, the diminutive husband grit his yellow teeth. Maintaining the ancient enchantment, he silently cursed the wretched bats as the swarm flew over them. Moving his gaze to Winnie, he met her eyes. With the demonic screams filling his ears, his small body shook from the wind caused by the bats' leathery wings.

Counting the hollow seconds, Winnie encouraged her husband with a look of adoration. She knew he was working so hard to protect them. She would have to make him his favorite root stew as a reward.

Watching with wide eyes as the last bat brought up the rear, Brynn bit her cheek to stop herself from screaming. Not only did they look and sound vile, but they smelled horrendous too. She didn't want to think what they would've done to her had they caught her.

Waiting until he was absolutely sure the bats wouldn't return, the husband ended the spell with a wave of his arms. Nearly collapsing from exhaustion, he couldn't help but chuckle. He knew he still had it in him. He might not be as spry as he once was, but he still had it.

"Did ya see that, Winnie?! Did ya see that?!" he asked.

Lifting her hand from the Sun Walker's mouth, Winnie nodded her head. She had a feeling he would be talking about this for years.

"Aye, Winston! I'm so proud of ye!" she replied.

Giving her husband a warm smile, Winnie turned her attention to the Sun Walker. Glancing down at the pretty human, she helped her to sit up from the damp forest floor.

"There ye go, dearie…an' remember, weapons are handy, but yer power is stronger than any knife…don't let yer fear dull yer gifts!" she exclaimed, handing her back the switchblade.

Taking the sheathed knife, Brynn stared blankly at Winnie. The creature's comments sounded incredibly similar to ones Yetta had made. She wished she understood what they were trying to tell her. Nodding as if she wasn't confused, she pushed the suggestion to the back of her mind. Taking in a handful of quick breaths, she smiled at the creatures.

"Uh…thank you…thank you so much for your help!" she exclaimed.

Puffing up his chest, Winston had a look of pride on his face. Not only had he saved a Sun Walker, but had also wiped his family's debt with the White Witch. It was a night that would be long remembered.

"Yer welcome, Sun Walker. Be sure to tell Clara that the trolls are now free folk…we have worked off our debt. Now hurry along before another one of those manmade machines finds ya again," he replied.

Carefully standing to full height, Brynn had a lightbulb moment. *Trolls,* she thought. Oh, God! Never in her wildest dreams did she ever think she would see an actual troll. They looked nothing like the lucky ones with the crazy hair.

"I will…do you…do you know where I should go?" Brynn asked.

Pointing towards his right, Winston motioned her to the remnants of an old stone path. If he had heard the White Witch correctly, it would take the Sun Walker to a hidden present.

"That way, good luck!" he replied.

Smoothing her free hand over the front of her now-short nightgown, Brynn nodded her head. Looking in the direction he was pointing, she swallowed hard. She didn't know what else was waiting for her. She would be lying if she said it didn't worry her.

"Thank you," she muttered, heading towards the path.

Wrapping his arm around his wife, Winston pulled her close. Kissing her temple, he whispered something into her pointed ear that made her giggle like the schoolgirl he had fallen in love with a century prior.

Catching the oddest laugh she had ever heard, Brynn glanced over her shoulder. Expecting to see the trolls, she was shocked to find two small stacks of rocks where they once had stood. Blinking her hazel eyes, a shiver raced down her spine. Had they actually been there? Or was the haunted forest playing tricks on her mind?

"This is so weird," she whispered.

Knowing she didn't have time to dwell, Brynn shook the thoughts from her head. Taking in a cleansing breath, she continued her journey. Running down the path that would hopefully meet up with her love, who was no doubt moving heaven and hell to get to her.

. . .

Staring at the blackened television screen, Christos motioned to it with a frantic wave of his hands. Only a second prior they were watching Brynn run for her life and then nothing. Total darkness.

"What the hell just happened?!" he yelled.

With a deep frown etched onto his face, Ulysses turned towards

Christos. He swore he caught the image of rock flying at the drone before the feed cut out. There was only one kind of creature in the forest that could hit a moving target with such accuracy using only a damn rock.

"Trolls," he growled.

Huffing under his breath, Christos folded his arms over his chest. *Trolls.* Of course. Nasty, smelly little buggers that we're extremely territorial. It wasn't the first time they interfered with a Hunt.

"Ugh…Leonardo…send in another drone! None of the static cameras are catching anything!" he whined. "You should have planned for something like this to happen, you imbecile!"

Pressing her crimson lips together, Helen forced her face to remain neutral as Christos continued to berate poor Leonardo. Inside, however, she was feeling quite smug. Their plan was working. She only hoped that Brynn would find her little gift before the next drone found her.

Typing away on the keyboard, Leonardo changed the coding on the second drone. Sending it to the last coordinates they had, he tried not to let the complaining Elders get under his skin.

"It will be there in three minutes, Sire," he said.

Audibly gasping, Christos instantly seethed. "Three minutes?!" he yelled. "She could get halfway into the fourth quadrant in three minutes!"

Shrugging his shoulders, Leonardo studied the cameras in the general vicinity where Brynn had been. He hoped that if any of them caught her, he could switch the angle before anyone noticed. It was the least he could do.

"I'm sorry, Sire! I'm sorry!" he said, not daring to look away from screens.

Hissing under his breath, Christos bristled. His rational mind knew it wasn't the youngling's fault. Unfortunately for Leonardo, his emotional mind was always louder.

"Oh. You will be," he promised darkly before reaching for his earpiece. "Anton, she's moving into the fourth quadrant. My guess would be near the ridge but who really knows. Just get there!"

Following Christos' lead, Ulysses contacted his own Proxy. Not wanting to be as outlandish as his counterpart, he kept his voice even and confident. Natalia would probably be the last one on the scene given her position within the Maze, but he had faith in her. Although her abilities were dulled within the forest, she was still incredibly powerful. She would secure the Sun Walker, of that he had no doubt.

"Natalia...move into the fourth quadrant as quickly as possible. Be vigilant. Trolls have already gotten in the way...I would be on the lookout for Fae, and other Spirts," he said, only paying attention to the concerns of his Proxy.

Pushing out a sigh, Helen took a handful of steps towards Leonardo's chair. Reaching out, she gave his shoulder a gentle squeeze. She hated that he was their favorite whipping boy. But not for much longer. While she couldn't sever his tie to Christos, she did have the ability to make his eternity easier. It was what he deserved for being turned against his will.

"You're doing well, Leo," she praised, her voice so low only he could hear. "Three minutes is all she needs."

CHAPTER THIRTY-FIVE

Sprinting down the worn path, Brynn nervously gripped her sheathed switchblade. Scanning her eyes through the woods, she felt her warm skin pebble in trepidation. There were sounds she had never heard before; smells she had never smelt. Everything around her felt ominous and evil. There was no doubt in her mind that the forest was truly haunted.

Turning a sharp corner, she reminded herself to remain steadfast. Nik was heading her way; she could feel it in her bones. She only needed to hide from Anton and Natalia until he found her. Honestly, how hard could that be?

Shaking the nervous thoughts from her mind, she followed her intuition. Moving right, and then left, she ran through a throng of mangled trees. Jumping over large rocks and broken limbs that threatened to trip her with every hurried step. She was suddenly thankful the Elders had allowed her to wear shoes. Although the ballet flats did little to support her feet, at least they were somewhat protected.

"Such a lucky girl," she whispered to herself.

Mindful of the prickly vines winding along the path. Brynn instantly perked at the sight of something unusual dead ahead. Slowing her steps, her hazel eyes widened when her brain finally registered what she was looking at. It was a small bouquet of pink peonies.

"Nikolai!" she exclaimed, running towards the flowers.

Relieved beyond measure, she knelt beside the bouquet. Picking up the fragrant blooms, her gaze immediately honed in on a bulky chain wrapped around the stems. Touching the silver pendant attached to the chain, she stared at it long and hard for a handful of seconds. She knew what it was, she was certain she had seen it before.

"Oh!" she said to herself. "It's a dog whistle!"

Feeling triumphant for knowing what it was, she furrowed her brow only a second later. A dog whistle? But, why? She couldn't make heads or tails of it.

Knowing she didn't have the luxury to dwell, she quickly wretched the chain from the stems with her free hand. Putting it on over her head, she hid the pendant under the neckline of her nightgown. Taking in a breath, she relished the way the cool metal felt against her overheated skin.

Giving the peonies one last look, she tossed them into the thick brush beside the path. Confident that the pink blooms were hidden, she stood from the dirt floor. As much as she would love to take a break from running, there simply wasn't time. She could rest once she and Nik were safely in Capri. Happy and safe under the Italian sun.

Mentally preparing herself for what might lie ahead, she soldiered on. Making her tired legs move, she unknowingly triggered a camera lodged in the crook of a tall tree. Off in the distance, a faint howl could be heard. Unfortunately for Brynn, she was too emotionally scattered to pay attention to either one.

. . .

"There she is," Ulysses growled, pointing to the center screen.

Squealing loudly, Christos clapped his hands together. Thoroughly pleased by the image of the Sun Walker stumbling over a fallen branch, he couldn't contain his excitement. He knew exactly where she was in the Maze. His Proxy was the closest to her. Things were working out quite perfectly.

"Anton! She's heading towards the Peak! She's about to box herself in...hurry! Hurry!" he exclaimed.

Narrowing his dark eyes at his counterpart, Ulysses reached for his earpiece. Natalia was just now heading into the third quadrant, she still had quite a way to go. He wished she could use her Gift. They were at a huge disadvantage that her ability to teleport was dulled by the magic of the forest.

"The Peak, Natalia…go there now. Anton will reach her first, but he won't be able to keep her. He's just a useless—"

"Rude!" Christos interrupted, giving Ulysses an offended look. "That's incredibly rude, Ulysses! As if your little bitch is any better!"

Lifting her fingers to her temples, Helen closed her violet eyes. Trying her best to ignore the bickering boys, she massaged away her slight headache. Nikolai was the furthest away from Brynn. And if what she had seen on the monitors was true, there were still a myriad of obstacles separating them. Her Proxy needed to hurry. Anton only had one threat standing in his way. Hopefully the Sun Walker was as clever as Nikolai had promised.

"Fututus et mori in igni! Would you just shut up! Ugh! You two are insufferable," Helen growled, opening her eyes. She had had enough of their incessant squabbling.

Darting his gaze to Helen, Ulysses became instantly enraged by her biting words. Slamming his fist onto the tabletop before him, he let out an ear-piercing yell. The monstrous sound caused the entire room to jump in response.

Unleashing the Demon within, his otherwise handsome features twisted and distorted into something not of this world. Scarlet horns pierced through the skin of his cheeks and chin, his eyes turned opaque onyx in color. Opening his mouth wide, his canines elongated into sharp, thick pikes. The sickening transformation commanded instant fear in both Helen and Christos. It was rare for Ulysses to show his true self.

After a moment that seemed like eternity, Christos bravely intervened. Knowing exactly what was at stake, he moved to Ulysses' side. Soothing the savage beast with his gentle touch, he slowly wooed his

Roman lover into returning. As much as he would love to watch him tear into Helen's throat, it would be to their detriment. They weren't in any position to begin their War. *Yet*.

"Our apologies, Helen…we will behave. Won't we, Ulysses?" Christos said, giving his counterpart a soft pat on the arm.

Grunting low, Ulysses swallowed back the last bit of the demon inside. Unbuttoning his black velvet blazer, he took in a much-needed breath.

Letting out a controlled sigh of relief, Helen straightened her posture in a show of faux confidence. If it had been anyone else, she would have put them immediately in their place. Although she was technically above Ulysses within the Hierarchy, she was surrounded by those that held his direct loyalty. It reminded her of just how dangerous the game truly was. She was tiptoeing on the edge of a very unstable ledge.

Remaining silent until he was fully calm, Ulysses refocused his concern on the television screens hanging on the wall. He could feel the heat of Helen's glare, but it mattered none. There was once a time where he worshipped her like a Goddess, but now? Now he couldn't wait to attend her funeral pyre.

"Yes, Helen. We will behave," he replied curtly, quietly seething as he noticed Anton nipping on the Sun Walker's heels.

. . .

Unable to keep up her hurried pace a moment longer, Brynn halted her steps. Bending over to grip her knees, she took in large gulps of air. Sweat dripped down her forehead, her lungs felt as if they were filled with fire. If she didn't know any better, she would've sworn she was spiking a fever.

Shaking with adrenaline, she closed her tired eyes. Trying her best to quiet her thoughts, she waited for the assurance of Nik's presence. To her surprise and dismay, she felt nothing. Not a single sign that he was with her. For the very first time since entering the Maze, she felt completely and utterly alone.

She prayed to God that he was safe and sound.

Finally catching her breath, she checked her surroundings. Wiping the perspiration from her brow, she glanced around the thick brush. Off in the distance she noticed a clearing with no sign of vegetation, not even a single blade of grass. For whatever reason, it called her, begging her to come closer.

Listening to the ethereal voice, she walked towards the barren piece of land without a single thought in her mind. Finding herself completely mesmerized, she dropped the switchblade as her autonomy slipped away. With every shallow step the white mist that had surrounded her through the Maze faded to nothing. Making the tall figure stalking her clearly visible.

Totally unaware of the Hunter, Brynn followed the melodic sound into the clearing. Once inside, a blast of golden light appeared out of thin air. Its sudden emergence made her jump, abruptly breaking her out of the hypnotic haze.

"Oh! Wow! Uh…hi? Woah…uh…what the heck are you?" she wondered, squinting her eyes.

Slowly gliding from side to side, the light flickered in intensity. Trying to seem as friendly as possible, it flew forward to tickle her nose.

Laughing lightly, she scrunched her face as the light touched her. Going cross eyed for a split second, she swore she saw a small creature hidden within the metallic glow. One with willowy limbs and gossamer wings. It reminded her of something she had read in a fairytale when she was a little girl.

"Wait…are you…are you a Fae?" she asked curiously.

Dancing upwards and downwards in the air before Brynn, the creature seemed to answer. Unable to speak the Sun Walker's native tongue, it whistled a cheerful tune.

Smiling brightly, she let out a sigh of relief. She was so thankful that another creature of the forest had come to her aid. Reaching up to tuck a sweaty lock of hair behind her ear, she kept her attention on the Fae as it hovered.

"How cool! Well, it's nice to meet you! Uh so…somehow, I got all turned around and I don't know where I am…I really need to find a place to hide until my love can find me…do you think you could help me? Please?" Brynn asked.

Mindful of the Vampire creeping closer, the Fae answered her in the same way she had only moments before. Needing the Sun Walker to move further into the clearing, it gingerly flew backwards.

"Wonderful! Ugh, I'm so thankful…so thankful," Brynn replied.

Following the Fae's lead, Brynn confidently headed into the barren space. With each step, she felt her anxiety settle and her hope return. Although she had no clue where she was being taken, she knew it was safe. She would have to find some way to thank the White Witch for all she had done.

"You really are beautiful," she said, utterly enamored by the tiny creature.

Fluttering before the Sun Walker, the Fae danced in a flirty pattern. Using its song once again, it charmed the woman into ignoring the dangers both behind and in front of her.

Humming along with the melodic lullaby, Brynn moved with the twirling Fae. Watching its light ebb, she felt the world around her fade away. Getting lost in the fairytale moment, her feet waltzed along the scorched earth. It wasn't until she felt only air under her right foot did she snap back to reality.

Instantly looking down, Brynn stopped herself before falling into the abyss. Hovering over the edge of a hundred-foot cliff, she pushed out a strangled scream. Falling backwards in a complete panic, she scrambled for solid ground, pushing herself away from what was almost her demise.

"Oh my God! Oh my God!" she squealed, continuing to scoot backwards to the safety of the middle of the clearing.

Enraged that its plan had failed, the Fae's golden light burned crimson. Zooming towards the Sun Walker like a spent bullet, it smacked into her forehead. Using its fury, it sliced into her skin again and again using its needle-like claws. Wanting to cause as much pain as it could.

"Ah! Ouch! Stop! Stop!" Brynn exclaimed, smacking at the angered Fae with her opened hand. "What…what the hell did I do?!"

Dodging every chaotic slap, the Fae continued its assault. Using all the energy in its miniature body, it wailed on her feverish forehead. Drawing small lines of blood with every terrible swipe.

"Holy shit! STOP! JUST…STOP!" Brynn screamed.

Waving her hands in front of her pained face, she growled as she was unable to make contact with the Fae. Squeezing her eyes shut, she prayed for the annoying insect to stop. Repeating the prayer over and over in her mind, it was seemingly answered. Just as quickly as it began, the attack on her ended. Leaving her bewildered and frightened.

Breathing hard, she opened her eyes. Wiping away sweat and blood from her forehead with the back of her hand, she frantically looked around the night sky. To her relief, the wicked Fae was nowhere to be seen.

"What the fuck was that about?" she wondered aloud, her voice shaking just as much as her body.

Blinking away sudden tears, she tried desperately to calm her erratic heartbeat. Taking in as much air as she could, she didn't have time to process what had just happened. Behind her, a masculine laugh rang out, causing her to freeze in triggered terror. She knew exactly who it belonged to, and it made her blood run to ice. How the hell did he find her first?

Jumping to her wobbly feet, Brynn whirled around to face the lowly Vampire. Trying so hard not to let her fear get the best of her, she met his dark eyes as he stalked forward. With all the faux bravery she could muster, she stood her ground by planting her legs and puffing her chest. She didn't want to give him even the slightest bit of satisfaction in knowing she was scared this time.

Adjusting the camera pinned to his black jacket, Anton made sure the Elders were getting a good view of his triumphant moment. Watching the blood trail down her face, he felt his mouth water in a mixture of physical and carnal hunger. He couldn't wait to lick her clean.

"Gotcha," Anton purred, curving his lips into a cocky smile.

CHAPTER THIRTY-SIX

"You haven't caught me yet," Brynn growled.

Quirking his head, Anton couldn't hide his amusement. Throwing his arms out wide, he laughed at her tough girl facade. He knew firsthand that she wasn't a fighter, nor a runner for that matter.

"There's nowhere for you to go, Brynn! Now be a good little girl and come to daddy," he said, motioning with his hands to come hither.

Giving him a disgusted look, she shook her head defiantly. Hearing him call himself that made her want to vomit. He was nasty on so many levels. There was no way she would let him claim her as his trophy.

"Ew...fuck that. I'm not going anywhere with you," she replied. "I'd rather be dead!"

Rolling his eyes, Anton stomped closer. Under different circumstances he might find her defiance adorable, but now? He was far too hungry to deal with any kind of attitude.

"Brynn," he warned, dropping his tone. "Come here."

Furrowing her bloodied brow, she took a couple of steps backwards. Slipping on a handful of rocks she had unearthed while crawling to safety, she let out a yelp. Quickly steadying herself, she felt her heartbeat quicken. There really was no getting around Anton, she knew she was trapped. But she would be damned if she didn't try,

Closing in on the disheveled girl, Anton let out a sigh. Caged animals were unpredictable. He didn't want to risk her accidentally throwing herself off the cliff.

"I promised Christos I would be gentle with you, and I want to make good on that promise. I swear to you that I won't hurt you...so come to me...before you do something that we will both regret," he said.

Darting her eyes to her left and to her right, Brynn tuned out Anton's empty words. If she could just make it to the tree line, she might have a chance. The fog was thick as pea soup in that direction. Even with his Vampiric sight, he wouldn't be able to find her.

"Brynn," Anton growled. "Come here."

Not giving herself a chance to chicken out, she jumped into a full sprint. Using the adrenaline coursing through her veins, she ran as fast as her feet could carry her. Successfully dodging Anton as he attempted to grab her, she raced towards the mangled trees. The taste of victory was sweet on her tongue, but quickly turned sour. Just as she hit the edge of the vegetation line, she was viciously yanked backwards by a grip on her tangled hair.

Twisting his fist into her chestnut locks, Anton pulled her to him. Wrapping his free arm around her lithe body, he brought her flush against his torso. Holding the squirming hellcat tightly, he pressed his lips against the shell of her ear.

"A for effort...but there's no way you will ever be able to outrun me, little girl. Remember that," he hissed.

Opening her mouth to respond with something flippant, Brynn was effectively silenced by the Vampire picking her up and throwing her over his shoulder. Losing the breath in her lungs from the rough toss, she purposefully went limp to regain her composure. Slowly catching her breath, she told herself not to give up. She still had her weapon...

Oh no, she thought, realizing that the switchblade wasn't in her hand.

"No! No!" she yelled aloud. "NO!"

Paying no mind to her protests, Anton spun in a lazy circle. "I claim this prize in the name of Christos!" he stated loudly, addressing the large audience he knew of was watching.

"You...son...of...a...bitch!" Brynn screamed.

With a tight hold on her legs, Anton chuckled darkly. Stepping through the thick brush, he gingerly walked towards the finish line located in the first quadrant. He still had a dozen kilometers to go, but the Sun Walker was in his possession. There weren't many rules for the Hunt, but there was one that still held true. Unless Brynn managed to free herself on her own accord, there wasn't anything Nikolai, Natalia, or the remaining annoyances of the forest could do. He had the luxury of taking his sweet time.

Letting the cameras get their fill of his victory walk, he whistled a few bars of a happy tune. After all these years, it felt so good to finally win.

"Cry all you want, Brynn...but you're *mine,* now," he said, patting her squarely on the ass. "All mine."

Gritting her teeth, Brynn balled her hands into tight fists. Letting her arms fly, she pummeled any bit of his body she could. Even with her gifted strength, it felt like punching against unforgiving cinder blocks. It pissed her off that she wasn't inflicting any pain.

Huffing in annoyance, the Vampire held onto her as she continued her feeble attack. Stepping over prickly vines and jagged rocks, he made note of the drone flying to their right. Giving the camera a wink, he moved his hand to pinch her ass.

"That's it, Sun Walker...beat me up," he said, his tone incredibly condescending. "Put on a show for everyone watching. They like it when the mortals are feisty."

Growling a response, she tried unsuccessfully to buck herself from his shoulder. Wincing as he tightened his hold on her legs, she wailed against him again and again. With her head dangling downwards, she felt her blood begin the pool. The dizzying sensation only intensified her anger, causing her body to overheat with a fever once again.

Lifting a brow, Anton noticed the side of his face growing warmer by the second as it pressed against Brynn's hip. Adjusting her over his shoulder, he enjoyed the way her body blanketed him with heat. It was pleasurable and comforting, almost like the hot water bottles Sara used during the winter.

"Mmm…you're feeling good, Brynn…daddy like. Tell me…is your cunt just as warm? It's been far too long since my cock has had a warm pussy. I'm getting hard just thinking about how hot you'll feel wrapped around me," he said.

Seething with instant disgust, she spit out a series of fowl curses. Met with his patronizing laughter, her rage took hold. Within a split second, a spark hidden deep inside suddenly ignited. Overcome by an intuitive power long buried, her entire body tensed as a phantom wildfire consumed her. With the flames fanning from her core outward, she screamed as they collected in her outstretched hands. Crackling with the mystical power of her bloodline, it exploded from her fingertips in a blazing flash of amber and citrine.

"What the hell?" Anton asked, only catching an intense light from the corner of his eyes.

Heaving with power, Brynn's chaotic mind became crystal clear. All at once, all the odd remarks tucked away made sense. Yetta was right. As was the Troll. *She was a God.* More powerful than any Vampire could ever be.

Filled with newfound confidence and bravado, she flicked a ball of fire towards Anton's legs. Missing her first couple of tries, she growled in frustration. Latching onto her anger, she raised her right hand. Narrowing her eyes in concentration, she wielded her power for a third time. With a single flame bursting forward, it caught his calf. Instantly igniting the cheap fabric of his black athletic pants.

Stopping dead in his tracks, Anton stiffened as his brain registered his burning flesh. Instinctively throwing the Sun Walker from his shoulder, he paid her no mind as her back made vicious contact with the sharp trunk of a broken tree. Looking down, he found his entire leg engulfed in flames. Screaming at the top of his lungs, he fell to the muddy ground in a panic.

Groaning in pain, Brynn's power evaporated as quickly as it appeared. Coughing and choking in agony, she slumped on her side like a tossed rag doll. Blinking back the tears welling in her eyes, she latched onto the delicious image of Anton rolling around on the forest floor. Counting the seconds, she made it to nine before the fire was successfully put out.

Calling Brynn every degrading name in the book, the Vampire looked over his badly injured leg. Watching as the scorched skin and muscles bubbled, he hissed low. Setting his livid gaze upon her, he made a show of releasing the bloodthirsty monster within.

"Oh shit," Brynn whispered, watching as his face twisted into something that terrified her.

Standing from the dirt path, Anton growled as he put weight on his injured leg. Although it was already beginning to heal, it would take days for it to get back to normal. Perhaps even weeks. How the fuck was she able to burn him to such a damaging degree?

"You fucking little bitch!" he bellowed. Forcing his leg to work, he stomped towards her. "I should fucking kill you!"

Hoisting herself into a seated position, she raised her hands defensively. Throwing her fingers wide, she willed her new power to return. But to her dismay, nothing happened. Not even a single spark. Looking at her hands in disbelief, she tried again and again. Whimpering louder and louder with every soul crushing failure.

"Come on! Come on!" she said, unable to stop the hot tears from streaming down her face.

Glaring down at the Sun Walker, the Vampire wondered what the hell she was doing. For a split second he was amused by her silly display. The feeling was fleeting however, replaced rather quickly by intense hatred. The bitch was more trouble than her worth.

"Where's the fucking lighter fluid and lighter?!" he yelled.

Shaking her head, Brynn met his undead eyes. Lighter fluid? Lighter? That's where his pea brain went? As if she could hide either in her tattered nightgown.

"Where would I hide those, dumbass?" she replied, scooting away to create some space.

Narrowing his eyes, Anton brushed off her common sense. Believing his delusions, he threw his allegiance to his Sire to the side. The bitch had tried to kill him, he was due some revenge.

"Fuck it! I'm going to suck you dry!" he growled, reaching for her.

Gasping audibly, Brynn pushed herself backwards in an attempt to escape. Rolling onto her belly, she scrambled onto all fours. Crawling as fast as she could, she yelped as she felt him grab her by the hair yet again. With her head jerking backwards, the necklace hidden within the neck of her gown jostled free.

Instantly remembering her secret gift, she felt a bright surge of hope. Almost on cue, a wolf howled in the distance. *Rikard's pack was prowling the forest.* Nik had reminded her of that fact multiple times.

Freezing for a moment, Anton glanced around the surrounding trees. He would be lying if he said that the Werewolves weren't a concern, especially after their last fight. To his defense, Remus had it coming. The Werewolf actually had the balls to think he could touch his Sara and live.

"Damn dogs," he muttered, dragging Brynn towards him by her hair.

Pulling her to him, he suddenly noticed her shoving something shiny into her mouth. Thinking she had another weapon at her disposal, he roughly tossed her onto the forest floor. Glaring down, he bent down to yank the object from her. Breaking it free from the chain around her neck, he brought it to his demonic face.

"What the hell is this?" he asked.

Swallowing hard, Brynn watched as he studied the whistle. She prayed to God that the Werewolves had heard her. She was only able to get in four good blows before he ripped it from her.

Looking over the hunk of metal, Anton's black eyes widened as he finally recognized what it was. Before he had time to process exactly what she had done with the inconspicuous weapon, the howls of multiple Werewolves echoed through the forest. Causing him to freeze in paralyzing fear for the first time in his whole undead life.

Noticing a distinct change in the Vampire, she couldn't help but smile. All around them the guttural sounds of excited canines filled the air. To her relief, it seemed as if her prayers were answered. Lifting her eyes to meet his, she gave herself permission to gloat. He deserved every bit of his wicked fate.

"Gotcha," she said, a smug look dancing over her face.

CHAPTER THIRTY-SEVEN

Sprinting through a throng of enchanted trees, Nikolai snaked his way towards the heart of the third quadrant. For whatever reason, his connection to Brynn had grown eerily quiet. He could no longer sense her emotions, could no longer feel her heartbeat. It was as if she had just…disappeared. To say that he was worried would be a gross understatement.

Visually scanning the tree line for anything out of place, he cursed the Elders as he noticed a second drone coming out of the woodwork to follow him. He knew he would be watched closely, but it still left him with a disgusting taste in his mouth. Once his love was safe in his arms, he would make a show of destroying every camera. This would be the last time they ever used him for their sick entertainment.

Dodging a handful of hanging vines, he moved forward with a catlike grace. Running through the thick fog, he used his muscle memory to jump over the various jagged boulders placed in his way. It was stupid of the Elders to use the Maze; he knew it like the back of his hand. Neither Natalia nor Anton had spent as much time here as he had. It was the only reason he had been able to move through it so quickly.

Not that they hadn't tried their best to derail him. He had to admit, throwing venomous vipers into the river was a nice touch. As was unleashing the zombie boar that chased him through the gully. But they were merely tiny nuisances. Nothing would stop him from finding Brynn. Nothing.

Rounding a sharp corner, he noticed a sudden flash of white to his left. Immediately turning his head, he perked as he noticed a figure running ten yards ahead. Instantly recognizing the brunette as she ran in the opposite direction, he turned on a dime. He couldn't remember the last time he had felt so relieved. Running towards her, he boldly called out.

"Brynn! Brynn! Stop!" he yelled. "It's me!"

Fully expecting her to heed his call, he was surprised to find her picking up her pace instead. Furrowing his brow in confusion, he doubled his strides. Although his otherworldly speed was altered by the forest, he was able to move faster than her mortal legs could carry her. It wasn't long before he caught up to her.

Saying her name once again, he quickly closed the gap separating them. Seemingly hearing him this time, he sighed as she slowed to a dead stop. Curious as to why she wasn't turning towards him, he lifted his hand to touch her shoulder.

"Brynn, my love…I knew I would find y—"

Before he had a chance to finish his sentence, she whipped around to face him. With a jagged dagger held tightly in her hand, she let out an ear-piercing scream. The unnatural sound caused her jaw to unhinge and fall to her chest, breaking the glamor spell and revealing the disgusting creature's true form.

Jumping backwards in surprise, Nik instinctively hissed at the demonic beast. Gone in an instant was the beautiful image of his love, replaced by something disgusting he had only encountered once before. It was an encounter that nearly cost him his undead life.

"Ghoul," he whispered.

Pulling back its shredded lips, the Ghoul screamed an archaic phrase in response. Eyeing the Vampire as he reached for his pocket, it raised its gem encrusted dagger above its decaying head. Without warning, it brought the weapon down in a fluid motion. Effortlessly piercing the blade deep into the Vampire's chest.

Widening his green eyes in shock, Nikolai coughed as the sharp metal sliced through skin, muscle, and bone. Missing his heart by only a scant inch, he realized the severity of the moment. Spitting out the black blood filling his mouth, he reached in vain for the hilt of the dagger. He knew the creature wouldn't miss twice.

Paying no mind to the Vampire's feeble attempt, the Ghoul easily wretched the golden hilt from his chest. Watching him fall to his knees, it snarled in heady triumph. Raising the blade one last time, it paused for a moment to admire its victory. The Vampire's head would bring a great reward. It would bring honor to its name.

Wincing in immense pain, Nikolai stared up at the Ghoul. With blood spilling from his mouth and chest in sticky, onyx waves, he braced for the bitter end. Closing his eyes, he stirred the image of Brynn to the forefront of his mind. He wanted her to be the last thing he saw before slipping into the gates of hell.

Lifting its gnarled arm, the Ghoul sneered at the pathetic Vampire. Going in for the easy kill, it was too focused on its task at hand to see a hulking brown wolf slinking through the lifting fog. Forcing the blade downwards, it bellowed in shock as the wolf leapt onto its torso with enough force to knock it from its clawed feet.

Replaying the last memory he had of his love, Nik froze as he sensed a familiar presence rush past. Snapping his eyes open, he locked his gaze onto the Werewolf as he crashed his large body into the Ghoul. Within the span of a single heartbeat, the Werewolf knocked the Ghoul onto its back. Viciously tearing into its long neck with his sharp teeth, he made quick work of dispatching the demonic creature.

Watching in stunned silence, Nik forced himself to stand. Ignoring the searing pain of his body stitching itself back together, he spit the last bit of blood from his mouth. With the sounds of screaming and snarling and the ripping of flesh filling his ears, he couldn't help but laugh. Never in his wildest nightmares did he ever think that Rikard, out of all the Werewolves, would come to his rescue.

Tearing the Ghoul's jawbone from its face, the Werewolf tossed it with a flick of his head into the woods. Confident that the immediate threat was eliminated, he eased his attack. Throwing his blood-soaked head backwards, he released a sharp howl to alert his Brothers of his successful kill.

Slapping his open palm over the wound on his chest, Nik took a step away from the gory scene. Giving the Alpha Werewolf a moment to relish his win, he prepared himself to eat a large helping of crow. He now owed Rikard one hell of a life debt.

Pulling himself from the Ghoul, the Werewolf shook the putrid blood from his mocha-colored fur. Closing his yellow eyes, he relinquished his power to the Night God. Instantaneously, the painful process began. Rearing up onto his legs, he yelped loudly as his body violently rearranged from canine to human. Turning the mythical beast into man in an evolution so grotesque that it made the Vampire watching offer his sympathies.

After what seemed like an eternity, Rikard stood to full height. Stretching the defined muscles of his nude body, his deep voice growled a series of lewd curses. Reanimating as human was always a bitch, but it was a small price to pay to hold such power. It was better than any illicit drug or drink. Better than having the privilege of bedding a talented whore. He would gladly endure the physical discomfort a million times over if it meant he had the honor of being Lycan.

Turning to face Nikolai, he wiped a smattering of blood and saliva from his mouth with the back of his hand. Meeting the Vampire's eyes, he hardened his sharp features.

"Let's get one thing straight, Nikolai…that was for Helen. It wasn't for you," he said, his tone cold and biting.

Maintaining the uncomfortable eye contact, Nik nodded once. Of course he only saved him for Helen's sake. His relationship with the Alpha had never been copacetic. Especially since his dalliance with Yetta over forty years prior.

"Thank you, just the same," he replied tensely.

Smirking at the Vampire, Rikard moved towards him. Tossing his brown locks over his broad shoulder, he stood unabashedly close. He knew damn well how his nakedness made the bloodsucker feel. It is as always so much fun to watch him squirm.

"Ever the gentleman," he said, his voice deep and gruff. "But don't thank me yet…the Hunt isn't over."

"No, it's not," Nik agreed, glancing around the eerie forest. "Where are the others? Have you found Brynn?"

Shaking his head, Rikard pushed out a sigh. "They're out prowling but no, we haven't found her yet. We can't catch her scent."

With a deep frown etched onto his blood-stained face, Nik said a silent curse. Werewolves were incredibly strong physically, but severely lacking mentally. They were all brawn and no brain.

"Well, that's not surprising in the least…Christos and Ulysses knew you were here. No doubt they've doused her in wolfsbane oil. You'll have to track her the old-fashioned way," Nik said.

"And we are," Rikard replied harshly. "It's just taking us a little longer, that's all. We will find her…we need the Sun Walker just as much as you do."

Balling his hands into tight fists at his sides, Nik reminded himself to stay calm. Rikard hadn't been able to breed in centuries due to a Warlock's curse. With the numbers of his Pack steadily dwindling, he was in desperate need of Pups. For whatever reason, the Alpha believed that a Sun Walker would restore his ability to sire much needed offspring. He was wrong, of course. But he'd be damned if he allowed him to test his theory. The Werewolf would never touch his Brynn.

Resisting the sudden urge to sink his fangs into Rikard's throat, Nik forced his attention to the Ghoul's mangled corpse. Finding the golden dagger still held in its hand, he stepped to the body. Kneeling, he yanked it from the Ghoul's dead grasp. Testing the weight of the hilt in his hand, he stood from the forest floor. The weapon would come in handy; he could already picture it cleaving Natalia's pretty little head from her neck.

"We should split up…you continue north, I'll head east," he said.

Lifting a black brow, Rikard gave the Vampire a critical once over. He could read Nikolai like an old newspaper; he knew exactly what the bloodsucker was trying to do. Like hell they would be splitting up.

"Nah, we'll head east together," he replied.

Hardening his features, Nik bit his tongue to keep himself from saying something scathing. *Fine.* The dog could follow. But Brynn would be leaving the Maze with him, and him alone.

"She's mine, Rikard. Don't forget that," he hissed, stalking towards the overgrown path.

Quickly catching up to Nikolai, Rikard let out a snort. Brushing past the Vampire, he made a point to stay half a stride in front of him. Sure. Brynn was his. Until she wasn't.

"Yeah, of course…of course," he said, a cocky smile lifting the corners of his rugged face.

Pressing his lips into a fine line, Nik silently stewed. Trying his best to ignore the dog to his left, he scanned his eyes through the dark forest. He would bicker with Rikard another night. His focus was getting to Brynn. The sooner, the better.

Stepping his bare feet over unearthed roots and sharp rocks, Rikard led the way towards the Ridge. Swiping his arm at a drone as it whizzed by, he easily caught the robot. Crushing it in his large hand, he flung the remnants into a blackened tree.

"Fuckers," he said under his breath.

Reluctantly agreeing with the Alpha, Nik matched his hurried pace. Moving through the forest in heavy silence, he kept his eyes and ears open. Covering a kilometer in no time at all, he tried not to let his thoughts spiral out of control. He didn't think it would take so long to find his love. It was irking him to no end.

Weaving through a throng of trees, Rikard motioned to his right with a flick of his head. Off in the distance he could hear the distinct sounds of members of his Pack rustling through the leaves of thorny bushes. They were onto something. A scent. Perhaps a visual imprint. Something was riling them; he just wasn't sure what. Spanning another thirty feet, he suddenly halted his steps.

Stopping next to Rikard, Nik gave him an odd look. He had never seen him look so concerned, so utterly intense. It immediately put him on edge.

"What is it?" he asked.

Shushing the Vampire, Rikard narrowed his amber colored eyes. Lifting his hand to cup his ear, he leaned his scarred torso forward. Swearing hotly under his breath, he nodded as he realized that he had heard what he thought he had.

"What? What is it?!" Nik asked again, growing impatient.

"Dog whistle. Half a mile ahead," Rikard replied.

Sucking in a breath, Nik all but jumped to attention. Instantly understanding the implications, he gripped the dagger tightly in his hand. Realizing that there wasn't much time, he said a single word before running towards the direction of the invisible sound.

"Brynn!"

CHAPTER THIRTY-EIGHT

Staring at the wall of screens, Christos gawked at the sight of his Proxy surrounded by six rabid Werewolves. Although the camera feeds were silent, he could read Anton's trembling lips. He was bargaining. Bargaining for his undead life. It was something the Elder never thought he would see.

"This...this shouldn't be allowed! We must put an end to it!" he yelled, motioning with his hands.

Folding his arms over his chest, Ulysses took his time to respond. He saw no problem with it. If the Werewolves exacted their revenge on Anton, so be it. The Youngling had always been a sharp thorn in his side.

"There aren't any rules against it," he replied nonchalantly.

Turning towards Ulysses, Christos gave him an incredulous look. He couldn't believe he was being so blasé. If the shoe was on the other foot, he wouldn't allow this to happen to Natalia. He knew his oldest lover was jealous of Anton.

"They're going to kill him, Ulysses!" he growled.

Humming low, Ulysses watched the screens as the Werewolves drew closer. While there was a good chance that they would tear Anton limb from limb, it didn't warrant their interference. Hunts were inherently dangerous. Anton knew exactly what he was getting into the moment he accepted his Proxy status.

"Perhaps...perhaps not. Have faith in him, Christos. You chose him for a reason," he replied flatly.

"I chose him to catch a Sun Walker! Not to fight half a dozen of Rikard's dogs!" Christos yelled, stomping his high heeled foot. "We must step in!"

Shaking his head, Ulysses narrowed his dark eyes. "We have never interfered in a Hunt, and we aren't about to start now!"

Trying her best to mask her glee, Helen eyed her counterparts as they quarreled back and forth. Things were progressing just as she envisioned, and it pleased her to no end. But if everything continued to go to plan, the situation would become messy very quickly. She couldn't allow her excitement over witnessing karma firsthand to cloud her judgment.

Casually stepping over to Leonardo, she placed a hand on the back of his computer chair. Leaning down towards him, she waited for Christos to shout before whispering into his ear.

"Be ready, Leo. I have a feeling we will be taking our leave sooner, rather than later."

. . .

Running at a breakneck speed, Rikard quickly caught up to his gathered Pack. Choosing to remain in his human form, he surveyed the scene as he waited for Nikolai to join them. Giving his Brothers a pleased grin, he moved his attention to the Sun Walker as she stood behind the held line. Though dirty and disheveled from everything the Hunt had thrown at her, there was no mistaking her divinity. She was beautiful and ethereal like the angels painted on frescos he loved so dearly as a child. Everything he had prayed to the Night God for.

"Are you alright?" he asked her, ignoring Anton's panicked cries for mercy. "Did the Vampire hurt you?"

Hearing an unfamiliar voice cut through her rushing thoughts, Brynn turned her head towards the sound. Immediately caught off guard, she jumped at the sight of a muscular, very naked man only a handful of feet away. She had no idea who he was, or how he got there without her noticing, but the second she met his amber colored eyes, she instantly felt at peace. True and pure peace for perhaps the first time in her entire life.

Nodding her head, she opened her mouth to answer the sinfully handsome man. Before she had a chance to say a single word, however, she noticed her love running into the clearing. Gasping in surprise, she couldn't help but smile.

"Nik!" she exclaimed.

Rushing past Rikard, Nik held out his arms. Mindful of the sharp dagger in his hand, he scooped Brynn up from the forest floor. Holding her tightly, he pressed his lips against her ear. Savoring the weight of her in his arms, he made her a solemn vow.

"I've got you, Sunshine…nothing is going to tear us apart ever again. *Nothing*. I love you…I love you so much."

Wrapping her arms around him, she melted into his embrace. But for whatever reason, she found her gaze being unexpectedly drawn back to the nude stranger. Time seemed to slow as she studied his rugged face, pulling her away from her much-wanted reunion. There was something familiar about the attractive man, but she couldn't quite place it. She could trust him, though. She knew she could trust him with her life. She felt it with every fiber of her being.

Basking in the odd serenity falling over her, she only caught the last bit of Nikolai's declaration; but it was just enough to break the spell. "I…I love you, too," she replied automatically, easing from his arms.

Suddenly noticing the dark blood staining his face and clothing, she let out a loud gasp. Reaching for his chest, she patted her touch to find the source of the bleeding.

"What happened?! Are you ok?!" she asked, fear tainting her tone.

Lifting his free hand, Nik cupped the side of her face. Gently forcing her to meet his eyes, he gave her a reassuring smile. Although her concern was sweet, he hated to make her worry. She had done enough of that to last two lifetimes.

"I'm fine…I'm fine. It's nothing to worry about, hmm?" he said.

Sighing in relief, Brynn nodded. It was probably for the best that he didn't elaborate on how he ended up drenched in dark blood. The important thing was that he was with her again. They were both safe and would remain that way. Nothing else mattered.

Clearing his throat, Rikard eyed the couple. If they were anyone else, anywhere else, he might have been moved by the heartwarming reunion. But it only left him with a bitter taste in his mouth. Pushing his rising jealousy to the side, he motioned towards Anton with a lift of his chin.

"I hate to interrupt this…sweet…moment but we have more pressing matters," he said, turning to face the cornered Vampire.

Moving in front of Brynn, Nik shielded her with his body. Drifting his gaze over the activity before him, he curled the corner of his lips into an evil smile. Snarling and growling, Rikard's wolves advanced upon Anton with their backs hunched and teeth bared. He was trapped like a rat with nowhere to run.

Lifting the jewel encrusted dagger, he pointed the tip of the blade at Anton. Narrowing his eyes, he slowly stalked forward. He knew Rikard would want his pound of flesh, but this was his kill.

Swallowing hard, Anton toggled his attention from the Werewolves, to Rikard, and then to Nikolai. With his hands raised in surrender, he stammered as they all slinked closer. He had no clue how this had turned so bad, so fucking quickly.

"Nik…you can't do this. You will violate our most cardinal rule if you do…think of Brynn…you know they will come after her if you do this," he said.

"Do *NOT* say her name," he hissed, moving in between two Werewolves. "And I hope they do come so I can kill them just like I'm about to kill you!"

Making sure Brynn was staying safe behind the line, Rikard followed Nikolai. Moving to flank his right side, he looked over his hungry Pack. Their excitement was palpable. He was afraid that the smallest thing would set them off. With a single thought, he ordered them to heel until he gave the command to attack.

"Nikolai…we expect you to uphold your end of the bargain," Rikard said, his voice rough and deep.

Glancing at the Alpha from the corner of his eyes, Nik couldn't help but bristle. If he wasn't completely loyal to Helen, he would have laughed in the dog's face. Reminding himself that it was a small price to pay, he gave a reluctant nod.

"I will uphold my end of the bargain. I will stake him, you and your brothers can tear him limb from limb and then—"

"Then I will burn the motherfucker to ash!" Brynn blurted out suddenly.

Almost in unison, Nikolai and Rikard looked over their shoulders at Brynn. Confusion fell over their faces, causing both supernatural men to furrow their brows. Neither understood her comment.

"You'll *what* now? Do you have a flamethrower hiding under that shredded nightgown of yours, Sun Walker?" Rikard asked, unabashedly raking his hungry gaze over her. "If so, I would love to see."

Shooting daggers towards the Alpha with his eyes, Nik stopped himself from grabbing his throat. The dog needed to be very careful from here on out. He didn't care for the lust written over his scared face. His loyalty to Helen could only carry so far.

Shaking her head at the stranger, Brynn swallowed hard from the intensity behind his eyes. Ignoring the nervous butterflies filling her belly, she lifted her hands. Taking in a cleansing breath, she released all the fear from her body. Remembering the hell Anton had put her though, she felt her rage bubble inside.

"Watch," she replied simply.

Clenching her jaw, she moved her hazel eyes to Anton's terrified face. Recalling every ounce of pain he doled, her heart began to pound against her ribcage. With every quick beat the fire within her grew. Stoking from a tiny spark to a raging wildfire in the span of a few scant seconds. Unable to contain her power, a small fireball burst from each splayed hand.

Jumping in surprise, Rikard stared at Brynn with wide eyes. Realizing the heady implications, he felt a shiver race down his spine. She had come into her power. It was a sign from the Night God that what the White Witch had said was true. Their fate together was intertwined and sealed. *She was ready for him.*

"Mio angelo," he whispered in reverence.

Focused only on his love, Nik found himself smiling. Yetta had left him with a parting comment that at the time he found ridiculous, but now it made sense. Brynn was magic. No, not just magic. This was so much more than that. She was a...

"Goddess," he breathed, awe painting his features. "You're a Goddess."

Shaking his head in disbelief, Anton spit a dark curse. The bitch hadn't burned him with a lighter or a match. The fire came from her. From her fucking hands! And just like that, any hope of his survival vanished into thin air. He knew he was truly fucked.

"You little cunt!" he yelled, knowing his cutting words were futile. Hissing loudly, his face contorted into something dreadful and demonic. "I'm going to rip into that throat of yours and drink you dry!"

Immediately turning towards Anton, Nikolai released his own monster. With his fangs extended and his eyes turning onyx, he allowed his bloodlust to consume him. That was the last threat he would ever make against his love.

Knowing Nikolai had officially snapped, Rikard quickly gave his order. Pressing his lips together, he let out a loud whistle that echoed through the forest. Watching his Brothers jump into action, he remained in his human form. It was best if Brynn didn't witness his transformation right then and there. It was something he needed to ease her into.

"Assalire!" he yelled.

Not having much time to think, Brynn gasped as the Werewolves made their vicious attack. Leaping onto Anton, they deftly knocked him to the muddy ground. With the sounds of masculine screams and canine snarls filling the night air, she watched with bated breath as the wolves grabbed onto his limbs with their teeth. Pulling his arms and legs at uncomfortable angles, they tugged in alternating jerks again and again. Causing the Vampire to beg and plead at the edge of every shrill scream.

Flipping the dagger like an expert assassin, Nikolai ran forward. Pulling back his lips into a snarl, he easily maneuvered around the hulking Werewolves to straddle Anton's splayed body. Staring down at him, he studied the look of true terror on his altered face. How many times had he thought of this moment over the past few centuries? He wanted to savor every delicious second.

Swearing hotly under his breath, Rikard followed suit. Running around his pack, he took his place above Anton's head. Falling to his knees, he roughly gripped the side of the Vampire's face to hold him still. Lifting his amber eyes, he spit out a gruff phrase in his mother tongue. The Italian words made the members of his Pack growl in response, their jaws eager to have their revenge.

Staring at the wicked display before her, Brynn stepped closer. Her adrenaline was spiking, feeding the wildfire within. Savoring Anton's frightened screams, she prepared herself for the savagery ahead. Tiptoeing around the large Werewolves, she noticed a new drone flying towards them. *Good,* she thought. The Elders needed to see what they were dealing with if they chose to revolt against them.

Glaring down at Anton, Nik leaned in low. Forcing more weight onto his torso, he stopped his counterpart from bucking. Looking into his Vampiric eyes, he moved the tip of the sharp blade over his heart.

"Give my regards to the devil," he hissed.

"NO! NO! NO!" Anton yelled.

Lifting the dagger high above his head, Nik swiftly brought the cruel weapon down. With the bloodstained metal piercing through fabric, skin, and bone, it easily found its target. Staking the protesting Vampire through his blackened heart.

Letting out a twisted and pain-filled scream, Anton thrashed beneath Nikolai. His face twisted into something vile as his executioner sunk the blade in deeper. True death was coming to claim him, it consumed him with rage instead of regret.

"I…CURSE…YOU…NIKOLAI!" he swore with his final breath.

Releasing the hilt of the dagger, Nikolai pulled himself off Anton. Making way for the Werewolves to claim their part of the bargain, he stepped over to Brynn. Standing by her side, he seethed while he watched the pack tear the body into pieces. A curse from a dying Vampire was a dangerous thing. He would have to talk to Clara as soon as they made it to Capri.

Twisting Anton's neck at a barbaric angle, Rikard let out an animalistic growl. Using only an ounce of his strength, he savagely ripped his head from his neck. Holding it in his hand by the Vampire's matted bleached hair, he stared into his empty eyes.

"This is for Remus and for Matteo," he said through gritted teeth. "May you rot in hell!"

Flinging the head onto the pile of mangled body parts, he stood to full height. Calling off his Pack from chomping away at the leftover bits of flesh, he ordered them to leave with a single howl. Immediately stiffening to attention, the wolves did as they were told. Licking their bloody chops, they cried out into the night before disappearing into the haunted forest.

Breathing hard from the afterglow of his retribution, he turned his head towards the pair. Ignoring Nikolai completely, he addressed Brynn in a voice low and husky.

"Your turn, Angelo Solare."

Meeting his reverent gaze, Brynn nodded her head. Lifting her chin, she stepped confidently to the mutilated body. Watching him be torn apart had excited her in a way she didn't think was possible. She was thrilled beyond belief to seal his death and send him home to hell.

Catching the blinking light of the drone whizzing by, she made a show of beckoning her powers. Using the emotions swirling in her head, the fireballs came easily this time. With one bursting forth from each outstretched hand, they were thrown at the pile of stinking flesh. Instantly catching the flames, a bonfire erupted before the audience behind the camera lens.

Caging the monster back in its cage, Nik felt nothing but pride watching his love. "Good girl," he praised, his voice heavy with awe.

Taking in a deep breath, Brynn allowed herself to smile. Watching her flames consume her attacker was liberating. She had no idea that revenge would taste so sweet. It made her crave more. Walking back to the men, she toggled her gaze back and forth between their handsome faces.

"Natalia…we have to finish this," she said.

Pushing out a sigh, Rikard took a step towards her. That was a fight he hadn't agreed to. While he worried about leaving her, he needed to make sure his Pack made it home safely. They now had targets on their backs.

"That's not my fight…I must leave you to it," he said, giving Nik a quick glance before meeting Brynn's eyes once again. "Be careful il mio bellissimo Angelo Solare. I'll see you back in Capri."

Not sure what that meant, she merely nodded. Feeling the heat of his intense gaze, her freckled cheeks blushed pink. Suddenly feeling guilty for enjoying the hunger behind his eyes, she forced herself to look away. Leaving him with a parting grin, she swiftly moved to Nik's side. Easing herself into his opened arms, she looked up at his face. He was trying so hard to mask his emotions, but she could see them straight away. He was jealous, and incredibly angry. It was a deadly combination.

Smirking at the sulking Vampire, Rikard swelled with a newfound confidence. Brynn felt the connection they shared, there was no doubt in his mind. Bowing his head at Nikolai, he made an attempt at civility.

"Nikolai," he said, his voice sounding more condescending than polite.

"Rikard," Nik replied, his tone icy cold.

Knowing time was of the essence, the Alpha gave the Sun Walker one last look before turning on his heels. Running at a full pace, he disappeared into the thick fog of the gnarled forest. Leaving behind all his trust in his enemy to keep his future safe.

Watching the dog scurry home, Nik squeezed his arms around his love. With visions of tearing into the Alpha's throat and drinking him dry, he looked to the drone as it flew over Anton's burning corpse. Letting the robot get to within a half meter of where they stood, he looked directly into the camera lens.

"Ulysses," he began, making sure to enunciate his words so that the Elders could read his lips. "Tell Natalia that she's next."

CHAPTER THIRTY-NINE

Falling to the hard floor, Christos wailed at the top of his lungs. Thrashing around in the most dramatic of fashion, his shrill screams filled the elegant dining hall. His beloved Anton was gone. Whisked home to hell by the winged devils he often dreamed of. He hadn't felt such searing, devastating pain in centuries.

"Anton...Anton...Anton!" he yelled again and again.

Stopping himself from rolling his dark eyes, Ulysses bent down beside his counterpart. Moving his hand to rub his shoulder, he tried his best to soothe him. Compassion was never his forte, a simple touch was all he could afford. Death, even with their kind, was inevitable. It didn't warrant such theatrics.

"Christos. Calm down," he said.

Halting his erratic movements, Christos looked up at the old Roman General. With hot tears causing his mascara to run down his face, he gave him a scathing look. When, in the history of ever, did telling someone to 'calm down' work? It only enraged him more.

"THEY KILLED HIM, ULYSSES! THEY KILLED HIM!" he screamed.

Letting out an annoyed sigh, Ulysses nodded his head. "Yes. They killed him. And making yourself sick with grief won't change a damn thing."

Remaining as quiet as a mouse, Helen waited until the two were deep in angry conversation. Casually glancing at Leonardo, she gave him the tiniest of nods. Nikolai and Brynn would find Natalia soon enough. With the Sun Walker's newfound powers, her death warrant was all but signed. The Hunt was effectively over. For her own safety, she needed to flee the Manor as quickly as possible.

Using one of her many Vampiric gifts, she created a blur in reality. Whispering an archaic phrase, a faux image of both she and Leonardo were magically created to take their respective places. It was a flimsy ruse, one of smoke and mirrors. But oddly real enough to allow them to escape.

Waiting until the doppelgängers were fully formed, she slowly backed away. Making a motion to Leonardo, she waited for him to come to her. Grabbing his arm, she cautiously led him from the room. Thankful that the two buffoons were too absorbed in each other to hear them leave.

"Natalia MUST kill them! She MUST!" Christos whined, pulling himself to a seated position.

Standing at full height, Ulysses folded his arms over his chest. Scanning the various screens, he grunted a reply. His Proxy was moving into Nikolai and Brynn's direct path. They would be running into each other in another dozen meters or so. The Sun Walker's new parlor trick was worrisome to say the least. He knew his Natalia was at a great disadvantage...*unless*.

Looking over his shoulder at Helen, he debated his only true option. Watching her smirk, he matched her with one of his own. Rikard and his pack were gone. Nikolai wasn't audibly connected to her. She had no allies of consequence in the Manor. Really, he had nothing to lose.

Opening his mouth to say something cutting, he noticed a tiny ripple marring her high cheekbone. Focusing on the defect, he spit a curse as the ripple widened to swallow half of her face. Instantly knowing she had duped them to run, he puffed in annoyance. He had been so looking forward to killing her and her Proxy before the sun rose.

"No matter," he said aloud. "I will find you."

Wiping his nose with the back of his hand, Christos glanced up at Ulysses. With confusion painting the fine features of his face, he narrowed his swollen eyes. "What? What are you talking about? Find who?"

Pointing to the wavering image of Helen, Ulysses remained silent. Nodding as his counterpart let out a sharp gasp, he lifted his hand to his earpiece. Calling his Proxy, he watched her as she moved through the wretched forest.

"Natalia…I am canceling my command. As Nikolai's Sire, you have complete power and control over him once again," he said, his eyes drifting to the image of Nikolai and Brynn walking hand in hand. "Use him to subdue the Sun Walker…then kill the bastard."

. . .

Leading his love through the warped trees, Nik scanned his eyes over the dissipating fog. The hairs on the back of his neck were standing on end, the feeling of impending doom taking root in his stomach. For the first time since the Hunt began, he felt the overwhelming need to run. It made him grit his teeth in frustration.

Feeling Nik's hand stiffen in hers, Brynn moved to walk beside him. Glancing up at his face, she scrunched her brow in worry. He had a cold expression that she had never seen. She didn't care for it one bit.

"What's wrong?" she asked.

Meeting her worried gaze, he instantly softened his features. Brushing off his anxiety as nothing more than anticipation, he shook his head.

"Nothing…sorry, I'm just…I'm just so damn ready to find Natalia and finish this once and for—"

Unable to finish his sentence, he was suddenly hit with a phantom punch to the gut. Wincing in pain, he was forced to halt his steps. It took a moment for him to realize what was happening. But as soon as he did, he couldn't help but rage.

"NO!" he growled.

Turning to fully face him, Brynn looked at him with wide eyes. "What? What the hell is going on, Nik?"

Squeezing her hand, he began to walk once more. Pulling her gently, he urged her to follow. Quickening their pace, he made a sharp left towards the edge of the third quadrant. His vengeance would have to wait. He needed to get Brynn out of the Maze *immediately*.

"I'm tired of being a puppet…the Hunt is over. I've won…we've won. Let's just get home to Capri, hmm?" he said, his words hushed and hurried.

Stumbling over a pile of slick stones, Brynn let out an exasperated sigh. Yanking back on his hand, she abruptly stopped walking. She didn't know why he was lying. Keeping her in the dark wouldn't shield her from the inevitable. Hadn't he learned his lesson by now?

"Stop it, Nik! Now tell me what the hell is going on. If something's wrong, don't you think I deserve to know?!" she spat.

Standing still, he met her angry eyes. She was right. Hiding the truth from her hadn't protected her thus far. It would be stupid if he thought it would do her any good now.

"It's Natalia," he said, trying to keep his voice low. "She…she's—"

"Right. Here," called out an all too familiar voice.

Looking frantically in every direction, Nik swore hotly under his breath. Dead ahead an unnatural glow emerged through a cluster of moss caked trees. Time seemed to still as an unmistakable silhouette strolled through the narrow pathway.

Shooting his love an urgent glance, Nik tried to tell her to run. To hide. But it was far too late. There wasn't anything either of them could do.

Staring at Natalia as she slinked towards them, Brynn missed Nik's facial cues. With an evil grin on her face, she planted her feet on the ground to ready herself for the brawl ahead. She was almost salivating at the thought of tearing the bitch apart.

Tightening his hold on her hand, Nik caught her wild eyes. Shaking his head, he leaned in close. She didn't understand the gravity of the situation. This was no longer a fight they could win.

"Ulysses gave her power back," he hissed. *"As my Sire."*

Blinking at him, Brynn soaked in his heavy words. Gasping as she finally understood the implications, she felt her blood run to ice. Wrenching her hand from his, she took a couple of steps backwards to create some distance. She was in grave danger. Not just of Natalia, but now of her own lover.

"Give me the dagger, Nik!" she urged.

Clicking her tongue against the roof of her mouth, Natalia snapped her fingers. Gaining Nikolai's attention like an obedient puppy, she motioned towards the expanse of trees behind him. Oh. She was going to have so much fun.

"No, Niky. Don't you *dare* give that dagger to her…throw it into the woods," she ordered.

Not giving it a second thought, Nik did exactly as he was told. Twisting his torso, he threw the dagger with an expert's hand. Within a blink of an eye, the blade sliced into the trunk of an ancient tree. Burying itself so deep that it would be hard for any mortal, enhanced or not, to pull it free.

Swearing loudly, Brynn's adrenaline spiked through her veins. Instinctively turning on her heels, she attempted to run into the heart of the forest. It was a futile, stupid attempt. A decision made from nothing more than pure impulse.

"Catch her Nikolai!" Natalia yelled.

Obeying his Sire, he quickly lunged towards Brynn. Catching up to her within a handful of long strides, he opened his arms wide. Capturing her in a tight embrace, he held her against his torso. Coming to an abrupt stop, he stood in place for a long moment. Shushing sweetly against the shell of his love's ear, he tried his best to soothe her as she thrashed wildly against him.

"Shhh…it's ok…it's ok Sunshine…everything will be ok. I promise," he said, not believing his own words one iota.

Whimpering softly, Brynn slumped in defeat against his chest. He had said that to her before. It was a lie then, and it was a lie now. They were both doomed. There was no need to sugarcoat it.

"Don't…don't say that," she replied through gritted teeth.

Closing his eyes, he held her reverently in his arms. He hated hearing the fear and hatred in her voice. There had to be a way for them to make it out alive. There just had to be.

Not caring to have Nik's back turned to her, Natalia let out a loud whistle. Folding her arms over her ample chest, she waited impatiently for him to face her with her prize. With Ulysses praising her through her earpiece, she couldn't help but smirk. *Yes.* She had done a fine job, indeed.

"Good boy, Niky. Now put her to sleep and bring her to me," she barked.

Shaking her head, Brynn arched sharply in her lover's embrace. Saying the word 'no' repeatedly, her mind went wild with terrifying scenarios of what would happen if he forced her into unconsciousness. Slipping further and further into despair, she suddenly had the smallest recall of a moment she had with him in Norway. A moment in which he gave her an invaluable lesson.

"Oh," she whispered.

Letting out a ragged breath, Nik gave his Sire a nod. Gently dropping Brynn on her feet, he encouraged her to face him. Reaching to cup her face in his hands, he studied her beauty through the filtered moonlight.

"I will be with you when you awake my love…I promise you," he said softly. "Now close your eyes and drift away…this dream will keep you safe until I am able to wake you."

Meeting his intense gaze, Brynn swallowed hard. Not wanting to tip Natalia off in any way, she let her eyelids fall. Within a few heartbeats she felt her lover brush against her thoughts in a gentle sweep. With his supernatural gift a hair's breadth away from taking hold, she quickly built a fortress around her mind. Exactly as he taught her back in their quaint little row house in Bergen.

Met with unexpected resistance, Nik internally perked. Keeping his expression neutral, it took him a split second to understand what she was doing. His Sire could force him to use his Charm but didn't have the power to make the recipient accept it. It was a loophole he had never considered.

Pulling back his useless influence, he leaned down to press his forehead to hers. Knowing Natalia couldn't see the tiny grin on his lips, he whispered a tender praise.

"That's my clever girl…now sleep."

Without skipping a beat, Brynn fell like a rag doll. Caught by his arms before reaching the ground, she kept herself as calm as possible. Putting on an act of blissful slumber, she reminded herself to keep her ears open. Nik might be powerless against Natalia, but she sure as hell wasn't.

Holding his love like a bride, Nik stepped towards his Sire. Hardening his handsome features, he stared at the woman he once worshiped. Natalia had caused him so much pain both in his mortal and undead life. He was looking forward to his retribution.

Smiling wickedly, Natalia unfolded her arms to give her Novice a tiny round of applause. Paying no mind to his sour disposition, she hummed an approval as he came to a stop before her.

"Good boy…now drop her right there," she ordered, pointing to the muddy ground to the left.

Giving a quick glance at the ground, he noticed a myriad of sharp roots protruding from the earth. Swearing internally, he twisted Brynn ever so slightly as his arms gave way. The tiny motion was just enough to ensure her head fell against dirt and not broken tree bits. At that moment, it was the only grace towards her he could give.

Swallowing a yelp as her hip hit a thick root, Brynn continued to play asleep. By the luck of the draw, her tangled hair fell across her face. Masking the micro expressions of pain and uptick in her breathing. Holding onto the sting as it radiated over her pelvis, she readied herself to use it to her advantage.

"There…you have her. You've won. Take her back to the Manor to Ulysses…enjoy her power," Nik said.

"Oh, I intend to…don't you worry. But you aren't going to get out of this so easily…you and me? We're not done yet," Natalia replied, giving a quick glance to a white drone as it zipped by. "I'm sorry to say this, my handsome boy…but I've been ordered to kill you."

Meeting his Sire's cold eyes, Nik straightened his posture. He expected nothing less from Ulysses. Someday he would draw and quarter the old Roman just as they had with Anton.

"What are you waiting for, then?" he asked.

Giving a small shrug of her shoulders, Natalia stepped forward. Closing the gap between them, she allowed herself to take in every inch of the man she still harbored love and desire for. Hearing Ulysses mutter the order had pained her in an unexpected way. She realized that she truly didn't want to hurt her beloved Nikolai. A realization that had unfortunately come far too late.

"Hmm…well…I suppose I'm waiting because I want something to remember you by," she replied, pressing her body to his. "You know…I was your first kiss…and I will be your last. Kiss me like you did at our wedding, Nikolai. When you were still madly in love with me…when I was the only thing that mattered to you."

Letting his eyes sweep across her face, Nik was suddenly taken back to their wedding night over three hundred years before. He was a fool back then. Blinded with what he thought was love. She truly was the only thing that mattered when they had promised eternity to one another. But not anymore.

Unable to fight the command, Nik roughly pulled her into his arms. Lifting her from the ground, he spun her around exactly as he had that fateful night. Pressing his lips to hers, he kissed her with a passion only a first love could create. Eager and greedy, wanting and hungry. Just as he remembered. Below the surface however, it was purposefully hollow. Much like the empty promises she had made to him.

Stilling his legs, he placed her back upon her booted feet. Moving his lips over hers one last time as a parting gift, he eased away. Sensing Brynn's white-hot anger as it grew within her aura, he suddenly understood why she had allowed the kiss.

"There…now let's get on with it, shall we?" he said, directing his words more towards his love than his Sire.

Licking the remnants of her Novice from her lips, Natalia hummed low. Although lackluster, the kiss would simply have to do. She had other memories that would sustain her. Surely another striking man would come along and take his place. At least she hoped so.

"On your knees, Nikolai," she said, reaching into the waistband pocket of her compression leggings.

Falling to the ground, he narrowed his green eyes as she removed an ornamental stake from her pocket. No more than eight inches long, the piece of lacquered mahogany was carved with an ancient curse that would send him straight to hell. The inconspicuous weapon was often something she would threaten him with whenever they would quarrel. He found it fitting that she intended to use it right then and there.

"Tell me you love me, Niky," she said.

"I love you," he replied, his voice deep and strained.

Pressing her lips into a fine line, Natalia nodded once. Committing the sound of his voice to memory, she gripped the sharp stake in her hand. Lifting it high over her head, she moved her gaze to the blood-stained fabric covering his chest.

"I love you, too…my sweet Niky," she said.

Hesitating for a split second, she didn't have a chance to carry out the death order. Before she knew what was happening, a bright ball of intense fire flashed in front of her. Not moving away in time, the flame licked the flammable fabric of her athletic wear. Catching her torso on fire so quickly she couldn't make sense of it.

Jumping up from the forest floor, Brynn pulled back her lips into a feral snarl. Containing her rage, she sent another pulse of fire from her hands, this time directing the flame towards Natalia's legs. Watching the Vampire flail around as the fire consumed her, she readied herself to use her powers once more.

Standing to full height, Nik turned his head to look into the forest. Ignoring the drone as it flew around them, he ran towards the tree that still held the dagger. Although fire would weaken her, it wouldn't kill her on its own.

"Move away, Brynn!" he yelled. "Stay away from her!"

Taking a handful of steps backwards, Brynn watched with wide eyes as Natalia dropped to the ground. With the sound of pained screams and shrill wails filling her ears, she took in a jagged breath. The scene before her was horrific, like something out of a nightmare. But again, as with Anton, she felt no fear or alarm. Only satisfaction.

Rolling over the muddy ground, Natalia tried in vain to snuff the flames. To her shock the ground only pushed the fire deeper within.

Roaring past her scorched skin, it burned deep into her muscles. Wreaking havoc to her undead body as the seconds ticked. Screaming as the embers kissed her throat, she gathered what remained of her dulled Gift. Collecting it as her charred body withered, she locked her bloodshot eyes on Brynn.

"I....WILL...KILL...YOU!" she yelled with what remained of her voice.

Shaking her head at the burning corpse, Brynn straightened her posture. She knew Natalia believed what she said wholeheartedly, but she couldn't be more wrong. No lowly Vampire would ever be able to make good on that threat. Not her. Not Ulysses. Not Christos. Nor any other ancient bloodsucker watching whatever footage the drone was capturing.

"You can't kill a God," she whispered to herself.

Unaware of the exchange behind him, Nikolai found the twisted tree that held their much-needed weapon. Grabbing onto the jeweled hilt, he yanked on the dagger. Gritting his teeth, he used his Vampiric strength to wretch it from the trunk. Quickly turning on his heels, he ran back to the fray with the blade in his readied grip.

Listening to Nikolai's footsteps with what remained of her hearing, Natalia balled her fading strength. Knowing she was mere moments away from certain death, she lifted her blackened arm. Using every ounce of power in her core, she called forth a rift in the fabric of their reality. With the hellfire still raging through her, she rolled through the barely opened portal. Much to the shock and dismay of her Novice and his whore.

"NO! NO!" screamed both Nik and Brynn in unison.

Running at full speed, Nik slid over the damp earth just as the rift swallowed his Sire. Coming to an abrupt stop, he hissed a bitter curse. He couldn't believe what had just happened. The bitch shouldn't have been able to jump.

"What happened?! What the hell happened, Nik?!" Brynn yelled.

Turning towards his love, Nik met her disbelieving face. Trying to keep his own anger from exploding, he walked to where she stood. This failure would always be a thorn in their side. Vexing them over and over again until they were finally able to make things right.

"I don't know…she shouldn't have been able to teleport," he growled.

"Well, where did she go?!" Brynn squeaked, her eyes jerking over his stoic face.

Holding the hilt tightly in his hand, he measured his growing rage. He didn't know if his love could control her power and didn't want to risk the chance of her riling her further. He had a suspicion of where Natalia had gone. There was an unholy Cardinal at the Vatican that was known to heal their kind. While he had never had the pleasure of meeting the man, his Sire had mentioned his gifts on more than one occasion. There was no doubt in his mind that she would need more than just her undead ability to heal from Brynn's fire.

"I don't know," he replied, standing before her. "But it doesn't matter. It will take her decades to heal…perhaps even centuries. She won't be coming back for us anytime soon."

Stammering for a moment, Brynn attempted to make sense of the situation. They were so close to killing Natalia. So damn close. And now they might have to wait decades…perhaps even centuries to finish her once and for all? The thought was perhaps the most bitter thing she had ever tasted.

"Well…what do we do now?" she asked.

Lifting his free hand, he gently caressed her flushed cheek. Making her meet his eyes, he gave her a small grin. There was nothing more for them to do. Not then, at least.

"We go back to Capri as quickly as we can…where we will live and love and prepare for whatever these fools bring to our door," he said, motioning to the drone with a flick of his chin. "And whatever it is…we will take it on together."

Pushing out a long sigh, Brynn turned her face to kiss his palm. While not satisfied with his answer, the idea of living and loving in an Italian Villa was extremely appealing. It soothed her annoyance over Natalia.

"Then take me home to Italy Nikolai," she said with a sly smile. "This Hunt is over. You have officially won me."

Leaning down, he brought his face close to hers. Running the tip of his nose along hers, he hummed happily. There was nothing more in the world that he wanted to do. Natalia and the Elders would receive their retribution all in due time.

"We've won each other, my beautiful Brynn," he replied, lightly brushing his lips over hers. "I hope you know how much I love you."

Nodding her head, she draped her arms over his broad shoulders. After all that they had been through, his love for her was something she would never doubt again. They still had an uncertain future, but she was confident that they could handle whatever came their way.

"I love you, too…with all of my heart," she answered, pulling him into a passionate kiss.

EPILOGUE

Nearly eight months later…

Letting out a sigh, Brynn placed her plastic binder upon the large dining room table. Pulling out the heavy walnut chair, she took a seat and opened the binder to the latest typed entry. Over the last six months, a local linguist had been transcribing ancient texts from Chinese, Sanskrit, Aramaic and Latin for her. Texts that Helen had been collecting over the last millennia for her vast library. Texts that held bits and pieces of long forgotten legends and lore describing what she truly was.

While nothing so far had given her any concrete answers, she was able to stitch together a consensus from the various myths. One, that she was indeed a God. Born of blood and flesh, transcended into power by otherworldly injustices. And two, that she was to restore harmony and balance to a world overrun and governed by the corrupt.

Whatever the hell that fucking meant.

Leaning over the binder, she scanned over the typed words. To her annoyance, the newest batch of transcription didn't say much of anything. Just more of the same solemn prayers and stories that even after all she had experienced firsthand, still seemed too fantastic to believe.

Flipping the page, she read through the next four paragraphs. With her frustration starting to rise, she stilled after the first sentence of the fifth. Three words instantly caught her eye, making her read them again and again and again.

Eradicate blood drinker.

Narrowing her hazel eyes, Brynn straightened her posture as she mulled over the heavy phrase. The linguist had often warned her not to take his translations as gospel. As he had said on more than one occasion, translation was a funny thing. Often thrown together using modern words that gave the general essence, but not necessarily the exact meaning.

Still, those three words gave her a serious pause. Eradicate blood drinker, singular? Sure. She could do that. No, she would do that just as soon as they located Natalia. But plural? As in eradicate all blood drinkers? How could she possibly do that? Especially when she and Nik had been having serious discussions lately over when she would be turned.

Chewing on the inside of her cheek, she slammed the binder shut. Pushing it to the center of the table, she sat with her bickering thoughts. Losing herself in a myriad of various wild scenarios, she was startled back into reality by the slamming of the kitchen door. Followed by a deep, animalistic growl that instantly brought her to her feet.

Pressing her lips into a fine line, she quickly walked towards the source of the outburst. Stepping into the chef's kitchen, she found the moody culprit facing a row of cabinets. Swearing loudly and swinging his closed fists into the air, he was in what she affectionately called Angry Alpha Mode.

"Uh oh. What now, Rikard?" she asked, clearing the space to where he stood.

Stilling his muscular arms, Rikard turned towards Brynn. Immediately struck by her teasing smile, he suddenly forgot about the burning sensation running along his bare chest. He was hoping to see her again before Nikolai emerged for the night. He was growing so tired of having to share her.

"Ah…il mio bellissimo angelo," he said, his voice deep and gravely. "There you are."

Meeting his intense gaze, her knees almost turned to warm jelly. Swallowing hard, she purposefully dropped her eyes. Noticing four claw marks marring his tanned skin, she let out a sharp gasp. This was the second time this week that she had seen him injured. She didn't like it. She didn't like it one bit.

"My God, Rikard...what happened?" she asked, all but running to clear the handful of steps separating them.

Relishing her concern, he shrugged his broad shoulders. While he hated to make her worry, he knew it was important for her to do so. Compassion would deepen their connection as future Mates. Whether she knew it or not.

"It's nothing...we're just training harder, that's all," he replied nonchalantly. "Miguel and I got a little carried away."

Huffing a reply, Brynn took his hand in hers. Leading him to the copper sink, she grabbed a clean hand towel from a basket with her free hand. Sparring sessions for both the Werewolves and Vampires were becoming more frequent, and more dangerous. With real weapons now replacing training equipment. Rikard had a maddening habit of escalating sessions to push the limits of his Brothers.

Turning on the kitchen faucet, she ran the towel under the warm water. Giving him a critical look, she began the process of cleaning his split skin.

"You have to be more careful...you're far too valuable to me," she said, instantly snapping her mouth shut after realizing what had slipped out.

Arching a scarred brow, Rikard couldn't help but grin. "I'm far too valuable to *you?*" he asked cheekily.

Clearing her throat, she felt her cheeks flush crimson with embarrassment. Continuing to wash the blood from his chest, she blinked away the flashes of fantasies flooding her mind. Feeling incredibly guilty for even having such thoughts, she reminded herself that it was normal to dream of others even in the happiest of relationships. Right?

Right.

"To *us*," she replied, her voice shaking ever so slightly. "You're very valuable to *us*, Rikard. Especially now with two more Clans siding with Ulysses and Christos."

Staring at her blushing face, he nodded his head. While her words were truthful, he knew his value to her meant much more than just being another weapon in Helen's war. All the time spent with her during the daylight hours was paying off. Just as Clara had predicted.

"Brynn…it's all going to be ok…I'll fight for you until my last breath," he vowed.

Lifting her hazel eyes, her breath hitched as she looked at his sinfully handsome face. "For me? Don't you mean *with* me?" she asked.

"Both," he said huskily.

Letting out a shaky breath, Brynn felt her stomach tighten. Standing in silence for a handful of seconds, she forced herself to continue cleaning his wounds. Every so often she caught a glimpse of the hunger behind his eyes. It was much more intense, more feral, than the way Nik looked at her. And God help her, she liked it.

Watching her intently, Rikard savored her delicate touch. Letting his gaze drift from her face to the deep v of her white tee, and even lower to the small swell of her abdomen, he instinctively licked his lips. He could smell her heady pheromones as she leaned in closer. She was ready and ripe. It annoyed him that another cycle was upon her and that it was completely wasted because of a damn Vampire.

"You know…you'd make an amazing mother, Brynn," he said.

Snorting loudly, Brynn shook her head. Running the towel under clean water, she wrung it out before making another pass over his skin. This wasn't the first time he had said something along those same lines to her. It always caught her off guard, but never in an uncomfortable way.

They had a very teasing friendship.

"Geeze, Rikard...you have a breeding kink or something?" she asked in jest.

Placing his large hand over hers, he stilled her touch. Pressing her hand to his torso, he narrowed his amber hued eyes ever so slightly. "Yes, I do mio angelo," he said truthfully, his voice taking on an edge of dark lust. "Would you care to indulge me?"

Rolling her eyes, Brynn playfully scoffed. Thinking he was only kidding, she brushed his comment away as nothing more than another bawdy tease. It was only when he didn't laugh along with her, did she realize that he wasn't kidding.

With a shiver running down her spine, she found it hard to come up with a reply. Melting under the heat of his gaze, she finally opened her mouth. But before she could respond, she heard a familiar voice call out from behind her.

"Am I interrupting something?" Nikolai asked, his deep voice laced with ice.

Looking over the top of Brynn's head at the Vampire, Rikard gave him a cocky smile. Letting her hand fall from his wounded chest, he straightened his posture. Shaking his head, he gave himself a mental pat on the back for pissing off the bloodsucker.

"No, Nikolai...Brynn was only trying to help me with my little scratch, here. But I should probably go take a shower, give it a really good clean," he replied before moving his attention to Brynn. "Come find me when you wake up and I'll take you into town for some gelato."

Licking her lips nervously, Brynn could only nod as she turned towards her love. Tossing the soiled towel into the sink, she watched Rikard as he stalked towards Nik. She felt incredibly guilty over her flirty interaction with the Werewolf. Fantasies were one thing, but teasing, no matter how seemingly innocent, was another.

Eyeing the Alpha, Nik hardened his expression. Balling his hands into fists at his sides, he mentally talked himself out of punching his smug face. The dog's overt lust for his love had been tolerated for far too long. Helen or not, there would come a time when he would no longer be able to hold back.

Purposefully brushing past him, Rikard bowed his head in a faux show of respect. "Enjoy your night, Nikolai," he said.

"Oh, I intend to," Nik replied, watching the trash take itself out.

Waiting until the dog was out of eyesight, he moved his attention towards Brynn. Watching her as she shifted her weight from her left foot to her right, he arched a dark brow. He didn't have to read her mind to know that she was embarrassed. It was written all over her beautiful face.

"Brynn. What was that all about?" he asked, stepping towards her.

Stammering for a moment, she shrugged her shoulders. "I was just trying to help him with a sparring wound...we can't risk our most powerful Werewolf getting an infection or worse just because he thinks he's too macho to clean a cut, now can we? Especially now, ya know?"

Letting out a sigh, Nik pushed the majority of his anger to the back of his mind. He hated to admit that she had a good point. They did need Rikard for his sheer size and power. It was probably the only reason why he hadn't torn his jugular. Yet.

"Yes, well...perhaps next time you should send him to see Clara, hmm?" he said, reaching up to touch her freckled cheek. "Oh...and I don't want you to go with him to get gelato...is that understood?"

Locking her eyes to his, Brynn nodded in agreement. He was right in wanting her to create some distance with Rikard. She would be just as jealous if he spent time with another woman. Especially if they were trying every trick in the book to get into his pants. Yes. Some distance between her and the Werewolf was needed.

"Yes, Sir," she replied.

"Mmm…that's my good girl," he praised, leaning in to kiss her forehead.

Giving him a small smile, she arched her brow. "So, what are the plans for tonight? Should we train? Read? Maybe go back to bed?"

"Oh, I'd love to take you back to bed…but there's something we need to do, first," he said.

"And what's that?" she asked curiously.

Pausing for a scant second, Nik let his eyes roam over her sweet face. They had settled into a comfortable routine together on the idyllic island. They were safe, and they were blissfully happy. He wished they had more time to just be.

"Helen has asked us to go and talk with her…now I don't know exactly why…but I saw Leonardo right before I found you and he gave me a heads up," he said.

Furrowing her brow, Brynn tried to ignore the sense of impending doom creeping upon her. There was a small twitch in his left eye. A tell she had figured out meant that he was worried.

"About what?" she asked, her voice suddenly tight.

"The five ancient families are meeting at the Carnival of Venice in three weeks' time. It's been over a millennium since they have all been together under one roof…and they are requesting an audience with us," he replied.

Taking in a sharp breath, she felt the blood drain from her face. Helen had told her stories about the ancient families that had made her skin crawl. The thought of meeting them terrified her to the core.

"Do you know what about?" she asked.

Shaking his head, he reached for her hand. Giving it a loving squeeze, he tried to reassure her with a tiny grin. He wanted to believe the ancient families had nothing but pure intentions for wanting to meet them, but the nagging voice in the back of his head warned him otherwise.

"I don't…but perhaps Helen will. But let's not put the cart before the horse, hmm? I'm sure everything will be fine, my beautiful Brynn," he said, lifting her hand to give her knuckles a soft kiss.

Nodding once, she pushed out a shaky breath. "Yeah, you're right…I'm sure everything will be ok…and besides, I have always dreamed of going to Venice…and during Carnival? I mean…how could we say no to such an invitation?"

"I have to admit…the thought of seeing you in a Venetian mask and gown is very appealing," he replied with a sly smirk.

"Oh, is it? Well then…the sooner we see Helen, the sooner we can look at costumes," she said, giving him a wink.

"Well then let's run to her room right now," he said, leading her away from the kitchen sink towards the hallway. "I'm looking forward to another adventure with you, my beautiful Sun Goddess."

Following his lead, Brynn snickered under her breath. Although she knew he was just as nervous as she was, she appreciated his positivity. Whatever surprise the ancient families had in store for them wouldn't be dull, of that she was certain. But just as long as Nikolai was with her, she could handle whatever nonsense came their way.

"Me too, my handsome Vampire…but I swear to God…if I see a golden birdcage, I'm lighting the whole city on fire."

ABOUT THE AUTHOR

A suburban wife and mother, Summer spends her days in a whirlwind of constant chaos, surviving on caffeine and carbs. No longer waterlogged in the Pacific Northwest of the United States, she now basks in the glorious sun and heat of the Desert Southwest. When not daydreaming of her own characters, she is often thinking of all things in a Galaxy Far, Far Away. Please follow Summer's socials to stay up to date on her latest projects!

Email: thesummerriley@gmail.com
tumblr: AffideCrystal
Facebook Author's Page: Summer Riley
Instagram: authorsummerriley

Printed in Great Britain
by Amazon